PRAY FOR US SINNERS

The Hail Mary Murder

FREDRICK KUNKLE

WARNER BOOKS

A Time Warner Company

Design and photo montage by Andrew Newman
Photo of car courtesy of Passaic County Prosecutor's Office
Photo of Solomine courtesy of the Bergen Record

0-446-60289-2

Warner Books, Inc.
1271 Avenue of the Americas
New York, NY 10020

A Time Warner Company

Printed in the United States of America

Author's Note

This book does its best to give an accurate account of the people and events surrounding the death of Robert A. Solimine, Jr. In writing this book, I have drawn on court documents, police records, and hundreds of interviews with some of the people involved, including members of the victim's family and three of the young men who took part in the murder: Frank Castaldo, D.M.S., D.S., and members of their families. (The names of the juveniles, whose identities were protected by the state's juvenile code, have been changed, and so have the names of their family members.) The recollections and court testimony of D.M.S. and D.S., who are currently serving twenty-year terms at the New Jersey Training School in Jamesburg, have been especially critical to creating this book.

The material facts and the dialogue in the book are drawn either from court records or interviews with participants. However, in dramatizing many scenes I have taken liberties to create a narrative that flows with the story, opting for simplicity in conveying many points of view. Indeed, the memories of many people, recounted in interviews and in courtroom testimony, often varied in regard to details, times, settings, and conversations. An examination of the trial record alone shows many times how one juvenile's testimony was at odds with the testimony of another—and sometimes with himself—over important details and sequence of events. Since it was impossible to reconcile differences in chronology of the boys' varying recollections, I have placed the events surrounding the murder in an approximate time frame that fits the facts as closely as possible. Where two people's accounts of a single episode diverged, I chose a version that seemed most likely, and I have freely transposed and edited conversations that people reported years after the fact. In a few places I have also created some dialogue based on reported conversations. Some scenes are compressed in time from many different accounts—such as the visits to Annie's Road—and some are a composite of facts and details drawn from people who do not always agree about what happened. In all, my aim has been to give a factual account of the story as the boys and other participants related it from different perspectives, while being fair to those involved and to the reader.

"I'm warning you, I'm going to get angry. D'you see? You're not wanted. Understand? We are going to have fun on this island. Understand? We are going to have fun on this island! So don't try it on, my poor misguided boy, or else—"

Simon found he was looking into a vast mouth. There was blackness within, a blackness that spread.

"—Or else," said the Lord of the Flies, "We shall have to do you. See? Jack and Roger and Maurice and Robert and Bill and Piggy and Ralph. Do you. See?"

—*The Lord of the Flies*

1

November 1991

TRAINING EVERY ONE OF THEIR SENSES ON THE MEREST SIGN OF the supernatural, the boys tramped across the black expanse of the cemetery, five teenagers in a crooked file, hunting for Annie's ghost. At times it became too dark to see faces and they could tell each other's position only by the sound of their voices. The group whispered in the darkness, and the air was sharp and clean and formed steam when they spoke. The moon glowed in the white granite of the headstones and made twisting shadows of the trees. They passed under the black arms of an enormous oak and two cedars twining upward and stepped into a broad clearing where stars began to emerge in the darkness. The trees were gaunt shadows, and the boys' footsteps crunched on the paved lanes as they went deeper and deeper inside the cemetery. As the darkness became almost like twilight, they could pick out the tan rectangles of freshly dug graves, and the sounds of the city vanished except for the soughing of the interstate. Spirits seemed to be all around them.

This was Stooge's first time at Annie's Road. It was old fun for the others, who came here almost every other night to prowl around the cemetery, smoke cigarettes, drink, talk, or just hang out in the open air with no one to tell them what to do. But for Stooge, who had turned fourteen years old only five months earlier, this was an awesome experience. The strangeness of it excited and frightened him. Things that appeared solid in the daytime had become ephemeral, subject to change in a glance. A leaf spinning in the wind appeared, just for a moment, to be a hand that stopped the heart. The votive candle flickering inside a red lantern on the hillside resembled a cigarette burning. Other shapes appeared and vanished. Something moved in the underbrush, maybe a skunk, and they almost ran back to their cars. It was very scary, but it was very cool too. Stooge had never had friends before, period, and certainly not friends who would take him places like this.

The boys had parked the Buick under the soaring concrete trestles that carried Interstate 80 over Annie's Road and the Passaic River just above Paterson, New Jersey. The drone of the traffic as it rushed overhead filled the narrow river valley with a low and mournful sound, an otherworldly roar broken now and then only by the sound of a truck bed rattling over a bump. They had walked underneath the eight-lane highway, which ran high above their heads over spans of green steel. They hurried past the graffiti-smeared retaining wall and climbed the bank alongside the overpass toward the cemetery. The noise of the highway became louder the higher they climbed. They crossed through the first chain fence—whose endpost had been uprooted, concrete base and all—and through a thicket of scrub pines and bare trees toward the brow of the hill. A hole had been chopped in the second fence that enclosed the cemetery, and the boys passed through it, stepping into a great clearing. As they walked, the interstate traffic streamed by to their left in a flood of light and noise, and just beyond it lay Garret Mountain, whose back was carpeted with the orange and green glow of a suburb. Ahead of them, in the direction of the mausoleums, the reflections from the headlights played off the tombstones. The lights from the traffic caught facets of polished stone at odd angles as the boys walked, so that it seemed as if spirits darted across the ground and vanished.

That night, Stooge met Tommy Strelka for the first time. Strelka was the group's wheelman, and he was never happier than when he was driving the guys all over Passaic County. It was Strelka's car—a 1979 Buick LeSabre—that had chauffeured them all first to Fun 'N Games, a huge video arcade in the county's largest mall, and then to Annie's Road. Strelka, who was seventeen years old, had a sharp, lemurlike face and straggly blond hair that fell into his eyes. He was a partyer who liked nothing more than a good time. Despite their age difference, Stooge soon found that he and Tommy Strelka had more in common than their first names. Strelka would laugh wickedly at whatever the other guys said that might be funny, but, like Stooge, he was otherwise pretty quiet, almost shy, and more adept at taking the part of the audience than a performer. Yet Strelka had dreams of becoming a heavy-metal rock star.

Then there was Frank Carboni, the firebug. Stooge had known Carboni the longest. Carboni also was only fourteen years old—he was about a month older than Stooge—but looked and acted years older. Sour-faced and tough, he had an olive complexion, glossy hair that was almost black, and features that, despite the bad attitude and his permanent five-o'clock shadow, were charmingly boyish. In temperament, Carboni was almost mulish, but he possessed a dark wit and brooding intelligence that easily surpassed the others'. His marks and test scores in school had earned him placement in advanced courses, and his middle-school teachers adored him.

All the same, Carboni had pushed himself through adolescence, equating maturity with hardness. He was a troublemaker, a thrill-seeker, a liar, and a bit of a show-off. He shot pool with a deadly eye, and he could shoplift as slick as any kid around. More than anything, fire obsessed him: He never went out without taking his Zippo lighter and at least one extra can of lighter fluid. Although Carboni was one of the smallest and one of the youngest, he had a way of holding his own and even controlling the rest of the group at times. It was Carboni who had introduced Stooge to everyone else in the group, including its leader: his cousin, Frank Castaldo.

Carboni worshiped his older cousin, but so did everyone in the group. Castaldo seemed to them suave and tough at the same time, and they regarded him as having an endless supply of street smarts. Castaldo was the eldest, having turned eighteen years old only a month or so back, and that alone was somehow impressive to the others. Although he could be very funny and ironic, Castaldo played the role of street sage, an old soul who was world-weary and wise, carrying himself with a menacing cool that teenagers everywhere admire in certain movies stars and try to ape. For Castaldo, this translated into slow nods of the head as he spoke and a raspy voice and a kind of stooped walk, as if he were imitating the early Brando. Perhaps he was. Castaldo was infatuated with the Mafia, particularly as it had been conceived by Francis Ford Coppola in the *Godfather* movies, and he frequently boasted that one of his relatives was highly connected. It was another story that allowed him to lord it over others. Laying it on thick, he told kids that he had pictures with members of the family beside prominent mobsters like John Gotti. Proud of his Italian ancestry, Castaldo equated the rise of the Mafia with the greatness that had built Rome.

Castaldo was not a big kid, and he was roguishly handsome, with a high brow and a cleft chin and a fine Roman nose. He had dropped out of high school after the ninth grade, and he had done a stint in rehab because of drinking—features that perhaps made it seem as if he was deeper than he was. On a few occasions, he bragged of selling drugs. This was probably not true, since he didn't use them—he didn't like any drugs except alcohol, and he was wary of that—and no one thought this strange, even after it became apparent that Castaldo couldn't manage a paper route or a steady job, let alone a large drug buy. But Stooge, who was perhaps typical of the others in this respect, admired the way Castaldo radiated power and authority, and the way the others looked up to him.

Wanger led the way through the darkness of the cemetery, talking all the while in professorial tones about the legend of Annie's ghost. Stooge had met Wanger for the first time on the way over. Like everyone else in the group, Wanger lived in Clifton. The other kids called him James, and from the first Stooge knew the kid was strange. There was something fussy and proper about him, as if he had been raised a hundred years ago. Wanger was odd, and he seemed to practice being odd. He dressed in weird getups, his posture was too erect, and his speech was mannered and unusually polite. His mild, bespectacled face seemed exactly what one might expect of the class nerd. He was dressed in a knee-length black trench coat, a white dress shirt, and mannish leather shoes. His gray-tinted aviator glasses made him appear older than seventeen, and on his head—which was enormous and somehow lumpy in appearance—he wore a cap with a small buttoned-up visor. He called it his "capello." Walking across the cemetery grounds in the long black trench coat, which he nearly always wore, Wanger seemed almost like a priest in a cassock. He habitually wore an expression that was self-consciously solemn, almost comically so, and it was clear from the way he acted in school or in public that he was in the habit of studying himself with an abiding sense of the absurd.

He was talking—James was always talking—and he was describing the research he had done about Annie in the library at the Clifton High School, where he was a senior. Wanger said he had looked up newspaper clippings about Annie's murder, and about anything in that area along the Passaic River that illuminated the legend of her death. The whole place had a spooky history that went back to the earliest days of the American pioneers, and before that to the Lenni Lenape Indians.

When the Laurel Grove Cemetery in Totowa, New Jersey, opened its gates in 1888, almost a decade before Totowa was incorporated as a borough, the final resting place for Paterson's citizens soon became a popular site for picnics and country outings, as well. City dwellers in horse and buggy rode out McBride Avenue, just above the River Lawn Sanatorium operated by Dr. Dan T. Millspaugh, for a day at the cemetery, and even small steamboats were launched from Bowers' Boat House at Passaic Falls to carry day-trippers to its lawns. The cemetery, which encompassed more than ninety acres, was bordered by River Terrace, which is now Riverview Drive, on the south; Totowa Road, which had wound from Paterson into the ridges above it; and the Delaware, Lackawanna and Western Railroad, which cut through the southwestern corner of the cemetery and crossed the Passaic River. It was here, just about a century after railroad engineers had thrown a wooden bridge across the Passaic River above Paterson, that another group of engineers chose the same site for a steel-and-concrete bridge that would carry a new superhighway over the river. The highway, which eventually would cross the length of the continent, was Interstate Route 80, and at this point in its course it followed the path of the railroad and a legendary bridge.

The wooden bridge where the Lackawanna Railroad crossed the river above Paterson was known as "The High Bridge." Carrying two lines of track, the bridge became the scenic backdrop for *The Great Train Robbery,* America's first motion picture. In the movie, four masked men board an Erie Lackawanna train, throw the fireman off the trestle, and make off with jewels before their apprehension by a posse. Until Edwin S. Porter had chosen it as his movie set, the High Bridge span's only mention of note involved the deaths of two repairmen in 1875 and the near-collision of a coal train with a horse trapped in the rails in 1888. But the bridge and the cemetery had also been tied to the legend of a young woman's ghost that haunted the area in billowing white garments. One legend had it that Annie had been a young girl carrying a lantern near the tracks, perhaps on her way to milk the cows one dark night, when the steam locomotive cut her down. Others said she had thrown herself onto the tracks over some romantic misfortune. Still others claimed that Annie had been around since Colonial days, having begun to roam the earth after she was struck by a horse-drawn carriage, which some people also had seen riding through the darkened cemetery. But Wanger subscribed to a more contemporary version of the tale. In the late 1970s, the High Bridge came down, and the interstate bridge went up in the same spot, and young people visited the site at night.

Wanger had learned that Annie had been a girl about his age when she died. Her beauty was such that everyone in those parts knew of it, although she came from a humble family. Her family had lived on Riverview Drive, a narrow two-lane that snaked along the Passaic River under a navelike canopy of tree.

Wanger told the boys that Annie's house was the small blue one that stood on Dead Man's Curve on the road beside the river. Legend had it that the sharp bend in the road there had claimed its own number of ghosts over the years, including a car full of teenagers who had stolen the county prosecutor's car for a joyride back in the 1950s.

One night, sometime around 1965 or so, Annie had been walking along the macadam road, attired in a flowing white dress for the high-school prom, when a car with some sailors drove by. The road was very dark, but the sailors saw her in the blades of light from the car. They stopped to have some fun. The sailors grabbed her and shoved her into the backseat. They drove up into the graveyard and raped her. That done, they killed her, tossing or dragging her body from the car as they sped along the macadam, ripping her head off and leaving a streak of blood across the asphalt. Some said the reason Annie's spirit was so restless was that to this day she was searching for her lost head. Others said they had seen the ghost of her intact body gliding with a lantern in the cemetery. Although she was considered to be a benign ghost, it was said that Annie sometimes took possession of people's souls. Wanger told them that she brought no harm to females. Annie possessed only boys or men and sometimes drove them mad.

Whatever the truth, the stories agreed on this: Her brutal death had made her spirit unquiet, and now Annie haunted the Laurel Grove Cemetery. Her name had also been linked to the interstate overpass, and the macadam road that ran beside the cemetery. Legend had it that an indelible streak of Annie's blood stained its asphalt on a straightaway near the old sewage-treatment plant, and that her spirit haunted Dead Man's Curve. Inside the cemetery James told the other boys that he had figured out where her body lay, and he led them farther down the sloping paths toward the mausoleum that contained all that was known of Annie's mortal remains.

It was a cockamamie story. But James Wanger—the group's creative genius, soft-spoken clown, and earnest peacemaker, who was known throughout Clifton's public high school as the oddball of oddballs—seemed to believe in Annie's ghost. Indeed, Wanger rendered to her spirit a degree of devotion and reverence that he did not express for the Roman Catholic Church, where he was deeply and officially involved, and so the others couldn't help but believe in Annie as well. Wanger had dug up every morsel he could find about Annie's ghost, and it was obvious that he had embellished on what he found, but he conveyed to them something essentially true. All of them at one time or another had acknowledged some unaccountable spiritual presence in the cemetery. All of them had at least once called out to her. To Stooge, the whole thing seemed a bit campy—but then it also seemed as if it might be true, because the entire place seemed immanent with a spiritual power. And anyway, who was he to doubt the supernatural? What seemed perhaps like a joke the first time he had been taken to the cemetery became, over time, almost an article of faith.

The boys lit cigarettes. They felt loose, almost exultant, as they walked farther inside the cemetery to a grove of trees. Tombs and monuments covered the ground in a dense welter of stone. At last they came to a mausoleum whose granite walls were shut up behind a door and a metal grating. In the darkness it looked like the opening to an underground passage.

This was it, Wanger said. The mausoleum, modeled after a Greek temple, stood in a field of carved tablets, miniature obelisks, and stone angels. There were three little stone steps and two rough-hewn columns, one on either side of the entrance. On the lintel above the door in raised stone letters was the name VAN DYK. Nearby, angels balancing atop the tombstones appeared to hover in the darkness like white birds. Wanger told Stooge he believed Annie's head had been buried elsewhere, possibly under one of the stone angels.

The boys lit more cigarettes and talked and joked. After standing around in the cold for about twenty minutes, Castaldo wanted to head back, and the others agreed.

"Do you have a cigarette?" Wanger said. Stooge realized Wanger was talking to him. Stooge pulled out his pack of Newports and handed Wanger a smoke. Wanger went around to the rear of the mausoleum, and Stooge followed him. In the rear of the mausoleum was a stained-glass window. On a sunny day the window glowed with a luminous picture of Mary as she knelt by the empty tomb on the morning of the Resurrection. This Mary was quite pretty and young, wrapped in flowing tresses of chestnut hair and purple robes, and she gazed off in the distance where three, or perhaps only two, wooden crosses tottered on the brow of Calvary. The colors were warm and the window, except for a chip in the glass, was in fairly good condition. Wanger laid the cigarette delicately on the stone ledge and stepped back.

"For Annie," Wanger said.

Before departing, Wanger always left a cigarette and sometimes a packet of matches for Annie. On occasion he would speak to her too, almost relishing the way the other guys might smirk or joke during his little ceremony. That was Wanger. He didn't mind playing the fool, because he seemed always to be on another plane, and he liked to remind the others of that. This was the group's place, they considered it almost their own, but most of all it was Wanger's and Annie's.

In a matter of months, however, another ghost would haunt the cemetery, the ghost of a young man whom all the Clifton teenagers had, at least at one time, considered a friend.

Now and then, regardless of the season or the time of day, the city of Clifton sends up a curious exhalation that floats invisibly in the New Jersey sky, drifts over the rooftops toward the Passaic River, and carries a surreal bouquet of chemicals along the city's streets. On some days, the cloud rolls over some sections of the town with an unpleasantly sweet and antiseptic smell, like heavy cologne or deodorant soap. On other days, the air is redolent with the aroma of warm bread or cinnamon. Sometimes the cloud eddies and swirls, wrapping its odor and a neighborhood for a time before disappearing, and at other times the strange mixture of odors lies heavily over parts of town like a bank of fog. These emissions of chemical compounds touch some areas of the town, but not all, and represent the unintended by-products of Clifton's great industrial might, which includes some of the world's largest makers of artificial flavors and fragrances. The plants give the town jobs and pay an enviable portion of its taxes. At one time, in fact, Clifton's tax base was the third richest in the state of New Jersey. These clouds that smell like rising bread or bubble gum or pine tar differed little from the toxic wastes expelled into the atmosphere by other companies in Clifton—such as the battery plant, the pharmaceuticals giant, or the steel mill—except that a layman could detect them, and they seemed somehow fitting for the place. For Passaic County, New Jersey, is a strange place, and Clifton is perhaps one of its strangest municipalities. Neither suburb nor city, Clifton is somehow both, and its citizenry embodies the extremes of both cultures in an almost willfully unreflective way. The place is both bland and quirky, lying only about thirteen miles west of New York City—and yet sometimes it seems as if the distance between Clifton and Manhattan can be measured only by decades.

Clifton itself is not big, occupying only 11¾ square miles of land, and its population—white, almost pure white, and very, very conservative—stood at approximately 72,000 in 1990. To the west of town lies Garret Mountain, whose cliffs inspired the city's name. Just south of that is First Mountain in the Watchung Mountain chain. Between them is a gap known as the Notch, which once conducted Dutch herders and today conveys thousands of cars along Route 46 toward the malls and distant suburbs. To the east of Clifton lies the Passaic River, which forms the city's eastern border and flows south toward Newark and the Atlantic Ocean. The city of Clifton boasts of twenty-eight parks and playgrounds, one golf course—the Upper Montclair Country Club—one recreation center, two movie theaters, two public library buildings, twelve shopping centers, thirty banks, and thirty houses of worship, the majority of which are Roman Catholic churches. There are thirteen public elementary schools, eight parochial elementary schools, two public junior high schools, and one public senior high school. Giants Stadium is two miles to the east, and the city of Newark is seven miles south. The city is generally clean, sheltered, and primly working-class. Wedged between the decrepit cities of Paterson to the north and Passaic to the southeast, the city of Clifton holds no remarkable claim on the great urban sprawl of New York City, except that it is a place intersected by dozens of highways where people can pass through. The Garden State Parkway bisects the city north to south, Routes 3 and 46 run east to west, and Highways 20 and 21 carry traffic between Clifton and Passaic and Paterson. Whereas its urban neighbors had grown in the age of railroads and canals, Clifton's fortunes followed the automobile.

Long ago, Clifton had been part of a Dutch settlement purchased from the Lenni Lenape for a trifling—some coats, kettles, blankets, and gunpowder. The deed was conveyed according to laws of the English proprietors of the East Jersey Colony, and the land—encompassing some of Paterson, all of Passaic and Clifton, and parts of other municipalities—became known as Acquackanonk. Derived from the original Lenape name, Acquackanonk signified a land made bountiful by the river running through it. The name stuck with the place from 1693 until 1917, when the city of Clifton was incorporated. Down the years, a few vestiges of Native American presence also survived in street names and the like. An Indian head was adopted as the city's symbol, a crude logo of which members of the police department wear on their arm patches.

The earliest places to be settled by the Europeans lay near a stream the Dutch called Wesel Brook, probably named after a town back home. The stream flowed southeastward from Wesel Mountain, which later became known as Garret Mountain, and emptied into the Passaic River. The brook powered one of Clifton's first manufacturing enterprises—grist- and sawmills—until a creosoting plant owned by the Delaware, Lackawanna and Western Railroad permanently polluted it. Years later, the brook would become known as Weasel Brook, and a county park of the same name would be established around it.

For years, Acquackanonk Township was a sleepy patchwork of settlements while its urban neighbors became manufacturing powerhouses. Thanks to the Passaic River, Paterson became the Silk City by the end of the nineteenth century, its mills flourishing with cheap power from the Great Falls, the second-largest waterfall east of the Mississippi. To the south of Clifton, meanwhile, Passaic became America's Wool City. As the two cities grew, people and some manufacturing plants spilled over into Clifton—but for the most part, Clifton remained mostly clover fields, a brief stopover on the Paterson Plank Road running between Paterson and Passaic. After the Delaware, Lackawanna and Western Railroad opened its Boonton Branch in 1870, industry followed the path of the rail line's distinctive, humpbacked locomotives into Clifton. Factories rose in an arc through the heart of what was still Acquackanonk. The railroad, which lent its name to a section of the town, lumbered from Hoboken on the Hudson River to Passaic. Then the trains continued through Clifton, into Paterson, across the Passaic River on the High Bridge, along the Laurel Grove Cemetery in Totowa, and then onward into

Pennsylvania and the heartland as far away as Chicago. The railroads gave Clifton a boost of industrialization that the canal and the river had not, and they also brought tourists and day-trippers from New York City to some of the small town's turn-of-the-century curiosities. They stayed in the Clifton Hotel, which stood where the Knights of Columbus building stands now, and relaxed in the picnic grove nearby. A racetrack opened on the site where the Christopher Columbus middle school now stands and became a nationally known venue for Thoroughbred racing. After its owners were indicted for harboring an illegal gambling enterprise, the track was converted to a velodrome for bicycle races. Not far from that was Fairyland Park, which contained a theater, a dance pavilion, a penny arcade, a miniature railroad, and a carnival of rides, including a Ferris wheel, roller coaster, and merry-go-round. There was also Olympic Park Stadium, where professional baseball teams of the Atlantic League played, drawing as many as 15,000 fans and bringing greats like Ty Cobb and Honus Wagner to Clifton. And in 1900, the United States Bureau of Agriculture opened the Federal Animal Quarantine Station in the Athenia section of town where the city's town hall and high school now stand. The center became the chief portal of entry for imported domestic and wild animals, keeping the animals there for up to thirty days to inspect them for signs of tuberculosis and hoof-and-mouth disease. The city acquired the land in the 1950s and 1960s for its high school and municipal complex.

But nothing contributed to the present-day shape of Clifton the way the highways did. After the highways went up, factories seemed to crop up everywhere, and parts of Clifton became a hodgepodge of residential and industrial areas. By the 1970s, huge corporations and manufacturing plants sat side by side, cheek by jowl, with split levels and ranch houses on Clifton's leafy streets. The juxtaposition was jarring, as if industry—including Fortune 500 companies like General Foods Corp., Pfizer Inc., Hoffmann–La Roche, Miles Laboratories, Union Camp Corp., American District Telegraph Co., a maker of security and alarm systems, and Automatic Data Processing, a payroll and computer service employing 16,000 people alone—lapped at the edges of the proud lawns filled with plaster saints and fake deer.

Clifton became an early suburb in a quintessentially suburban state, and yet—because of the number of large manufacturing plants—it never became strictly a bedroom community. Many of Clifton's residents had been at one time or another European immigrants who had worked the mills and plants in nearby Paterson and Passaic. These laborers gathered their wages, picked themselves up, and built modest frame houses on half-acre lots in the town next door, a little farther away from the factory whistles, the smokestacks, the bustle and the grit. No doubt their struggle toward prosperity shaped their faith in traditional values such as self-reliance, loyalty, and self-sacrifice. To this day, Cliftonites radiate pride in their civic achievements and the quality of their schools. Cliftonites are stolid, traditional, slow to change, almost reactionary. In 1964, for example, in an episode now known as the "Washline War," irate housewives in the Richfield Village apartments drew widespread attention when they mounted a protest against the landlords who tried to replace their backyard clotheslines with newfangled drying machines. In 1988, the city council refused to repeal a 37-year-old ordinance banning the sale of condoms except by doctors and pharmacies.

Cliftonites tend to view themselves as a big raucous family—prone to loud squabbles but bound by ties as deep as blood. More than most municipalities, Clifton residents bestir themselves to attend council and school board meetings, to speak out against waste, and to keep an eye on what their leaders and their local government are up to. Many people grew up in Clifton and lived out their lives there, and many returned to settle down. People who move away return to watch the Mustangs play high-school football games. This is what makes their town special, they would say. But the flip side was a detectable air of self-satisfaction in the city, an aura of the smug bourgeoisie. People in Passaic and Paterson still remark on it—this sense that Cliftonites never tire of feeling a little superior to the people and places they have left behind. Some put the town down as having an Archie Bunker mentality. This perception, fair or not, became more complicated the more one openly examined the specter of race. For one thing seems almost indisputable: The Lenape were probably the last nonwhites to inhabit Clifton in numbers. Although blacks who moved to Clifton would often say that they generally did not encounter overt discrimination, getting in the door seemed to be the entire battle, and many blacks did not bother looking in the city because of its reputation for intolerance.

In Clifton, there was nothing like the wild rate of homicides and other violent crimes one found just over its borders, and many Cliftonites were not ashamed to link the two to race. Clifton almost never reported violent crime as Paterson and Passaic did. Indeed, in 1990, in one of its most bizarre and gruesome years, Clifton had seven murders, while Paterson and Passaic reported a combined total of 23. When murders did hit Clifton, they almost always had a new wrinkle to them, as if the long drought had been time to store up more than an ample amount of bizarre, horrid, and sometimes kinky details. In the mid-1960s, for example, the murder of Judith Kavanaugh, the wife of a wealthy publisher who lived on Hazel Street, would become one of the most sensational crimes in the history of the county, and perhaps the state. Her partially clothed body was found in March 1966, on an embankment off the Garden State Parkway and Hazel Street, a month after her disappearance. Police suspected she had been abducted and sexually assaulted. A hapless dishwasher at the Daughters of Miriam rest home was viewed as a suspect. In a matter of time, however, her murder was linked to the gangland execution of a small-time Paterson hood, and much more besides. Before it was all over, the Kavanaugh case would have it all: allegations of wife-swapping, a multimillion-dollar counterfeiting ring, Mafia involvement, crooked cops, and corruption in the county government. A Passaic County grand jury indicted Judy's husband, Paul Kavanaugh, wealthy upcountry publisher Harold Matzner, and a decorated Clifton police detective, Sgt. John DeFranco, for her murder, and a veritable Who's Who listing of local and national eminences played parts in the drama. Even F. Lee Bailey jumped into the fray. In the end, after two trials, there were acquittals all around and accusations that the defendants had been framed by a corrupt investigator in the prosecutor's office. In later years, the New York City news crews raided Clifton after three members of a deaf family were slain—leaving only an infant survivor—and after a serial killer was apprehended for the murder of his wife. But these were rare instances, almost freak events.

Clifton residents were proud of its many accomplishments. There is pride in the city, pride in its industry, pride in its property values, pride in its schools. It was, everyone said, a good place to raise children.

Tommy "Stooge" Stujinski remembered his heart pounding the moment he heard the key turning in the lock. His father was home from work. Tommy slipped out of the living room. He left the TV on. The after-school cartoons were playing, it was Huey and Louie at that hour, and the quaint cuckoo clock on the wall swished back and forth. Tommy went down the narrow hall to his bedroom, where the paneled walls were plastered with car posters, and pulled the door shut. The cars in the pictures were brand new and sleek and photographed to seem almost alive, as if they contained speed inside their polished skins. Between the posters of automobiles he had hung posters of Dwight Gooden and Jose Canseco, who was taking a mighty swing. On the corner shelf at the foot of his bed, Jesus held a lamb in his arms. Jesus was golden-haired and young.

Outside, the wind stirred the leaves on the trees. Tommy's room had been the kitchen once. There was a door leading outside, but he would never be bold enough to sneak out or leave. He snapped on the tiny black-and-white TV in his room. He didn't want to think about his father, who sometimes could be actually nice to him, throw a ball around in the backyard with him, but the anxiety seemed to mount up inside his chest, and crowd his heart.

There had been a time when Tommy wasn't afraid, and when his family had been happy. His parents had come from Yugoslavia, they had worked very hard in factories and blue-collar jobs, first in Brooklyn and then in New Jersey, and they had secured enough of the trappings of American middle-class success for his father to boast about them to friends and family. Then their lives became hateful.

His father drank more and more, and he beat Tommy's mother and he beat Tommy. His father was forced to leave after he beat up his mother one too many times, and the old family crumbled, until it was just he and his mother and his younger brother alone in a dark house near the railroad tracks in Clifton. For a long time Tommy had no close friends, merely a few acquaintances, and then he found the best and most loyal friends he could have imagined, in Carboni, Wanger, Strelka, and Castaldo. They became like family. They even renamed him. Tommy's surname was Czech in origin and had been adopted by some Croats—although it was rare among the Serbs, to whose ethnic group he belonged. Because no one in America pronounced it properly, his last name sounded somewhat like "Stooge." And so, inevitably, that was what his friends called him. In time, even his mother would call him Stooge.

Her name was Mary. It had been a variation of Marina, in Yugoslavia, where she had been born during the later years of Tito's reign. One of five children, she grew up on a farm with two sisters and two brothers. She was happy, and her family was close. They kept cows, horses, and geese, grew vegetables and crops, and drew their water from a spring. For some reason, her Eastern Orthodox parents christened all the children except Mary and her sister.

She met her future husband, Velimir, a steelworker whose nickname was Mica, when she was twenty-two and he was twenty-seven years old. After a relatively short engagement, they were married on September 25, 1976, in a government office in a suburb of Sarajevo, not only because church marriages were discouraged, but because neither felt any strong emotional tie to religion. They had barely settled in a Sarajevo apartment when Mary's family members emigrated to the United States, and she and Mica decided to follow. They arrived in New York on a Thursday, and by Friday Mica was working in a knitting factory in Brooklyn. Mary soon found work as a cleaning woman. They stayed a few weeks with Mary's sister, and then a few weeks with Mary's brother until they could find an apartment. They were soon going to need one with enough space for three.

Their first child was a son whom they gave a Serbian name. He was born June 26, 1977, and his nickname was Tommy. Mary did not stay home with the baby for long, because she and Mica could not afford it. Other family members helped to watch the baby, and eventually he was put in a Lutheran church's nursery school. When Tommy was about three and a half years old, Mary gave birth to a second boy.

Meanwhile, the family's prospects improved. Mica was working better and better factory jobs, and Mary started a fabric company with her sister. Each woman took home $200 a week of their earnings and plowed the rest back into the company; before long, they owned ten sewing machines and they put on more workers. Mary and Mica furnished a simple but decent apartment in Greenpoint with new, store-bought furniture that looked like something one would find in a hotel chain. But it made them proud all the same. A mixture of articles from home—European lace curtains, bric-a-brac, needlepoint, and handmade crafts—lent some warmth to the cramped quarters. In time, they were able to consider buying their first home.

In the mid-1980s, Mica and Mary moved to New Jersey. They bought their first house in Paterson for $86,000. Mary's business continued to thrive, and Mica found a job with a Clifton company assembling prefabricated wooden furniture from Yugoslavia. By 1988, they were ready to move out of the city, and they bought a homely wood-frame house in the Athenia section of Clifton, on Fornelius Avenue, for $232,000. The huge backyard, which was low and often mushy, ran almost to the embankment of the old Erie-Lackawanna railroad tracks.

Over the years, as their economic status rose, their private lives were still shaped by the humble rhythms of the Old World: there were inexpensive outings at Rockaway beach and Coney Island, family gatherings at Christmas and Easter, parties at home for the boys' birthdays. Simple things, usually involving their children, brought them pleasure. In Clifton, Mary and the boys spent hours kicking a soccer ball up and down the backyard behind their house. Mary brought home scraps of fabric from the factory and sewed a huge cocoon for her and her boys to roll around in, in the backyard. They filled albums with snapshots that caught Tommy smiling, wearing a parochial-school uniform, lugging around his stuffed E.T. doll and—almost always—hugging his mother or his little brother with a look of contented pride.

Their roles were defined by tradition, but not entirely: Mica helped with the laundry, and Mary knew how to fix a leaky faucet. Yet the child rearing fell mostly to her. She was somewhat indulgent, without being a pushover. If the boys misbehaved, Mary would spread some dry corn on the floor in a corner of the room and make them kneel on the kernels. The boys knelt, the kernels biting into the thin flesh of their knees, for fifteen minutes. Sometimes the punishment lasted an hour. She didn't, as a practice, strike the boys, and she seldom needed to punish them at all. Tommy was a very good boy, as he had been a good baby—even-tempered, not prone to fussiness, a good sleeper. He helped take care of his little brother.

"He tricked me into having a second one," Mary told her friends, but she had no complaints. Except one.

Mica's drinking was the one constant and malevolent force that unbalanced their lives. When he was sober, he was a kind man and attentive husband, and he was gentle with his sons. When he drank too much, he became abusive and sometimes violent. Tommy knew the warning signs: His father's voice grew thick. His face appeared swollen and red, until it became the mask of a mean-tempered man who would scream at him, lash out at him, or strike him if the least thing went wrong. If a bowl of sugar tipped onto the floor, his father might give him the back of his hand. If Tommy's little brother got into something he wasn't supposed to, his father screamed at Tommy, who was supposed to look after his younger brother. As foul-tempered as he might be with his sons, however, Mica was worse with Mary.

Mica usually started out as a convivial drinker. When friends came over, he poured the rounds until he became a little tipsy. His tongue wagged, and he was particularly fond of showing off the trappings of their success. They owned two cars. They bought an enormous TV in a wooden console. They gave Tommy and his brother computer games galore. It was all toted out for friends and family to see, and when they left, he would grow dark. He continued to drink by himself. He became pushy for sex. At night, he would wake her from sleep and demand sex and slap her around if she didn't comply. Or he would rape her. Alcohol poisoned Mica's mind until he became steadily more isolated from everyone, and he became paranoid. He started to believe Mary had lovers and that her shopping trips were excuses to meet other men. If she bought new clothes, if she had her hair permed, if she painted her fingernails, it was all because she was having an affair with someone. It got so that he forbade her from using makeup or lipstick. He told her she could not buy new jeans and decreed she wear his old pairs. He restricted her showers to once a week—anything more than that, he believed, was a sign that she was pampering and preening for another man, and he would not have that in his home.

There were terrible scenes in front of the boys. Mica told his sons their mother was a whore and a bitch, and he accused her in front of them of running around with other men, and it was only a matter of time before he battered her in front of them too. Once, in the fall of 1985, Mica choked Mary until she passed out. For two weeks afterward, Mary wrapped a scarf around her neck and wore extra makeup to conceal the black and blue marks from her coworkers. She worried as much about deflecting their questions as she did avoiding his blows. When he wasn't attacking Mary, Mica took out more and more of his frustrations on Tommy—perhaps because he was the eldest. Tommy became gun-shy of any loud voice. By the time Tommy was twelve, he would show the beginnings of standing his ground with his father, but for the most part he quivered at his father's step. The family came unglued, and each of them retreated into themselves or, in Mica's case, into the bottle.

It was a familiar American phenomenon: As the family's prosperity grew, their happiness diminished. Mica's drinking grew heavier, and his interest in work and family life waned. He drove a truck now, but his work habits became spotty. Mary carried more and more of the load. She worked as a cutter at Swedra Knitting Mills in Passaic, New Jersey. Their last year together, she earned $34,701, while Mica was coming home drunk.

It seemed as if their marriage could not grow worse until, on July 19, 1989, it came apart entirely. Some people came by, and Mica became drunk. That night he demanded sex. Mary refused. He began to smack her around, and she jumped out of bed. She sat down in front of the TV, hoping he would fall asleep and leave her alone, but he followed her to the living room. He beat her again and again, and he choked her. Fearing for her life, Mary dashed out of the house into the backyard. She hid in the bushes as he cursed her and crashed around the yard. In bare feet and pajamas, she began to run.

Mary ran in the direction of Paterson. She had a friend there who would shelter her. She ran until she made it to Route 19, a lightly traveled highway at the base of Garret Mountain between Clifton and Paterson, and she kept running until a Paterson police car saw a crazed-looking woman in nightclothes on a highway at 2 o'clock in the morning and stopped to find out why. Mary was driven to the Clifton Police Department headquarters, where she swore out a criminal complaint against her husband. The police noted the evidence that corroborated her story: the chain around her neck had left an impression on her skin from Mica's choking her, and his fingerprints were visible too.

The police arrested Mica and took him to the Passaic County Jail. A Municipal Court judge granted a temporary order of protection that forbade him from returning home. He spent several days in jail before Mary bailed him out, and then—because he called from an apartment and made threats over the telephone in violation of the restraining order—the police locked him up again. Altogether Mica spent seventeen days in jail in the late summer of 1989.

That September, Mary filed for divorce. Mica took off midway through the proceedings. Mary last heard he had gone to Austria, and she assumed that eventually he returned to Yugoslavia, but she never heard from him again. Neither did Tommy. Even relatives on Tommy's father's side in Yugoslavia no longer bothered sending letters or birthday cards. The three of them—Mary, Tommy, and Tommy's younger brother—were on their own. Mary worked two jobs, besides renting out part of their house, to get by. Since Tommy was her eldest son, she treated him like a friend and companion, particularly after her husband left.

Meanwhile, Tommy retreated further inside himself. Not yet thirteen, tall for his age and mousy-looking, he had black hair and thick black eyebrows above a pair of windshield-size glasses. Most of his life was unfolding in the bluish glow of a television screen. When he wasn't watching TV, or playing computer games, he spent time in his room, reading Tolkien's trilogy or Stephen King mysteries. He was making the transition from a boy to a teenager in awkward and tentative steps. He kept a collection of beer and soda cans and his baseball cards on a shelf near stuffed animals of Donald Duck and plastic figurines of Bart Simpson and the Smurfs. To the wall full of car posters and baseball heroes—he taped up the covers from several *Playboy* magazines.

Despite his troubled family life, Tommy did fairly well in school, especially in math and science. He liked reading, too, but he detested writing and found it too much work. Aptitude tests placed him in the top 10 percent of the population in verbal reasoning and numerical ability, but his grades were average. Some of his teachers believed he was wasting his talents, not in a wanton or reckless way, but simply because of indifference. In his last year at the Woodrow Wilson Elementary School, just before entering Clifton High School as a freshman, Tommy earned a C average, getting Bs in science and math but Ds in reading and social studies.

In the time since Mica left, Mary had become mother, father and friend to her boys. Mary played Monopoly or card games with them. Now and then Mary treated Tommy and his little brother to the movies. She wanted to instill the proper values in her boys, and above all she required that they be normal. She would not go in for hippy hair on her boys or pierced ears—although she also could be persuaded to bend. On the one hand, it suited her fine that Tommy spent so much time at home. If he wasn't watching cartoons—his favorite was the adventures of Huey, Dewey and Louie—he was playing computer games on his Nintendo. His favorite game simulated Dungeons and Dragons, the fantasy game that sent players on role-playing quests in a world of medieval knights, trolls, and sorcerers. On the other hand, Mary fretted that he was shut off from the world. Part of being a normal boy was having friends, and Mary wanted Tommy to get out more.

One day at the grocery store, as Tommy helped his mother haul the groceries to the car, they saw a boy riding up on a bicycle. He was a dark-featured, waifish-looking kid. The boy's long bangs dabbed at the corners of his eyes like wingtips.

"Hey, Tommy," the boy said. Both boys waved, and the one on the bike pedaled away. His name was Frank Carboni, and he lived almost in Tommy's neighborhood.

"Who's that?" Mary asked.

Tommy shrugged. "Oh, that's a kid from school," he said. Tommy told her that they had shared a couple of classes together during their first year at Woodrow Wilson School—world history and gym. He said Carboni was an honor student. In fact, Carboni had impressed Tommy as a very bright kid whose head was crammed with interesting facts and ideas, yet he didn't seem like a show-off. Tommy liked that about him.

"How come you don't play with him outside school?" she asked.

"Oh, Ma, I don't know. He took the bus. You picked me up at school," Tommy said.

In time, however, Tommy Stujinski would get to know the boy on the bicycle better. Sometime before the beginning of his ninth-grade school year, in the fall of 1991, Tommy bumped into Carboni on a rainy day, when both of them were looking for something to do. They went to the movies to see *Batman* together. So their friendship began, and in time they would sleep over at each other's house and idle their days away on bicycles, hanging out in local stores, sleeping out with another kid who kept a collection of knives, or laying pennies on the railroad tracks that ran behind Stooge's home for the passing trains to flatten. Tommy would soon become just "Stooge." Through Carboni, he would meet other boys whose lives seemed so much more interesting than his own.

James Paul Wanger was known by several names that changed, like protective coloring, in accordance with his surroundings. At home, he was Jimmy, although sometimes he was Jim. Some relatives and neighbors called him Jamie. As he grew older, he became James to his friends, acquaintances, and classmates. Often, with a bit of distance or a note of derision, he was just Wanger or—with an unmistakable strain of ridicule—The Wang, The Wag, or The Wanger. To make matters worse, at least for a young boy, it sounded very much like *wong* or *wang,* just a few of the common slang words for the penis—not to mention that his last name also sounded like *wanker,* the British slang for masturbator. By almost any standard, his surname was clanging and odd, and it was about all he retained from his father. But to the delight of other kids, Wanger's name was a great name for making fun of, and it was only the beginning. Wanger's oddities and frailties drew plenty of unflattering attention, and his last name became just one more reason for children to torment him.

The first and only child of Paula and Samuel D. Wanger, Jr., James was born on July 22, 1974, almost nine months to the day after his father had filed for divorce. His mother was a licensed nurse working part-time at the Daughters of Miriam Home, a Jewish senior citizens residence on Hazel Street. His father was a warehouse worker at Levitz Furniture in Fairfield. Their very brief and stormy marriage was terminated by a Superior Court judge's signature before James was a month old. The reasons for the divorce and Sam Wanger's departure aren't clear.

The couple was married on January 20, 1973, at St. Clare's Roman Catholic Church on Allwood Road in Clifton, the church where James would learn the rudiments of Roman Catholicism. But by April 8, 1973, Sam Wanger was gone. In his divorce pleadings, Sam Wanger sketched Paula as a crazed woman who interfered with his easygoing life and went ballistic when he stood up to her. Even after he left her, Paula alternately harassed him or threatened to kill herself if he did not take her back. And although there was more than one attempt at reconciliation, these ultimately failed.

Sam Wanger's pleadings stated that he and Paula fought an astounding number of battles in a remarkably short period of time. In quick succession, there were fights when she grabbed the TV, took it in the bedroom, and locked him out because he wouldn't go to bed early with her; when she pounced on him while he was dozing in an easy chair and hit him because he had gone to sleep acting as if he had won an argument; when she winged measuring spoons at him in a quarrel. Another fight ended when she spat on him, and in still another she bit and scratched and kicked him in the groin. It was hard to believe, considering that she was five feet, six inches tall, but Sam Wanger complained that she kept coming after him in one violent or manic episode after another, even after he moved back in with his parents.

Paula drove there one day demanding to speak with him. When Sam Wanger's mother told Paula that her son was out with a male friend, Paula insisted that he must be inside the house, being held against his will. She banged on the doors and windows, screaming and ringing the bell until his mother called the cops. Another time she stood at his parents' front door ringing the doorbell while his parents ignored her. Furious at getting no response, she opened the door of her car and removed a heap of Sam Wanger's clothes, dumping them on the front lawn. Twenty minutes later she came back, and for some reason threw the clothes in the backyard. Another time she tracked him down at work and almost wrecked his car trying to get him to stop and talk to her.

Of course the divorce papers, which he filed on September 25, 1973, suggest that Sam Wanger had done nothing at all to precipitate any of the conflict—other than having exactly *two* beers after playing basketball with some friends, or helpfully, giving her the number of a local tavern where he could be found after he walked out the door one night. (He said he had even gone out of his way to drive her there so she would know where it was, only to have her rip up the slip of paper with the bar's phone number and launch into another fight.) In her papers, however, Paula Wanger denied all of Sam Wanger's charges—and in particular his assertion that there were no children from the union. In her reply to Wanger's pleadings, she pointed out that she was more than four months pregnant.

By the time James was a year old, Samuel Wanger disappeared from the boy's life for good, ceasing to acknowledge his son with so much as a card at Christmas or on his birthday. Other family members would say Samuel Wanger never acknowledged the boy as his flesh and blood, and in fact Sam Wanger promised in his divorce papers to dispute the child's paternity. But the long battle over child support in the years that followed the divorce suggested that he had never disproved paternity, either. Many years later, James would tell friends that he had never met his own father and that he never wanted to meet him, either.

Faced with being a single-parent mother at the age of twenty-two, Paula threw her heart into the project of raising a son, as if by sheer effort a single parent could become two. She got him involved early with St. Clare's Church, where he attended preschool classes and catechism. She helped him set up lemonade stands, took him to art museums, played board games like Monopoly with him, and took him trick-or-treating with other children from Sunday school. She was warm and vivacious, with a personality so effervescent that she seemed forever a teenager. She worked tirelessly to care for the boy and earn a living, sometimes working double shifts as a personal attendant caring for sick and terminally ill people in their homes. Later she also found work as a barmaid. Eventually, the lifting of sick and handicapped people into beds and wheelchairs took its toll on her, crippling her back to the extent that she would require surgery. Yet, for all her hard work, Paula liked a good time. Auburn-haired, blue-eyed, and petite, Paula was an attractive woman who remained hip and pretty at forty, and she liked to have a drink at a local bar. Some thought she was a bit flaky, and members of the Clifton police force knew her because of her habit of making complaints—sometimes justified, and sometimes not—about strangers harassing her, or about a fleeting altercation with another motorist that she feared could escalate.

Given the burden of raising a son alone, Paula turned to her parents, Paul and Martha Colombo, and they would eventually take James into their home and raise him as their own. Before his retirement, Paul Colombo had been a painter who worked at the Meadowlands racetrack. As a young man, Paul wanted to join two brothers serving with the Navy in World War II, but he had been too young to enlist. Instead, after the Japanese surrender, Paul enrolled in the Merchant Marines and acquired a love for the water that he would pass on to his grandson. His wife, Martha, was a homemaker and devout Roman Catholic. They lived in a squat clapboard house with brick facing and aluminum siding that they had purchased in 1962 in Clifton's Delawanna section. There was a shrine of the Virgin Mary in the front yard and a birdbath in the back. The Colombos lived in the second floor of the house, and Anne Kellman, who was James's great-aunt, lived in the first-floor quarters.

James's grandfather became his surrogate father. From the time James could sit up in a boat, Mr. Colombo took the boy fishing on the lakes in Passaic County. He also introduced his grandson to stamp collecting, showed James how to be handy around the house, and took him on nature outings to collect rocks. As James grew older, he and his elderly grandfather trooped to local hotel ballrooms for baseball-card exhibitions and trade shows whenever they came around. Paul Colombo was unfailingly generous as a neighbor, and he imparted his generosity to his grandson. Many years later, his neighbors still recalled how Mr. Colombo took care of a problem with birds in their chimney. One cold winter, the starlings had been perching on the chimney to warm themselves. The fumes intoxicated them and they fell in. The neighbor told Mr. Colombo about the problem, and one day—unbidden—he leaned a ladder against the side of their house and hammered a screen over the flue to protect the birds.

Hand in hand with their devotion to James, Mr. and Mrs. Colombo also were strict and extremely protective: If it was too hot and humid in the summertime, his grandmother ordered him inside, fearing for his asthma. Sometimes James's neighbors heard Paul Colombo's voice booming as he corrected his grandson, or they heard his grandmother calling loudly and impatiently now and then for James to come in. But no one ever saw James's grandparents deal roughly with him—and no one ever heard James talk back or raise his voice to them, or to his mother for that matter. He seldom strayed far from his backyard, and his grandparents always seemed to be close by.

When he was a boy in elementary school, one of James's first and only friends was his next-door neighbor, Christiane

Tempio, who lived with her family next to the Colombo's house. Christi was four years younger than James, and her father, Charles Tempio, thought it a little strange that James, who was around ten years old, found the girl so interesting. But he knew James too, and he saw no reason for alarm. The Tempios attended the same church as James and watched as he participated in the ceremonies first as an altar boy and then as a lector, reading passages from the Bible to the congregation and tending to the candles by the altar. As they saw him mature, the Tempios viewed James as a model child whose worst failing, if it could be seen as that, was that he seemed extraordinarily meek and somewhat sheltered. James invariably spoke to Charlie Tempio and his wife, Diane, in formal address as "Mr. and Mrs. Tempio," and he salted his speech with plenty of "ma'am"s and "sir"s. He was perhaps the only child in the early 1980s in New Jersey who played in neatly creased corduroy pants and man-tailored shirts. The Tempios liked James, and they were forever inviting him to join them in their above-ground swimming pool, and James was always declining because, he told them, his grandmother didn't think it would be good for his frail health.

As for Christi, she adored the boy next door and the brotherly attention he showed her, sometimes referring to him as "my James." To her, Wanger also was "Jamie." She and James spent whole summers together playing in each other's yards and houses, and James was unfailingly patient and polite to her. Despite their difference in age and gender, he never picked on her. He never got fresh. He never even swore. When they played indoors, Jamie showed off the boyish treasures that interested him, like his stamp collection and a truck full of military gear. Outside, they would play for hours together, skipping rope or inventing other diversions; one of their favorites was "Snail," a form of hopscotch whose numbered squares curled into a shell. Planting flowers in the flower beds around the Tempios' house and garden, James showed Christi step by step what to do, and he went into great detail explaining about how the flowers germinated and grew.

The Tempios were impressed about how much he knew his subject, and they found it amusing the way James could sound at times like a pint-size encyclopedia.

But where the Tempios and some neighbors saw an angelic child whose species seemed rare in late twentieth-century America, others saw a boy who seemed excessively withdrawn, weirdly self-absorbed, and maybe disturbed. James agreed to perform stunts to get other kids' attention, but it was more than that. He seemed forever lost in his own world as he played in his yard or pedaled his bicycle around the block, never straying off the curb in front of his house. The bike took him everywhere and nowhere. Until he was nearly thirteen years old, his grandparents forbade him to cross the street. So James would pedal to the brink of the curb, and his playmates would cross, leaving him behind. Other kids thought they would go crazy driving over the same stretch of sidewalk and taunted him for being so goody-goody. But James obeyed his grandparents and kept to his limits. He rode back and forth, wearing the same blank, dreamy face, all the way up to Terhune Avenue, to where a stone fence had been built like a castle wall, complete with crenellated towers, and then back to South Parkway. He rode back and forth so much that the neighbors who lived on the corner suspected James pedaled by all day with the purpose of annoying their dog, which would bolt around his pen yapping out of its head at the flashing bicycle. On days like that Sam Jacalow, who was about three years older than James, observed his young neighbor with a mixture of pity and mild revulsion. James acted like an annoying and very warped kid, and Jacalow didn't pick on him as the other children did simply because James wouldn't react. Wanger was too pathetic to bother with.

But most kids couldn't resist tormenting James—and torment him they did. Everything about him seemed fair game. He dressed nearly always in a quaint outfit of slacks and man-tailored shirts, never blue jeans or a T-shirt. For this alone he was mocked as a "sissy," a "moron," or a "baby." Kids were forever daring him to do things—act up on the bus, say something silly, eat something horrible—and James would do it. On the school bus, the older students would invariably ask James to sing some goofy song that he knew, and James would comply. Sincerely, as if unaware that he was being played the fool, James would sing at the top of his lungs while the other children howled and jeered. If kids brought shaving cream as a prank, it was only a matter of time before everyone ganged up on James and covered him with the stuff. For kicks, when all else failed, older boys on the bus piled onto him in his seat until he was almost smothered and gasping for air. Yet, the more the older children picked on him, the more James seemed to enjoy it—or at least the attention it brought. From his earliest days, being weird was the way he shined.

To add to his troubles, Wanger also was frail, at least as a child. He suffered from allergies that required him to go to the doctor's office once a month to get shots; he had sinus problems that sometimes led to blockages in the Eustachian tubes to his ears; he received speech therapy for about a year at the age of five; he was myopic (testing at 20/70 vision just before he turned twelve years old); he was afflicted with orthodontic problems, and a doctor diagnosed him as having mild curvature of the spine. Even as an infant he had been sickly, having suffered febrile convulsions at birth. Whether as a result of medical problems or nervous habit or both, by the time he became a teenager he seemed to be a collection of nervous tics and ritualistic gestures. Sitting in the classroom or church, his eyes blinked hard from time to time in a sudden exaggerated spasm, which also caused him to scrunch up his nostrils like a feral animal. If he sneezed, he was apt to rap lightly on his chest with his knuckles, as if to restart his heart. By the time he was in high school, he told friends that he suffered from brain seizures of some sort, and he claimed he could die if he didn't take the medication that had been prescribed to control them. In fact, when James had turned fifteen years old, a doctor prescribed the drug Tegritol to control mild, nonepileptic seizures. It was a medicine that he wasn't always very good about taking—and later, when he decided he wanted to join the military, he stopped taking it because he felt it might harm his chances of getting in. But Wanger also told his friends that if he didn't take the drug, he might simply "snap" or do something horrible without knowing what he was doing.

Everything in his childhood, however, pointed to a gentle person who was fond of animals and noble causes. He once found a caterpillar and kept it in a jar, nurturing it every day with milkweed until the creature spun its cocoon and emerged as a monarch butterfly. He cared for a dog and a cat. He participated in a poster contest in middle school on an antidrug theme. His poster won and municipal officials ordered it displayed in City Hall. As a boy of eight or nine, he got it into his head that he would grow up to be a missionary. What this meant to him—a life fulfilled in its holy commitment to God's will, the sense of belonging among a group of like-minded believers, or the promise of foreign travel and adventure—wasn't entirely clear. But he volunteered a great amount of his time to the church, and he couldn't wait until he could enroll in a program that would train him for his work. Other kids made fun of him for his desire. But Wanger persisted. If the teasing bothered him, he didn't let on.

Wanger worshiped with his family at Saint Clare's Roman Catholic Church on Allwood Road, across from a cemetery and close by Main Avenue where it crossed under Route 3. The sanctuary, which resembled an abstract igloo, had been built on the site of a former school building that the congregation had purchased in 1913. In the following years, St. Clare's added a parochial school and a convent. For much of the time when Wanger was growing up, the church's pastor was Monsignor Brendan P. Madden, an Irish priest who had been drawn to the church as a young man by the beauty and mystery of the Roman Catholic rites. Madden, whose pink face with wire-rim glasses and frosting of white eyebrows belied a sturdy will, did not suffer fools gladly. Educated by Irish priests and nuns, he had obtained a literal understanding of the Bible's admonition about sparing the rod, and he believed in firmness in dealing with the children in the church.

But Wanger, who became an altar boy and talked about entering the priesthood, never presented him with any problems. James was nothing if not dutiful in his work for the church. If Father Madden asked James to cut the grass out back, James cut the grass out back. Wanger was always compliant and obedient. In fact, he had a dreamy quality that set him apart from other boys and made him seem to be always outside himself. It wasn't that he was just going through the motions. He seemed earnest. But unlike other children his age, Wanger became wholly lost in his private reveries as he went about performing his rites at church services or carrying out his chores on the church grounds. Who knew what was going through his head, but it also didn't seem as if he was transported by his faith. Wanger almost never discussed the Bible or the teachings of Jesus in a way that betrayed an intellectual engagement with his religion, and if he wanted to be a priest or a missionary, he seldom discussed it with Madden. The priest viewed Wanger as a good kid but nothing extraordinary—strictly *vin ordinaire*. All the same, Madden instructed Wanger in the arts and duties of being an altar boy, and later a church lector. By the time he was a teenager, Wanger had begun to teach grade-school children about Catholicism in CCD, or catechism classes.

Outside the church, James threw himself into one altruistic or moneymaking project after another. He mowed the lawn free of charge for his disabled neighbor. He set up lemonade, Kool-Aid, and hot chocolate stands in front of the house and sent the proceeds to charity. He busied himself with projects to alleviate world hunger. He once came across a flier asking for $2 to help missing and abused children, mass-produced a batch more, and raised $550, which he gave to the organization. When Paula gave him cuttings from her plants, James tended the growths until he had an array of mature blooms. Then, in advance of Mother's Day, he and his mother set up a bench outside the house to sell them, and James donated the money to another agency doing the Lord's work. If he wasn't donating his blood, which he did regularly once he was old enough, he sent money to a children's hospital or to organizations in support of research for heart disease, lung cancer, and other diseases.

There was hardly a wholesome activity that James didn't throw himself into, carrying his participation beyond the place where most kids stopped. He joined the Cub Scouts and advanced nearly to the level of Eagle Scout. On February 7, 1988, when he was thirteen years old, Wanger received the Ad Altare Dei Award along with twenty-three other area scouts. The award, which means "To the Altar of God," was presented personally by Paterson Bishop Rodimer following a mass at St. Therese Roman Catholic church in Succasunna. James had devoted six months to obtaining the award, and he was the only boy from Clifton to do so. By the time he was seventeen, he was close to achieving the rank of Eagle Scout when his interest, competing now with other projects in high school, began to wane.

Along the way, in addition to his interest in the priesthood and his commitment to philanthropy, Wanger became a patriot. Wanger believed that everyone should serve his country in some fashion or another, and for him this meant the military. He liked the idea of joining the Navy or the Marines. For a time, James did some work at the Navy recruiting station in Clifton. Paula, who had come of age in the rebellious 1960s and early 1970s, found the notion of patriotic displays and unquestioning allegiance personally distasteful, but she stifled her own reservations and went along with her son, encouraging him in whatever he wanted to do. As James showed greater and greater interest in the armed services, particularly the Navy, Paula put aside her Vietnam-era disgust with all things military to encourage him to join the United States Naval Sea Cadets, a preenlistment and recruiting organization.

As James grew older, the Tempios would see Paula dropping James off at her grandparents', and he would be wearing his Boy Scout uniform or his Sea Cadets uniform, but they saw much less of him now that he had apparently found other teenage friends of his own. Now and then, the neighbors still saw him playing in the backyard, throwing around a football with his grandfather. To the Tempios, it was a memorable and poignant sight as the old man moved around the yard demonstrating the rudiments of a rigorous sport to an awkward boy. They noticed that Paula always seemed to be rushing off somewhere, busy with this or that, and James always seemed to have some project or other going. Nothing seemed to be amiss. Only, a few neighbors noticed now and then that James would pull up at the curb in a friend's car and get out, acting very drunk.

In the middle of October 1991, Tommy "Stooge" Stujinski ran into Frank Carboni at the Main Avenue street fair, an event awash in the pungent aroma of overheated fry vats and Italian sausage. Both boys were fourteen years old. Having met by chance, the boys pulled up to each other on their bicycles and started talking. Carboni told Stooge he was thinking about buying a knife at one of the displays. Tommy was interested, so he wheeled his bicycle around to follow Carboni to the knife. The Main Avenue Mall, as the one-day event was known officially, was a twice-annual affair. Police would close off eight blocks of Main Avenue, between Luddington and Grace, and approximately 200 vendors would join the local merchants in setting out tables of handicrafts, T-shirts, musical recordings, jewelry, antiques, and other wares. There was almost always a DJ or some form of entertainment adding to the carnival atmosphere. The open air alone made the sidewalk sales so pleasant that it was almost forgotten that the event was a last stand by local shopkeepers in the battle against suburban shopping malls.

The knife that had caught Carboni's eye features a long blade with a special sheath that allowed it to be concealed inside a boot or under a pants leg strapped to an ankle. It was going to set Carboni back about $25. The guy who ran the stand had no problem showing the knife to the two young boys, but he refused to sell it to them. You had to be eighteen years old to buy it, the man said, or you could get your parent or a guardian to buy it for you. Carboni had someone in mind.

"Let's go to Frank's," he said.

Stooge had heard Carboni talk about his cousin Frank Castaldo in the past, but Stooge had never met him. He had heard through Carboni that Castaldo like to hang out at the pool hall. In fact, a chance meeting at the pool hall had allowed Carboni and his cousin to become reacquainted. Lately, Carboni and Castaldo had been hanging around together more often, and Carboni had been spending more and more time at Castaldo's place. What he described there sounded to Stooge like an adolescent boy's dream. At least during the day, the Castaldo home operated like a boy's clubhouse: The rules of the place were more or less laid down by Frank Castaldo. His parents, both of whom worked, either were never home or never seemed to bother themselves with what Castaldo and his friends were doing. If they did complain, Castaldo usually backed them off or ignored them. But for much of the time, a guy could hang out with no adults around to hassle with, smoke cigarettes, meet girls, drink now and then, and be cool.

2

It took almost no time for Stooge and Carboni to pedal their bicycles the three or four blocks from the Main Avenue street fair to Frank Castaldo's house, which was located in a working-class neighborhood near Clifton's border with the city of Passaic. Sitting about halfway down a short side street, the Castaldo home was a boxcar flat armored in white siding that had turned the color of old snow. The Castaldos occupied the first floor and rented out all but one room on the second floor to tenants, usually single women. There was a blacktop driveway on the left leading up to a slight bank. Stooge and Carboni parked their bikes and walked up the front stairs. The brick stoop was crumbling, and there was only a half-inch lead pipe as a banister. One of the family's dogs, a German shepherd/collie mix named Rebel, was always barking in the back. Carboni rang the doorbell and Castaldo let them in.

Castaldo seemed smaller than Stooge might have guessed from all the advance billing. Castaldo stood only about five feet, seven inches tall and weighed about 160 pounds. He had a habit of shuffling around with his chin jutting out and his shoulders stooped. He smiled easily and had a good sense of humor. Since he didn't have a job, he spent most of his time watching television. Above the television set and the VCR were some blown-up color photographs mounted in rough-hewn wood frames. Time had bleached out the color in the family snapshots, but the Castaldos still beamed on their wedding day, and Frankie peered upward at the camera as a toddler with a child's suspicious look. Another picture showed Frankie as a bespectacled schoolboy wearing a radiant smile and a tie.

Carboni told Castaldo why they had come. Castaldo said it was no problem, that he would gladly buy the knife for his cousin. It wasn't unusual for him to help out his younger friends by buying cigarettes or booze for them. They chatted in the living room as Castaldo prepared to go.

Stooge stepped across the tiled foyer into the living room and looked around in amazement at the clutter. The house was crammed with bric-a-brac and junk. The living-room couch was covered with clothing, and there were ashtrays brimming with cigarette butts and dirty dishes strewn over the coffee table by the remote control and some videotapes. A peep through the dining room into the kitchen beyond promised even worse. There were dirty pots in the kitchen sink, food had spilled on the stove, and the counter was grimy, as if it hadn't been wiped with a clean cloth for a while. It was not squalor per se, just chaos, but definitely not the kind of place Stooge was used to. You were taking your chances reaching into the Castaldo refrigerator that a carton of milk had spoiled or something. In contrast, Castaldo himself was dressed neatly. Usually, he wore clothes that the kids at the high school would call "guido" style—dress shirts or clothing with B.U.M. logos, Cavaricci pants. Now and then he wore a clean white T-shirt and blue jeans.

"Where's your room?" Stooge asked.

"You're sitting in it," Castaldo said.

They chuckled. But it was true. The living room was Castaldo's bedroom and the couch, a velour affair tucked against the front windows, was his bed. Except for a few infrequently used dress suits, Castaldo kept most of his stuff in a heap on the floor in the closet of his little brother's room, off the kitchen. But it didn't matter where Frankie slept. For a sizable part of the day he had the run of the house. He also had a lot of visitors. Frank Castaldo's house was the place to be, and it sometimes didn't matter whether Frankie was even home.

The first child of Italian immigrants, Frank Castaldo was born on September 19, 1973, at St. Mary's Hospital in Passaic. His birth certificate listed no middle name. By the time he entered elementary school, records appeared listing him as Frank Anthony Castaldo. His mother, Alfonsina Andreana Castaldo, was nineteen when she gave birth to Frankie, as the family called him. His father, Giuseppe, was then twenty-five years old. Blond and ruggedly handsome, Giuseppe Castaldo had left Italy after a stint in the Army to find work in the United States. He came over on a boat with one of his younger brothers and some distant relatives. His first job in the United States was working for a company in Garfield, New Jersey, that imported *cararra* marble. Giuseppe's American coworkers called him Joe, and the name stuck. Across the Passaic River, Alfonsina set up housekeeping in an apartment on Parker Avenue in Clifton.

Either because of homesickness or because Giuseppe's new job could not be counted on for the long term, they returned to Italy for a time. Frankie was about six months old when Alfonsina and Giuseppe returned to the small town where both of them had grown up. They had lived in a village named Baiano near Avellino, Italy, a modest-size town in the Apennines mountains east of Naples. Their village, set in countryside that was rugged and picturesque, was so tiny that it seemed as if everyone there shared a blood tie. In fact, Alfonsina and Giuseppe were second cousins (Alfonsina's maternal grandfather and Giuseppe's paternal grandfather were brothers, but their families had been distant), and their marriage had been arranged by their parents. When Alfonsina was a teenage girl taking secretarial classes, Giuseppe's parents came by her family's farm in the summer of 1972. Taken with the girl, whose strong Mediterranean face was distinguished by prominent cheekbones, dark eyes, and a broad toothy grin, the Castaldos decided it would be best if she and their son married. The formal proposal of marriage—Giuseppe gave a ring—was made on August 22, 1972. The Roman Catholic wedding ceremony, resplendent in all the customary trappings and traditions of a splashy Italian celebration, took place on December 10, 1972.

When the Castaldos returned to Italy, their families, particularly Alfonsina's parents, were mad with joy over the young couple's first son. The Castaldos stayed with Alfonsina's parents. Traditional gentry, her parents lived in a wealthy villa, raised dairy animals, pressed their own cheeses, and baked in coal-fired brick ovens. Their cash crop was hazelnuts, which were harvested and then dried on rooftop terraces. In February 1975, about a year after returning to Italy, Alfonsina gave birth to a second child, Angelina, and the young family talked once more about settling in the United States. Again, they went off to America, and again they settled in Clifton in circumstances that were impoverished compared with what they knew in Italy.

This time the family rented an apartment on Getty Avenue in Clifton. Alfonsina raised the children, while Joe went to work as a millman at the Bay State Milling Company, a job that he would hold for nearly two decades. It wasn't bad work, and often he lugged home five- and ten-pound sacks of flour or sugar that he purchased from the plant at prices cheaper than at the supermarket. But Joe put in twelve-hour days sometimes, repairing machinery or feeding grain into huge machines that milled flour for pizza chains and local bakeries. He was up by 7 A.M. and out the door, and when he came home around the dinner hour he headed straight for his bedroom to rest. Until her children approached their teens, Alfonsina stayed at home.

After a few years the couple bought a two-story frame house on Prescott Avenue, just off Main Avenue, and rented out the upper floor. It was in one of the poorest sections of town, with two-thirds of the families there earning less than

$25,000 a year. Most of their neighbors also were of Italian descent. The houses were drab and shabby, and Clifton's border with the ailing city of Passaic was only a few blocks away. But the street was peaceful. Because it was so short, almost like a cul-de-sac, Frankie and the other kids in the neighborhood could play football, baseball, and kickball on the pavement, stopping only for the cars that occasionally came through. In April 1978, Alfonsina Castaldo gave birth to the couple's third and last child, whom they named Stefano.

As a clan, the Castaldos were a hot-blooded, hot-tempered lot. They were fairly close to each other, spending hours standing around the kitchen and talking while their mother fussed at the stove, and they spent even more time together in front of the TV, with Mrs. Castaldo watching whatever the kids were watching. Mr. and Mrs. Castaldo's marriage was a traditional one in which the roles of husband and wife had been fixed by convention long ago. They sometimes conversed in Italian, using the Neapolitan dialect, and their children picked up a little of it. Alfonsina called her husband "Penuch" and deferred to him on the grander issues the family faced, but on a day-to-day basis she ran the household. There was not a lot of money. Family vacations consisted of day trips in the family car to Sandy Hook down on the Jersey shore. They played simple games together around the kitchen table. Mrs. Castaldo liked to have her children play at home with their friends so that she could keep an eye on them. She enjoyed her children, too, and she was the kind of mother who would get up and dance like mad with the teenagers at her daughter's birthday party. They laughed a lot together, and liked to tease each other. But when the Castaldos clashed, they let loose freely. A disagreement could become a squabble, escalate into a quarrel, and a quarrel sometimes snowballed into an out-and-out fight, with bouts of screaming or worse. One visitor to the house remembered long afterward how Angie had flown at her father and choked him during a fight.

Frankie's childhood seemed ordinary, or at least little different from that of any of the other scrappy kids who lived on the block. When Castaldo entered kindergarten at School 12, he earned an A in behavior—a pinnacle that he reached at the age of five and never again matched. By the end of the following school year, his conduct marks had started slipping, and his first-grade teacher was suggesting that Frank be held back a year. His father agreed.

But Frankie never improved. He seemed always to be lagging, despite standardized tests that suggested that he was of normal intelligence and, in some areas, quite bright. For example, by the eighth grade, he had settled to the bottom 20th percentile in language skills—but he also ranked in the top 20 percent in abstract reasoning. He liked numbers and he had a decent recall for historical dates. By the time he entered the sixth grade at the Christopher Columbus School, he showed an interest in computers, although this went only so far. Monkeying around with a Commodore keyboard and a monitor, Frankie played games and ran a few simple programs, and he borrowed friends' disk drives to make it work. But on the whole, school bored him out of his wits. He wriggled in his seat, studying the clock. The classroom confined him, and he hated it, although he also was at a loss to say what it was he wanted to do otherwise. By the end of middle school, he had learned that it was much more interesting to cut classes than attend them.

Early on, Frankie encountered another distraction from his studies: girls. In the fifth grade, when many boys still wanted nothing to do with girls, Frankie started fooling around with them. He had sexual intercourse for the first time when he was a seventh- or eighth-grader; she was three years older than he. What her last name was, he didn't know. He didn't care, either. They had sex and he never called her or spoke to her again. He already had moved on. For Frankie was not only sexually precocious, he was—at least by his own account—promiscuous, too. He bragged of having sex with sixty-five different girls, most of whom were younger than he, before he turned eighteen. True or not, Frankie soon acquired the reputation of a Don Juan, and he played it for all it was worth. Nothing could be better than prowling suburbia for girls, driving around in his friends' cars eyeing girls, trolling Main Avenue on foot for girls, hanging out at the pool hall to impress the girls, and—especially—hunting the local shopping malls for girls. His parents shared a resigned sense of pride that their son should be a ladies' man. Charming the girls also happened to be one of the few things Frankie could boast about. Another was brawling.

Around town Frankie became known as a tough kid who liked to fight. He boasted that he had never backed down in a fight and never shied from helping a friend. He wore with pride small scars above his left eye and on his right cheek from fights he had been in as a kid. Fighting was part of the code of honor, something that had to be done from time to time to restore the balance. Friendship meant, he would say, to stand by someone in trouble. Yet Frankie liked to say that he didn't hold grudges after a fight. You did it and moved on. He brawled once with a kid named Steve Kraviec—over what, no one remembers—only to become one of Kraviec's best friends later. Once, when a buddy of his was arguing with another teenager, Frankie took it upon himself to step in.

"Why you talking to him?" Frankie said in his friend's ear. "Don't waste your time. Just hit him."

And Frankie showed him how.

When Castaldo entered Clifton High School's ninth grade in September 1989, he was fifteen years old, already a year behind, and known as a troublemaker. It was only a matter of time before Detective Chris Kelly, a member of Clifton Police Department's Youth Services Bureau, who was assigned to the high school as a liaison to the youngsters there, came to know Frankie as well. Kelly, who had an office just outside the principals' office near the main entrance, came to like many of the kids. His door was always open. A lot of girls came by to flirt or gossip or complain about trivial matters at home, but most of the time Kelly was dealing with kids in trouble. Most of it was run-of-the-mill stuff: runaways, fights, vandalism, thefts, teenage drinking, and drug abuse. Kelly took a go-easy approach, preferring to handle most crises as a counselor rather than as a cop—on more than one occasion, he found himself fending off school officials who wanted criminal complaints filed against kids caught smoking cigarettes on school property. Building a rapport with the kids gave Kelly an important vantage not only on what happened behind the scenes at the school, but on what was happening in the community at large: Kelly knew which kids were using drugs, who was drinking, who was running away, and often what their parents were up to, besides.

When Kelly met Castaldo he thought the kid had an angelic face, which would seem wildly out of character later on. Not that Frankie got in serious trouble all the time. The kid was even likable. And despite his brushes with the law, Frankie was never charged with a juvenile complaint. It was just that Castaldo was at the lower strata of the high school and seemed to like it there. He carried himself like some minor character in a Damon Runyon sketch. Too smooth by half.

Kelly had Frankie come in one day after a boy's car had been "keyed"—that is, someone had taken a key or similarly sharp object and cut a long vicious scratch into the paint. Word had it that Castaldo had done it. Frankie slumped into a chair in Kelly's office, and Kelly asked him what he knew about it.

"I don't know nothing," Castaldo kept saying.

Kelly and Castaldo were in the office for a long, long time, with Castaldo insisting on his innocence as firmly as Kelly believed he was the one who had vandalized the car. Castaldo stonewalled so long that Kelly was impressed. Finally, Castaldo threw up his hands and agreed to pay for the damage. But he wouldn't admit to being the culprit.

Well before Frankie entered high school as a ninth-grader, his flair for handling himself in a fight and picking up girls had made him ever so cocky, particularly in his dealings with girls. He knew he was handsome. His face was lively and distinctive, with wide-set, almost sleepy, brown eyes. He had a firm, square jaw, a cleft chin, and good teeth, although they had yellowed a little from smoking cigarettes. Devoting considerable energy toward mastering the nuances of skirt-chasing, Frankie believed he knew when to move in and when to play hard to get—which was often, since he subscribed to the notion that it almost never hurt to ignore a girl in order to pique her interest. He knew how to make girls laugh, and he didn't mind breaking the ice for somebody else. Other boys his age might be tongue-tied and uptight, but Frankie could be spontaneous, silly, and unafraid of appearing ridiculous if it got a girl to smile. Girls seemed to appreciate his direct manner, and they definitely appreciated that he would pick up on things that were important to them—stuff like who their favorite rock singers were, what their favorite color was, and so on. It also helped that he wasn't afraid to dance. He loved going to the local dance clubs, and he collected dance music by groups like Clear Touch, Johnny O, and Cynthia.

Yet, even as a teenager, Frankie seemed to show two faces to the girls he liked: One minute he would be charming and protective, but the next he could be defensive, jealous, or angry, liable to blow his temper at the slightest provocation. In 1989, for example, Frankie started dating a girl. She was thirteen years old. Frankie was sixteen. Frankie wooed her, making a point of knowing that her favorite color was red and her favorite musical artist was Phil Collins. It was the girl's first love, and she became consumed with Frankie and the awesomeness of their shared destiny, elevating their teenage romance to the status of a religious event. She made Frankie wait eight months to have sex. They virtually lived together, and it should have been obvious that they were sexually active. Apparently no one raised an eyebrow.

But she and her mother also found out that Frank's personality could go south in a flash. During one fight, Frankie struck her. The fight began one day when Frankie got a call from another girl. There was hell to pay. Angie Castaldo ran upstairs to get their neighbor to help her break up the fight.

The neighbor came downstairs, and the girl appealed to her to take her home. The neighbor agreed.

Hands on his hips and glowering, Frank continued yelling as the girl pulled away in the neighbor's car. The look on his face seemed to suggest that he had the power to order her back if he wished. After that they started fighting all the time. Later that summer, they fought after Frankie saw her dancing with another guy at a club. Frankie told her he was done. He hung up the phone when she tried calling. He refused to see her again when she came by. Three days after the scene in the dance club, she attempted suicide. She spent time in a hospital and then in a rehabilitation center. Frankie softened his stance, and he met with a psychologist, but his relationship with her was finished. Long afterward, the girl's mother felt that her daughter needed counseling to get over the affair.

Meanwhile, Frankie went about his business, which consisted of skipping school and loafing. His parents railed at him but without effect.

"You leave for school, and you don't get there," his mother would say. "What happens?"

What happened was that Frank went to the pool hall, the Willowbrook Mall, uptown, friends' houses, driving around—anywhere but school. By March 16, 1990, Frankie had missed ninety days of school—or a little less than half of the entire school year to date—and the school called in his parents, who seemed muddled, supportive, alarmed, and indulgent at the same time. There was no way Frankie would pass the school year, school officials said, and it seemed as if the problems were more intractable than study habits.

Everyone agreed that Frankie should go to the Family Recovery Center in Paramus for evaluation and therapy. There Frankie admitted to drinking a little bit, but that was it. The shrinks accused him of denial. They recommended that he go to an inpatient rehabilitation facility in the Pocono Mountains for further evaluation. Grudgingly, to get the doctors off his back, Frankie agreed to go—but on the understanding that the stay would last no more than ten days.

Once Frankie got there, he felt the staff harped on him to face up to a substance-abuse problem that he didn't have. He submitted to the urine test, which came back negative, and he insisted that his only problem was his dislike of school. The staff didn't buy it, and the center decided to make the stay last thirty days—at least that's what Frankie's family heard from him. His parents, who agreed that he should go, were on his side again. Deciding that some plan was afoot to keep Frankie indefinitely, Alfonsina made up her mind to go get him. Frankie's family had never been convinced that Frankie's problems were anything more serious than a bad attitude, and they believed the talk of a drinking problem was overblown.

Frankie returned to Clifton and made up his schoolwork in summer classes. In boyishly crabbed handwriting, he wrote to the high school's principal, Robert P. Mooney, that summer, asking to be reinstated.

"I will abide by all the schools rules and Regulations," Frankie wrote. "Attend school Regularly, and try to be the best student I possibly CAN. I will also participate in school activities and try to be more a part of the school.

"I would appreciate your consideration in this matter."

Thanks to summer school, Frankie came back in the fall of 1990 without falling another year behind. But he only seemed to be more of a junior hoodlum. Frankie dressed in sinister-looking getups that made him look more dangerous than he was: lots of black, usually a long black trench coat. On the other hand, Frankie was respectful enough in the halls, greeting Kelly, for example, as "Detective Kelly" and acting decently.

But Frankie's summertime pledge to become an upstanding citizen of Clifton High School lasted no longer than the first grading period, when he turned in Fs in every single class, including Creative Living. No longer postponing the inevitable, Castaldo quit school midway through tenth grade. On February 8, 1991, his father signed an acknowledgment that his son was quitting, stating as a reason that Castaldo was seeking employment.

Despite dropping out, Frankie still came around the school. If anything, he seemed to be there more often. When Detective Kelly spotted Castaldo lurking around the school grounds, the detective would say hello, ask how he was doing, and tell him politely to leave. But Frankie kept up friendships with kids in the high school, mostly with younger kids who could not seem to fit in anywhere else. Even when Castaldo was nowhere to be found around school, he still exerted some influence, if only because his house soon became a hangout for the slacker crowd. If a kid cut school or ran away, it was a safe bet that sooner or later he or she would turn up at Castaldo's. Kelly heard about it all the time: Castaldo's place was Party Central, especially for the pool-hall crowd.

In fact, Kelly would occasionally turn to Frankie to reach kids in trouble, asking Frankie if he knew where so-and-so was.

"They better get home before I find them or they're in trouble," Kelly would say. Or Kelly would ask Frankie to pass word to a runaway girl to have her call home or call Kelly so at least her parents would know where she was.

And Clifton Billiards was Frank Castaldo's home away from home. A down-and-out landmark located on Main just below Harding Avenue, the pool hall was not one of these yuppie joints that were springing up on every corner in Manhattan at the time. This was the real thing, whose down-at-the-heels decor and blue-collar, leather-jacket, 'Boro-smoking clientele exuded a sense of danger and expertise. A sign in the back said "Clifton Billiard Lounge." Gum-snapping girls in doorknocker earrings and black leather stood around talking tough while clumps of teenage boys chalked cue sticks and talked tougher. Here and there were a few old-timers whose faces barely emerged from the gray fog of tobacco smoke. Kids who were too young to drive pulled their cue sticks like weapons from tight leather cases, screwed them together, and settled down to shoot games for money. Although signs on the wall warned that there was no gambling, strangers who walked off the street and up the dirty scarlet plush on the carpeted stairs could expect to be hustled at least for the price of a table.

"You don't need a table, honey," a guy named Hank would say at the counter to some of the girls who came through. "You need a rack of balls."

There was a refreshment counter, a bulletin board with the standings of local tournaments, and a clock whose hands advanced over twelve billiard balls to count the hours. There were about fifteen pool tables in the cavernous space, and the lighting was terrible except directly above the felt. There were six narrow windows on the west side of the room. By the time the kids would start getting out of school, the sunlight slanted sharply through the venetian blinds and cut geometric shapes in the fog of cigarette smoke. The walls, covered in muddy brown paneling like a rec room from the 1960s, contained a few posters of Jackie Gleason and Paul Newman from *The Hustler*.

The staff kept a blacklist of unwelcome guests somewhere behind the counter, but Castaldo wasn't on it. His father told the staff to throw him out by 10 o'clock at night because he was supposed to get home by then, but Castaldo wasn't considered a troublemaker, not by a long shot. He had a lot of pull, in fact. Frankie was a regular who knew almost everybody in the pool hall. He loved the joint and he liked the thrill of hustling there. He bragged of having seen $1,500 wagered on a single game and $500,000 cash thrown on a table in a match. When he wasn't playing pool, he played chess with some of the guys behind the counter. Castaldo was reasonably good at chess; he knew enough opening gambits and lines of play to wager twenty dollars a game. By his own admission he was only average at billiards. But he was still the best of the group. He could beat his cousin Carboni, who was probably closest to him in ability, and he could beat Stooge, too, although Stooge also had a pretty good eye.

Frank Carboni was a bright kid. By almost any measure, he was easily one of the brightest in the group of six boys, with the possible exception of Stooge, or Wanger before Wanger discovered alcohol. But Carboni, perhaps uncomfortable assuming the conventional role of the gifted student, chose to become a wiseguy instead of a brain.

Until that day in September 1991 when Carboni walked into the pool hall, he and Frank Castaldo, separated in age by about three and a half years, had been only nodding acquaintances. Castaldo and Carboni got together at weddings or funerals or other large family gatherings, and that was about it. After meeting in the pool hall, however, they shot a few racks of balls and went over to Castaldo's house. For Carboni, it was just about the first time he had been to the Castaldos' on a visit that didn't involve the whole family. From that day on, however, Carboni started going more and more.

It was a coincidence that Carboni and Castaldo shared the same first name. What made it interesting was that Carboni seemed to want to be Castaldo. By the age of fourteen, Carboni idolized his older cousin, a tenth-grade dropout who split his time between his home and the pool hall and wherever someone with a car was willing to take him.

Carboni was born May 20, 1977, to Stephen and Maria Carboni. He was the eldest of three children: His mother gave birth to a second son a little less than two years later and a daughter five years later. His mother had immigrated to the United States from Italy in the late 1960s when she was twenty years old. In her native country she had attended school as far as the fifth grade, but she studied English after arriving in America. She found work as a sewing-machine operator in Garfield, receiving her wages based on the pieces she produced. She held the job for ten years until being laid off sometime around 1991. After losing her job, Carboni's mother became a full-time housewife.

Maria Carboni was related to the Castaldo family through Frank Castaldo's father, Giuseppe. Her father and Giuseppe Castaldo's father were brothers. That made Maria Carboni and Giuseppe Castaldo first cousins, and by extension Frank Castaldo and Frank Carboni were second cousins. Both families came from the same area of Italy. Indeed, Maria Carboni's husband, Stephen Carboni, also had been born and raised in Italy in the same town as Giuseppe Castaldo. Stephen Carboni dropped out of school after the ninth grade and joined the military. Frank Carboni's parents married in July 1975, the same year that Stephen came to the United States. He took the oath of United States citizenship three years after leaving his homeland, and he became a factory hand at Fritzsche, Dodge & Olcott, a chemical company that employed 120 workers in Clifton. The company, which manufactured chemical flavors and fragrances used in foods and cosmetics, exuded nauseatingly sweet odors that residents were often at a loss to describe. Some said the plant smelled like cinnamon or suntan lotion. Having worked at the company more than thirteen years, Carboni's father became an assistant shop foreman.

In November 1975, they bought a two-story, three-bedroom house on Clinton Avenue for $42,250 and gave their son a bedroom in the attic. It was everything a kid could want: Under the eaves at the top of a zigzagging set of narrow stairs, Carboni's room was divided into a space for his desk, his books, and his school things, and an entertainment area with a sofa, a stereo, and a television set. He had a battery of Nintendo games and decorated his room with gleaming, cast-metal replicas of automobiles.

His parents were kind but also strict, forbidding Carboni to be out after dark—although this changed after he began to hang around with Stooge. Carboni was expected to work around the house, and in return he received an allowance. He cut the grass, he painted, he did what needed to be done, and he learned to work hard. He also learned that he could bend the rules a bit more if he pitched in with chores around the house.

By his freshman year, Carboni stood five-feet-eight inches and weighed 132 pounds. He resembled a young Al Pacino: He had glittering brown eyes and hair that was almost black; thick eyebrows and long, almost feminine eyelashes; a slightly downturned mouth and a brooding aspect that was heightened by his fondness for speaking in blunt, foreshortened phrases. His hair was cut close to the skin in the back and parted down the middle in the front, where his bangs flared to the sides. On his upper lip was a vain, almost imperceptible mustache. Neighbors who remembered a skinny kid patrolling around the streets on his bike, indistinguishable from other kids, suddenly took note of his new habit of wearing gold jewelry and a long black trench coat. By that time, Carboni also had his own pool cue, and he often skipped classes to go to the pool hall with Stooge. They played eight ball and nine ball for hours. Then they would drop by Castaldo's. Carboni's parents imposed a curfew of 9 P.M. on weeknights and 10 P.M. on weekends. This was a constant source of friction in the household, with Carboni frequently arguing for permission to stay out longer. His parents eventually agreed that he could stay out to 11 P.M. on weekends. On special occasions, he could stay out later. But whatever the curfew, Carboni also had his own key and sneaked out after hours anyway.

When Carboni was of school age, he entered public grammar school near his home. That was School 15, an imposing old building that sat on a hill on Gregory Avenue beside Weasel Brook Park. Carboni was a good student who gave the teachers no problems. Most knew him as a shy, quiet kid with soulful eyes. But he had a high opinion of himself, which steadily emerged as a kind of sullen cockiness. No doubt this was a consequence of his abilities, for he was smart, and when he entered the Woodrow Wilson School as a sixth-grader, Carboni was enrolled in the gifted and talented program. He earned mostly Bs, except for As in social studies, art, and science, and he was testing in the 90th percentile in almost every subject. Leaving Woodrow Wilson School where he had first met Stooge, Carboni entered high school with the freshman class of 1995 and performed about as well. His gift for language earned him entrance into honors English. His vocabulary included words like "malevolence," "pliancy," "qualm," and "paradoxically." At school, he read Jack London's *White Fang* and Greek myths. On his own Carboni read Stephen King mysteries—but by the beginning of high school it was clear that his attention had strayed far from school and literature. In December and January of his freshman year, he also started working after school at Ploch's Garden Center for $4.25 an hour.

Since September 1991, Carboni and Stooge had been spending more and more time at the pool hall and at his cousin's house, and Carboni's grades reflected it. Well aware that it wasn't the material that was giving him difficulties, his teachers became troubled by his performance.

"Are you studying?" one teacher asked after Carboni bombed an English test. A surly, disruptive, and angry side of Carboni began to emerge. He had frequent run-ins with the guidance counselor and at least one teacher by the name of Irene Falcone. Clashes with the faculty led to Carboni's receiving two in-school suspensions and one three-day, out-of-school suspension that fall. His rage toward Falcone grew. One day he filled a sheet of notebook paper with the words "Kill the Bitch," written over and over.

At best, Carboni could be devilish, relishing his ability to get under the skin of kids his own age and especially authority figures, and at his worst, he could be malicious. Among his friends, Carboni was famous for his stubbornness. Once his mind was made up, it was difficult to persuade him to change it. As an exercise for school, he once wrote an assessment of himself. It was written throughout in the third person:

> He's high-strung. He always thought he was better than everyone in one way or another. He was annoying and always gave people an attitude. He always stole . . . He always wanted people to like him. He tried to be popular. He thought he was tough. He would start trouble but need help getting out of it. Tried to act older than he was . . . He always tried to act as if he was in power.

Had a drinking problem . . . Blamed his mistakes on others. He always carried a knife.

The one thing Carboni omitted happened to be his deepest obsession: fire. His friends thought he was a pyromaniac, but no one knew why, and Carboni either was unable to articulate—or uninterested in explaining—the poetry he saw inside the flames. He owned a Zippo lighter and kept the plastic box and cardboard liner it came in, propping them up on the banister of his bedroom like a kind of shrine. Besides the lighter, which he always carried, he sometimes packed an extra can of lighter fluid. He was always playing with the lighter, practicing and showing off how he could hold it between his thumb and two fingers and snap open the metal hood in one quick gesture by squeezing his hand.

Once, he doused his boot with lighter fluid while he was wearing it and lit it on fire. He squirted lighter fluid on people's floors, on the ground, or almost anywhere, and then torched it, watching the flame zip across the line of fuel like a fuse. When autumn came, Carboni poured lighter fluid from one pile of leaves to another as he rode by in a car or on a bicycle, and then he would light the fluid, setting off a chain reaction of smoke and flame. Another favorite stunt was to dip his fingers in rubbing alcohol or lighter fluid and light them on fire. All five fingers would go up, a wild candelabra that looked like a movie stunt, and he would spread his fingers and watch as the blue flame swirled, yellowed, and died. The fire seemed to consume his entire hand. But the trick was to make sure the fingertips were soaked, really soaked, with alcohol. The alcohol would flame off without burning the flesh. But still the fingers would get hot, and he'd blow them out, and everyone would tell him he was crazy.

"People are going to know me," Carboni had said to Castaldo more than once. "People are going to know me. They're going to know my name."

"Yeah, yeah," Castaldo said. "I know."

During the fall of 1991, as Castaldo's friendship with Carboni and Stooge grew, the two younger boys showed up more and more often at the pool hall, and eventually both Stooge and Carboni purchased their own cue sticks.

Unaware that Castaldo was half the reason their son headed to the pool hall, Carboni's parents had told Castaldo to keep an eye on their son and make sure he didn't get mixed up in drugs or anything. But Carboni was always cutting school or stealing or lying to his parents, calling up and telling them he was at Castaldo's when he wasn't. They played straight pool or games of eight ball and nine ball, usually for money. There was "Race to Three," where the first to win three games in a row would pocket ten dollars. Or they played "Buck a Ball."

At first, it was fun to have his cousin coming by the pool hall or the house, but after a while Castaldo had had enough. Castaldo felt as if every time he turned around Carboni and Stooge were in his face. Carboni and Stooge, Carboni and Stooge, Carboni and Stooge. Whatever Carboni did, Stooge did. Sometimes they called him at his girlfriend's to track him down, and Castaldo began to mock them as "The Dynamic Duo" and make jokes about how they were attached at the hip. Before Carboni could stand up from Castaldo's couch and say "Let's go," Stooge would be on his feet. Besides feeling as if he had a shadow, Castaldo also grew annoyed with Carboni's mouthy attitude. One day, hanging around the pool hall, Carboni and Stooge were shooting pool together when Carboni made a wiseass remark to a kid he didn't know. Sizing up the kid's girlfriend, Carboni tilted his mouth and cracked: "Is that your girl, or is that your dog you're walking?"

Whether it was meant to be heard or not wasn't clear, but it was heard, and the kid was going to take Carboni outside. Castaldo came over and broke it up. He knew the kid, and he apologized on behalf of his cousin. But it was typical of Carboni, and as much as Castaldo enjoyed a good fight, he was getting sick of the way Carboni was always running his mouth and getting into a scrap and expecting Castaldo to help him out.

"Don't come up here no more," Castaldo told his cousin.

But of course, when their tempers cooled, that's where Carboni came almost all the time, looking for his cousin and usually finding him. Because as screwy as the logic might be when Castaldo said he was leaving school to get a leg up in the working world, the truth was different. Frankie Castaldo was in no hurry to find a steady job and settle down. He took odd jobs—helping people move, cleaning horse stables at a place on Garret Mountain, and the like, and for a time he worked in a pizzeria in Garfield and a bagel shop on Main Avenue in Clifton. But the pizzeria shut down and the bagel shop didn't work out. When Frankie had been about sixteen, his mother had taken work at the Daughters of Miriam, a Jewish nursing home, and she wasn't around to watch over him all the time. As the home's nutritionist, Alfonsina was up at 6 A.M. and worked to the dinner hour and sometimes beyond. So both his parents were gone all day. Frankie's laziness galled them, and Alfonsina and Joe would ride him about it.

"Frankie, you're going to be eighteen now. It's time to settle down," his mother said. She warned him that his foolishness and idle habits were going to get him into trouble. She told him the world wasn't going to treat him like a kid anymore.

But being a kid was lots more fun. Frankie was living it up, pulling "break nights," as the family called them, by staying out at the dance clubs until dawn. During the day he would be hanging around watching TV and cluttering up the house. How he spent the day was anyone's guess, because he got almost nothing done. In fact, Frankie never got a driver's license. The reason, he said, was his vision. What this really meant was that he needed to wear corrective lenses in order to obtain a driver's license, but personal vanity stood in the way. He refused to wear eyeglasses. Frankie told his parents he wanted contact lenses. Fine, Joe told his son. Go to work and get some. Joe would pay for his son's glasses, but he was not going to shell out the extra money for contact lenses. Frankie promised he would find a steady job. When Frankie finally got around to filling out the application at Bayside Milling, where Joe worked, his mother and father were relieved. Eventually, Frankie went for the interview, and things looked good. In the meantime, Castaldo took a job at the Robin Hood Inn in Clifton busing tables. Although he griped that the pay barely covered the expenses of his taxi fare to work and back, Castaldo seemed to like it for a while—perhaps because he soon made the acquaintance of some of the other busboys, including James Wanger and Tommy Strelka.

At the sound of the key twisting in the lock, Susie Strelka stubbed out her cigarette and waited. She hadn't heard his car on the street or his footsteps on the porch. He had probably parked around the corner to avoid detection. But now, late one night in December 1991, Tommy was turning the key very, very slowly, teasing the lock open as quietly as possible, and Susie was waiting for him in the dark. The anger that had been smoldering for almost three hours as she waited up for her son now threatened to blow, but she waved her hands to clear the smoke and listened for his next move. A thin silhouette pushed open the door and tiptoed inside.

This was a very delicious moment—an ambush in the making. Momentarily, when she pounced, she would enlarge her already considerable reputation for motherly omniscience. Her eyes had sprung open around 1:30 A.M., perhaps because in the back of her mind she knew that Tommy hadn't come home. She got out of bed and checked his bedroom. Nope. He was still out, and at least an hour past curfew. On school nights he had to be in by 9 or 10 o'clock, but on weekends she let him go until 1 or 2 A.M. because of his job. At first she didn't get too excited, because it wasn't really a fixed curfew, and Tommy often straggled in around 2 A.M. or so with a good excuse. She told herself not to get crazy about it. After all, the boy needed some room to grow up. He worked at the Robin Hood Inn busing tables until midnight, generally, and so she didn't see any harm in letting him go to McDonald's or something for a hamburger after he was off. All work and no play, and all that.

Susie went downstairs to the living room, expecting him any moment. Her husband Ray was upstairs sleeping. She lit a cigarette and found a late movie on television and waited. And waited. And waited. The movie flickered, the clock ticked, and she grew angrier as she waited. After a while, her emotions spun between worry because something might have happened to him and anger because he had defied her. It got so that she could barely sit still. She smoked cigarettes and looked out the window at the street, where neighbors had strung Christmas lights. She snapped off the movie because she couldn't focus on the story anymore and turned out the lights in the living room and waited, because there was nothing else to do but wait. The red coal of her cigarette winked in the darkness. The clock rolled around to 4 A.M. when Tommy's key stirred in the lock.

After stepping through the door, Tommy crept up the stairs like James Bond, and it was amusing to watch him be so sly in the dark. As a child, Susie had known the tricks too. She had sneaked out of her house, knowing by heart which steps creaked and which steps didn't so that she could slip past her parents. Tommy was not as devious, in general. She followed him into his room. She let Tommy lie down on his bed. She let him settle a moment. No doubt he was about to drift off in a heavy slumber of relief. Then she grabbed him by the collar.

"Okay. You're dead," she said, yanking his shirt.

Tommy was like a fighter clearing his head.

"Good morning, Thomas," Susie said. "Do we have a job as a milkman now?"

Tommy was speechless.

"You do not come into my house at this time of the night," she said. "Where the hell have you been? I want to know where you've been, Tommy."

Susie could see that he had had a few drinks. She asked if he had been drinking, but Tommy denied it.

"We were in Castaldo's house," he said thickly.

"You were in Castaldo's house?"

"Yeah."

"Who was in Castaldo's house?"

"Me, Stooge, Frank—"

"Doing what?"

"Nothing."

"Nothing? Don't tell me nothing. You were drinking."

"No, Ma, I wasn't."

Susie flicked on the light. Tommy was swatting at the light as if it were swarming around his head, and his eyes were glassy.

"Yes, you were drinking, Tommy. I can see it," she said. "What kind of household is this that a bunch of kids are in the house till four in the morning? These parents just let a bunch of kids party all night? Something's wrong here, Tommy."

Susie had a few things she wanted to tell him right now, as he lay in his bed half drunk, but she decided they would wait until tomorrow. She would have to deal with this creep Castaldo—but she knew that she would have to be sensible, too. She wasn't going to put up with this nonsense, but she wasn't a dictator with her kids, either. It was like the time she had found his cigarettes. Tommy denied everything that time, too.

"Tommy, cut the bull," she had said. Susie had found the cigarettes mangled in the wash. But she smoked—she smoked a lot, in fact—and her husband smoked. It wouldn't do to be hypocritical, so she sat at the table one night and leveled with him.

"Tommy, I'm not going to tell you you should or should not smoke, because I smoke, but let me tell you—it's the worst mistake me and your father ever made," she said.

Tommy seemed to listen, but if her words had made any impression, it didn't show, because Tommy continued to smoke. But Susie and Ray decided there wasn't a whole lot they could do about it. You couldn't stop a kid from growing up.

And that was Susie's approach. She wanted to keep open the lines of communication. But tomorrow she would deal with this Castaldo. She would talk to Ray about it, too, but one of the things that was definitely going to change around the Strelka household was Tommy's friendship with this thug.

Susie Strelka was a Jersey girl, having been born a fraternal twin in 1948 in Jersey City. She lived with her brother and her parents above an A&P supermarket in Journal Square. She was fourteen when her mother gave birth to a second son. When she was three years old, her father, an executive with the Bendix Corp., moved the family to Lodi, a Bergen County town whose principal business had once been converting human waste from New York City privies into fertilizer. Susie's parents raised the children in the Roman Catholic Church, but she converted to Protestantism as an adult. Her childhood had been unremarkable, although as she grew older and became rebellious, she sometimes left the house and stayed away on her own for days, exploring places like Greenwich Village in New York City.

On December 28, 1970, she and Ray married. He had been born in Passaic and raised in Clifton. That same year Ray had taken a job with PSE&G, a major utility in the state, and in time he became a supervisor. Their first child, Thomas Strelka, was born on August 8, 1974 in Boonton, where once-thriving iron forges had depended on the Morris Canal and the Lackawanna Railroad. About a year after Tommy was born, the family moved to a three-story house with a backyard in Clifton's Lakeview section. Two more children followed after Tommy: a sister, who was born almost exactly five years after Tommy, and a brother, who was nearly eight and a half years younger than he.

The Strelkas were a close, working-class family. Dad worked; Mom stayed home with the kids. They sat down to dinner every night and they piled into the car for occasional treats at the local hamburger or ice-cream stands. Without fussing over their children, the Strelkas gave them everything that was needed to get on and, they hoped, secure the things they hadn't had as kids. There were the usual family diversions: barbecues in the summer, splashing around in an above-ground swimming pool, playing summer games with neighborhood kids until the fireflies came out, doing chores like housecleaning and taking out the garbage. When the children grew old enough for a pet, the family chose a toffee-colored mutt from the pound. She was shaggy and high-strung; they named her Candy. They spent summer vacations at Lake George every year until Lake George became a Strelka family tradition; Tommy looked forward to these trips so eagerly that he would toss and turn, unable to sleep, on the eve of their departure for upstate New York.

Little else troubled Tommy's sleep. As an infant he cried easily, but as he grew older Tommy became such a quiet child that almost everyone outside the family wondered if he knew how to speak. He was meek, obedient, and good-natured. He was a good kid. The worst thing he had ever done was shoplift a cassette, for which he felt terrible afterward although he hadn't been caught. Later he discovered he had a fairly hot temper, but he suppressed it usually, choosing to ignore people who made him angry rather than make a scene. He was fastidious and kept his room extraordinarily neat; if his mother so much as moved a single knickknack out of place, Tommy would return it and mention it to her. He filed schoolwork away in metal filing cabinets, where dozens of manila folders bore carefully lettered headings such as "7th Grade Science Tests" and "English Composition 11th Grade."

As a little kid, Tommy played ball in the street in front of his house and collected Garfield comics, but his primary interests lay in video games, model trains, and music. He and his father both liked collecting model trains. Together they constructed an elaborate toy world on a plywood platform in the basement, threading the miniature track past depots, granaries, signal towers, spotlights, and engineer shacks. It wasn't exactly "Roadside America," but it was pretty impressive. There were all sorts of cars—cattle cars, tankers, and flatbeds hauling lumber, or spools of cable, or a crane—and he had replicas of the locomotives that once upon a time had pulled trains for great railroads like the Santa Fe Pacific, the Baltimore & Ohio, and the Erie Lackawanna, whose locomotives were particularly handsome in their maroon-and-gray paint. The main control panel held an industrial-size transformer and an assortment of levers, buttons, and toggle switches that controlled the throttle, coupled and uncoupled the trains, or activated the track-switching junctions. The platform rumbled when the trains started rolling along all six tracks, and when Tommy hit the whistle or the smoke, the sound carried through the house.

"Where are you—the train station?" a friend said once when Susie called her on the telephone. It was a pretty cool place to spend the afternoon fooling around.

Tommy envisioned himself as an engineer in the cab of a locomotive, his hands on the throttle as tons of steel thundered down the rails, and he told people that's what he would be when he grew up. Sometimes he grew frustrated assembling the tiny parts that required great dexterity and patience, but the outcome—creating a tiny world that was both ordinary and fantastic—was always satisfying. Relatives learned how to draw him out of his reticence by bringing up the train collection. It was one of the few things that Tommy would discuss and become animated about. But he was not comfortable talking about anything, if he could do it instead. Perhaps that was why he read a decent amount of books and mystery novels but mostly liked toying with his microscope or telescope or studying rocks and minerals.

People who knew him would describe him as a sweet kid who did what he was asked and never drew attention to himself. He felt close to his family, and when he was thirteen years old, Tommy bicycled across town to keep his grandmother company after his grandfather died. As a member of the Hungarian Reformed Church of Passaic, Tommy impressed the Right Reverend Zoltan Kiraly with his obedient and gentle demeanor in attending Sunday school or volunteering to help and supervise other kids at the church socials. If Tommy's mother had to step out for an errand, she could trust Tommy to look after his younger siblings without tormenting them. If she was blindsided by a migraine that knocked her off her feet, which was often, she could send Tommy downstairs to watch his little brother and little sister. He cooked for them, looked after them, kidded around with them, assuming the ironic tone adults sometimes take dealing with very little children. At worst, he got a kick out of playing practical jokes on them. He charged them quarters once to borrow books from the shelves in the family's house. He told his little sister that he was the guy who had written the words to "Blowing in the Wind"—and no doubt he wished he had.

Early on, Tommy Strelka fell in love with music. One of the first memories he had of growing up was beginning kindergarten the year of a big hurricane and taking an interest in a record that a girl had. It was "Disco Mickey Mouse," and Tommy went nuts for it. He got his parents to buy the record for his own collection, and he kept it for years, long after his taste in music had shifted to Led Zeppelin and Pink Floyd. When Tommy was about thirteen, he started playing guitar. Eventually, Tommy's room would contain various musical instruments, including a drum kit, and he spent hours practicing.

Like so much else in his early youth, Tommy's school days were virtually indistinguishable from those of countless other permanently average students who went through Clifton's public schools. Tommy was a dutiful student who kept out of the way and out of trouble, and that was about it. Standardized testing suggested he was of average intelligence, and from grammar school on he earned grades that were average or better. Now and then he would excel—he won an award for excellence in history when he was a sophomore, and he displayed the citation on his wall—but for the most part he occupied the solid upper-middle rank of the student body that earns Bs and sometimes Cs year in and year out.

* * *

In 1986, at the age of twelve, during his second year at the Christopher Columbus Middle School, Tommy met a gangly kid with furry eyebrows and a constant patter of ideas and wisecracks. The kid's name was Robbie Solimine, and they became friends after Robbie had been transferred into Tommy's reading class. Robbie seemed like a pretty cool kid. They talked in school, and soon Tommy started spending time with him after school and going by Robbie's house, which was also in the Lakeview section of town. Robbie's parents were divorced, and he lived with his mother and stepfather a few blocks from Strelka's. Robbie's family lived on East Seventh Street, and the Strelkas lived on East Eighth. After the dismissal bell rang, they would walk home together and spend hours poring over their baseball card collections, debating the merits of various players and working out swaps and deals, and listening to music together. They liked a lot of the same bands—Metallica, Def Leppard, Guns 'N Roses. When they went outside, they whiled away the hours riding their bicycles or hanging out in a park down by the DPW tubes, where the city's Department of Public Works had some garages. The old Lackawanna Railroad cut through the city near there, and in the side of a railroad embankment, which was braced with creosoted pilings and grown over with brush, were a series of huge concrete culverts lined up side by side. It was known all over that kids from that part of town went down there to drink and fool around, and it was close to a small city park.

Tommy was so quiet and Robbie was so outgoing that it was difficult to know what the two boys found in each other. Sometimes, when Tommy went to visit Robbie's father and stepmother in North Haledon, Robbie's parents would forget he was there. Tommy was usually absorbed in whatever they were doing and quiet, and it would come as a surprise to hear Robbie talking to someone. Sometimes Robbie's stepmother, Arlene, would find herself actually coaching Tommy to be more assertive when Robbie got fresh.

"Tommy, say something back to him," Arlene might say, or she would tell her stepson to lay off.

Before long, Robbie and Tommy became best friends. They went to the movies, stayed at each other's houses on sleepovers, cruised the local five-and-tens, played baseball or football in the ballfields near their houses—just doing whatever, the regular boy stuff that seems fantastically vivid until a teacher asks at the end of the summer to write an essay about it. Occasionally, the boys stirred up trouble in their neighborhoods, tormenting an old guy across the street from Tommy or, when they were juniors in high school, winging chunks of Play-Doh at a window, which drew the attention of the police. The officers took statements from the boys and let them go. Robbie's father paid for the window. On another occasion, the boys egged the house of Tommy's ex-girlfriend, and when Robbie's stepfather found out about it, he chewed them out and told them to go over and clean up the mess, which they did. Robbie's stepfather considered Tommy a third son, and after a while, Robbie's mother and stepfather added a third desk in the house because Tommy spent so many nights sleeping over. Robbie and Tommy seemed inseparable, even as they grew out of adolescence. Robbie's grandmother, Lee Yakal, who lived just around the corner from Robbie's house, had always treated Tommy as her own grandson. Tommy was so meek and unassuming around them that she would almost have to plead with the boy to take some cookies or have a piece of fruit when he and Rob visited. Years later, when Tommy turned seventeen years old and finally got his car—Rob had gotten wheels first—Tommy announced it to Rob's grandmother, and it was so uncharacteristic of him that she thought she was hearing things.

"Mrs. Yakal," he said shyly, "I got a car, too."

Robbie's grandmother told him how thrilled she was for him, practically gushing as Tommy beamed.

No one in Robbie's family ever heard Tommy so much as raise his voice, and they came to see him as a follower, not a leader, usually doing what Rob wanted to do. It would take a long time before their friendship burned out, but for five years or more, Tommy Strelka would be Robbie's most constant, and perhaps his only, friend.

3

At the age of seventeen, Robbie Solimine's life had settled uneasily into the twilight between boyhood and manhood, an unstable and painful region where he, like most of his peers, was struggling to establish an identity. But Robbie encountered other difficulties besides the awkwardness of his age, and these isolated him further from the people around him. He seemed very alone and always to be caught *between* things: between his mother and his stepfather, who were on the verge of divorce; between his mother and biological father, who had been divorced when he was an infant; between the lifelong bonds of family and the new ties to friends between the Clifton public schools where he had spent most of life and the regional high school where he transferred after eleventh grade; between life as a student and life in the working world; between sobriety and booze; between the rigid order of the military, which he longed to join, and the chaotic mess of his private life, which he couldn't escape. In short, in the fall of 1991, as he began his senior year of high school, Robbie Solimine was a misfit, a haunted boy who had been battling demons for a long time. Through it all, he seemed to crave two things most: attention and a sense of belonging.

He had a way of looking askance at things, with an ironic,

impious, almost wiseass grin. He was gawky—while growing up some of the kids called him Salamander—but he was growing into his features: prominent nose, thick eyebrows, full lips with a slight pout. He had a thin face and straight black hair that he wore either short in a crew cut or moderately long, with his bangs parted to the side or down the middle. He was a talker and a charmer, a generally bubbly kid at times who considered himself a bit of a ladies' man. He wore a gold stud in his left ear. He smoked Newports. He worshiped his car—first a black Chevy Camaro, and then a white Plymouth Laser—and he worshiped the New York Jets. He sometimes left the house in full Jets regalia: Jets jacket, Jets shirt, a Jets cap. He listened to heavy-metal music and taped a muddy excerpt of it on the answering machine to his private telephone line. He had fooled around with drugs—petty stuff: mostly marijuana, and Coke and aspirin—but in a tentative way, in a manner calculated more to fit in with peers, or to blanket his insecurity, than as an adventure to transport him. Alcohol seemed more his style; he drank so heavily that for a while he thought he was an alcoholic in need of professional help. Most people considered him quite bright, although he was an average student, an indifferent student, who had finished his junior year at Clifton High School with barely passing grades. He was somewhat athletic and played noncontact sports, signing up for volleyball in high school. Outside of school he took up bowling and joined a league at a Fair Lawn bowling alley with his elder brother. In early 1992, he took his first job, working as a busboy at a Friendly's restaurant. Most of all, he continued to serve with gusto in the U.S. Naval Sea Cadets, a preenlistment organization for the Navy. The Sea Cadets had been the brightest passion in his life since he was fourteen years old, and it helped him keep his eyes trained on joining the Navy after graduation.

If you liked Robbie, you would have said he was a fun kid, a high-spirited young man who liked people and wanted very much to be liked in return. He at least wanted to make some sort of impression. He liked to have a good time, and he always was quick to reconcile if he made someone angry. He was funny, vivacious, moody, earnest, industrious, and temperamental. He had a knack for sensing in an instant where another person's strengths and vulnerabilities lay, and he was equally talented in directing his charms to those areas, in the hope of either winning the person over or making mischief. He was, in short, fairly intuitive, and perhaps somewhat impulsive as a result.

If you didn't like him, you would say Robbie Solimine was a hyper kid who could be a real pain in the ass. He could be smart-alecky, whiny, and boastful. Among peers he sometimes seemed like a chameleon, altering his identity to survive the shifting cliques and alliances of high school. Worst of all, he could be a tattletale. He had a habit of passing things to one teenager that had been told to him in confidence from another, with predictably unhappy results. Others said he was just a snitch. Whatever the case, he liked to stir the pot. He could make people—adults and peers—laugh and grit their teeth at the same time, and he knew it. Whenever he was in the mood to be loud, abrasive, silly and spastic, Robbie got so wound up that the only recourse would be to tell him to leave. Robbie sometimes seemed to be testing the world's patience merely to make sure that someone was paying attention.

He was born Robert Anthony Solimine at Beth Israel Hospital in Passaic on August 29, 1974, at about the time his parents' marriage had begun to crumble. He was known most of his life as Robert Solimine, Jr., and usually, just "Robbie" or "Rob." His parents, Margaret and Robert Solimine, lived in the Passaic Park section of Clifton. Their first son, William, had been born three years earlier. Margaret stayed at home taking care of the children. When Robbie was born, Bob was working at two gas stations as a mechanic: It seemed sometimes that he fit two weeks of work in one. He possessed the patient curiosity of the tinkerer, and he honed his skills working on jet engines for the United States Air Force. He had served in Vietnam in 1968, a watershed year for the war, and on several bases in the United States back home. The war left him with mostly unpleasant memories and two other things besides: a marketable skill and a middle initial. He had been born without a middle name, but the military insisted on three of them, so he had thrown in the letter *J*. While crawling under cars or pumping gas at Esso and Sunoco gas stations day and night, he was hoping to use what he'd learned in the military to land a job as an aircraft mechanic at one of the local airports.

Robbie's parents had met in December 1967 at Bolero, a nightspot that later became a Ford dealership. They went for a ride together and soon started dating. There was not a lot of time to get to know each other. Bob had enlisted in the U.S. Air Force in 1967 after his graduation from Clifton High and jetted to Vietnam the following May. After he left, he and Maggie wrote to each other, and he looked her up when he returned on a thirty-day leave. Following his discharge, Bob picked up with Maggie, and in November 1967, they were married at St. Brendan's Roman Catholic Church on Lakeview Avenue in Clifton.

Margaret had been the only child of Lena and William Yakal. They adopted Maggie when she was five. Lena, who was known as Lee, had grown up in Clifton a few doors down from the Favas, whose grandson would go on to make a distinguished career as a Paterson municipal court judge and Passaic County prosecutor. Lee's father, who had come from Italy, was a butcher; Bill's father, who had come from Germany, was a butcher. Lee, who worked for Ma Bell as a telephone operator, was goodhearted, soft-spoken, easygoing, and patient. A hotheaded man who brooked little disagreement, Bill Yakal was a softy with children but just about no one else. In 1942 they met at a public swimming pool in Clifton, not long before Bill Yakal volunteered, at the age of seventeen, to serve in the Navy. Having married at the end of the war, the couple discovered that they could not have children. During his days in the military, however, Bill once served with a unit whose custom was to treat the local orphans to a Christmas outing. Bill liked the experience so much that when he returned to New Jersey, he and Lee arranged to do the same for a child there. A nun at a home operated by the Immaculate Conception Roman Catholic Church in Lodi said she had a child in mind. It was a smiley little girl named Margaret; the Yakals called her Maggie.

The Yakals started visiting Maggie when the child was five years old. Her command of the English language wasn't so good, perhaps because the place had been run by Polish nuns who had recently come to the United States, but Maggie was an irrepressibly happy child. The Yakals took her out of the orphanage every chance they got. They looked into the possibility of adoption—although Lee told her husband that if it came to a court fight, she would not be able to stand face-to-face with another woman and take away her child against the woman's wishes. It would have to be consensual or not at all. In this case, Maggie's mother agreed to relinquish her parental rights. So without ever meeting the woman or even learning her name, the Yakals took Maggie as their daughter.

Maggie was proud of her adoption, proud that she had been "picked" by a family. She wasn't shy about telling people that she had been adopted by the Yakals, and she liked to play it as a joke that she had been born two months before her parents were married. Perhaps taking after her adoptive father, Margaret was strong-willed and fiercely independent. As a young woman who had grown up with an interest in flying, Maggie wanted to be an airline stewardess, but she was too short to meet the height requirement.

When Maggie and Bob Solimine met, Clifton was still the sleepy suburb it had been when they were growing up, although it had swollen to the largest size in its history and it was bursting with industry. When Bob had been a boy, he and his family lived in the Albion section near Garret Mountain. There were still farms, and the Albion section in particular was undeveloped. Bob Solimine and his two brothers played in the woods and climbed its slopes. Now the city was crisscrossed by highways.

Bob and Maggie's life together was humble, with modest

comforts. They had two cars, both of which Bob had bought secondhand and fixed up, but he also earned enough money to afford a vacation for the family at Disneyworld or the beach. But money became a sticking point in their relationship, as Maggie pushed Bob to improve himself and improve their lot. She told him he should attend trade school at night to get his electrician's certification, so he did. She urged him to climb the ranks of management, take night classes if need be, and make more money for the family. To Bob, it seemed as if she just didn't like the idea of being married to a blue-collar guy, or at least a laid-back blue-collar guy. In the meantime, Bob's brother was working at an instrumentation company in Teterboro and helped him land a job there. In no time, Bob became a top technician, but it didn't seem to smooth things at home.

The troubles took Bob by surprise. He had thought that he and Maggie had a reasonably good marriage. At least he had been pretty content. Then, it seemed to him, she gradually became a scold who wanted more, more, more. Bob suspected that their problems could be traced to Maggie's father, who always seemed to have his daughter's ear. Bob and Maggie began arguing more frequently, and eventually Maggie started sleeping on the couch. Bob moved out sometime in late 1975 or January 1976. At the time, Robbie was about a year and a half old. William was about four. Margaret filed for divorce, and Bob, not being much of a fighter, chose not to contest it. The divorce became final in 1978.

Robbie and Billy stayed with Margaret, who retained legal custody. Bob had visitation rights. But both parents, no matter how disagreeable their relationship, worked hard to make the best possible arrangements for the boys. They tried to make up for the blow by providing extra attention to the boys, and neither parent brought around a prospective partner or a date to meet their sons until a fair amount of time had passed. Nonetheless, like perhaps half of the population in the late 1970s, the boys embarked on dual lives. From Monday to Friday, they lived with Maggie in Clifton. On the weekends they lived with their father. In time, they would have a bedroom in Maggie's house and a bedroom in Bob's house, and they would keep enough clothing and personal articles at each place to make them feel at home. From here on out for Robbie and Billy, no family bond would be as stable, and the only real constant was the presence of a brother in each of their lives.

From the time they were tiny, however, Robbie and his brother seemed worlds apart. Billy was aloof, something of a loner. Robbie was gregarious and almost clingy. Billy talked slowly, and sometimes, it seemed, hardly at all. Robbie talked fast and talked a lot. Billy went along with things to the point you often wouldn't know he was there, and Robbie could be argumentative, raising a ruckus because he wouldn't clear the table when he was asked.

Robbie was the sort of kid who needed something to do. Billy was laid back, content to let the world go by. If Bob Solimine started working on something or puttering around the house, Robbie would join his father without having to be asked. Like his father, he never seemed to grow bored of taking things apart, seeing how they worked, and putting them back together. To pick up pocket change, he went around the neighborhood gathering newspapers to recycle. He wanted to get things for himself, try things for himself, do something, do anything. The two brothers carried on a rivalry that was bitter and friendly by turns. In their likes and dislikes, for example, it always seemed as if Robbie would become a fan of whichever team his elder brother hadn't picked. If Billy liked the Giants, then Robbie liked the Jets. If Billy picked the Yankees, then Robbie took the Mets. And so on. (Robbie had the New Jersey Devils all to himself because Billy didn't like hockey.) Sometimes they fought, of course, as all brothers do, but they also enjoyed doing things together. They spent hours shooting hoops in the driveway behind his mother's house. Or they would walk down the hill to Currie Park with other neighborhood kids to play football. When they were teenagers, they both found Howard Stern endlessly amusing and listened to him together on the radio. Halfway through his senior year of high school, Robbie took up bowling, and so did Billy, and they joined a league at a Fair Lawn bowling alley where they were known as "The Tailgaters." They were very different, and not necessarily close, but their parents' divorce unexpectedly had thrown them into the same lot. Of the two boys, Robbie showed the effects of his parents' broken marriage more than Billy, but both seemed to be doing about as well as expected.

Less than a year after Bob moved out, he met Arlene Dean, a blond, softhearted, giggly party girl from North Haledon. They dated about five months before Arlene met the boys, and by then things had become serious enough that Arlene and Bob decided to move in together. Arlene adjusted quickly to motherhood. The first night the boys slept over, they were tossing around a baseball in their bedroom—which might have been okay except that it was 2 A.M. Finally, on August 18, 1978, Bob and Arlene married and settled down at 119 Overbrook Drive in North Haledon, the family home where Arlene had grown up. That same year Bob started his own company, Intercontinental Avionic and Instrument Corp., in Elmwood Park. At his shop, which was littered with dials and gauges and tools, he tested, repaired, built, and calibrated aeronautical equipment to precise standards. In no time she discovered that Robbie was the more outgoing of the two brother and Billy was shy. Billy, who was already in school, kept to himself when Arlene showed any affection. But without much coaxing, Robbie gladly cuddled up in Arlene's lap. Always the boys called their stepmother "Arlene," not "Mom," but they made her feel as if she were their mother all the same. No matter how unpleasantly they might argue over the years, the boys never spat back in her face that she wasn't "really" their mother, and she too became more certain of her role ("I'll gladly to go jail for this one," she would joke when the boys tested her patience). They had a close relationship, as close as a relationship formed over many years and over many weekends can be.

As for Maggie, she had been faced with the prospect of raising two boys almost on her own, and so she began to spend a lot of time at her parents' home. Maggie had always been close to her parents, and Bill Yakal especially took a keen interest in his grandsons, showing them how to work with their hands and, in particular, sharing his love of sailing. Around the Yakal household Robbie was always game for a project. Anything Bill told him to do, he'd do. When a limb needed to be cut down from a tree, Robbie clambered up the tree with a handsaw before his grandfather could say a word.

"All right," his grandfather said. "I'll give you a good funeral if anything happens."

"Okay, Grampa," Robbie said.

Befitting an old Navy man, Bill Yakal loved boating and took his two grandsons out on the water in a thirty-five-foot cabin cruiser dubbed *Rum Runner*. They piloted the boat up the Hudson River, down the Jersey shore, and over to Long Island. Robbie grew to love it. When Robbie was about seven years old, they took a voyage to the Caribbean aboard the *Falcone*, a four-masted tall ship that had been rebuilt with the hull of a Navy destroyer. Robbie chased a kitten around the ship as the crew sailed Nassau and Bimini and through the Devil's Triangle. Every day the captain of the ship, a Scotsman, appeared in kilt and full regalia to explain what the passengers would encounter on that day's leg of the voyage. As was customary at the end of one such session, he asked for questions. Robbie, who was never shy, put up his hand.

"Yes, Rob," the captain said. "What is it?"

"I'd like to know why you wear a skirt and a handbag," he said.

Meanwhile, to make ends meet, Maggie became a secretary at Shulton Inc. on Colfax Avenue. Shulton, a subsidiary of one of Passaic County's largest employers, the multinational chemical and pharmaceuticals company American Cyanamid, carried out the research to develop and manufacture common household products and cosmetics. These included items as varied as Breck shampoo, Pine-Sol, Old Spice, Pierre Cardin perfumes, and Combat, the roach killer. The plant, a sprawling compound situated in the middle of Clifton where the Garden State Parkway and Route 46 intersected, was just down the street from the high school. Later, after the division was sold by Cyanamid and closed down, she found work with Tsumura International Inc., a fragrance and bath products maker in Secaucus, as a promotional payments analyst.

About the time that Robbie was in first grade, Maggie met a man named Manny Chircop through a mutual friend in a cocktail lounge called Maggie's Dockside in Butler, New Jersey. Chircop drove cement mixers for Herbert J. Hinchman & Son in Wayne. A working man with a sun-reddened face, an owlish nose, and deep blue eyes that fixed on people with uncomfortable frankness, Manny was both blunt and wary in his dealings with others. But he knew how to have fun, too, and he and Maggie hit it off almost from the start. In the process of courting Maggie and her sons, Manny took the boys for rides on his motorcycle and treats at the local hamburger stands. The first time Manny met the boys, Robbie was off the wall. He was bouncing on the bed, showing off. All boy, Manny thought. His brother, Billy, was more subdued, and it took a while for Billy to be at his ease around Manny. About a year after meeting each other, Manny and Maggie decided to marry. Unable to obtain annulments and marry in the Catholic Church, they were married by the mayor of Wayne township in a civil ceremony on October 16, 1982. Margaret adopted Manny's last name.

As the new family settled in together, the boys soon learned that Manny had exceedingly firm ideas about the right way and the wrong way to raise children. Shortly after he and Margaret were married, he sat the boys down at the dining-room table and gave them a choice: they could call him "Dad" or they could call him "Mr. Chircop." It was going to be one or the other. Whatever their choice, he would not have any of this "Manny" stuff from his own kids. So the boys called him "Dad"—at least to his face. When Bob heard about this, it hurt him a little, but there wasn't much to do about it.

As could be expected, it took a while for Robbie and Billy to get used to their stepfather; they regarded him with a mixture of fear, respect, and, at times, derision. Manny did not like the boys stepping out of line or messing with things they had no business messing with. Manny snored quite loudly, but woe to the boy who shut the door to the master bedroom at night. As part of his way of doing things, Manny padlocked a basement workroom because he did not want his tools to wander off. He locked the air-conditioner thermostat, setting its timer to begin cooling at a fixed hour every night and to shut down at a certain time in the morning. Robbie and Billy, who arrived home from school to a sweltering house, were forever looking for ways to switch the timer without getting caught. When Robbie slammed and locked the door to his bedroom in a huff one time, Manny got a screwdriver and took it off its hinges.

These were the ground rules: The house was to be kept neat and orderly, the boys must learn to pick up after themselves and take care of themselves, and above all, there would be no backtalk. But Manny, despite his gruffness, also built a rapport with the boys. He worked at it. He wanted to win them over. When talking to coworkers or friends, Manny never referred to Billy or Robbie as stepsons. They were his *sons*. One time, when Robbie was visiting him at work, Manny introduced him to a friend, who looked the boy up and down closely.

"He looks like you, too," the coworker said. It was a remark that amused Manny and Robbie and made them proud. In time, Billy and Manny would get along quietly, as if both were neutral observers in the family. Robbie and Manny would oscillate between treating each other like best buddies and mortal enemies.

As a kid, Robbie spent a lot of time watching TV, usually the comedies and the shoot-'em-ups. His favorite show was "The A-Team," and he talked and acted like the orphaned, wise-talking star of the series "Webster." He also spent hours playing video games. He played so much Donkey Kong, the video game where the Charlie Chaplinesque construction worker leaps barrels and climb ladders to rescue a beauty from a gorilla's clutches, that Manny sometimes thought he would lose his mind if he heard its jingle one more time. But Robbie also started piano lessons and kept at it until he was pretty good. He kept animals of all kinds: gerbils, hamsters, fish, a dog and a cat. The dog was a Lhasa apso-schnauzer mix named Chopin. The cat was a black cat Robbie had found as a kitten and brought home as a present for Manny. Robbie named it Maxine, although no one was sure of its sex, and eventually it turned out to be a Max. Robbie loved baseball, playing shortstop and first base on a Clifton Little League team. Manny, who was the coach, played him all the time, despite the fact that Robbie was his own kid, because Manny believed he was good enough. Robbie filled box after box with baseball cards, until he had thousands of them, all painstakingly catalogued by the players' names, teams, and years. The cards were so dear to him that one routine punishment was to take them away from him. To guard against such contingencies, Robbie would hide his prized cards inside a Bible.

In December 1983 the Chircops settled in at 216 East Seventh Street, a mustard-colored, aluminum-sided frame house with a brick front porch and a mansard roof. Margaret liked antiques and filled one of its rooms with them. Their life together was comfortable—two kids, two cars, some pets—and when they went on family vacations, they traveled to places like Disneyworld, Lake George, Virginia Beach, and Washington, D.C. Once a year, although Manny did not like the Jersey shore much as a vacation spot, he would take the boys down to Point Pleasant for a chartered fishing trip for bluefish or fluke. They never came back empty-handed in the three years they had made it an annual ritual. Wherever they went, the Chircops returned with memories of some event that became family legend long after as the good times had vanished. In the summer of 1985, for example, when Robbie was about to turn eleven, the family spent some time at Lake George and Robbie took part in a junior rodeo's calf-catching contest. As children swarmed after the bawling, bucking animal, Robbie grabbed its tail. To the delight of his family, Robbie held on as the animal leaped and dodged and bucked all over the corral, Robbie flapping around like a tail on a kite. He won the prize, and he was tickled. Everybody said it was just like him to grab hold and keep on to the end, and it was the kind of story they liked to tell years later.

When Robbie entered school, his high spirits ran head-on into the rigidity of parochial school. From his earliest years in a Catholic school just up the street from home, through the middle grades at the Christopher Columbus School, and into his high school years, Robbie's problem always seemed to be his mouth—particularly with female teachers. He entered kindergarten at St. Brendan's School, where the nuns expected the children to study, pay attention, and eat lunch at their desks, and otherwise comport themselves with old-fashioned formality and discipline. This wasn't going to work for Robbie. He talked back to the teachers and spoke out of turn, until the disruptions became so frequent that Margaret thought it necessary to take Robbie to a psychiatrist.

No doubt part of the problem was that his life had been complicated by the entrance of Manny, who did not think his stepson needed therapy. In Manny's eyes, psychiatry amounted to throwing away thousands of dollars so that some stranger could take his kid to the candy store or play video games with him and talk. Then the doctor would report that Robbie's problems stemmed from too much chocolate or caffeine, or that his misbehavior was a way of crying for attention. Instead of a headshrinker, what Robbie really needed was a challenge, Manny thought, something that might interest him. Rather quickly after joining Maggie and the boys, Manny learned that the best way to keep Robbie out of mischief was to keep him busy. Once, when Manny was putting up walls, he told Robbie he could help him pound nails. He gave the boy some nails and a hammer and showed him what to do. The minute Robbie ran out of nails, however, he just kept banging away, poking holes in the plaster. To Manny,

Robbie always seemed like a bright kid who was so much smarter than most that he got bored too easily. While Robbie coasted along getting Bs instead of As, all the lost energy was converted into mischief.

Whatever the cause, Robbie's rambuctiousness created serious problems. In February 1984, when he was more than halfway through the fourth grade, Robbie was taken out of St. Brendan's. It was felt the school didn't have what Robbie needed, and he was placed in the public schools. Nonetheless, his behavioral problems surfaced again in public school, and from time to time they became serious enough to warrant letters home about rude and disrespectful behavior. One note in sixth grade reported that Robbie had exploded in a tantrum after a gym teacher told him he could not play a game but could keep score instead, since he had forgotten his gym shoes. That same year, school officials alerted the family that Robbie had singled out a new boy in the class as a target of ridicule. Perhaps Robbie was trying to build himself up at the weaker boy's expense, because he suffered his own share of torment. Other kids frequently picked on him, and more than once threw him into the pond by the Christopher Columbus Middle School. But whatever the reason, Robbie constantly made fun of the new boy and enlisted other boys to do the same.

During his second year at Christopher Columbus Middle School, Robbie Solimine met Tommy Strelka, and they became friends. But Robbie also met another interesting kid in middle school, James Wanger, through an organization that most kids hadn't ever heard about.

One day during the 1987–88 school year, all the eighth-graders at the Christopher Columbus School, including Robbie Solimine, met for a period-long assembly. On the program was a presentation by the United States Naval Sea Cadets Corps, a youth organization sponsored by the U.S. Navy. Members of the group, wearing colorful military regalia and moving with spit-and-polish precision, appeared on stage with an honor guard and flags. Then the lights flickered out, and the students watched *Lanes to the Sea*, a promotional movie designed to excite their interest in seafaring and stir their patriotic fervor. The movie, whose footage dated to the 1960s, told the story of the Navy and Coast Guard in bold and impressionistic segments: Here were courageous young men in action, safeguarding democracy on the high seas and along the nation's coasts. The movie also showed pictures of boot camp, SEALS training, and so on, and it explained what the Sea Cadets were.

When the movie credits ran, the adults and the young people, including a teenager from Clifton named Jennifer Clayton, stepped forward to talk to the students about their experiences in the Sea Cadets. Kids who joined the organization would travel to ports on the East Coast and spend weekends aboard Navy ships. They went to boot camp. They marched in local parades. There would be dinners and events. Most of all, the organization instilled values and discipline that would be beneficial to a person's career no matter what it was. And being in the Sea Cadets was fun. At the conclusion of the assembly, the Sea Cadets on stage invited interested students to sign up to obtain further information about the group and attend a regular meeting.

The romance of a life at sea seized at least two youngsters in the auditorium that day: Robbie Solimine and James Wanger. Robbie and Wanger put their names on the roster of potential recruits who wished to learn more, and soon after they were invited to a meeting at the Alexander Hamilton Army Reserve Center in Lodi, the group's local headquarters. Robbie and James both went. Sensing the promise of an interesting future, they signed up for the Sea Cadets and embarked on a venture whose traditions went back to the earliest days of seafaring and the inception of the United States Navy.

The U.S. Naval Sea Cadets had been set up in 1958 by the Navy League, a volunteer organization of former service members, at the request of the Department of the Navy. The Sea Cadets' purpose was to encourage boys—and later, girls—to embark on a maritime career, civilian or military, and to instruct them in the basic arts of seamanship. The Sea Cadet were modeled heavily on the U.S. Navy and Coast Guard, and almost every activity directly or indirectly prepared them for enlistment. There was no obligation on members to join the Navy, but many did. The organization was open to all United States citizens of sound moral character between the ages of fourteen and eighteen. To become a Sea Cadet, youngsters underwent two weeks of basic training. This was boot camp, and it was like the real thing in almost every way, except that it was shorter and it was for kids. The training, some of which was conducted by military personnel, took place on shore and aboard the ships. They also were expected to master the manual of Basic Military Requirements given to regular Navy recruits, known as the BMR, in addition to the rules and regulations of the Sea Cadets. By and large, the Sea Cadets was for enlisted men and women what the ROTC was for the officer class.

No doubt Robbie's fascination with the military and sailing piqued interest in the Sea Cadets. He admired members of his family, including his father, uncle and grandfather, for serving in the military. And from the time he was a young boy, Robbie had always loved the water, an avocation shared by almost all the men in his family. He loved the ocean's salty sting, he loved the calm of freshwater lakes in northern New Jersey and upstate New York, and he loved to fish. His brother Billy could take it or leave it—when he went out with Bob and Robbie, Billy might slip on the earphones of a Sony Walkman and zone out—but Robbie would fish and fish and fish. In 1985, when Robbie was about nine years old, Arlene and Bob bought a country house on a lake in Pennsylvania where the boys could fish and play in the hills. Robbie loved it. He couldn't seem to get enough of fishing and sailing. Back home, he begged his aunt and uncle to take him to the Jersey shore whenever they could, whiling away the day fishing and crabbing behind their shore house. Manny took the boys out on Greenwood Lake in West Milford, New Jersey, in a boat that was dubbed *There Goes Paris*, because its previous owners had been planning a trip to the French capital when they decided to buy the nineteen-foot craft instead. Robbie knew how much fun sailing could be and now the Sea Cadets promised to prepare him for a lifetime of it.

Having signed up at the same time, Solimine and Wanger attended basic training together at the Recruit Training Center, Naval Construction Battalion Center, in Davisville, Rhode Island. When they arrived at the old Seabees base, their luggage—or "sea bag" now—was dumped on the floor for inspection. The boys packed only the essentials listed on a Sea Cadets checklist. This meant uniforms, some undershirts (white only), gym shorts (black or blue only), and toiletries. Their names were supposed to be stenciled on their clothing. The boys also were required to bring stationery and stamps ("Cadets must write home"), but they were forbidden from bringing virtually everything else except a baseball mitt or a camera. They were not permitted to bring cigarettes, candy, food, jewelry, or even civilian clothes.

In their first days of basic training that summer, seaman recruits Solimine and Wanger learned how to make a bed and keep a locker. Their days began at 5:30 A.M. with reveille and ended with taps. They were drilled in the proper way to stand at attention—head erect, chin drawn in, heels together, toes turned out at forty-five degrees—and in the proper way to march. As part of their training, Seamen recruits learned how to salute, when to salute, what to salute, and whom to salute. They learned to count the hours by the twenty-four-hour military clock. They learned an entirely new lexicon, whereby a floor became the "deck" and the ceiling became the "overhead." Going upstairs or downstairs was going "topside" or "below." Walls became "bulkheads," beds were "racks" or "bunks," and the toilet was "the head." In the classroom, Wanger and Solimine were exposed to a knowledge of naval history and lore. They were quizzed on ship nomenclature and exposed to other skills as well: basic navigation, firefighting drills, sending messages by semaphore. One of the first skills the boys would learn was how to tie a knot properly—a subject known as marlinspike seamanship. The square knot came first, and more exotic forms followed. It was essential that a sailor know how to tie the square knot, not only because of its versatility, but because the kerchief on their uniforms had to be tied this way. The bolen came next, followed by the becketbend, the double becketbend, the clove hitch, and then on through a dizzying assortment of knots whose variety of designs and uses were testament to the working man's ingenuity.

Above all, they learned discipline and obedience. Like a Navy recruit, they learned that the first step to getting along was deciding that they would do exactly what their commanding officers told them to do, when the commanding officers told them to do it. Both boys seemed to derive unusual satisfaction from mastering the ability to obey.

Wanger failed boot camp, however, and had to be sent home. It was through no fault of his own. He had collapsed during one of the physical exercises and required hospitalization in the infirmary. The staff at the base attributed the fainting spell to the heat and humidity, but an infirmity was grounds for sending a youngster home. No doubt the disappointment came as a great shock. Some time later, Wanger told friends that the collapse was a turning point in his life—not because it held him back in Sea Cadets, because it did not. In fact, Wanger went on to progress through the ranks on a schedule almost simultaneously with Solimine. But Wanger told his friends that the incident revealed the existence of some sort of neurological condition—mild epilepsy or seizures of some kind—that required him to take an anticonvulsant medication. It would also stand as an emblem of how his health might sabotage his dreams of becoming a soldier.

By contrast, Robbie passed boot camp with aplomb. His enthusiasm became apparent early on to his superiors, and his success conferred a new distinction on him that he wore with pride: He was entitled now to call himself a full-fledged Sea Cadet.

Both Wanger and Solimine became active in the events and regular meetings, which at times seemed as formal or demanding as boot camp. Everything had structure and (at least it was said) a purpose. The Sea Cadets were divided into units whose chain of command stretched, at least in theory, all the way to the Secretary of the Navy and then to the President of the United States. The units were broken down into divisions and companies. Solimine and Wanger's unit in Lodi was named the DeLong Division. Solimine was assigned to Alpha Company. Wanger was assigned to Bravo Company. The division was headed by Lieutenant Commander Joseph T. Hamlisch, a gruff bulldog of a man who had lied about his age forty-some years earlier so he could enlist in the Navy when he was only sixteen. Having served for more than forty years, he approached things from the old school: There was always a right way, the wrong, and the Navy way. Behind his back, the cadets called him "Teddy." Just below Hamlisch was the division's executive officer, Lieutenant Junior Grade Donald J. Clayton, another former Navy man; his wife, Judith A. Clayton, was the administrative officer; Ensign Gregory J. Kits, a young man in his twenties who had not served in the Navy, was the unit's personnel officer; Jennifer Clayton, whose parents had imbued her with a deep love for the Navy and the Sea Cadets, had joined in 1985 and rose to become the unit's leading petty officer; her younger brother also became a member. At their meetings, the cadets wore uniforms that resembled the regular Navy seaman's uniform in every respect but the "flashes"—the insignia that marked them as Sea Cadets. Boys wore the white, "Dixie cup" cap, bell-bottom trousers, and the jumpers with the distinctive square collar-flaps in the back. Girls wore skirts below the knee and a garrison cap, a sort of winged beret that resembled a school crossing guard's hat. Haircuts and other grooming had to conform to the Navy code. Everyone referred to everyone else by rank. The cadets spent hours drilling and parading.

To some of the supervising officers, rookie cadet Solimine looked like trouble from the first regular meeting in Lodi. He horsed around all the time, cracking jokes or making faces when the ranks were forming, acted rambunctious, and got on the nerves of his superiors. Clayton, a big-boned girl with smiling eyes and a slight speech impediment who helped train the cadets, went head to head with Solimine over his inability to follow orders. Kits also thought Solimine was a clown. Kits kept a dish of candy on his desk and put it up when he saw Solimine coming: He was convinced the sugar made him go nuts.

When he wasn't actively creating a disturbance, Solimine was often distracted, and his inattention interfered with exercises the leaders were trying to do. At first, Robbie and Jennifer's clashes also contained a sexist undertone, as though Solimine was uncomfortable taking orders from a female—especially one who was only a little older than he was.

"Rob, you gotta settle down," Clayton told him. "If you don't settle down, you're out."

Clayton's father, Kits, and Hamlisch all had to have sit-downs with Solimine at one time or another. Threatened with expulsion, however, Solimine came around. As he knuckled down, he also showed another side of himself. He still liked to be rowdy now and then, but he also liked to be in control, to achieve a measure of competence that earned him some respect. As time went on, Jennifer and Rob became friends. Robbie grew also to respect her, not just as his superior officer, but in her own right, for her thoughts and opinions and advice about other things. In turn, she grew to respect him. In fact, Jennifer discovered something. The more that was expected of Rob, the more he expected of himself.

One day, when the unit was cleaning up around the reserve center, Kits got the idea that they should put Solimine in charge of the work detail. Make him a leader. At the time, Jennifer Clayton thought Kits was out of his mind.

"No," Kits said. "I want you to let Solimine do it. I can see a lot of myself in Rob Solimine. He's got a lot of potential. I know if you give him something to do, it'll keep him out of trouble."

To Clayton's surprise, Rob took charge. Kits and Clayton followed up the experiment by giving Rob more and more responsibility. Robbie welcomed the opportunity, and he responded well to new challenges. As he settled down in the organization and directed his energy toward useful ends, the side of Solimine that endeared him to people also emerged more and more readily. With his charisma and his energy and his charm and his discipline—when he wanted to show discipline—Jennifer thought she saw the characteristics of a potential leader.

The transformation that Robbie underwent in the Sea Cadets soon affected the rest of his life, and his plans for the future. His parents noticed, and not without some astonishment. The first time Bob and Arlene Solimine saw Robbie marching around in uniform, snapping to attention and saluting, they almost fell over.

"Is that really him being told what to do," Arlene said, whispering to Bob behind her hand, "and he's really doing it?"

In no time, Robbie seemed to live and breathe the Sea Cadets and the Navy, stuffing his room with maritime paraphernalia: an American flag, plastic models and pictures of fighting ships, a dud artillery shell. He started talking about enlisting in the Navy after he got out of high school; he said he would sail as a cook. Bob Solimine told him he might think about the Coast Guard instead, because he thought the Coast Guard might be more interesting for his son, but Robbie had his heart set on the Navy. It became a habit of his to say, "When I get in the Navy, I'll . . ."

All the while, Wanger too became an ardent Sea Cadet, although he was far less flamboyant than Robbie and displayed his enthusiasm in more conventional ways. He was obedient and disciplined and seldom, if ever, caused problems. Although he occasionally screwed up in his dreamy way—he fell asleep at a computer screen once and filled forty-two screens with punctuation marks—he did what he was asked to do with a salute and a nod. He was good under pressure and seemed generally to be on an even keel. Nothing could throw him off, very little seemed to bother him, and he was so mild as to be virtually harmless. Just as Robbie earned more and more responsibilities, so did James.

One summer, for example, James returned to the boot camp in Rhode Island to help supervise the training of the recruits. Kits had him helping with the paper work. It was hot in the office where the staff was working, and the windows were propped open. Suddenly, James stopped typing and stood up. He stepped away from his seat and bent over something near his desk. Then, very carefully, James picked up an insect of some kind, a bug so small it seemed invisible, and carried the creature between his two fingers to one of the windows, beyond harm's way. Then he released the bug outside. He returned to his typing, unaware that anyone had been watching.

"Did you see what he just did?" one of the workers whispered to Kits. Kits had, and the memory stayed with him long afterward.

The Sea Cadets became one of the few places in Solimine's and Wanger's lives where they felt entirely comfortable. It was there that Solimine acquired the discipline and attention he seemed to crave or felt to be lacking elsewhere. As for Wanger, no one in the Sea Cadets picked on him or made fun of him for his eccentricities, as they did in high school. In this unusual setting, a friendship grew between Wanger and Solimine, a friendship that bloomed although it was complicated by rivalry. Some of the leaders dubbed them the Bobbsey Twins, because they seemed so close. It would not be free of bickering or occasional quarrels during the long car rides on field trips, but for the most part they got along very well. At meetings and on field trips, they seemed to do everything together and follow each other everywhere—especially Wanger, who did most of the following, at least at first. For one thing, Solimine was the first popular kid—not popular like the captain of the football team, but in the sense that he was widely known and fairly well liked—ever to pay attention to Wanger and take him seriously. Wanger, who had been a geek in the shadows, was grateful for the attention. So was his mother.

Although she was working two jobs, as a barmaid and a private nurse, Paula Wanger became one of the most enthusiastic and loyal parents in the Sea Cadets group. Kits, who was always hunting up parents to drive the boys on field trips, could almost always count on her to volunteer. Whenever there was a Sea Cadets benefit dinner or ceremony, Paula would appear, exhausted but happy, carrying a covered dish or a plate of cookies—usually bringing a double batch to cover for the cadets whose parents couldn't or didn't take part. On those occasions when Paula Wanger couldn't be with Wanger at a Sea Cadets affair, Wanger's grandparents were. Although the military bearing was something foreign to her, Paula endorsed the Sea Cadets because Jimmy did. She wanted him to have good role models, and she felt that the Sea Cadets had plenty.

Happy-go-lucky and youthful, Paula Wanger related easily to the cadets and always seemed eager to lend a hand. She especially liked Robbie from the first time she met him. Robbie won Paula over with his humor and his charm, and she encouraged her son's friendship with him. After a while, Paula treated Robbie as though he were her other son. The Colombos treated Solimine as if he were also their grandson. Yet Paula also considered herself a friend of Robbie's, an authentic contemporary; it was as if she was able to bridge the gap in years, and not merely to overlook it. She and Robbie talked often, and during those talks, Robbie perceived that she listened carefully to him. She sympathized with his family problems. Robbie's conflicts with his mother especially struck a chord, no doubt since some of his complaints focused on his wish that his mother be as involved in the Sea Cadets as Paula was. Although Bob Solimine had driven Robbie and the other boys on various outings, Rob complained that his mother did not participate, or that he would call her up asking for rides home after regular meetings and she would tell him he could walk. Paula Wanger took it upon herself to be another mother in Robbie's life.

Side by side with the friendship between Solimine and Wanger, however, their rivalry, which generally was collegial, also grew. No doubt their competition had been generated early on by their different experiences at boot camp, but it also became apparent as they followed each other closely through the ranks. As friends go, their personalities could hardly have been more different. Wanger was straitlaced and usually quiet, almost never letting go unless he was completely at ease with the people around him. Solimine was chattering all the time and seemed eager to jump from one activity to another. Wanger possessed endless amounts of patience in dealing with the younger recruits. Robbie did not, and he had a tendency to pick on the younger ones. Wanger almost never cursed; Robbie cursed freely. Wanger seldom if ever blew his stack. Robbie could be temperamental. Like most of the cadets, Robbie liked marksmanship training and scored well enough with the .22-caliber rifle—a modified M-16—to qualify as a good shot. Wanger, perhaps because of his poor vision and glasses, was a lousy shot and didn't like it very much. On recruiting trips to local middle schools, Robbie always scooted over to the cute girls and came away with a new phone number. Wanger seemed too shy to speak to a girl, and whenever he tried it almost always seemed to get all gummed up. Robbie was more at ease physically and more animated, having developed an athletic build that was broad-shouldered and thin at the waist. Wanger was physically gawky. No matter how hard he worked on his military bearing, he always seemed to be off-kilter, his face slack-jawed and inscrutable, his legs too long and rickety for his body. Even their choice of service eventually diverged. Although at the time of his joining the Sea Cadets, Wanger talked of wanting to be a priest, he later decided that he would join the Marines. Robbie stuck with the Navy.

They differed in other important respects too. Although Wanger always seemed to be private and somewhat inscrutable, Robbie talked at length about his life, his ambitions, and the things that troubled him. Before he had his own car, he would bum rides home from Kits, and they would talk man-to-man about many things. A frequent topic between them concerned the turmoil in the Chircop household. By the time he was a petty officer, Robbie also was confiding regularly in Clayton. He had some problems with his father, it was true, but nothing like what was going on with his mother and stepfather. He was often upset about the fighting with his mother, mostly over the usual things kids run up against with their parents—housekeeping, study habits, what have you. Robbie told them he felt as if his mother favored his brother over him. Robbie also fretted that his mother didn't like his friends, even his friends from the Sea Cadets, and he complained that she had threatened to yank him out of the organization because she felt some of the kids were a bad influence on him. Clayton saw him cry sometimes, and every once in a while at home she took desperate calls from Robbie on the telephone. It disturbed him the way his mother and stepfather fought with each other, and he also told Clayton he wondered whether his mother and stepfather drank too much. There were nights when Jennifer Clayton knew who was calling before she could get to the telephone.

"I need to get out of here," Robbie would say, "can I come up there for a while?"

In contrast, Wanger seemed to have no great desire to unburden himself to others. When he talked about what he wanted to be and do, he sketched out the plans without much detail: It was enough to say, as he did not long after he became a Sea Cadet, that he wanted to be a priest. Though he sometimes canceled out of Sea Cadet events because of his duties at church, Wanger seldom discussed religion or his beliefs or what it was about religion that had launched his dreams of joining the priesthood. What's more, Wanger almost never talked about his family. It was clear that he was devoted to his mother and his grandparents, that he respected and loved them very much. But he seldom brought up matters pertaining to his life with them, or their pasts, or the absence of a father. People knew that he didn't have one, and that was about it.

As time went on, Wanger and Solimine found they had another thing in common besides an interest in joining the military: They liked to get drunk. By the time they were in high school, Robbie and Wanger were drinking to excess whenever they could get it or sneak it, and Wanger in particular loved to boast about his drunken exploits. Neither of the boys ever brought alcohol to a Sea Cadets affair or appeared drunk during a drill or outing, but Kits and Clayton and the others all knew that they occasionally drank. Wanger, who was nerdy enough to look middle-aged at times, happily discovered that he could buy liquor in several different places, usually in Paterson or Passaic, simply by walking into the liquor store, picking out a bottle, and paying for it as nonchalantly as a legal customer. Wanger liked Jack Daniel's whiskey and even had a taste for gin. He and Robbie drank down the street from Robbie's house at the "DPW tubes," the huge cylindrical pipes by the garage for the city's Department of Public Works. When they drank, they got bombed.

For Wanger, drinking seemed to be a rite of passage that demonstrated that he had finally arrived. Certainly, his views of boozing weren't much different from those of his high-school classmates. To be a man meant being able to drink—and to be a real man meant being a hard drinker. Or so it seemed from the tough-guy way Wanger had of talking about booze. Just slinging the brand names around seemed to give him a charge, and he liked playing the part of the drunken ox. He regaled his friends with tales about drinking until he blacked out or pulled crazy stunts.

As for Solimine, he liked to drink, too, but his interest in alcohol seemed more complicated, as though he had been seeking something more elusive inside the bottle than Wanger had found. For Solimine, drinking seemed like a more inward exercise, something more medicinal and needy.

In their years of participating with the Sea Cadets, Robbie

and James also met plenty of other kids from Clifton or nearby towns. They became good friends with several of them. One young man who joined the unit was Tommy Stujinski. Stooge was assigned to Solimine's company, and while he was in the group he was obliged to follow Solimine's orders. But Stooge didn't stick around very long. Not long after joining the Sea Cadets, Stooge quit. He just didn't like the regimented style of the thing.

Another who came through the Sea Cadet ranks was a boy named Stevie Castaldo, a thirteen-year-old kid who lived over on Prescott Avenue. Unlike his elder brother Frankie, Stevie Castaldo was a not a fighter and he was not a dropout-in-the-making. A quiet, hulking kid who laughed easily when someone drew him out, Stevie Castaldo did well enough in school that he had hopes of going to college someday. Stevie joined the Sea Cadets in 1990 and attended the meetings regularly. He liked Wanger and Solimine and brought them both to his house. Perhaps because both Wanger and Solimine were older than Stevie, it was only a matter of time before Solimine and Wanger gravitated toward hanging out with Stevie's brother, Frank, as well. At first, everyone got on well, even Frank and Rob, although they were as different as two young guys could be. But it didn't last very long. Robbie and Frankie just didn't mix.

One night, Frank and Robbie sat up drinking, and Robbie poured out his heart. Frank, who had started out the night liking Solimine, felt differently before it was over. During their discussion Solimine had crossed a line, revealed too much, admitted too much, so that all Frankie took away from the conversation was an appraisal of the other kid's weakness. Frankie felt mild disgust, as if he were embarrassed for Rob's sake at the way Rob had gushed—especially Robbie's confession that he was a virgin. The encounter left Castaldo feeling cool toward Solimine. There was no clash that night and no feeling of animosity between them. They watched television and they drank. But it would be as close as they would ever get to being friends.

Some time later, on a weekend before a Sea Cadets trip, Robbie came over to spend the night at Stevie Castaldo's house. The next morning they were supposed to go see an aircraft carrier somewhere. Robbie had brought some liquor, either for the sleepover or the trip to the port, and he left it in Stevie's bedroom in the desk. While straightening up in Stevie's room, Mrs. Castaldo disturbed Solimine's belongings and heard glass clanking around. She opened the bag and found two bottles of booze. Joe Castaldo forbade drinking in his house; he was not a big drinker himself. On New Year's Eve, his kids made fun of him because he bought nonalcoholic champagne. Mr. and Mrs. Castaldo knew, however, that kids drank, and on occasion, friends of Frankie's showed up at the Castaldos' house already drunk. The Castaldos didn't like it, although they didn't do much about it, either. But Mrs. Castaldo didn't want it going on in her house. In anger she closed the bag and waited for the boys to return.

"Rob," she said angrily, "I appreciate that when you come to my house you no bring no liquor in my house. I got little kids in the house, and I don't want no one drinking here."

Robbie apologized. But after being chewed out by Mrs. Castaldo, he was reluctant to come around for a while. Still, he continued to drink, raiding the booze from his father's liquor cabinet in North Haledon or getting it from package stores that didn't care who they sold their liquor to.

Strelka, too, could drink. He had experimented with alcohol for the first time with Robbie, and he liked the way it messed him up. Only Wanger seemed to be his match. Wanger would drink himself into a stupor and be proud of it.

One summery night Billy was home watching TV when Rob dashed in the door looking for him. Billy was generally so calm all the time, he could seem slow on the uptake. Rob started to tell him what was going on.

"Me and Wanger were drinking, and he drank a lot," Rob said, and there was urgency in his tone. "Can you give him a ride?"

Rob told his brother that Wanger was down the street in Currie Park. Wanger was so drunk that he was out cold. Rob was worried Wanger might run off, get in trouble or worse. To keep that from happening, Rob said, he had handcuffed Wanger to a metal tube.

Handcuffed? Billy couldn't believe it.

Billy followed Robbie down the hill to the park, and sure enough, there was Wanger, flat out on the ground in his Army fatigues and combat boots. Wanger, who still was in his Persian Gulf warrior incarnation months after the war, was an utter mess. He was lying in the mud, which had been softened by recent thunderstorms; a big swatch of puke stained the front of his white T-shirt. He was not unconscious—but he was not exactly alert, either.

Robbie and Billy tried yelling at him, but that didn't work, and they couldn't budge him, either. They obviously couldn't leave him like this. And it was getting late. Against his better judgment, Billy agreed to give Wanger a ride to his grandparents' house. Robbie unlocked the handcuffs. Wanger lay in the mud like a toad. Wanger started mumbling stuff, but neither Billy nor Robbie could make out what he was saying as the two boys started trying to move him out of the park.

"He's too big!" Billy said. "I'm just going to leave, and he's going to have to find his way home."

Billy guessed that his brother had been drinking too, but he couldn't tell for sure. Maybe the dilemma of what to do about Wanger had sobered him. What's more, Billy was having second thoughts about his brother's friend fouling up the car. Wanger was one big dirty, sopping, nauseating pile of stink by now, and the last thing Billy needed was Wanger rolling around on the seats and heaving all over the place. Billy had the idea to make an anonymous call to the cops, tell them there was a drunk in the park, and let them take it from there.

They stood in the small park for half an hour trying to decide what to do. They were pissed off, too. But as much as both of them might have wanted to leave Wanger where he lay, Billy and Robbie knew they couldn't do it. Wanger's grandparents would flip as it was, if they found James in this condition. God knows what would have happened once the police got involved. Finally, Robbie and Billy decided that the only solution was to do whatever it took to get Wanger into the trunk. Billy had a black Oldsmobile Cutlass, which probably had room enough in the trunk for a drunk Wanger's size. The only question was whether they could get Wanger in there. Straining to lift him without getting coated with muck, Billy and Robbie eventually flipped Wanger inside. But before they could shut the lid, Wanger came to life.

"What are you doing?" Wanger yelled. "What are you doing?"

Billy and Robbie slammed the trunk lid and drove off. Wanger was thumping around in back and banging with his fists. When Wanger was sober, he seemed to get a kick out of riding in the trunk of a car, or at least proving that he wasn't afraid to do it. Now he was making a holy ruckus. Billy turned the stereo on. His thinking was that the stereo would keep Wanger awake—as Billy and Robbie had no interest in hauling Wanger's carcass out when they got to Wanger's house—and it would drown out the noise he was making. Then—why not?—just to bedevil him, Billy and Robbie couldn't resist cranking the volume. Up it went, and the speakers, which were mounted just ahead of the space where Wanger was clunking around, filled the Cutlass with a groove that almost blew the windows out.

It was really a hoot, the whole scene—until a cop started trailing Billy's car. Billy and Robbie had no doubt the cop was onto them, and that they were all about to be busted. Billy cut the music and kept an eye on the rearview mirror. They yelled at Wanger to pipe down because there was a cop behind them. Wanger wised up and quieted down. A few blocks later the cop turned off, and Billy and Robbie drove on. When they pulled up by Wanger's house, Billy opened the trunk. Wanger was scrunched up like a baby between the wheel housings.

"You're home," Billy said. "Get out."

Wanger didn't budge. Either he was sleeping, dead to the world, or he was pretending to be asleep. Billy couldn't tell.

"Get out, Wanger," Billy said, louder.

Wanger still didn't move.

"Wanger, if you don't come out of there, we're going to get your grandfather out here. You'll be in deep shit."

Like Lazarus awakened from the dead, Wanger stirred. He stirred at the word "grandfather" and stepped out of the trunk, blinking in the cool orange light of the streetlamps. Robbie and Billy gave Wanger's handcuffs back to him and got him going in the direction of his grandparents' house. They watched him going up the walk. Then Wanger went inside.

By the spring of his junior year, in 1991, Robbie Solimine was drinking so much that he feared becoming an alcoholic. He had reached the point that he was drinking almost every weekend with his buddies. Robbie confided his fears to his parents, who expressed surprise. If Robbie was an alcoholic, neither Bob nor Maggie had seen the obvious signs. Bob had seen the kid down a beer on a fishing trip or something, but that was about it. But Robbie was sincere, and his parents supported him. Robbie began consulting with a psychologist.

Outwardly, Robbie didn't seem different. He was halfway through his junior year of high school, and he still seemed high-spirited and active. But in ways that would appear obvious later, Robbie's life was unraveling, and so was Manny and Maggie's marriage. For starters, Robbie and Tommy Strelka's friendship, which had been tight for at least four years, was showing strains. It may have been simply that they grew apart, but at least three other factors played a role as well: alcohol, music, and a girl. Strelka had taken his first drink with Robbie, and now he was drinking all the time. Drugs did not interest him, other than a few experiments with prescription medicines that he and Robbie found around the house, but Strelka learned early on that he liked to drink. Other kids at school started to view him as a burnout. With drinking as a catalyst, Tommy's life was growing a little more wild—not reckless, not out of control by most kids' standards, but more rebellious. And Strelka's drinking habits were becoming more troublesome just about the time Robbie started to think he should quit.

Then there was music, which now took center stage in Tommy's dreams. Since the age of ten, Tommy had imagined becoming the lead singer or guitarist in a band like Def Leppard, which he idolized. Def Leppard became the Led Zeppelin of the 1980s, its popularity and its legend magnified by eerie mishaps and deaths that shadowed its monster-size success, and Tommy followed their career with almost religious devotion. Watching Def Leppard's videos on MTV or listening to them on his stereo, Tommy slashed at his guitar. He sang along as singer Joe Elliot rasped hits like "Pour Some Sugar on Me" and "Armaggedon It." He became a metal head and dressed the part: ratty jeans, flannel shirts over a rock-and-roll T-shirt, long hair, baseball cap with the brim turned backward. Tommy became such a fanatic of heavy-metal music in general, and Def Leppard in particular, that when guitarist Steve Clark overdosed on booze and painkillers in his London flat on January 8, 1991, Tommy mourned the star's death as if he had been a close friend or member of the family. Tommy also jammed to groups like Anthrax, Pearl Jam, and Nirvana. Listening to the music took the edge off his nerves, and he believed literally in the music's ability to heal him. If he had a cold, for example, he would slip in a CD and crank the volume, and the cold would begin to vanish.

"It makes me feel good because I feel I have accomplished something in life," Tommy wrote in an essay about his love for heavy-metal music.

While Tommy focused more and more on music, joining a band and dreaming of hitting the Big Time, Robbie became more and more of a nuisance. They just weren't in sync as they had been as young boys. It seemed Robbie had nowhere else to go but to Tommy's house. Tommy would be practicing guitar in the solitude of his room, feeling the music rising from his fingertips, when Robbie would intrude, wanting to do something and wanting Tommy to pay attention. Tommy felt as if Robbie wanted him to drop whatever he was doing and bow down to his commands. Worst of all, Tommy felt Robbie was interfering with his progress as a musician. They quarreled more, and for the first time, Tommy started to tell Robbie to buzz off.

Finally, there was one girl in particular whom Robbie and Tommy liked quite a bit. Her name was Chrissie Bachelle. Her friends called her "Cat"—and in fact her handsome face appeared somewhat feline, and her almond-shaped eyes beheld the world in a vacant blue stare. She was blond, and her hair hung down in self-consciously long bangs and curls that drooped to her shoulders. One day, she hoped, she would be an actress; she was very proud of having starred in a McDonald's commercial as a child. She talked out of the side of her mouth, and she had strong opinions about everything. Yet, it was odd to hear her talking tough in her squeaky voice. Her thoughts were apt to conclude with a weary "whatever." When words failed her, which was seldom, she screwed up her face in amazed disbelief—a sort of can-you-believe-it irony—and flashed the cheerleader's Beauty Queen smile, as an expression of disdain played at corners of her mouth. She knew more than she told, and she was intuitive and cagey, particularly about the opposite sex. Indeed, she had mastered the art of flirting, knowing the way to propose and withhold—not necessarily to manipulate, but to hold people at bay.

Chrissie and Rob first got to know each other over the telephone. Robbie started calling her up in October of 1990 because he was interested in one of her friends. He talked for hours, asking what he should do about the other girl, and Chrissie would tell him, and then Rob would try it, and if it didn't work, they would talk over another plan. If they weren't talking about Rob's crush on Chrissie's friend, or school gossip, then they talked about their families. Chrissie's family life had been turbulent, and she told Robbie about her stints in foster homes, shelters, mental wards, and the like. The state Division of Youth and Family Services long ago had intervened in her case. She said she had been sexually abused. She also became sexually precocious. She ran away and she looked for thrills. She got high, she got drunk, she got laid. Social workers would try to patch things up. All of the things that had made her vulnerable, however, had also made her wise, and they certainly made her attractive to Robbie. As his life at home became more difficult, Robbie leaned more on Chrissie and seemed to identify with her unhappiness. Rob spent hours on the telephone with her and liked to walk over to her house to see her. A few times he brought his buddies, including Tommy Strelka and Wanger.

At school, meanwhile, Robbie was flunking American history, just getting by in French, and earning Cs in marketing and metals. He had never been a model student, but he was not a dummy, and his parents considered him an underachiever. They believed his biggest problem was his attitude. In ninth grade, chronic run-ins with his teacher in the metal shop had sidetracked his hopes for making the honor roll. The metals teacher requested referrals to the guidance office, parent conferences, and detention; in the end, Robbie pulled out a final grade of C. Now, however, the degree of his alienation was perhaps best shown by his performance on an Otis Lennon School Ability Test. Although standardized tests in middle school ranked him as an average learner, a test in April of his junior year suggested he was capable of reading only at the fifth-grade level. Then a guidance counselor at the school caught the problem. The answer sheet—containing the familiar egg-shaped blanks that students fill in with No. 2 pencils—had been used to draw obviously ridiculous patterns. Whether out of boredom, anger or frustration, Robbie had blown off almost the entire test, filling in whole rows or creating letters and geometric shapes with the dots.

At home, too, Robbie and Billy both were struggling to cope with Maggie and Manny's fraying marriage. Robbie's mother and stepfather were fighting more often, usually over the things everyone fights over, such as money. But another source of conflict was the boys, as Manny and Maggie quarreled over how to raise them. Maggie thought Manny was too much of a disciplinarian; Manny thought she was too lax. What's more, Manny felt as if his role as parent was called into question. He complained that Maggie could seldom resist pointing out that he was not the boys' natural father, as if therefore he lacked the full authority to deal with them as he saw fit.

"You're living under my roof!" Manny would say to the boys during an argument.

Then Maggie would get upset.

"It's *our* house," she would say.

As both Maggie and Manny were somewhat headstrong, they would go days without talking to each other after a particularly nasty row. On two occasions that fall, Manny ripped the phone out of the wall, Maggie would later claim.

When things became too unpleasant at home, both boys availed themselves of their grandparents' house. They were warmly welcomed there, and the place became like a sanctuary. Their grandmother adored her grandsons, and in her eyes they were faultless. She did everything in her power to make sure they were fed, worried over, and loved. They worked with their grandfather on their cars or the boat. They shared their anxieties over the strife at home, which was complicated all the more by the fact that Bill Yakal and Manny all but hated each other. Manny felt that Yakal always was butting his nose into business that didn't concern him, and if he wasn't doing it directly, then he was trying to force the issue by telling Maggie what to do.

As things worsened between Maggie and Manny, the conflicts became more frequent between Rob and his parents. Maggie and Robbie always had a complicated relationship, and as he approached adulthood, it only became more complex and more racked by contradictions, misunderstandings, and pain. Since they had been boys, Billy was closest to his father, and Robbie was closest to his mother. Part of it could be explained by compatibility: Billy and Bob were quiet, relaxed, and almost like loners. Robbie and Maggie were more gregarious and open. Manny sensed that Maggie favored Robbie. Yet despite her closeness with Robbie—or perhaps because of it—Maggie was also the source of Robbie's greatest turmoil. They were both iron-willed when their backs were up, and that accounted for some of the trouble. In telephone conversations with girls or while talking to Kits at Sea Cadets, Robbie complained about his mother more than anyone else in his life. He told friends he often felt that she did not love him, that she favored his brother, and that she didn't care if he lived or died.

Whatever the reason—Maggie's marital problems, Manny's building anger, or Robbie's teenage existential crisis—arguments exploded regularly over almost anything. Maggie might ask Robbie if he studied for his exams, Rob might say, "Later," and around they'd go. They clashed over friends and over household duties, as Margaret seemed forever to be after her son to clean up his room, fold his laundry, clean up after himself, and pitch in around the house. It was an issue for Manny, too. To Manny, it seemed as if Robbie's idea of cleaning his room was piling the clothes under his bed. But Robbie complained bitterly to friends that his mother was a neat freak who would tell him he had to clean the bathroom tiles with a toothbrush. And if it wasn't about the house, then Robbie felt his mother was nagging him about his friends. Meanwhile, Rob was clashing with Manny, too, and to make things worse, he had a way of playing one parent off the other, making an already unhappy marriage positively volatile. It got so bad that Rob and Manny got into a scuffle on one occasion. Robbie gave his stepfather a nosebleed.

"Good for you," she said to Manny.

Things seemed to be coming to a head, and the fighting grew worse. The day Robbie was supposed to get his school picture taken for the yearbook, he and Maggie quarreled, and she refused to take him for the portrait, so he called Susie Strelka and she took him. Another time after a fight at home, as Susie Strelka would later say, Robbie showed up at the Strelkas' in tears, spaghetti or some sort of food dripping on his clothing. Susie, thinking that maybe Robbie could use a cooling-off period, said it would be okay if Robbie spent the night at their house. Because Robbie was hungry, he and Tommy Strelka went to a chicken place over on Lakeview Avenue together. While they were gone, Maggie showed up at the Strelkas' in a rage. She demanded to know where Rob was, and she accused Mrs. Strelka of harboring him. She threatened to call the police and accuse her of kidnapping. Another night Robbie called his stepmother Arlene in tears from a pay phone. He said he didn't want go go home because of the fighting. In February 1991, Robbie and Maggie got into a fight and Robbie took off. He didn't come home, instead spending the night at Chrissie Bachelle's. Maggie went to the police and filled out a missing persons report.

As the fights between Robbie and his mother grew in intensity, Robbie spent more and more of his time either going by his friends' houses or pouring out his troubles over the telephone. His troubles seemed so immense that Robbie was threatening to commit suicide. On several occasions, he told friend he was going to overdose on pills. Once, with Tommy Strelka, he found a gun in the house, held it to his head, and threatened to kill himself. Another time after a run-in with his mother, Robbie went to Chrissie's in tears with a vow to slash his wrists. Chrissie asked if Robbie had a knife, and Rob showed her two of them. Chrissie kept him talking. She asked to see the knives herself and if she could hold them. Rob handed her the knives. The crisis passed. They talked the rest of the night, but Robbie was convinced he couldn't stay at home and he couldn't live with his mother. He told Chrissie he wanted out.

One night, toward the end of the 1991 school year, Manny called home. Maggie was upset about something and didn't want to talk to him.

"Don't bother me now," she snapped. "I'm having big trouble with Rob."

"Where's Rob?" Manny said.

"He's with his father," Maggie said. "You finally got your way."

That wasn't what Manny had wanted, but Robbie had moved out, and his departure came as another blow to their marriage. Robbie moved in with his father in North Haledon in June 1991, just before the end of his junior year. Robbie withdrew formally from Clifton High School on July 17, 1991, and enrolled in Manchester Regional High School in Haledon. The high school, which educated about 700 students from three small towns north of Paterson, had only a so-so reputation. Robbie didn't know anyone at the school, and he wasn't thrilled about the prospect of spending his senior year there, but what could he do. After he turned seventeen years old on August 29—a date that he awaited with giddy impatience—he could get his driver's license, and then maybe a car, and he would still be able to get back to Clifton. He had only moved about eleven miles from home.

As for Arlene and Bob, it was no big deal that Robbie was moving in. Billy had lived with them for a time also and returned to his mother. Both boys had bedrooms in their house. If this was what Rob wanted, and if it was okay with Maggie and Manny, then it would be okay with them. They knew about Robbie's problems in the Chircop household but they minded their own business, knowing it was more complicated than assigning blame to anyone. They knew well enough that Robbie wasn't a saint. To make sure there would be no confusion, Arlene and Bob laid down the ground rules early on. There were curfews: On weeknights, Robbie had to be in by 10 P.M. On weekends, he could stay out until midnight, maybe an hour later if there was a special occasion or a party and he cleared things in advance with Arlene or Bob. They wanted Robbie to find work. When school started, they expected Robbie to pull Cs at the very least.

The change of place seemed like a reasonable solution to the growing tensions in the Chircop household, and everyone worked to make the transition smooth. From the earliest days of her relationship with Bob, Arlene had become the mediator with Maggie. The two women got along well, and Robbie's move was handled as amicably as possible. Although Maggie had been upset at her son's leaving, she also thought that the move might be in Robbie's best interests. She didn't like the crowd of friends Robbie had been hanging around with in Clifton, anyhow. But Robbie's devotion to his mother became clearer still now that he lived with his father, and he came by Clifton to visit when he could.

Disaster struck not long after Robbie had moved in with his father in North Haledon. It was July 1991, and Bob Solimine wanted to let some air into the house because of the heat. He opened up Robbie's bedroom door. Robbie was sleeping on the bed in his blue jeans and T-shirt. Bob called to Robbie, but Robbie didn't stir. Bob tried again. He stepped closer, called Robbie's name and shook him. But Robbie wouldn't wake up. Growing more anxious, Bob telephoned Arlene at work. He suspected the kid might have gotten himself drunk, but he was puzzled because he had cleaned out all the booze. He was not the kind to panic. Arlene came to the phone wondering what was going on.

"Something's wrong with Robbie," Bob said. "He's not waking up."

"Did you call his name?" she asked.

"Yes."

"Did you shake him?"

"Yes," Bob said.

"Bob, call an ambulance," she said.

"No," he said, "come home."

Normally during the rush hour, it took Arlene half an hour to get back and forth, but she zoomed home in twenty minutes or less. Inside her stepson's room, Arlene bent over Robbie and saw that he was breathing.

"Robbie," she said, "Robbie, can you hear me? Are you okay?"

Nothing.

"I'm calling the cops," she said. "We've got to get an ambulance in here, because there's something terribly wrong."

When the police and the ambulance crew arrived, they noticed right away that Robbie had vomited some hours earlier. Projectile vomiting, someone said. It had dried by then, and neither Arlene nor Bob had noticed it. One of the ambulance attendants shook Robbie, trying to see if they could get a response, but Robbie wouldn't come to. The police right away suspected an overdose of some kind.

"Does he do drugs?" a cop asked.

Bob and Arlene told the police that Robbie had been seeing a psychologist because of a drinking problem, but they had never known him to take any drugs. An ambulance attendant told them that Robbie must have overdosed on something and told them to search the house.

Sirens wailing, the ambulance transported Robbie to the Wayne General Hospital emergency room. The medical staff pumped his stomach with charcoal to neutralize whatever it was he had taken, and Robbie started vomiting up black stuff. But he was still unconscious. Indeed, he had slipped into a coma. The doctors put him in intensive care. Back home, Bob told Arlene or Billy to tear apart Robbie's room. Eventually, they found a bottle of prescription medicine that Arlene kept for migraine headaches. From the size of the bottle, they figured Robbie must have taken about ten pills.

Whatever it was he had taken, it almost killed him. Robbie lay in a coma for more than twenty-four hours. His parents and stepparents kept a vigil; the doctors advised them their son might not survive. As the clock ticked off the hours, Arlene and Bob shook their heads: It had been only by the grace of God that they had even looked in on Robbie that morning.

Strelka's mouth dropped the next day when Billy Solimine told him what had happened to Robbie.

"No way!" Strelka said.

"Yeah, he did."

"Really?"

"Yes."

Strelka was shocked. He couldn't believe it. It really threw him that Solimine was in the hospital. In a coma, no less. But perhaps it shouldn't have.

"I thought he was kidding," Strelka said.

"Why did you think he was kidding?"

"I thought he was making it up," Strelka said.

Strelka had known that Rob was taking some pills the night before, but he just didn't think about it all that much. He had popped pills himself now and then. Maybe that was why Robbie had called him the night before, wanting to talk. Strelka and Robbie were more and more on the outs, so Strelka wasn't in the mood to talk about Robbie's problems. Robbie said he wanted to get messed up, but all the booze was out of the way, and all he could find was Arlene's medication for migraines. Robbie knew that Tommy Strelka's mom took the same kind of medicine—he thought they were barbituates or something—so he wanted to know what Tommy thought. Tommy thought Robbie was a nuisance.

Strelka, who was growing sicker and sicker of Solimine's friendship all the time, had someone else on call waiting. He put the other friend on hold and told Solimine that the pills were powerful enough to kill you and not to take too much, and then he switched over to the other friend on the other telephone line. An hour later, Strelka called back and Solimine's line was busy. So Strelka let it go.

Strelka had no idea that Robbie was nearly killing himself. He thought Robbie was shooting for a little buzz.

Billy got angry when he realized that Strelka had known about Robbie taking the pills in the first place. Strelka should have known how messed up Robbie was then—that he was seeing a shrink because he thought he was an alcoholic. But what was Strelka supposed to do?

"If it ever happens again, call somebody," Billy said.

Robbie stayed in intensive care for two days. He spent at least another week in the hospital recuperating. Afterward, Robbie told everyone that he had just been fooling around, that he had taken the pills for a crazy high. He told his folks he took a couple of pills, nothing happened, he took a couple more, nothing happened, and so on until he blacked out. He didn't mean to go under. He was adamant about it, and he denied up and down that he had tried to kill himself, although some of his friends believed that was exactly what he had been trying to do.

Meanwhile, Paula Wanger called up Arlene and Bob as soon as she heard Robbie was in the hospital to find out how he was doing. Arlene and Bob recognized the name, of course, but neither knew Wanger very well, let alone his mother. Bob had met Wanger on trips to naval installations, but the kid had been distinctly unremarkable: another voice in the back of the car, another mouth devouring hamburgers at a pit stop on the highway.

Paula told Arlene how she felt close to Robbie, how she liked him a lot, how he was a good kid. Arlene, who had never met Paula face-to-face, was struck by her youthfulness. It was like talking to a teenager, Arlene thought. Paula told Arlene that having Rob around was especially important then because she had been having problems with James. Arlene was touched by Paula Wanger's concern. Paula also visited Robbie in the hospital, with her parents, making sure he had candy and magazines. Once a week, as Robbie recuperated, Paula called Arlene to ask how Robbie was doing.

Robbie was doing better with each passing day, but Arlene and Bob were already thinking about what to do after Robbie left the hospital. They were afraid of bringing him back home right away, where neither would be able to keep a twenty-four-hour watch over him. Maggie and Manny's household wasn't the solution either. So they decided to enroll Robbie in the Carrier Foundation's clinic, an inpatient rehabilitation center in Belle Mead, New Jersey. Robbie was placed under the care of a psychiatrist from the Robert Wood Johnson Medical School, who prescribed an antidepressant as part of the therapy. The clinic offered intensive treatment. In addition to

Robbie's private therapy, his family—or at least Bob, Maggie, and Arlene—drove at least fifty miles every week to meet with counselors and participate in family therapy sessions. The course of treatment for Robbie lasted approximately three months. It cost a bundle, too. Bob would have to come up with $60,000 before it was all over. But that was the least of his worries. It broke Bob's heart the day they left Robbie there. His room contained a bed, a straight-backed wooden chair, and just about nothing else. It looked like a prison.

4

When the 1991–92 school year began at Clifton High School, Robbie Solimine was still in rehab, miles away from his classmates, his teenage friends, and all their ordinary preoccupations. His parents and therapists would have liked to keep it that way, too. Yet Robbie's family knew that keeping him apart from Clifton and the old crowd wouldn't be easy—except during the school day. Since he would return to living with his father in North Haledon, Robbie would enter Manchester Regional High School. Strelka, Wanger, and Chrissie and all his other pals would be attending Clifton High School. Everyone knew Robbie hated the thought of spending his senior year of high school in an unfamiliar place. Keeping up with his friends was on his mind, and he no doubt wanted to see them once he left the Carrier clinic. But his parents and his therapists had other plans.

For one thing, Robbie's treatment would not cease the moment he left rehab. After returning to North Jersey, Robbie was expected to attend Alcoholics Anonymous meetings to keep his head on straight—three months of daily AA meetings, as a matter of fact, a regiment they called the Ninety-Ninety. What's more, as part of his treatment, Robbie also was to sign a contract for a self-imposed quarantine. In the name of building new habits for a healthier future, he pledged to discarded all vestiges of his self-destructive past. That included his friends. Which meant no more Wanger. No more Strelka. No more Chrissie.

Robbie wouldn't hear of it. He had submitted to everything else, and he had a commendable attitude toward his therapy, but no matter how many times his parents reasoned with him or argued with him, no matter what the therapists told him, he steadfastly refused to break with his friends. He felt strongly about maintaining his friendship with Wanger and Strelka and Chrissie. He could not just abandon them—her, especially.

Of course, he had no way of knowing yet that the world he refused to let go of already had drifted in his absence, that his friends had been forming new allegiances. While Robbie was away attending to his inner demons, his best friend, Tommy Strelka, had been hanging out more and more with Wanger, and both of them were spending time at Frank Castaldo's. By the time Robbie left the Carrier clinic, Strelka was moving in faster circles and living it up with his new pals. Eventually, he also started spending more time with Chrissie Bachelle.

Tommy Strelka had turned seventeen in August of 1991, but he looked three years younger and appeared almost undernourished. At the beginning of his senior year, Strelka stood five feet seven inches tall and weighed 115 pounds. His pronounced features seemed especially sharp. No matter what he did, his dirty blond hair appeared genuinely a little dirty, or at least stringy. he had a snaggle-toothed grin that communicated a tentative quality about him, a shyness that went deeper than any words, or lack of them, could express. All the same, he was gung-ho about forming a rock band in the hopes that it would lead to something big—and if it didn't, then it would be good experience toward achieving his backup plan, which was to make it as a record producer. Strelka had wheels now, too, a silver 1979 Buick LeSabre his father had given him in return for getting a job. The family called it the Silver Bullet. His friends called it The Tank. As with all teenagers, the car gave him some stature, despite its condition. There was only an AM radio inside the Buick, and the car had an unquenchable thirst for gas, but the seats were like sofas—he could pack in just about everybody he knew and then some—and it ran smoothly. Strelka was such a runt that when he got behind the wheel, he looked like a little kid. His mother joked that maybe he should sit on a telephone book when he drove.

Strelka's plans for the future were humble: Except for his rock-and-roll fantasy—and he mostly understood it as that—Strelka wanted to get through high school and get a job. He was pretty well assured of getting his diploma. Although he had discovered he liked to party more than he liked school, he did okay in the classroom, and what modest successes he had were entirely his own, since he felt almost no pressure at home. His parents were realistic. They knew Tommy wouldn't split atoms, but they also knew he wasn't dumb. He did not have to earn As, but they didn't want him bringing home anything below Cs, either. Most of all, they would not tolerate his being a slacker.

Although he passed most academic subjects, Strelka steered increasingly toward vocational classes as he proceeded through high school. His attendance record was good, except for a string of absences necessitated by health problems, and he achieved reasonable success in courses like English, biology, history, accounting, and marketing. His teachers graded his citizenship as "commendable," and he never got a suspension. High-school principal Robert P. Mooney signed off in May 1991 on a Bronze Merit Award for Strelka's participation in the Distributive Education Club of America (DECA).

When Strelka started his senior year in the fall of 1991, he took part in DECA's work program, which permitted him to leave school early for a part-time job. He found work busing tables at the Robin Hood Inn on Valley Road in Clifton, a dark place with a traditional menu that paid him $3.35 an hour, plus tips. A bit of a space cadet, Strelka was always losing the black bow ties that the busboys were supposed to wear, but he also was known as an excellent young worker who treated the customers well. He liked the work, putting in about twenty-five hours a week and averaging about $50 to $60 a week in take-home pay. Most of the clientele were regulars. Strelka got to know them, and vice versa. The job put money in his pocket and gas in his car, and it also gave him a chance to make friends with another busboy at the restaurant by the name of James Wanger. He was not a complete stranger to Strelka, as they had known each other at least since their days at Christopher Columbus middle school, which Solimine also attended. Wanger had been in Strelka's seventh-grade English class. The two talked, but they didn't hit it off in middle school, and never became more than nodding acquaintances. And Strelka already had become best friends with Solimine.

As a junior in high school, though, Strelka became reacquainted with Wanger, who sat two seats ahead of Strelka in their marketing class. Wanger had a reputation as a buffoon. Strelka found him amusing. They both joined the school's DECA program. They went on a class trip and shared a motel room with a couple other guys. What's more, they shared a connection through their mutual friendship with Solimine. After they started working together at the Robin Hood Inn, they became friendlier still. Strelka started giving Wanger rides home in The Tank. One of the first times Wanger came by Strelka's house was to pick up a work shirt or a bow tie that he had left in the trunk of Strelka's car. Susie Strelka, who answered the door when Wanger called, had never quite met a teenager like James Wanger before. She sized him up and down as Wanger stood on the front porch on a rattan welcome mat that said "Go Away!"

"Is Tommy Strelka home, ma'am?" Wanger asked.

"*Ma'am?*" she thought.

Susie invited Wanger into the living room, where the family was watching TV, and called upstairs to her son. "Get a load of the trench coat and the hat," Susie said under her breath to her husband. "He looks like a hit man." In no time she also got the full flavor of Wanger's extremely polite manner. It seemed like a put-on to Susie Strelka, although it was amusing at first. *What's with this kid,* she wondered—it was as if Tommy had invited Eddie Haskell over.

"Tommy," she said, "what's with this kid? What's with this 'Yes, ma'am, No, ma'am' business?"

"His grandfather and grandmother are raising him, and his grandmother is very religious," Strelka said.

Strelka admitted that Wanger was stuffy, but also funny and odd. Wanger had his Sea Cadets business and that spit-and-polish jazz, but Wanger did and said things that nobody else would think of saying or doing. Strelka liked him, and soon they started hanging out after work.

Then, during the early fall of 1991, Wanger drew in Strelka. One night after they finished working a shift at the Robin Hood Inn, Wanger invited Strelka to drop by Castaldo's house. Strelka did, and it didn't take long before it became his habit. Strelka and Wanger dropped by Castaldo's house every day at the end of work at the Robin Hood Inn, and on other occasions as well. For Wanger, it was as if an orphan had found the ideal father. All his life he had been a geek on the fringes, and now he was in the company of someone whose notoriety carried widely around Clifton. Strelka also enjoyed standing in the reflected light of Castaldo's outlaw status. Castaldo introduced them both to the manly arts of playing cards, playing pool, and loafing. Wanger was an idea man, which came in useful for the Castaldo crowd. Strelka had some cachet, too, because he had something extremely beneficial to Castaldo and the others: a car. For a time, all three teenagers worked at the Robin Hood Inn—until Castaldo quit, deciding that low pay was worse than no pay, after all.

The friendship between the three boys grew quickly. It seemed to Strelka's parents as if one day they heard Castaldo's name and the next thing they knew Tommy was spending all his time there. On November 6, 1991, Strelka invited his mother to come to the Robin Hood Inn to celebrate her forty-thirty birthday and meet his boss. Ray and Susie both went, and they took Strelka's younger sister and brother.

"I want you to meet Frank," Strelka told her. Susie, who kept her ears open to what the young people were saying about the things that went on downtown and in the school, had heard enough stories by then about Castaldo to know he was a troublemaker. Besides, Castaldo already was showing a degree of entitlement to Strelka's car. Strelka and Castaldo hadn't known each other all that long, but if Castaldo called for a ride, Strelka scooted out the door. Already, Susie had taken to needling Strelka about being Castaldo's lackey, and she hadn't even met the kid.

Now, as Strelka escorted his friend across the restaurant to meet his parents, Susie Strelka got an eyeful. One look at Castaldo's swagger was enough to convince her that her suspicions were correct. He was the picture of cool in a monkey suit. His eyes were half-masted with boredom, and he strode with a slow, rolling bounce, as if a hip were out of place. Susie leaned toward Ray.

"Here comes trouble," she said.

"Get a load of the shit-eating grin," Ray said.

There were introductions all around, and Castaldo at least was polite. Still, Susie had the feeling he was trying to put one over on them. You could tell it was a command performance. Job or no job, bow tie or no bow tie, Castaldo seemed as if he had the makings of a car thief.

Castaldo returned to work. Strelka bused tables and swung by the table from time to time. They had ordered a cake with candles for Susie, and everyone sang "Happy Birthday." Susie met Tommy's boss, who was full of praise for the young man. The woman told Susie that Strelka was hardworking and respectful.

But afterward, she told Strelka that she wasn't happy. Believing that first impressions are often correct, Susie wasted no time in warning Tommy about his new pal Castaldo.

"Tommy, this kid is streetwise," Susie told him. "And you most certainly are not streetwise. This kid is going to get you in trouble. You mark my words."

"Oh, Ma."

"He's not your nature," she said, well aware he wasn't listening.

All the boys—Stooge, Strelka, Carboni, Wanger—were coming to Castaldo's now. They came after work, they came after school, they came when they cut school, and they came almost at all hours. Stooge had started visiting Castaldo after meeting Carboni at the Main Avenue Mall, and now they all had settled into the place. Castaldo's house became their playhouse, their clubhouse, their hangout. The diversions there seemed endless, even when they were bored. Castaldo held court in the living room with the TV going. Carboni and Stooge seldom showed up without the other one. Strelka came by all the time, usually with Wanger, and Wanger was a nut, who knew how to liven things up. He came by Castaldo's every day, his bass voice sounding at the door.

"How you doing today, bud?" he would say, and Castaldo would invite him in. Wanger dressed all the time now in his black London Fog trench coat and his cap with the snub brim. If Mrs. Castaldo was home, Wanger invariably greeted her and asked for a cup of espresso. After a while, Mrs. Castaldo, who liked Wanger a lot, would offer it to him when he came through the door. The other boys stayed on the sofa in front of the television with Castaldo. But Wanger made himself right at home. It was not unusual for him to lift the lids on the pots on the stove to see what kind of dish she was preparing, while Mrs. Castaldo would take down the stovetop espresso maker and boil Wanger a cup of coffee. The espresso was strong and black, made from the 500-gram packages of Kimbo coffee her family mailed from Italy. Wanger fancied his with a lemon twist. Then he would sit at the kitchen table, sip the espresso, and gab as if he were a little old man at a social club, one of the hangouts on Cianci Street in Paterson or Mulberry Street in Little Italy.

Mrs. Castaldo generally welcomed the boys, although sometimes the racket and the commotion got on her nerves and she disappeared to play bingo at one of the local churches. At Castaldo's house—and at Stooge's house, too, their other haunt—the boys spent afternoons and evenings playing cards or board games such as Monopoly, at least when there was nothing on television. One of their favorite diversions, which usually drew in Mrs. Castaldo, was *tombola*, the Italian form of bingo. Everyone at the table received cards containing numbered squares. For hours at a time they took turns shaking numbers out of a little red plastic jug to fill up the squares. They played for pocket change.

If it wasn't *tombola*, then it was poker, which Mrs. Castaldo did not play. All the boys loved to play poker. Strelka never seemed to understand how the odds worked, but Stooge and Wanger played card for card against Castaldo, who usually won. Castaldo taught them all the games, from the standards like draw poker and stud to more hokey variations. There was Seven Card No Peek, Follow the Queen, Baseball (both Night and Day versions). They also played Football (like Baseball, but with numerical values corresponding to the gridiron instead of the baseball diamond), and they played plenty of Blackjack, or 21. Stooge learned to shuffle and deal a deck of cards like a sharpie, and he caught on quickly to the art of gambling. Wanger was hard to beat because he had an unbeatable poker face, but he would also kill himself with his own perverse style of play. If his luck was going badly, for example, Wanger would make it worse. Absurdly worse.

"Hit me," Wanger said when Castaldo came around to him while dealing a hand of blackjack. Castaldo pointed out to Wanger that Wanger's cards were already showing nineteen.

"Hit me," Wanger said, straightfaced. To no one's surprise, Wanger went bust.

"Hit me," he said, and everyone would howl.

They spent hours sometimes just talking among themselves, dreaming up things to do, gossiping about other kids in school, ragging on teachers they hated, airing their gripes about each other, and smoking pack after pack of cigarettes. As the room filled with smoke, most of the time was spent talking about where they were going that day and what they wanted to eat next. One time they discussed starting up a business selling beepers. Sometimes they hatched plans to beat someone up over a perceived slight. There was the time, for example, that some jock had made some smartass remarks about their group, and the group vowed to get him. Castaldo said they should stove the kid's head in with a pipe. Pipes were obtained, and the band of teenagers followed the jock home from school every day for a while to learn his route and his habits. The day the group decided to jump the kid, however, the jock couldn't be found. The target of their animosity, of course, had no idea that he had been singled out for their hatred, and the whole affair died of its own accord because something else grabbed their attention at the roundtable. It as like communal living. They dumped their cigarettes and butane lighters in the middle of the table and shared until someone had to run to the store to buy more. It was a standing joke that the lighters always seemed to end up with Strelka, who was accused of being a kleptomaniac.

If they were staying in, the boys would get Mrs. Castaldo to cook some pasta. Or they would order a pizza. More than once, Wanger would get on the telephone, pleading with San Remo's pizzeria down the street to send over a pie, despite the fact that he had called a minute before closing. He got a kick out of seeing if he could persuade them to come through.

"Come on," he said, pleading and pleading with them as if his life depended on it. "Come on, you guys. One more pie."

Sometimes it worked, and sometimes it didn't.

"You don't even have to put it in the oven," he would say. "Just bring it over. All right, then, just bake it halfway."

When the pie arrived, the kitchen would erupt in merry bedlam. Wanger would be the first to start shredding up chunks of pizza and dropping it on the floor for Barney, the chihuahua he and the boys loved to torment. (Sitting in the living room watching a movie or something, they all got a kick out of putting their shoes right in front of the dog's face, knowing that for some reason it provoked the creature to paroxysms of barking.) The whole scene at Castaldo's on an average night was loud, and it was fun and—unless somebody woke up Mr. Castaldo, who always had to be up early in the morning for work—there weren't any problems. They stayed at Castaldo's until it was time to go home or until they had enough.

On almost any evening of the week or on a weekend afternoon, they might go to the pool hall, leaving Castaldo's house and walking up Main Avenue, the heart of Clifton's downtown. This was a taste of the small-town America that was steadily vanishing in Clifton. Down the street to their left was the headquarters for the *North Jersey Herald & News*, a small but feisty newspaper that paid particular attention to Clifton and Passaic, and to the right, in the direction of Clifton Avenue, was the former City Hall. There was a grungy storefront office for City Taxi and just a few doors down was the Clifton Theatre, a small movie house whose crumbling marquee teetered above a dark lobby. Across the street, at the dime store ("5 & 10 J.O. Grand Stores 25¢,"), the display window showcased heaps of costume jewelry, artificial flowers, spools of sewing ribbon, and dusty Matchbox cars. At the corner stood Moe & Annie's Menswear, a shop that had been around since God knows when. On the other side of the street was "Ronnie I Productions Music Record Shop," a peculiar place that sold nothing but old 45s of R&B and doo-wop. The walls were plastered floor-to-ceiling with yellow record jackets containing hits by the Pharaohs, Bill Harris and the Continentals, the Five Saints, the Mellows, the Ebb-tones, the Castaleers, the Harptones, and hundreds more. A placard in the front door warned shoppers looking for anything contemporary to go elsewhere. Most curious of all, the display window contained a tombstone. It was billed as "The Official Headstone of Frankie Lymon," who had been immortalized by the Motown hit "Why Do Fools Fall In Love?" Fame dumped him when his angelic voice had changed. It was an honest-to-God gravestone, which almost no one noticed anymore. The inscription read:

> In memory of Frankie Lymon
> Sept. 30, 1942–Feb. 27, 1968
> We promise to remember
> Dedicated by his fans and friends

Castaldo and the other boys must have passed the store and the other quaint shops around it hundreds of times while going to the Clifton Billiard Lounge, a monument itself, where the boys spent hours before going back to Castaldo's or heading somewhere else.

When they tired of being around Castaldo's house or the local neighborhood, they jumped in Strelka's car and drove. It didn't matter where. They just drove. Carboni usually brought along a boom box to play music, since The Tank had only one radio station and nobody but Strelka liked the heavy-metal music it played. Some nights they went to the movies, either at the malls or at Cinema 46 behind the Holiday Inn in Totowa, which also was the turnoff to get to Annie's Road. Or they cruised around Clifton until they got hungry enough to stop for pizza at San Remo's or hamburgers at the White Castle. They drove down Route 21 along the Passaic River, past the vast reservations of public housing on the outskirts of Newark, or to some of the tonier Essex County suburbs and their parks, or out of town on Route 46, to the valley of diners and strip malls, or to the mammoth shopping centers in Wayne or Paramus, or they drove to the cemetery. Besides Annie's Road, there were other spooky places like "Gravity Hill," where kids swore that you could put a car in neutral at the bottom of the grade and the car would miraculously move up the hill. They liked to take girls to Annie's Road, or Gravity Hill, or other deserted haunts and play pranks that scared them half out of their wits.

If they got their hands on some booze, they would go out to the overpass by Annie's Road and crawl deep inside the ledge, just up under the interstate, where no one could see them from the road. The whine of the traffic drowned out all but their voices. Other kids used the spot too, and the concrete ledge was littered with half-burned candles other kids used to invoke black magic. Usually Castaldo and the boys brought forty-ounce bottles of Budweiser, although they also liked Sambuca, Absolut vodka, and Jack Daniel's—especially Jack, since it was Wanger's favorite. When they drank, the boys restrained themselves from acting drunkenly—at least everyone except Strelka, who sometimes got so lit he had to let Stooge drive the car, and Wanger. The group's credo, in general, was that it was better to nurse a slow buzz instead of carrying on. (In fact, Castaldo hardly drank.) But Wanger loved boozing, and he would become more talkative or more twisted the more he drank—up to a point. One night while they were drinking, Wanger started chain-smoking like a machine. When he finished one smoke, he crammed another into his mouth. He stuck a bunch of cigarettes behind each ear, like a cartridge belt. He lit another and another and another, all the while reloading from the smokes tucked into the crease behind his ears, and stuffing more back there, so that his head bristled with a crown of white cigarettes poking out at the sides. Everyone was much amused.

There were times, however, if he wasn't yakking or clowning around, that Wanger drifted away in utter silence. Eventually, the others would notice and razz him, but Wanger wouldn't respond.

"What's wrong with you?" the others would say. One night when they were drinking at Annie's Road, one of Wanger's weird spells came over him. He wouldn't talk. Then Wanger put his hand to his head and discovered that his cap was missing. Whatever it was the others were talking about or doing, he hadn't been paying attention, and he suddenly broke in.

"I gotta go back to the car," Wanger said.

"What's wrong?"

"It's my capello," Wanger said.

Wanger was alarmed, amusingly so, because he couldn't find his hat. No one could understand why he had become so agitated, almost panicky and fixated at the same time, about having to go back at that very moment to retrieve his cap, but they couldn't talk him out of it.

"Wanger, the car's about a mile away," they said.

But Wanger got up alone and walked off in the darkness to the stores down by the bridges to get his hat.

If it was just the guys driving around in Strelka's Buick, they talked about cars, girls, or drinking, or just teenage stuff from school. When Strelka opened his mouth, it was usually about music, and if it was about music, it was usually about Def Leppard. Besides rhapsodizing about heavy-metal rock bands, Strelka also spun tales about the girls that he allegedly had slept with.

"Uh-huh," said Castaldo, who made it clear that he spoke with true conviction and knowledge about girls. "I'll take your word for it."

And then Castaldo rode Strelka for having a crush on Chrissie, saying Strelka was one of those unfortunate lads who was pussy-whipped without actually getting any. Strelka denied everything, saying nobody understood the kind of relationship that he and Chrissie had.

"Wake up," Castaldo said.

Meanwhile, Carboni, the junior big shot, usually tried topping what everyone else was saying. If he wasn't doing that, he would try bossing everyone else around or meddling in Castaldo's relationships with girls—usually by telling him what he should do and sometimes by giving orders to Castaldo's girlfriends about what they were supposed to do. Stooge, wedged into a corner of the backseat, usually said almost nothing but took everything in. And Wanger—no one knew what Wanger would come up with.

Sometimes Wanger talked about teaching the kids at church, delighting in the questions they would ask him about religion, but he usually just joined in talking guy stuff—he loved talking about drinking, for example, or about the military. But Wanger also talked about things from the past that the boys had never heard of. He would bring up all the stuff about Annie's Road, for example. Or he would talk about old movies and music—*really* old movies and music. For some reason, Wanger had a head full of knowledge about movies from the 1930s and 1940s, which seemed ancient and impossibly boring to the other guys. Now and then, Wanger would just burst into song, usually some corny number from the movies or a Broadway musical. One standby, for example, was "Follow the Yellow Brick Road," from *The Wizard of Oz*. Wanger sang it all the time, his basso profundo voice booming the lyrics, screeching upward into a falsetto, until the singing became infectious. Everyone would join in. If it wasn't *The Wizard of Oz*, then he would belt out a rendition of the "Chattanooga Choo Choo," perhaps the song he sang most of all. Wanger sang this Glenn Miller standard so often that the other kids learned the lyrics to that song too:

Pardon me, boy, is that the Chattanooga Choo-Choo?
Track twenty-nine, boy, you can gimme a shine,
'Cause I can afford to board a Chattanooga Choo-Choo . . .

The boys laughed a long time afterward about the time Wanger started singing "Chattanooga Choo Choo" from inside the trunk of the car at a gas station. Wanger—who had hopped in the trunk of the car on more than one occasion, either because there wasn't enough room up front or just because he felt like it—had been bumping around inside for a while as the attendant filled Strelka's car. Then he started singing. The attendant couldn't figure out where the sound was coming from, and then Wanger started banging and yelling.

"Help me!" he shouted. "Help! They got me trapped."

The attendant, looking concerned, came up to Strelka's window.

"Is there somebody in there?" he said.

Sometimes during their nomadic jaunts, about twice a month or so, they headed into New York City, mostly around Rockefeller Center, looking for stuff to do. There was something glorious just about being young and walking around the big city, and being together. Wanger surprised everyone one night when he took out twenty dollars and pressed it into a bum's hand, while Castaldo was on the prowl for girls. Once, when it was only he and Wanger, they met some college girls on a summer night in the city and talked their way into the girls' apartment. Castaldo homed in on a tall shapely brunette with long hair. Wanger picked a blonde. They were watching television, having a few beers, and Castaldo eventually took his date into her bedroom. When Castaldo was through, he got up and opened the door to the living room to see how Wanger was doing. James was doing fine. Castaldo would later recall that Wanger's pants were pulled down around his ankles, and he turned around to see Frank with a big shit-eating grin on his face. Bare-assed and grinning, Wanger was humping the girl doggy style. Wanger grinned, kept going. To top it all off, Wanger was still wearing his big black combat boots. Castaldo couldn't believe it. He laughed and shut the bedroom door.

In mid-November, Castaldo started dating a girl named Melanie Garzielik. A month earlier, they had met outside a drugstore when he was buying cigarettes. Two of the friends she was with introduced them. She was fifteen years old. They talked that day and met a few more times around the pool hall. Castaldo made a point of knowing that her favorite rock singer was Prince, that she liked the color purple, and other details that were important to her. On November 17 they officially began dating, and she became part of the

Castaldo crowd. It wasn't unusual for her to be hanging around at the same time the boys were, and she joined in a lot of their games. When they played poker, she usually found herself trying to explain the game to Strelka.

When Castaldo and company weren't driving to Annie's Road or all over Passaic County, they went to Fun 'N Games, a video game arcade in the Willowbrook Mall across from the Sears Auto Center—and they drove some more. Their favorite game, which they played obsessively, was a simulated race car track.

Inside Fun 'N Games was a madhouse of coin-operated make-believe. The arcade had everything you could imagine, and it drew kids from all over the place. There were city kids and suburban kids, black kids and white kids, Latinos and Asians, all milling around observing each other's moves on the joystick. The scent of burnt reefer rose sweetly from the folds of black jeans and black T-shirts and mixed in the room with the odor of tobacco and teenage sweat. Only an airport could be noisier, what with the pumped-in rock and roll and the growling, whining, howling din of simulated combat, simulated car engines, simulated jet rockets, and simulated cries of pain. It was hard to talk—no coincidence, surely—and people had to holler in each other's ears to be heard above the racket.

When Castaldo and Wanger and the others came to Fun 'N Games, the boys skipped all the other amusements to play Final Lap. Positioned under a huge photograph of the Pocono International Raceway, the video game allowed eight players to take seats side by side and race. Each driver had a gearshift, an accelerator pedal, and a brake pedal. If a player drove aggressively enough, his time on the machine would be increased. If he drove too fast or carelessly, the car spun out or crashed. The cars whined through the screen at speeds in excess of 400 km an hour. The tailpipes spat fire. There was even a Goodyear blimp floating above chartreuse infields.

But the allure of this game was not just the illusion of driving in a race car. What made the rush all the keener was that this game hooked up several video screens together so that the players could compete. Each player could race against the clock and race against his buddies, keeping an eye on them by watching his rearview mirror. There was also an aerial view showing each player's location on the course. Players could drive through a Le Mans–style track, an American oval, or two other types of tracks.

The boys slid into the hornet-green bucket seats and paid their money. Stooge was a good driver, and so was Strelka—as one might expect, since he spent half of his teenage life driving the others around. All of them spent countless hours and dollars racing each other through the television tubes. It was an escape—such a good escape that one night they almost forgot they were ducking Solimine, who had finally come back from rehab. Even if they had taken their eyes off the video screens, they couldn't have seen him coming, since the windows were plastered with larger-than-life posters of sports heroes like Joe Montana, Michael Jordan, Magic Johnson, and Don Mattingly. The sunlight had faded and discolored them. But there he was, in the flesh.

Carboni's face said it all.

"Great," someone said. "Solimine's here."

5

INDEED, SOLIMINE WAS BACK. BUT NOW, AFTER HIS ABSENCE, HE had become almost an onlooker as a newly reconfigured group of his friends had taken shape around Castaldo. By mid-October, the group's bonds had tightened considerably, and as the ring constricted, it squeezed Solimine out and pushed him farther away.

But Solimine had moved away from the others too, of his own accord, since leaving the Carrier clinic in September. The experience had shaken him and, in some ways, transformed him in ways that went beyond attendance at AA meetings. True to his word, Solimine would not leave his friends, as the Carrier clinic contract had required. Yet Solimine seemed to shift between being needy for Strelka's friendship and acting as if he had outgrown it. Strelka, too, showed signs of his old loyalty. He drove Solimine to the AA meetings or picked him up because Solimine didn't have a car yet. Occasionally Strelka sat in on the meetings. They still drove around together looking for girls and looking for trouble. But Strelka was more interested in Castaldo and Wanger these days.

As Solimine settled in again at home, he also resumed his activities with the Sea Cadets. It was a testament to the amount of respect he held among the DeLong Division's leaders and cadets that he was welcomed back with open arms. One of the requirements of Sea Cadet membership was high moral character, and Solimine had obviously put those virtues in doubt by his overdose and his acknowledged alcoholism. It was rare for the Sea Cadets to take someone in, or take someone back, after such a failing. But Kits and Jennifer Clayton and the others welcomed Solimine. They also recognized a monumental change in him. His attitude had become extremely positive. Rarely talking about his work with AA—bringing it up only with Jennifer Clayton and never Kits or the others—Solimine poured himself into the group with renewed vitality. He no longer needed much pushing. He wanted to excel. He seemed very proud of the progress he had made in therapy.

Indeed, Solimine started bugging Strelka about drinking and other things. Solimine, seeming excited with the idea of pulling his life together, had been acting like a superhero or a religious convert who sees a disciple in every new face he meets. At least that's how he seemed to Strelka. Solimine would lecture Strelka about this or that, tell Strelka that he was going to get in trouble if he kept it up—and it was hard to imagine a form of behavior more annoying to a teenager. It got on everybody's nerves. Even at home, Solimine would nudge his parents about alcohol. Bob Solimine wasn't much of a drinker to begin with. But when he and Solimine went out to eat at a restaurant, and Bob ordered a beer, Solimine frowned.

"Do you really need that?" Robbie asked. His father sent it back. Although he was careful not to show anything but support for his son, Bob was almost bemused at his son's newfound zeal for temperance. Strelka and the guys were not. Especially Castaldo.

Although drinking wasn't that important to him, Rob Solimine's preachiness got under Castaldo's skin, and it wasn't long after Solimine's return from the Carrier clinic that Castaldo became disgusted with everything about Robbie Solimine. At least initially, the reasons for Castaldo's hatred for Solimine seemed indefinable. It was no more specific than that Castaldo did not like the way Solimine talked, the way he walked, the way he stuck out in a crowd.

Whatever it was, Castaldo nurtured a cancerous loathing for Solimine that soon infected the others. Wanger and Strelka had their own problems with Solimine, but Castaldo's hatred became a catalyst that intensified their feelings. Solimine had done nothing to Carboni or Stooge to kindle anything that could amount to intense dislike, yet they hated him too. No one could say why. Compared with the others, Carboni and Stooge hardly knew Solimine. It was true that Carboni had no patience for Solimine's habit of kissing up to adults, and he despised Solimine's inflated opinion of himself as a lady's man, and even more, Solimine's lack of self-respect that kept him poking his nose around where he wasn't wanted. But hate him? The first few times Solimine and Carboni met, Carboni thought Rob was all right. Then he heard the others running him down. Then he started to see for himself: Solimine acted like he was the man, like he was *it*, when it was obvious he was nothing but a geek. He was pathetic or so it seemed to Carboni. Stooge came to share Carboni's opinion on this, as he did on so many other things, although there were times Stooges seemed to like Solimine's company. Yet Stooge couldn't stand the way Solimine acted like a baby—bouncing around all the time, always yapping, getting too cute and too chummy with Stooge's mom, as if he thought he could be her son, too. As they closed ranks with the older boys, binding themselves ever closer to Castaldo and to each other, the more their dislike grew into a consuming hatred of Solimine.

As for Castaldo, it never became clear why he disliked Solimine so much. It may have been because Castaldo, who had been preening as a tough guy at least since he was sixteen, despised Solimine's weakness and vulnerability. On top of everything else, Solimine was nosy, always wanting to know what Castaldo was up to. In a word, Solimine was fatally "uncool." To make matters worse, Solimine was always whipping up trouble around the Castaldo house. Once, he lit a fire in the garbage cans, which drove Castaldo's father up a tree. Other times he messed with Angie, flirting with her in a way that grated on Castaldo's nerves and sometimes her nerves. Even if all he did was drop by and sit on the couch watching TV by himself until the others showed up, he had a knack of taking over the place as if it were his, thereby irritating the whole Castaldo family. They wondered if the kid had a home. It got to the point that Castaldo's mother told him that she didn't want Solimine coming around anymore getting everyone in an uproar.

Yet Solimine still tagged along. The others would try to shake him a hundred different ways, but he kept coming, kept coming, kept coming. His resilience to their slights—or his imperviousness—amazed the other guys. Everyone was goofing around at Castaldo's when the doorbell buzzed. Someone went to the peephole, saw who it was, and yelled out, with a tone of great disapproval that certainly must have carried through the door: "Solimine's here."

A groan would go up from the table where everyone was playing cards or playing Monopoly or eating dinner.

"Oh, man—why did he have to come down here?"

And in Solimine would come with his dopey grin.

Most of the time, Castaldo ignored Solimine—or, at least, he seemed to be ignoring Solimine. When Solimine would make one of his off-the-wall remarks, Castaldo would scrunch up his face in a sour expression, look off to the side, and squint, as if trying to see where it could have come from. But even while pretending Solimine wasn't there and giving him the silent treatment, Castaldo regarded Solimine with a barely suppressed rage. It was maddening that Solimine couldn't detect how much Castaldo disliked him. It was more maddening to think that Solimine noticed but stuck around anyway. He was just *there*, wherever you looked, whenever you didn't want him, like some shameful act from the past or an unpleasant duty, until Castaldo couldn't take it anymore.

"He's around again," Castaldo would say. "I don't want him around."

Sooner or later, someone would tell him to get lost, and sometimes Solimine got the message—but if he disappeared for a day or two he always resurfaced. It came to the point that the other boys started to amuse themselves by being rude to Solimine and ditching him in more and more inventive ways. They would try to shake Solimine in the car, and it would become a game of cat and mouse. Strelka would streak off in the LeSabre with a car full of people, and Solimine would give chase. They might speed down Route 46, turn off through Clifton, race upcounty around Solimine's house, and then back downcounty and sometimes south of Clifton and Passaic into Essex County. Most of the time, they waved through Clifton, stopping now and then for gas, hamburgers, or just to get out and smoke a cigarette and shoot the breeze at a park, all the while looking for Solimine to appear. If Strelka worked his way around to come up behind Solimine, they exulted in getting the drop on him. Having gained an element of surprise, Strelka would sneak up to Solimine's Plymouth, which might be sitting at a red light or a stop sign, and give it a good bump. Nothing to wreck the car, usually, but enough to scare the shit out of him. It was all like a big high-speed game of tag. Then it would be Solimine's turn to blaze off, waiting for Strelka to give chase. If the gang was in the mood for Solimine, they might pursue him. If one of the group was riding with Solimine in the car—say, Carboni or Wanger—there was no doubt that Strelka would gun his car after Solimine's. But if Solimine was alone, and if they had gotten sick of him, they would pretend to chase him until Solimine was out of sight, and then just let him go.

"Good riddance!" they would hoot. "The idiot's gone!"

If they didn't want Solimine to find them at their favorite haunts, they would take precautions to avoid him. When Strelka hauled everyone up to the mall, he sometimes parked in the farthest corner, and they would all duck inside, looking over their shoulders to make sure Solimine didn't see them.

They knew Solimine cruised their hangouts, driving past Castaldo's house or Stooge's house or the mall, looking for Strelka's car. And there had to be thousands of cars in the parking lot, particularly around Thanksgiving, but who should turn up? Solimine, of course, and he would manage to park near Strelka's car, too. Inside, he would find them at the arcade or the food court, and he would stride up to them, tail wagging, goofy grin, funny speech, asking questions and interrupting everyone's good time. It drove them crazy.

All of this was the stuff of high-school cliques and the politics of teenage identity crisis. But now another element was beginning to stir the group's animosity toward Solimine—jealousy. At least since early autumn, Strelka had been drawing closer to Chrissie Bachelle. It was ironic, since Solimine had been the person who had introduced Chrissie and Strelka the previous year. Strelka had, in fact, been smitten with Chrissie since the first time he met her. That was before they had cars. Early one autumn evening in 1990, Solimine and Strelka walked over to her house, and Solimine talked the whole time, joking around and trying to impress her, while Strelka hung back and watched. Chrissie was only fourteen. She sat on the steps with a girlfriend from Nutley taking it all in, basking in Solimine's attentions, and watching the quiet blond boy chuckling to himself.

"Shut up, Tommy, you're talking too much," Chrissie said.

He seemed hangdog for a moment.

"I'm only kidding," she said. "Don't you talk?"

"Sure, I talk," Strelka said, and they laughed some more.

They met again after Strelka started driving. One night, after Solimine came out of the Carrier clinic, he and Strelka drove over to some girl's house because Solimine wanted to talk to her. The girl was one of Chrissie's friends, so Chrissie was there. As Solimine talked to Chrissie's friend and some other girl, Strelka stayed in the car. Chrissie sauntered over to his window.

"Why are you sitting in your car?" she asked.

Strelka liked the friendly lilt in her voice. She smiled and talked to him. Eventually, everybody cruised around that night, and after Strelka dropped off Chrissie and went home, he got a telephone call from her. Chrissie said she wanted to thank him for dropping her off at home. They talked some more, and Strelka asked her if he could start driving her to school in the mornings. That was the beginning. Soon enough, Strelka and Chrissie were sharing hall locker trysts between certain classes. In the middle of the bustle Strelka sometimes hugged her and told her he loved her. They talked after school on the telephone. On Mondays, when Strelka didn't have to work at the Robin Hood Inn, he would pick up Chrissie after school and hang out with her. He loved her very much. She felt strongly about him too, but insisted that they were only friends.

Strelka drove Chrissie to the mall a lot during the fall of 1991. They walked around for a while, split up to do their own things, and hooked up together later whenever their courses happened to coincide. Chrissie and her friends cruised around the shopping center, hanging out most near the food court and looking for guys they knew. Strelka raced the grand prix cars over at Fun 'N Games until he had had enough. Then he went looking for Chrissie.

One time, they were standing by the Food Court when half the Clifton High School football team came by.

"Hey, Tommy," Chrissie called out. "Is that a little pencil in your pocket or are you just happy to see me?"

"That's *three* pencils in my pocket," Strelka said, "and no, I'm not happy to see you."

Like other kids their age, Strelka and Chrissie joined the pack of mall rats, hanging out, goofing on each other, trying to embarrass each other in front of friends and total strangers. Chrissie and Strelka were at the Willowbrook Mall when she heard Strelka mention Castaldo for the first time.

"I was hanging out with Frank," Strelka said.

"Frank who?"

"Frank Castaldo."

"And?"

"Hanging out," Strelka said.

Chrissie had heard of Castaldo, because Castaldo was known for causing trouble, and she knew some of the wilder kids hung out at his place, but she hadn't been aware that Strelka was in with that crowd. Strelka was a naive, quiet kid who didn't seem right with a dropout who had a reputation for fighting and destroying things, Chrissie thought.

Meanwhile, Strelka was telling some of his friends that Chrissie was his girlfriend. And although Chrissie had other ideas, she seemed to return Strelka's interests. Her life was endlessly complicated with emotional difficulties, some of which were her own doing and some of which owed to her family. The state Division of Youth and Family Services, which had opened a file on her some time ago, had deemed her to be virtually incorrigible. Her family seemed very different from Strelka's, but they had other things in common. Chrissie had a withdrawing manner. She didn't ask a lot of questions, she didn't pry, and God knows, she didn't have much in the way of advice. Her style was a good fit with Strelka, who barely spoke a word the first time they had met. In turn, Chrissie liked Strelka's way of listening to her problems. He really listened. He seemed mature. He had sound ideas about how things had become the way they were and how she might change them. Certainly, Strelka seemed more stable than Solimine, who had threatened to kill himself more than once. Chrissie liked Solimine too, but Strelka seemed to have his head on straight, and there was only so much one basket case could do for another.

So Chrissie started spending more and more time with Strelka and visiting his home. She marveled at the domesticity of the place and envied it. She wasn't used to a family that sat down to a home-cooked meal together, and the good-natured bantering put her at ease. For Chrissie's amusement, Strelka usually cracked jokes about his mother's cooking or elevated them with letter grades.

Kids at school, everyone it seemed, would see Chrissie and Strelka in the halls talking, and it was going around that they were boyfriend and girlfriend. No doubt Strelka thought so. But Chrissie was hard to pin down. She fluttered off. She never quite gave herself up to the idea of dating Strelka. They were best friends, she said. Nothing more. Strelka seemed to understand that, at least in his dealings with her. He never gave up but he came at her in a more subtle way than Solimine, and that was nice. Solimine, though, never stopped trying. Of course he was a flirt, everyone knew he was a flirt, and you couldn't take him too seriously, but he made it clear he was starstruck with Chrissie. Her friends noticed Solimine's crush on Chrissie and needled her about it.

"Rob really likes you," a girlfriend told Chrissie.

"We're friends," Chrissie said.

"No," the girl said. "He *likes you* likes you."

But Solimine wasn't Chrissie's type, and she warded off his advances.

"So when are you and I going to get together," Solimine would say. "You and me together. What do you think?"

"Like, no," Chrissie said, making a face.

"I mean it," Solimine said.

"Yeah," Chrissie said. "Whatever."

This much was becoming clear: Solimine's attentions to Chrissie drove Strelka wild, and Chrissie knew it. In fact, she knew both of them were jealous. It certainly didn't take much to get a rise from Strelka. Once he gave her a ride to the mall and left her stranded there because she was talking with another guy. Then Solimine once told Strelka to stop hanging out with her—or something to that effect. Strelka had a fit. Whatever it was Solimine said, Strelka carried it around with him for days. Chrissie felt caught in the middle. She thought each of them had made too much of his relationship with her. All she wanted was to be a *friend*—although if forced to choose, she had to admit her deeper attraction to Strelka. By late fall, it was clear that Solimine thought Strelka had stolen Chrissie away from him.

* * *

Word was out that Castaldo wanted to pound Solimine something fierce. There had been tensions over Chrissie, after Castaldo warned Solimine that Strelka wanted him to back off. When the weather was still warm, for example, Strelka became furious about something Solimine had said or done with Chrissie, and he aired his beef to Castaldo. Castaldo blew. It was just the kind of thing that might give him the excuse to kick some ass. No one was going to mess around with one of his boys' girlfriends. Castaldo wanted to assemble a war party on the spot. Ginny, the Castaldos' upstairs tenant, who was walking her dog, saw the commotion.

"What's going on?" she asked.

"We're going to get Solimine, because he tried to put the moves on his girlfriend," Castaldo said, and he gestured toward Strelka. Nothing came of it in the end. But now Castaldo had his own reasons for wanting to beat up Solimine.

That October, someone from the Sea Cadets called the Castaldos about kids drinking in the Castaldo home—or at least that was how Castaldo understood it. As he had heard it, some lieutenant had been complaining about the Castaldos being a bad influence. The lieutenant had heard that young people were drinking openly at the Castaldo home. The Castaldos denied it. But the lieutenant—or whoever he was—then called up Mrs. Castaldo—or in some way communicated with her—to say that if these stories were true, then what she was doing was illegal. He reportedly advised Mrs. Castaldo to put a stop to it.

Whether there had been such a call or not, no one knew for certain. All that mattered was that that's how Frankie had understood things. His brother, Stevie, thought perhaps everything began one night on the way home from Sea Cadets. Ensign Kits was carpooling everyone when Wanger asked to be dropped off at the Castaldos' place. Wanger asked Kits if Kits wanted to come along. To which Kits replied, "What do you want to do at Castaldo's? Drink?" Kits's remark took Stevie by surprise. The implication was clear enough, that his parents were running a speakeasy for local kids. Stevie

Castaldo felt he had to defend his family and adamantly denied the charge. There was an animated discussion as they drove through New Jersey about what happened or did not happen in the Castaldo home.

Whatever version was accurate, when word of the controversy got back to Castaldo, he became furious. It was one thing to rip him for being a bum, but it was another thing altogether to attack his family. Although it may not have seemed that way from his behavior, Castaldo professed to respect his parents. The way he looked at it, his father had worked every day in his life, and his mother had been good to the kids, and he would not sit down for attacks on them. The Castaldo family honor was at stake. Frankie was prepared to defend it. Castaldo also knew exactly whom to blame.

Not long after the Castaldo home had been tagged as a disreputable teen hangout, Strelka and Castaldo paid an unexpected visit on Chrissie Bachelle. Castaldo stayed in the car. Strelka found Chrissie eating dinner. He wanted to see if Chrissie would come out for a ride when she was finished. It was a school night, but he wanted to drive around or go to the mall or something, and it was like he wanted Chrissie to drop everything. At one point he hurried her along by saying she was keeping Frank waiting. But Chrissie was waiting for someone too. Not fifteen minutes before Strelka had come around, Solimine had called her and asked her to come by. He was on his way, she said.

As Chrissie explained this to Strelka, she saw that he became angry. Strelka didn't go into details about what his anger was about—perhaps, Chrissie thought, because it might have to do with his jealousy over her. But, in fact, Strelka was fuming just as much as Castaldo over Solimine's tattling to the Sea Cadets about drinking. Strelka wasn't sure—no one had ever checked out for certain that Solimine was the source for the Sea Cadets rumor—but everyone in the group by now was going on the assumption that it must have been Solimine.

To Chrissie, it made no difference. She told Strelka that he and Solimine should patch things up. Wrong, Strelka said.

"Well, you're going to have to," Chrissie said.

Suddenly Strelka's face lit up with an idea. Castaldo just happened to be hunting for Solimine, and woe to Solimine when Castaldo caught him. Frank was going to kill him, Strelka said. Here was the chance to do it.

Chrissie listened with annoyance. She never took Solimine for much of a fighter. Or Strelka, for that matter. When Strelka got mad at someone, he clammed up, ignored the person. Now Strelka was talking about fighting. He had even gone outside to break the news to Castaldo about their good fortune—that Solimine was on his way over to Chrissie's house. Whatever it was that was going on, Chrissie didn't want any part of it. She certainly didn't want two of her friends fighting at her house.

Chrissie walked outside. Sure enough, there was Castaldo sitting in Strelka's car. Strelka had parked the Buick in the lot of a church nearby. Strelka told Castaldo to sit tight until Solimine got out of his car; after that, Castaldo could jump him.

Just then, Solimine pulled up to the curb in his Camaro—but Castaldo got out of Strelka's car too soon, Solimine saw him, and peeled rubber.

Chrissie went over to Strelka's car and met Castaldo for the first time. She wanted to know why Solimine was in trouble. But she didn't have a chance to find out. The telephone rang, her stepfather called from inside the house that it was for her, and she went inside to answer it. When she picked up the receiver, she heard Solimine's voice.

"I'm around the corner," Solimine said. "Will you come around and meet me?"

Strelka and Castaldo were sitting in Strelka's car waiting for Chrissie to get off the telephone when they saw her leave the house. Instead of coming back to Strelka's car, however, she hustled around the corner. The snub increased Strelka's anger. Castaldo, who hardly knew her, was mad too.

"Where's she going?" Castaldo said.

"She's going to meet Rob!" Strelka said. "Let's go, Frank!"

By then Chrissie had turned the corner and climbed into Solimine's black Camaro. They took off before Strelka and Castaldo could do anything. Strelka started the Buick and hightailed it after Solimine.

"We're going to kick his ass!" Strelka said.

"What do you mean, 'we'?" Castaldo said.

For the next two hours, the four teenagers played a dangerous game of cat and mouse. Solimine drove the Camaro like a lunatic, sometimes hitting speeds of sixty miles per hour in residential areas, and Strelka chased after him. They circled endlessly around the Athenia section of Clifton. The whole time, Castaldo was promising to cream Solimine when they finally caught up to him. At times, Strelka would park the Buick and lie in wait for Solimine—then gun the car to cut him off. Solimine managed to scoot by every time. Castaldo, who had been angry before about Solimine, became furious at the way Solimine stayed just out of grasp, as if playing him the fool. Castaldo pounded his fists on the dashboard and shouted and directed Strelka in the hunt—although Strelka didn't need much encouragement. Strelka grew nearly as angry and frustrated as Castaldo.

"He's probably laughing at your ass," Strelka said. "He's probably calling you all kind of shit."

Indeed, whether Solimine was taunting his pursuers or flirting with danger in self-destructive fashion, he kept the chase going long after he could have gotten away for good. Solimine knew Castaldo wanted to beat him up. There was no doubt about that. As they drove, Solimine told Chrissie that Castaldo would kick his ass—but didn't tell her why Castaldo was so angry.

Chrissie was beyond caring. Whether or not the big chase was fun for the boys, Chrissie was scared. She was scared of the way Solimine was driving, and she was angry too, because he wouldn't just leave the other two behind. She demanded that Solimine let her out. She asked again and again, but he refused. He kept driving until Chrissie became as worked up as they were, and finally he agreed to drop her off.

Meanwhile, Strelka had broken off the chase and parked near Chrissie's house to lie in wait for Solimine. They knew that sooner or later, Solimine would have to drop her off. They waited a long time. Finally, after it had gotten dark, Solimine—perhaps guessing how his onetime best friend might think—dropped Chrissie off a distance away from her house, so that she had to walk part of the way home. When Chrissie got near her house, Castaldo and Strelka saw her coming. She was crying. She came over to Strelka's car, and the other two boys got the gist of what she was upset about. Castaldo vowed to get even.

Not long after the cat-and-mouse duel around Clifton, Strelka called Chrissie from the Robin Hood Inn, changed out of his work duds, and tooled over to her house. It was about 4:30 in the afternoon on Halloween, and the two of them had been planning on going out together trick-or-treating—or at least just going out together. When Strelka showed up, he was dressed as he was always dressed—T-shirt, black leather jacket, jeans—and Chrissie was dolled up like a strumpet. Her idea was to go as a slut. Strelka offered to be her pimp.

Before they could leave Chrissie had to wait for her mother to come home, so she and Strelka sat on the stoop of the house talking. Then they started talking about Solimine. Strelka explained to her why he and Castaldo had been so furious, and why Castaldo wanted to beat him up. Now Solimine would have to pay both for ratting on Castaldo to the Sea Cadet lieutenant and for the cat-and-mouse game the previous week. Strelka was still smoldering. But now Chrissie was fuming too. After Solimine's stunt driving around Clifton in the car with her, Chrissie had become angry with him. She had told him to stop the car about a dozen times and he didn't, and she thought he was going to kill them both. As she talked with Strelka, she could also understand now why Castaldo was so angry. She would have been angry too if she were Frank, with

Solimine spreading the word all around town that the Castaldos were nothing but drunkards.

The telephone rang and Chrissie went inside to get it. It was Solimine. He was full of pleasantries. Chrissie was withholding, letting it all go one way. Solimine wanted to stop by. Could he?

"Yeah, I'm bored," Chrissie said, and she hung up. She knew what she was doing. She knew she had just set him up. But she was pissed at him and in a reckless kind of mood: a little selfish, perhaps, a little interested in seeing a fight, a little bored. She didn't expect Castaldo to massacre the kid anyway. Frank said all he wanted to do was hit him a couple times and that would be it. She had hardly come back out on the porch when she told Strelka that Solimine was on his way.

Strelka's eyes lit up with the glow of unexpected good fortune.

"Can I use your phone?" Strelka asked. He ducked inside, called Castaldo, told him the good news. They had a second chance at ambushing Solimine. Castaldo needed a ride, though, so Strelka hustled over to Castaldo's with his car. A few minutes later, Strelka and Castaldo were looking for a strategic spot to waylay Solimine in front of Chrissie's house. Strelka parked his car a block away so Solimine wouldn't see it. Then they hid themselves in the bushes at the top of the stairs at Chrissie's house. A few minutes later, Solimine pulled up in his car and stopped. But he didn't open the door.

"Come on over," Solimine said, calling to her from the window of his car.

"No, you come on over," Chrissie said.

"No way," Solimine said. "I passed by Tommy's house, and I didn't see his car, so I know he's probably around here somewhere with Wanger and Castaldo."

The only part he was wrong about was Wanger, who had a church event or something.

"Frank's probably hiding in some bushes and wants to jump me and kick my butt," Solimine said.

Chrissie laughed.

"No, that's not going to happen," she said. "Come on out. Besides, my mother needs to talk to you."

"No, I'm not getting out."

"They're not here, Rob. Really. They're not here. And my mom really wants to talk to you."

Chrissie knew this ruse would probably work. Chrissie's mom and Solimine were on very good terms, and the idea of grown-ups around would probably put him at ease. But Solimine was wary. Perhaps he sensed that Chrissie was still furious with him too.

Eventually, Chrissie persuaded Solimine to get out of his car.

Solimine was walking up her front porch when Castaldo sprang. Castaldo flew at Solimine, taking the other boy completely by surprise. Solimine covered up like a boxer. But before he did, Castaldo popped him once right in the face.

"Don't you ever do that again!" Castaldo bellowed. Castaldo tried to hit him again, but he had trouble lining up a punch because Solimine already had sunk to the ground in terror. Castaldo was cursing through clenched teeth and swinging hard, trying to get at Solimine's face and body as Solimine lay on the pavement in a fetal position, covering his face with his arms. Solimine was begging Castaldo not to hurt him. Castaldo kicked him in the ribs a few time, but there was no use. Solimine lay there like a worm.

"Please! Please! Please!" Solimine cried as Castaldo swarmed over him.

Strelka sat on the top step with Chrissie. They were enjoying the spectacle so much that they pretended to be eating imaginary popcorn from an imaginary bag. Getting into the spirit of things, they tossed some imaginary puffs of popcorn into the air, smiling gaily when they caught them in their mouths, and then dueled to see who could throw the pretend popcorn into the air the highest, while Solimine's thrashing continued.

"I'm sorry!" Solimine was saying, "I'm sorry! I'll never do it again!"

Castaldo reached down and jerked Solimine by the shirt.

"Get up!" Castaldo screamed. "Get the fuck out of Clifton! If you ever come back here again, we'll kill you."

Castaldo turned Solimine loose. Solimine looked at Strelka. It almost seemed as if Solimine should have started crying, but he didn't. Solimine turned around, said nothing to Strelka or Chrissie, and started to walk away. Strelka, Castaldo, and Chrissie watched him go. Just before Solimine got into his car, he turned and looked over his shoulder at the trio and tugged at his jacket with a flick of the lapels—the classic Hollywood tough-guy gesture. It got a laugh from the other three. Chrissie rolled her eyes. It was as if Robbie was grabbing for the last shred of pride or something, and it also showed how cocky he was. To Chrissie, it seemed as if Solimine was trying to act as if he had just kicked some ass, and nothing could be further from the truth.

"Hi, James," Chrissie said, stepping into Strelka's car. She looked at Wanger, who had said nothing—a very unusual occurrence for him.

"What's up, James?" Chrissie said.

Wanger regarded her with a solemn and distant look. His lips were pressed primly together. Wanger turned his head toward Castaldo as if expecting a cue but said nothing. Chrissie looked around for an explanation.

"James isn't speaking," someone said.

The Tank was already off and flying to Annie's Road. They sped out Route 46 through the Notch above Little Falls, which overlooked a broad basin glowing with commerce. Castaldo had gotten out of the front passenger seat so Chrissie could sit there, and now all the boys were wedged into the backseat of the Buick. Someone said they had just grabbed some burgers at the McDonald's in Nutley, which explained the garbage swimming around on the floor and the smell of sweet grease. Everybody was acting normal except Wanger, who refused to speak.

"What's going on?" Chrissie asked, and she tried to get an

answer out of Wanger. Wanger kept quiet. He looked over at Castaldo.

"You may speak, James," Castaldo said.

Wanger spoke. Everyone in the car laughed.

Chrissie asked another question, but again, Wanger wouldn't answer. Instead, Wanger looked once more at Castaldo.

"Don't say anything," Castaldo said.

Wanger fixed Castaldo with a stare. This was a new one, although Chrissie knew Wanger well enough to expect that he was pulling some stunt.

"What's going on?" Chrissie said.

"You may speak," Castaldo said.

Wanger spoke. He said he was Frank's right-hand man. Whatever Frank said to do, Wanger did.

Chrissie looked over at Strelka to see if it was true. It was true.

"Whatever," Chrissie said.

Strelka turned off the highway at the Holiday Inn and drove through the lot in the rear. They descended the serpentine driveway behind the Holiday Inn and turned left onto Riverview Drive. When Wanger and the boys drove to Annie's Road, they often parked on Norwood Terrace, a settlement near the overpass that they referred to derisively as Midgetville. White plastic grocery bags whipped around high up in the naked trees, having fluttered down from the highway like ghosts, and in the wintertime you had to listen overhead for snowplows, which would dump potentially fatal avalanches of ice and dirty snow over the side of the overpass to the ground below. Strelka raced along the river and drove past Midgetville, past the abutments scrawled with graffiti, under the Route 80 overpass, and then pulled off about midway between the stores and Dead Man's Curve. This wasn't the usual way for the group to go inside the cemetery, but they used the entrance now and then, usually after someone in Midgetville had yelled at them and threatened to call the cops.

Strelka parked off the side of the road, not far from where some kids had dumped a streak of red paint, and everyone got out. They climbed through a hole in the fence, walked through a border of small trees that surrounded the cemetery, and stepped into grass. They walked past a line of graves and crossed one of the unpaved roads. A huge lawn opened before them. Overhead the sky became dark enough to observe Orion's Belt and the Great Bear, but it was livid at the edges with the orange wash of city lights. The roar of Route 80's traffic grew fainter as they walked, until only the moan of trucks reached the broad plain. Old, old hemlocks stood like skeletal fish against the sky, and the streetlights along Annie's Road shrank in the darkness.

They jumped over a ditch with a trickle of water and climbed the slope toward Annie's tomb. Chrissie always got freaked out coming here. Strelka had told her plenty of stories about the place, and about the things that had happened to them there—too many things that could not be explained except by the supernatural. Once, for example, when the boys were walking across a clearing in the cemetery, a bank of fog seemed to follow them as if by magic. Then there was the time Stooge and Strelka saw a white shadow at the top of a hill inside the cemetery, moving much too fast to be a person or an animal.

In the house where they had seen the shadow of a woman in the window, the boys also saw a girl in a pink prom dress as they drove past in Strelka's car. But by the time they turned around and drove by again, it was gone. Another time, while returning from a jaunt to New York City, the boys drove past looking for a spirit and Strelka's car got a flat tire. After they limped to the gas station in Paterson, Strelka and Wanger and the boys examined the flat tire and found three tiny holes, as if jabbed by a pin in a straight line across the side of Strelka's tire. More than once, Strelka claimed to have been paralyzed by some force. This happened once while he was driving The Tank, and everybody began screaming until someone grabbed the steering wheel and hit the brake and got the car through a turn and onto the iron bridge that crossed the river into Paterson. And, of course, they all swore they had felt Annie's heart pounding through the soles of their feet while walking in the cemetery past a row of small mausoleums.

But now Chrissie and the boys stood around and smoked cigarettes and talked. Wanger and Strelka and Stooge went off among the tombstones, looking for the place where Annie's body was buried. After a while they came back, and Wanger explained that Castaldo had released him from his control for the evening. He had been learning to take orders. The whole exercise, Wanger told them, had to do with the Mafia and the discipline necessary to survive in organized crime. If Wanger had told them once, he had told them hundreds of times about his dream of becoming a soldier—not a *soldier* soldier—but a gangster. Maybe even a hit man.

"You can do anything in the Mob," Wanger said. "Look what it did for John Gotti."

This explained Wanger's getup—the black trench coat and the cappello. It also explained his fascination with all things Italian—the language, the coffee, the food—and it certainly explained his insistence that he was a full-blooded Italian whose grandfather's family could be traced to Sicily. He was eager to learn Italian from Castaldo and Carboni and envied their ability to converse with their parents in their native language. All three of them, in fact, shared an intense interest in La Cosa Nostra, and perhaps it had something to do with their pride in being Italian. More than once, for example, they pointed out that Stooge and Strelka couldn't dream of joining—not that they wanted to—because they weren't Italian. What's more, even though the family would later make clear that this was all fantasy, Castaldo was forever bragging about an uncle or a cousin, or some relative anyway, who was a wiseguy. Castaldo promised to get Wanger inside the Mafia through this relative, and that was all Wanger needed to hear. Wanger talked of almost nothing else. He adored the Mafia and regaled everyone with his knowledge of it. Between him and Castaldo, they must have watched the *Godfather* movies countless times. They adored Gotti, the Dapper Don whose reputation from sartorial elegance and extreme violence made him a favorite front-page story for the New York City tabloids. According to Chrissie, Castaldo had boasted of having a snapshot that showed a member of his family standing beside Gotti. Of course, Wanger either didn't know or didn't care that Gotti that fall happened to be sitting in a roach-infested cell at the Metropolitan Correctional Center, awaiting trial on federal racketeering charges. Gotti—whose luck in winning several acquittals had earned him the sobriquet "Teflon Don"—appeared glamorous and powerful, and it took only a small leap of the imagination to transform Castaldo's tawdry white house on Prescott Avenue into their version of the Ravenite Social Club, Gotti's haunt on Mulberry Street in Little Italy.

Chrissie had heard the Mafia shtick from Wanger many times, so it didn't really surprise her. She had known Wanger since Solimine once brought him around to her house a couple years earlier, and ever since he had struck her as a cutup who did and said odd things. Sometimes Wanger called her to chat, and they would spend part of the conversation scheming to pull off the perfect bank robbery. Or some other fanciful crime. It didn't mater, so far as Chrissie was concerned, if it could finance the beginnings of a Hollywood career. She was only kidding, of course, but Wanger seemed to get a thrill out of the idea of planning the perfect crime. It was the challenge of the thing. When he discussed the Mafia, he spoke with admiration about their ruthlessness, their pledge of silence, and especially their notion of unity. The concept of Mafia brotherhood appealed to him strongly. When he talked to Chrissie or the boys about becoming a mobster, Wanger often dwelled on the Mafia's promise of lifelong belonging and protection.

"You know what it takes in the Mafia to get out?" Wanger once asked Stooge. "Three bullets."

Stooge had no idea what Wanger as talking about.

"One in the head, two in the chest. The only way out is to be killed," Wanger said. "Sort of like our group."

Stooge believed him.

* * *

That November it became clear that the Halloween fight achieved legendary status. Castaldo once more had proven himself to be a man of action and a man of his word, and everyone extracted a measure of glee at the thought of Solimine wriggling around on the ground like an insect. Among them all there was a sense of justice and relief because Solimine the snitch had met his comeuppance, and because the moral balance in the teenage order had been restored. Everyone knew that tattling was about the lowest thing a teenager could do—perhaps Solimine would learn a lesson. No, a few lessons, they thought, like keeping his mouth shut and staying away from places where he wasn't wanted.

In fact, Solimine did move further away from the group. The weekend after the fight, Solimine didn't go out. He asked Arlene if there was any Ben-Gay in the house because he had strained some muscles while lifting weights, but his stepmother sensed there was something more to his request, that something was bothering him. On nights that he normally would have been out with his friends, he stayed home and watched television with her and Bob. He spent more and more time with his father down at the Volunteer Fire Department's firehouse in North Haledon.

But somehow the Halloween incident and Solimine's absence only whipped up the group's hatred for him more. It wouldn't have taken much at this point to make a clean break with Solimine once and for all: He would have gone his way, and the Castaldo clan would have gone theirs. But Wanger and Castaldo weren't through with Solimine yet. They seemed obsessed with him, and the obsession spread to the others. A mysterious irony was at work. While the five teenagers grew more close in friendship, transforming themselves from individual misfits into a powerful little group, at the center of their union was the figure of a pathetic and lonely young man. Yet he had an inexplicable power over them that even Castaldo couldn't match. Castaldo might direct Strelka about where to drive, or decide when they would leave or what they would do, but Solimine controlled them in a more profound way. Even in his absence, the group devoted much of their time to Solimine—berating him, mocking him, hating him, discussing his personality and cataloging his weaknesses. Their interest in Solimine assumed the form of a perverse cult, as if they had given themselves over almost entirely to Solimine and the feelings of disgust and rage that he aroused. Without consciously thinking about it, perhaps, the group's hatred of him became an object of worship. Otherwise, how could one explain the way they would not let him go?

No, Wanger and Castaldo had other ideas. There were ways to torment Solimine that they hadn't even tried; they might at least amuse themselves at his expense for a while. If they planned things well, they might have both: They could do crazy stuff to Solimine and have fun—until the time came that they would ensure, once and for all, that the pest wouldn't set foot in Clifton again. So they didn't want Solimine to leave their circle just yet. They needed, in fact, to draw him in a little closer again. As if lifting his strategy directly from *The Godfather*—"Keep your friends close; keep your enemies closer," the Corleones said—Wanger promised to settle the feud with Solimine. Wanger would peace things up, as he put it, so that Solimine would come around again—so that they could do something worse later on. It would be a false truce, Wanger said, and a subterfuge. Everyone liked the idea, especially Castaldo, who nevertheless told the others to make sure Robbie wouldn't come around more often than once a week. Then, everyone agreed, they could make Solimine's life miserable.

6

THE LUMINOUS DAYS OF AUTUMN SOON PASSED. NOVEMBER brought heavy skies, rain, and streets filled with the brown scurf of dead vegetation. Now and then it remained warm and bright, with goose-down clouds scattered across a pale sky—but the gray days had come. The cold provided a respite from the late summer's haze and smog, and on some nights, from certain vantages, Manhattan's skyline hung like a starry jewel in the sky, but for the most part, it was a depressing time of the year. Darkness fell early, the rain washed oily rainbows into the street and blackened the leftover mounds of dead leaves, and the five boys spent most of their time, when they weren't in school, hanging out in Castaldo's living room watching television or playing video games at the mall.

True to his word, Wanger had patched things up with Solimine. Wanger had acted the peacemaker before, he was good at it, and so Solimine had no reason to doubt that the gang would welcome him back. Outwardly, things stood as they had stood before. Solimine once more wormed his way into their fun, annoying them as usual, but now there was a secret purpose behind having to put up with him. Stooge was the only one who hadn't been completely aware of the reason for the phony truce—perhaps because he was busy gaming on the Nintendo in Stevie's room while the other guys were talking—or maybe he had forgotten. But Solimine started coming around again.

"Don't make him mad. It'll ruin things," Wanger said, and he made it a special point to warn Carboni, whose stubborn streak made it difficult for him to change directions very easily.

So it was that for the sake of a ruse, the five teenagers exercised a remarkable degree of tolerance for Solimine that hadn't been possible before—all the while as they were sitting in Stevie Castaldo's bedroom, thinking about what it would take to bring Solimine down a peg and wipe that stupid grin off his face. As if in pursuit of a complicated problem that could only be solved through collaboration, they studied ways to make Solimine miserable and discussed the options that would hurt Solimine the most.

Naturally, they thought of his car. Solimine had smashed the Camaro on Route 20 in Paterson, but not long afterward he borrowed some money from his brother and mother and bought a used Plymouth Laser. His dad, who had bought the Camaro and given it to him, told Rob there would be no more freebies or bailouts. Solimine would have to buy the second car and he would be on his own paying for its upkeep. So now Solimine was paranoid about anything happening to his car, and the boys knew it, and they debated the merits of dumping flour or baking soda into the gas line, or maybe using sand, sugar, or even cement. Taking a more direct approach, someone suggested bashing in the windows of Solimine's car with a baseball bat. Someone else floated the idea of handcuffing Solimine to a tree at Annie's Road, somewhere far inside the cemetery where no one could hear him for a while, and just leaving him there. But for the most part, they fixated on the idea of wrecking his car.

Carboni said they should flatten all his tires, stranding Solimine like an idiot at some remote place. The proposal would be simple to execute—all he needed was a pocketknife—and it wasn't a novel trick for Carboni. When he and Stooge and another kid were sleeping over, Carboni and the kid trampled all over Clifton slashing tires just for the hell of it. The boy had kept a dazzling collection of blades inside a trunk, along with handcuffs and other junk. Now Carboni kept his own collection. Usually he was carrying a two-inch blade with a fake wood handle and brass hinges. Carboni proposed getting Solimine's car at Annie's Road, where Solimine would be in the middle of nowhere, and everyone agreed it was an excellent idea. They would go up to Annie's Road in two cars. Once at the cemetery, they would split into two groups. The group with Solimine would take one path up to Annie's mausoleum. The other group would take a different path, sneak back down to where Solimine was parked, and slit the tires. Then they would race back to the mausoleum, arriving just as the other group did, to make it seem as if nothing had happened. Since people were always yelling at them near Norwood Terrace, and since other kids hung out up there, they could blame the prank on someone else and it would sound more or less believable.

There was no denying that the elaborate maneuvering posed certain challenges and provided a certain thrill to the venture all its own—so they talked about giving it a dry run. The five went up to Annie's Road, split up, and tried it out. They parked at the different places on Annie's Road and took two routes into the cemetery, with Wanger doubling back to the cars to see if he could catch up with the others and meet them at the mausoleum at the same time. Carboni timed him with a watch, to see if he would have enough time to do what was necessary. The concept seemed sound.

The next day, when it came time to carry this plan out, Solimine balked. He never liked Annie's Road that much—he thought it was boring, that there wasn't anything to do up there—and no one could convince him to go. He simply refused, and the plan had collapsed. Whether because this plan now seemed impracticable or simply had failed to capture their imagination wasn't clear, but they let it go. However, they were not going to give up on the overall goal. They continued to think of ways to get Solimine. Still focusing on his new car, the group had as their object some kind of malicious mischief, something along the line of flattening the tires or keying the paint, and nothing worse, and a recognition among themselves that this was risky enough.

The group cruised past Stooge's house on Fornelius Avenue one day and spotted Solimine's car parked out front. They could hardly contain their glee. Through no doing of their own, they had found Solimine's car unattended, parked there like a sitting duck, just waiting for them to mess it up. And Solimine would never be able to prove it was them. Strelka thought it would be hilarious if they stole one of Solimine's tires as a practical joke. Carboni suggested swiping the lug nuts, so the tire would fly off on its own.

Everyone was hooting it up as Strelka drove around the block to have another look. Melanie was there too, but she just seemed bored or disgusted. They cruised by Solimine's car again slowly, craning their necks to see if Solimine was around, which he wasn't. At last, a solid opportunity had come to mess up his car; they couldn't believe their good fortune.

Strelka parked a little way off. He opened the trunk of the Buick and lifted out the heavy-duty jack. They went back to the rear of Solimine's hatchback, set up the jack, and started cranking. The car jerked upward in little spasms as Carboni pumped the hand crank. The rest of the group yucked it up or shushed each other, all the while keeping an eye on the front of Stooge's house to make sure Solimine didn't catch them. Strelka lifted off the tire. The jack, which wasn't built for Solimine's car, started ripping the piece-of-shit Plymouth like a garbage bag. Wanger saw the bumper ripping and grabbed the jack and pumped harder.

"Just lower it and leave it!" Strelka said.

All of a sudden Wanger started having second thoughts.

"No, no," Wanger said. "Leave the jack! We can't put the axle down on the ground—it'll mess it up."

"I'm not leaving my jack!" Strelka said.

They stood around arguing about what to do, and even

Castaldo agreed they should put the tire on again. Strelka tried refitting the tire onto the wheel, but now the jack had come down somehow. Castaldo and Carboni staggered under the Plymouth and tried lifting it, but it wouldn't budge. Wanger tried too. Melanie, who was cold, watched the entire escapade from the Buick.

But just about the time they had the tire going back on, Stooge's mom saw the group of kids from her bedroom window doing something to Solimine's car. She went to the basement door and ducked her head down the stairwell, calling to Stooge, Solimine, and their friend, a girl named Terri.

"Rob," Mary called. "You better come up here. It looks like some kids are fooling with your car."

Solimine bounded up the steps, Stooge and Terri close behind. The front door banged against the house as he dashed out onto the street, flailing his arms and bellowing.

"What the fuck are you doing to my car!" Solimine shouted. "What are you doing? Put the tire back on! Put it back on now!"

For a moment, it looked as if a fight could break out. Everyone told Solimine to calm down, to take it easy, that it was all just a big gag. They laughed a little nervously and made a few tenuous wisecracks. Everyone agreed to fix his car. To keep from ripping the bumper further, they got around the back of the Plymouth and lifted. With a collective groan, the teenagers lifted the tail end of the hatchback while Strelka zeroed in on the wheel rim to line it up and fit the tire back on. It took some doing, but they eventually succeeded. Then they tightened the lug nuts and put the hubcap back on. Solimine was still hot, although he also seemed a little full of himself now that he had stood his ground and forced the whole group to put the tire back. He lectured the group about how messed up they were. Strelka tried taking the sting off by reminding Solimine of all the other pranks they had pulled over the years, and eventually Solimine cooled off.

"Take it easy, Rob," Strelka was saying. "We didn't mean anything. We were just playing with you."

* * *

A few weeks after the tire incident, the group crowded through the door of Romeo's Pizza and shook off the chill of an autumn day. Just over the Passaic border from Clifton, the pizzeria was tidy and well-lighted, almost too bright, with large windows that looked out on Main Avenue and the parking lot of an auto-parts store. Baskets of artificial flowers hung from the walls, and there was a large color television atop a cigarette machine. Everything was painted tangerine and white, and there was a sugary seascape hanging in a frame by the back of the shop.

Wanger held the door for the other four teenagers and ushered them in with a theatrical gesture. The others were shoving each other, putting in orders at the counter, horsing around. Wanger ordered last and offered to pay for everyone. He made small talk at the counter, addressing the pizza maker with belabored civility, and shelled out the cash. Everyone crowded around a wood-grain Formica table and started shoveling down pizza and talking.

It was looking as if it would be a fun day, and then Solimine's name came up. Everyone started reciting the now-familiar litany of his offenses. They just couldn't get rid of him. It was the way he talked. It was the way he acted like a baby. He was too hyper. He was obnoxious. He was a geek, a momma's boy, and a goody-goody. Worst of all, he was a tattletale and a snitch. What was it with him? He had become nothing less than a pest, and no matter what they did or said, he couldn't take a hint. It filled them all with disgust the way Solimine craved to be a part of their group, the way he seemed to disregard their ill will. Just the other day it had taken almost forever to ditch him at the video arcade. It was almost as if he were *harassing* them.

Strelka was jamming a pizza slice into his mouth, and he was saying he couldn't believe how Solimine had changed since rehab. Ever since then he had been acting like a superhero, as if he was somebody he wasn't, like he was better than the rest of them. It was fine if Solimine didn't want to drink, but now he was all preachy about it, Strelka said. To top it off, he was getting holy about Chrissie, too. Then the next minute he was doing something to hurt her. Strelka had grown to feel more and more protective of her, and he didn't like the way Solimine treated her. You would think Solimine was his girlfriend or something. Strelka was still fuming because of the time when Solimine suggested that Strelka leave her alone. And to top it all off, all of their plans to vandalize his car had failed.

"That's it," Wanger said. "We should just kill him."

It was an old line, but everybody laughed. Wanger said it so often—and so did just about everybody whom Solimine annoyed—that "kill" might have been Solimine's middle name.

"No, I mean it," Wanger said. "We'll kill him."

Wanger's habitually morose expression revealed no hint of whether or not he was kidding—but there was something in Wanger's tone that suggested he had meant what he had just said. But you never knew with Wanger. Wanger would say the wackiest things in complete earnestness. Deadpan. They peered closely at Wanger, trying to read what was going on behind the tinted aviator glasses. This sounded like just another morbid joke. But everyone at the table sensed that there was more to it—that Wanger wasn't really kidding. Or was he kidding them too well? No one knew what to make of it. Strelka stopped chewing. He looked around the table at the others, and they were looking at him. Someone chuckled, and they were looking at Wanger to see what he was going to say next. Wanger was looking at them with a steady gaze.

"I'll do it myself," Wanger said.

Strelka, who had just been making the most fuss about Solimine, made an absurd face. Everyone objected.

"That's crazy!" someone said.

"That's too serious!"

"Get real!" Stooge said.

Wanger persisted. He said it several times. He suggested they just shoot Solimine and get it over with. Everything else they had tried so far had failed. All they had wanted to do was mess up Rob's car, flatten the tires, make him look like an idiot, do something, and they couldn't seem to do that. Wanger kept going until everyone told him to pipe down because someone might hear him and call the police or something.

Castaldo said nothing. Carboni didn't react, either.

"You're crazy, James," Strelka said.

Stooge couldn't figure out if it was real or not, though. Wanger's face was like stone. Just the other day, Wanger had been telling Stooge and the others that the group should be more organized, that it should be more like the Mafia, more serious, so that they could get things done. But this was very serious. Stooge had never heard anything so radical in his life. It was wild.

Wanger let his proposal slide, but not without some disappointment—at least he looked disappointed, Stooge thought. The conversation about Solimine's annoying habits moved on, and then it was on to something else altogether. But time would show that Wanger wasn't kidding anymore.

One day Wanger asked Strelka to drive him to Sikora's, a store in the Dundee section of Passaic. The neighborhood along that stretch of Market Street still bore traces of the Slavic community that had settled there in huge numbers during earlier waves of immigration, but it was becoming more Latino. A blue storefront with a statue of the Holy Family in the window, Sikora's had been in business for more than sixty years, but it would be easy to miss if you weren't looking for it. Inside was every manner of religious article: crucifixes for the home; crucifixes as jewelry; rosaries in every color; Bibles in every color, shape and size; religious books and pamphlets; prayer cards and stationery; bins and glass display cases full of jewelry, medallions and dimestore religious trinkets. In the rear of the store was a church-supply center where priests could purchase clerical garb and objects necessary for the sacraments, such as chalices, monstrances, and decanters. The racks flowed with a rich assortment of ecclesiastical stoles and chasubles.

It was almost a dizzying experience to walk its aisles. Throughout the store, hundreds of Jesuses in various incarnations gazed down from picture frames on the walls. There were Eastern Orthodox icons and there were statues—a remarkable array of statues—from the tiny figurines of the Virgin, or St. Michael slaying the demon, that one could affix to a dashboard to yard-size fiberglass statues of the Holy Family. Indeed, the variety seemed endless, as if the entire Bible had been poured into plastic, fiberglass, or ceramic molds and then assembled into a gaudy host: St. Francis communing with the animals was popular, and there were Saints Dominic, Anthony, Joseph, and Jude; there were statues of Jesus of the Sacred Heart and Our Lady of the Sorrows, her huge scarlet heart extruded surrounded by silver gloria; statues of St. Elizabeth Seton and obscure religious figures.

Wanger picked out a bunch of tiny gold religious medallions. He had a bag full of them. Wanger gave one to Strelka and said that he had a purpose for them that he said he would explain later.

"This is our membership," Wanger told him. "This is our sign that we are together and that we will keep silent about anything we do just between us."

Strelka took the medal and didn't pay much mind. Wanger always did so many weird things that this seemed almost normal. He really knew the Bible, it seemed, and once he pulled it out to quote from a passage about Eve being Adam's helpmate and inferior. This, he thought, would settle a dispute Castaldo had been having with his girlfriend, Melanie. Now he was buying religious medals. A bagful. No one knew what to make of Wanger anymore, what with his obsession with joining the Mafia and his stuff with the church.

In the closing shots of *Godfather II*, Michael Corleone sits alone as the screen darkens and the light draws close around his face. Having at last vanquished his enemies, he holds cold dominion over the factions of his own crime family, the underworld at large—and solitude. The last great crime of the movie turns out to be a replay of man's first: fratricide. With the report of a hit man's gun across a glassy lake at dawn,

Michael Corleone has dispatched his only living brother, Fredo, in retribution for the sin of betrayal.

Although foreshadowed (by a kiss, no less), the finale comes as a shock all the same—and so does the twist of having Fredo, played by John Cazale, recite the Hail Mary moments before his death. The Hail Mary is one of the Roman Catholic Church's most revered prayers of supplication. Since he had been a boy, Fredo recited the prayer in the belief that it helped to catch a fish. Sitting in a boat on a Nevada lake after dawn, Fredo recites the prayer until he reaches its last line—"Pray for us sinners now and at the hour of our death." A gun cracks, and Fredo is gone.

It is a disturbing scene, and no doubt it had an effect on Wanger, for Wanger watched it many, many times. He loved a lot of gangster movies, but none like *The Godfather*. At the Castaldos' one night, Wanger called the local Blockbuster video store just minutes before closing and begged them to hold a copy of the movie until he could get there. Then Wanger sprinted out the door to the store to rent the videotape so he and the others guys could watch it that night. When he wasn't obsessing with *The Godfather* he rented other contemporary gangster movies, such as Martin Scorsese's grim and blackly humorous masterpiece, *Goodfellas*. But mainly Wanger loved Francis Ford Coppola's luminous family portrait of the Mafia. By his friends' estimates, Wanger had rented the movie at least ninety times. Even Castaldo, who liked anything about the mob, didn't like the movie that much. Stooge could take it or leave it, and Strelka, whose favorite show of all time was "The Honeymooners," was more interested in comedies. But at home and at Castaldo's house, Wanger, and Carboni, too, watched *The Godfather* straight through, almost hypnotically, from its opening shot of a hand working a marionette, to the first murder (the garroting of a Coreleone soldier), to the bloody climax of Michael's coronation as the new Godfather. It was easy to see why: Besides being a classic, the movie articulated many of the themes that dominated the group's life. With all the majestic elegance and charm Hollywood could summon, the movie depicted the Mafia's obsession with respect and ethnic identity, loyalty and insularity, and violence. The code of honor, which was cloaked in regal masculinity, was nothing if not the code of a holy brotherhood. The movie also implied that the Mafia's values were no more extreme or immoral than those held by the rest of society. This point in particular had a strong effect on Wanger, who believed the government was not run much differently from the Mafia. That was just the way things were, Wanger felt. As part of its social critique, *The Godfather* stood for the proposition that the most outrageous crimes could be justified not by emotion, but simply as another way of doing business. And finally, the movie set the luxurious mysteries of the Roman Catholic Church against the hypocrisy of the gangsters who worshiped in it.

No doubt the juxtaposition of the Hail Mary prayer and Fredo's murder shocked moviegoers (at least Roman Catholic moviegoers) nearly as much as the climactic quick-cut finale in *The Godfather*, when scenes from the baptism of Michael Corleone's first son are interwoven with a ferocious series of gangland executions. Except perhaps the Our Father, or Lord's Prayer, no other prayer is as significant in the life of a Roman Catholic as the Hail Mary. Known also as the *Ave Maria* and the angelic salutation, the prayer is addressed to the Virgin Mary, who holds a central place in Roman Catholicism. Existing in its present form since 1514, the prayer incorporates verses from the Bible (Luke 1:28 and 1:42) that tell of the Annunciation of Christ's birth by the Archangel Gabriel and the greeting to Mary by Elizabeth, the mother of John the Baptist. Perhaps because the prayer beseeches Mary—a mysterious and complicated figure who stands as the Sorrowful Mother, the Mother of God, and the Mother of the Church—the Hail Mary became one of the most popular and emotional devotions. As a lector in the church, Wanger certainly must have had a feel for this, and even the most irreligious among the group knew it word for word.

* * *

A few days after Wanger had bought the religious medals at Sikora's, everyone dropped by Stooge's house. Christmas was just around the corner, and Stooge's mom had put up decorations around the house. Wanger, Strelka, Castaldo, and Carboni were playing poker at the dining-room table with Stooge. Melanie was there as well. Stooge's mom was upstairs, and the TV was blaring in the little sitting room just off the dining area. Gold and silver tinsel was draped over the hutch where his mother displayed miniature beer steins. The telephone rang in the kitchen around the corner from the dining room and Stooge picked it up, almost shouting into the receiver to be heard over the noise. Then he hung up. It was Solimine calling to say he was coming by, Stooge said.

Castaldo flipped. "He's coming down again! I can't believe it. I've had it with him!"

There was discussion about whether they should take off before Solimine got there. But Wanger, saying there was nothing they could do since the pest was already on his way, suggested they make plans to wreck Solimine's car again. Melanie listened with some detachment and wondered why no one just told Solimine to his face to stop coming around.

As everyone waited for Solimine to appear, they developed a plan that added a twist to the idea of splitting up in the cemetery. They would try to slash Solimine's tires, but this time Wanger and Carboni would accompany Solimine. Wanger offered to persuade Solimine to make the trip, since he had known Solimine longer than anyone else in the group except Strelka, and he had, after all, brokered the peace. Wanger would tell Solimine that he needed a breath of fresh air. He would say they could go up to Annie's Road, not for too long, and he would see to it that that's where Solimine went. Carboni, who had become like Wanger's alter ego when it came to dirty tricks, offered to ride along. They would make sure Solimine parked in a conspicuous spot in Midgetville or, even better, along Annie's Road where fewer people would see them. Then they would take Solimine inside the cemetery and wait for Step Two.

Meanwhile, Strelka and Castaldo would give Solimine,

Wanger, and Carboni a head start—at least fifteen minutes, or enough time for the three to make it out to Annie's Road, climb the bank beside the overpass, and walk to Annie's tomb. Then Castaldo and Strelka would jet out to Annie's Road, find Solimine's car, slash the tires, and take off. Stooge would wait at his house with Melanie for Solimine's expected distress call. As they pictured it, Solimine would walk out of the cemetery, lay eyes on his busted-down car, see all four tires flat on the ground, and start blubbering his way to a pay phone on Totowa Road. That would be the signal to go out and get them—not because anyone gave a shit about Solimine, but because no one wanted to strand Carboni and Wanger. It would also divert suspicion, since they also didn't want to let on to Solimine—at least not yet—that his own friends were making his life miserable.

Soon enough, Solimine arrived at Stooge's house. He took a place at the table, joining in the poker game. The group played kid's games with adult-size pots. There was a $5 ante to play, and they dealt lots of wild cards and used fanciful rules. The money was very real, however. Wanger had recently blown $500, the second time in a year he owed Castaldo a big chunk of money because of gambling. The first time it happened, Castaldo told Wanger not to worry about it, but Wanger insisted on coming up with the dough. This time when Solimine sat down to play, he didn't know that the game had been rigged against him. The way it was set up, it wasn't going to matter if Solimine won or lost. They simply intended to stiff him. No money was changing hands. Instead, a running tally of who owed what was kept on paper at the table. Even if Solimine won, the boys would simply refuse to pay him. If he lost, they would collect. As it happened, Solimine was losing—badly. Before the evening was over, he owed each boy at the table $50.

The real excitement, though, lay in the plans for getting his car. After playing enough hands to sink Solimine, Wanger stood up and asked Solimine if he wanted to take a ride to Annie's Road. Wanger said he could use a breath of fresh air, and Stooge almost had to laugh at the way Wanger followed his own script, word for word. But Solimine wasn't interested.

"Come on, Rob," Wanger said.

"It's boring up there. Let's stay here and play cards."

"Come on, Rob. Just for a while," Wanger said.

Wanger had to work on him for a while. But he had a way of wearing people down, and eventually Solimine gave in. He drove off with Wanger and Carboni, who looked like twins in their dark trench coats.

After Solimine had left, Castaldo and Strelka could barely contain their mirth. They went back and forth over how to slash the tires and who would do it. They agreed that Strelka would take out two tires and Castaldo would cut two tires. Each would take a knife. They waited at least fifteen minutes, and then Castaldo and Strelka took off in Strelka's car.

"They're not going to do anything," Melanie said.

"Yeah, they will," Stooge said.

Stooge and Melanie watched MTV, played cards, and waited for the telephone to ring. Nearly an hour passed. Stooge and Melanie waited, but the telephone never rang.

Suddenly, the screen door slammed against the house as if it had been kicked by the wind, and it scared the bejesus out of Stooge and Melanie. Stooge turned to see Castaldo barreling into the kitchen, his fists balled up in fury. Castaldo paced across the kitchen floor, cursing up and down. Stooge could see that Castaldo wanted badly to pound something. But Castaldo, who had a habit of slamming his fist into things when he had a tantrum, seemed to be controlling himself, perhaps because he was in Stooge's house.

"He got away!" Castaldo thundered. "He got away again!"

Strelka stalked in not a minute later, and he was pissed too. But the size of Castaldo's fury was such that it seemed almost theatrical, like some character going off in Wrestlemania. He kept saying over and over again that Solimine had gotten away.

"Yeah, we looked all over the place, and they weren't there when we got up there," Strelka said.

Strelka said they had cruised up and down Annie's Road about four times looking for Solimine's car. They had driven through Midgetville, past the overpass, down to the shops on Totowa Road, behind the shops, and back up to Midgetville, but there was no sign of Solimine's car.

"I can't believe it!" Castaldo said. "That kid's too fucking lucky! He got away again!"

Castaldo had been going wild since all the way back on Annie's Road. He erupted in Strelka's car, pounding his fist on the dashboard hard enough to crack it. Castaldo sat down at Stooge's dining table, banging his fist now and then on the lacy white tablecloth for emphasis, and continued to fume. It sent chills down Stooge's back and reminded him of the days when his father went nuts.

"There's got to be a spirit out there looking out for him," Castaldo said, and with him, it wasn't just something to say. Everyone in the group knew Castaldo was deeply superstitious—the whole group was, really—and Castaldo wasn't fooling now, Stooge thought.

"The only thing left is to kill him," Castaldo said.

Half an hour after Strelka and Castaldo returned, Wanger and Carboni came through the door of Stooge's kitchen. Solimine was with them, revved up for a night of fun. Everyone wondered what had gone wrong. After a few minutes, Wanger and Carboni stood to the side and talked something over in Italian. At the first opportunity, Strelka grabbed Wanger and dragged him into the downstairs bathroom to find out what had happened. Wanger told him that Rob wanted to stop at his house to pick up some weed. They went by his dad's place in North Haledon, but by the time they got to Annie's Road, Castaldo and Strelka had come and gone.

So it was another case of bad timing. Or Solimine's luck. Or Solimine's flighty personality. But the night wasn't a complete loss. The group played cards and hung out for a while. Solimine's cards kept heading south, which made it easy to take his money, and then everyone got into Solimine's and

Strelka's cars and cruised the city. When exhaustion set in, they all split up. Solimine stayed over night at Stooge's, despite Stooge telling him not to, and the others went their separate ways.

In the giant shopping mall that had become northern New Jersey by 1991, the Christmas season germinated sometime between Halloween and Thanksgiving. By early December, all the holiday regalia—the crèches, the strings of lights, the electric candles, the lawn Santas and the plastic snowmen, and the rest of the red-and-green hooey—had metastasized overnight to almost every lawn, front porch, shopping center, shopping mall, and bargain discounter in the land. The highways connecting suburbs and malls were jammed with the heaviest traffic of the year, and no matter what night of the week it was, it was hard to find parking. This of course did not hinder Strelka and the boys from driving out to the Willowbrook Mall. On trips like these, Strelka finessed the dials to get the best sound he could out of the AM radio, or they listened to Carboni's jams on the boombox, or talked, or let Wanger prattle about whatever entered his mind.

One thing Wanger loved talking about was Jack Daniel's whiskey. He liked to talk about it almost as much as he liked to buy it. God knows what Wanger really knew about the stuff, but he regaled them with inside knowledge, the kind of thing real aficionados know, such as the fact that it was not bourbon, but Tennessee sipping whiskey; that there was a real Jack Daniel; that he was an orphan; and that he had learned how to make whiskey from a preacher when he was thirteen years old. Stooge, for one, was impressed with Wanger's knowledge about the whiskey, but really, it was comical too. Once Wanger got started on a topic like that, he was off and running. It was as if Wanger had been writing a term paper on the subject.

"That's good stuff, man," Wanger would say.

Who knew if he was making it all up, but it sounded interesting. Driving west on Route 46, they passed "Rocky's Hot Dogs," a fast-food joint run out of a small trailer by a blind guy who, ever since anyone could remember, filled the lot out front with Christmas trees for sale every winter. He'd string some lightbulbs and put up a snow fence, and the place would be crawling with customers standing up the trees and looking them over. At Ploch's Garden Center in Clifton, where both Stooge and Carboni had started working, it was all they seemed to do now, loading Christmas trees onto customers' cars for $4.25 an hour plus tips. Stooge had his mom come by to buy one, proud that he could get one for the house at a discount. There would be several more spots at the Willowbrook Mall selling trees.

The traffic was always bad at the interchange, but it knotted up especially thick at the Route 23 interchange during the Christmas season. Just before the cloverleaf was The Fountains of Wayne, a landscaping business that was chock-a-block with all sorts of cement statues and doodads for people's yards; birdbaths, *putti*, and assorted lawn sculpture. Lighted Christmas trees sprouted from the rooftop, and a twenty-foot fiberglass Santa stood waving to the traffic that passed along the highway. Santa's mouth was open, and he stood holding his belt, an arm thrust into the air, like Mussolini in his signature pose as Il Duce.

It always took forever to find a place in the Willowbrook Mall parking lot, and they drove around while rent-a-cops cruised slowly in four-wheel-drive vehicles with flashing yellow lights. Strelka parked near the Sears and they walked through an outdoor center, where people were inspecting fresh-cut wreaths and Christmas trees, into the Sears store. Once through the doors, the chilly fragrance of cut pine vanished in a blast of plasticized air from the shopping mall. There was a huge display called Christmas Town nearby featuring giant light-up Magi and astroturf Christmas trees bathed in spray-on snow. They turned past the heavy appliances—the dryers, washers, and stuff—and walked through the store in the direction of the mall entrance. Somewhere in the midst of this consumer overdrive, however, Wanger stopped Carboni, or at least slowed him to a near halt, to give him something. He jostled around inside the pocket of his trench coat for something until he fished out a plastic bag bulging with gold jewelry. He pinched out a charm and held it for Carboni to see. It looked like the booby prize from a carnival, at least at first glance.

"Here," Wanger said, pressing the charm into Carboni's hand. "Wear this."

The object gleamed in the bright store. Carboni examined the trinket. If not for their halos, the people on the medal resembled a bearded guy in a bathrobe holding a baby. There was a shock of wheat or grass or something on the reverse.

"It's a St. Joseph medal," Wanger said.

Carboni could see it wasn't real gold.

"Keep it with you always," Wanger said. "It's a sign of our unity, that we're all together. Nothing can separate us except death. We're a group now." Wanger used a name, too: Il Consigliere. The counselors.

"We can't be split apart, no matter what," Wanger said.

No doubt Wanger was aware that St. Joseph, the earthly father of Jesus, was revered as the saint of workingmen and carpenters, and was the patron saint of a peaceful death. Typically, he was depicted as an old man cradling the Blessed Infant in his arms. Because he was a carpenter, he often was shown holding a set square, and he was associated with the lily, whose image graced the reverse side of the medals Wanger passed out. The church considered St. Joseph the patron saint of departing souls. There were standard prayers begging his intercession before Christ's throne in heaven. Wanger had already given similar medals to Stooge and Strelka. He had given one to Castaldo, too, but Castaldo believed that gold brought him bad luck, so he wouldn't wear it. But Carboni took Wanger's offering quite seriously. Carboni took off the gold chain around his neck, put the St. Joseph medal on it, and never took it off.

One night that winter Candy started yapping, and Susie's eyes opened. She hadn't been sleeping anyway, because she knew Strelka wasn't home. Then she heard banging and slamming—an unbelievable amount of noise, really—as if Strelka were trooping around downstairs like a herd of elephants. The door slammed, there was more banging, and she looked over at Ray, who was out cold. As if all the other commotion weren't enough, Susie wondered why Tommy, who was already past curfew, would be getting the dog all worked up, when suddenly Candy yelped as if she had been kicked.

That's enough, Susie thought. She got out of bed in her nightclothes and bounded downstairs, intending to give Tommy an earful about his rudeness. She stopped at the top of the stairs in the living room. It wasn't her son Tommy in her house making the racket. It was Solimine. It figured, too. Solimine seemed to get a special kick out of teasing the dog when he came over, and Susie was convinced he had done something now to torment her.

"What the hell's going on, Rob?" Susie said. "Do you jerky kids know what time it is? How come you're making so much noise? And what'd you do to the dog, Rob? She's going nuts here. What'd you do—kick her? Where's Tommy?"

Solimine was holding Strelka's keys in his hand, and he was trying to shut the dog up. Susie turned on more lights, and Solimine was all Boy Scout.

"Tommy's outside in the car," Solimine said. "He's been drinking."

"I'll give him drinking. Tell Tommy to get his butt in here."

"He's really drunk," Solimine said, and he seemed to take a tone with her as if he were the voice of wisdom itself. "He's passed out in his car."

Then Strelka stepped in. He made it to the doorway, leaning against the jamb, door open and letting the heat fly into the night, a big goofy grin on his face. He was laughing, and Susie's anger increased.

"Get in here, Tommy, and shut the door," Susie said.

"See," Solimine said. "Your son drinks."

Solimine said they had met up with the group at the mall,

and they went drinking in a park. Strelka denied drinking anything.

"Look, Rob," she said. "You're no better. You're with him. He's drunk, and you're half drunk."

Susie told Solimine to leave. Strelka was in the door, and she didn't need lectures from another stupid kid, so she told Solimine to go home.

Solimine left and Susie woke her husband. Ray came downstairs and started hollering: Didn't Strelka realize how dangerous it was to be drinking and driving? After threatening to take the car away for good, Strelka's father grounded him on weeknights and moved the weekend curfew to midnight until further notice, and he promised Tommy that they would be discussing the affair much more when Strelka was fully sober and his father was fully awake. Then Ray went back upstairs.

Susie had been a teenager too, so she couldn't play it as if she didn't know that her kid was going to fool around and drink now and then. She had done it herself when she was a girl. But she was not going to put up with Strelka coming home at all hours of the night or driving the Buick all over town after he had been drinking. She started the interrogation, trying to find out where he had been, but Strelka was sullen and angry. He only told her that they had been drinking vodka—he didn't name names except to say Solimine, too, had been drinking—in a park. Strelka said it was Brookdale Park, and Susie didn't recognize the name until Strelka said it was the one over in Bloomfield, which she pictured in her head as the huge park that was aflame with cherry blossoms every spring.

But Strelka wouldn't say much more. He sat down on the couch and turned on the television, and Susie went back upstairs. Then she heard Strelka on the telephone. He was talking quietly, and she tried to listen to see who it was. Unable to hear what he was saying, Susie went to another telephone and picked up the line to listen in.

"She's so strict," Strelka was saying. "I'd rather be in jail than live with her."

It was Castaldo on the other end. He wasn't saying much, but the little bit she heard was enough for Susie. She broke in.

"Go to hell!" she said.

Then she marched over to Strelka, who was practically spitting with rage because she had cut in on his telephone call, and slammed down the phone. He ran out the door and headed down the street in the direction of a girl's house where Chrissie was staying.

Susie got in her car to go after him. She started the car, pulled it out of the driveway, and drove over to Lakeview Avenue. Eventually, she saw Strelka heading back toward her. Chrissie and her friend were leading him back home, trying to calm him down, but when Susie stopped, Strelka went wild again. He refused to get in the car. He was swinging his arms, screaming at his mother to leave him alone, and screaming at Chrissie too because she was telling him to listen to his mom. All, it seemed, right in the middle of Lakeview Avenue. The cops came in a matter of minutes.

"What's the problem here?" one of the cops said.

"He's drunk," Susie said. "I'm trying to get him home, and he's acting like Mr. Macho Man."

The cop squared off with Strelka. Strelka had calmed down, but Susie could see he was still willful, still seething because of the whole turn of events, but especially because she had interfered again with his friendship with Castaldo.

"Tommy," the cop said, and finally Strelka seemed to be listening, "get in the car with your mother. She cares about you."

Castaldo couldn't believe his ears. Strelka was leaning on the kitchen counter at Castaldo's house, recounting the whole night again, up to and including when Susie had snapped off their telephone call, and then further into the scene with the police and the consequences of the following day. These included Strelka's being grounded for a month on school nights. His weekend curfew, which had been flexible to say the least, had been snubbed up to twelve o'clock sharp. If he was late, or if he didn't call to explain why he was late, he was in big trouble. And it was all Solimine's fault.

Strelka's mother believed that Solimine had kicked the dog. Maybe he had only been banging doors or snapping on the lights or something, but this much was clear: he had made so much racket it seemed as if he wanted to wake up the entire household. Strelka's dad went ballistic, and then he just took off. With everyone listening in disgust, Strelka ignited the fuse. He told Castaldo how Solimine had been saying to his, Strelka's, mother what a bad influence Castaldo was on everybody—including Strelka—and how it had to do with the drinking.

Castaldo's eyes were on stems. He punched the kitchen cabinet with his fist.

"That's it!" Castaldo said. "That's it! I want him dead!"

Everyone in the group understood that Castaldo was prone to such outbursts, but Castaldo's banging on the cabinets in his kitchen signaled the beginning of something new. From this day forward, Castaldo wanted Solimine dead, and Wanger took him at his word. What had been just talk and braggadocio had now evolved into reasoned discussions about getting rid of Solimine. They began meeting secretly. Standing in his brother's room, Castaldo posed the issue to the group regularly now, and he wasn't kidding around about what they were planning to do. Castaldo wanted ideas about killing another kid. Castaldo's words and his fist in the cabinet left a lasting impression on them all.

"He's dead!" Castaldo said. "That kid is dead!"

So far as Stooge could tell, Castaldo really meant it.

After New Year's Day, 1992, the group's discussions became more businesslike and focused on the Solimine problem. Ever since the attempts to wreck Solimine's car had failed, and since the time Solimine got Strelka in trouble, the talk had shifted from discussion only about damaging his car to talk of inflicting harm on Solimine himself, and even killing him. What's more, in a matter of months, their hatred of Solimine had grown to monstrous size.

To Stooge, the meetings took on an almost formal air, resembling something one might see on TV when the board members of a corporation met to conduct business. Castaldo was running things, and Carboni and Wanger had infused the proceedings with more and more stuff about the Mafia. No one ever really gave the group a name, except for the time in the Sears store, and perhaps there was even a campy element to their self-styled junior Mafia: Wanger called Castaldo "Don Franco"; Castaldo called Wanger "Don Giuseppe." Castaldo, who sat at the head of the table or stood in the room as he spoke, was the leader. He was considered the caporegime, or captain, of the group. Wanger was his right-hand man—although Carboni at times became Wanger's rival for second-in-command. Carboni—because he was Castaldo's cousin, and also became he had more than a touch of the fanatic about him—followed next in the chain of command after Wanger. There was debate now and then about this point, since Strelka, who was eleven months younger than Castaldo, outranked Carboni by virtue of his age. But it went without saying that Stooge was dead last. Stooge knew it, and Stooge didn't mind. As long as he was out having his fun, having big adventures that most fourteen-year-old boys would never dream of, Stooge didn't care about anything. Where he fit in mattered a good deal less than having someplace to fit in, period.

For a while, the discussions seemed like only some big talk. Stooge certainly didn't think much of it. By the middle of January, however, as they crowded into Stevie Castaldo's bedroom, they were talking openly among themselves about killing Solimine. Of course, no one ever really referred to these sessions as meetings per se, or called the gatherings to order. They had no "colors" or secret handshake, as gangs sometimes do. They were looser than that, much looser, but held together by one theme. Their conversations flowed this way or that with nearly aimless monotony—just as always, just as their nightly journeys around the county—until Solimine's name entered the picture and someone pulled the door shut to Stevie's room.

Everyone seemed to enjoy pitching in and deliberating the best way to carry out a murder. As it had been with the tire-slashing, the group's taste for plotting ran to the fantastic: It would not do to have a straightforward scheme if a wildly contrived plan could work instead. Wanger had plenty of ideas, and Carboni was clever enough to have some of his own, usually involving something combustible. Fake suicide seemed an obvious choice, given that it looked as if Solimine had tried one time and threatened to do it more than once. They could get Solimine drunk, preferably up at his father's house in North Haledon, and slash his wrists, make it look as if he had done it himself. If that plan didn't work, they could get Solimine drunk, cruise out to someplace like Garret Mountain, and push him off a ledge. The idea of handcuffing Solimine and doing something to him was popular: They could jump him at Annie's Road, handcuff him to a tree inside the cemetery, and beat the living daylights out of him. Round and round the ideas went, and whatever else the others might invent, Carboni usually promoted a grand finale: blowing up the car.

The scheming seemed to take on a life of its own. What a rush it was to think about setting something up that would work like a military operation or a gangland hit! And then really pull it off! All this whispered talk of homicide brought them closer together. Invoking the gold medals he had given them, Wanger pumped them about sharing an unbreakable bond. The St. Joseph's medallions symbolized their unity, he said, and he policed the others to wear them all the time. Carboni put the St. Joseph's medal on his neck the day Wanger gave it to him, and never took it off. Stooge kept his inside his wallet. Strelka wore his St. Joseph's medal for a while, and then he'd tire of it and put it aside. When Wanger pressed him, Strelka started wearing the medal again. It was like a cycle. Eventually, Strelka stuck the medal in a filing cabinet in his bedroom and nearly forgot about it. The only person Wanger didn't pester was Castaldo, both because he knew better and because he accepted the fact that gold brought Castaldo bad luck. It didn't matter that it wasn't real gold—it was just the color itself that jinxed him, Castaldo said. Castaldo put it on top of the microwave in his kitchen and forgot about it.

It was about 4 o'clock on a school day in January, and everyone was hanging out in Stooge's basement watching TV, when Carboni started with the fireballs. Carboni, who never quit monkeying with his Zippo, was creating a blowtorch using his cigarette lighter and a can of Stooge's hair spray. Carboni waved a tip of flame near the nozzle, blew the aerosol spray through it, and the spray burst into flame. Wanger was amused, and Strelka was cracking up, watching Carboni messing round with his little homemade flamethrower. Stooge was so used to it, he didn't pay Carboni much mind. It didn't occur to him that Carboni could burn the place down, and anyway, Stooge had made fireballs himself in his house now and then. It was no big deal.

Watching the flame licking at the air, Castaldo started thinking. All of a sudden he got up and went into Stooge's bathroom, poking his nose around.

"Where does you mom keep her cleaning chemicals?" Castaldo said.

Stooge opened the cabinets, and Castaldo rummaged around through the aerosol cans, plucking out this one and then that one, and reading the labels as he went. Castaldo trooped into the living room, a few bottles and cans in his arms. Stooge thought Castaldo wanted to find something really interesting for Carboni to play with, something that would make bigger fireballs, but then Castaldo told Stooge to go upstairs and get the encyclopedias. He wanted volumes A and G.

"What for?" Stooge asked.

"Just do it," Castaldo said.

Stooge and Strelka both went upstairs to Stooge's bedroom and returned with two 1963 World Book Encyclopedias. The edges of the pages were shiny gold. Stooge handed Castaldo one of the volumes. Castaldo flipped through the pages until he found the article he wanted. It was about cars. A colorful breakaway illustration depicted the insides of an automobile.

There were black-and-white pictures of engineers and other busy-beaver types in crew cuts and pockets protectors working on the cars, and there were wildly outdated sketches showing cars of the future. Castaldo started reading bits and pieces of the articles, and he was studying a schematic diagram of a car's power train. Stooge handed him the second volume. Castaldo leafed through an article about gasoline. Castaldo read from the book.

"The liquid hydrocarbons commonly used to produce gasoline have from 4 to 12 carbon atoms in each molecule, and *vaporize* (boil) at temperatures from about 38ⱣC. to about 204ⱣC.," the encyclopedia said.

Stooge had no idea what Castaldo was up to. Then Castaldo looked up at the other boys in the room and started jabbering about gasoline's boiling point, and how it gets up to 1,500 degrees alone inside a car's engine. Stooge was trying to see for himself what Castaldo had read and couldn't see anything in the encyclopedia that came close. Then Castaldo picked up one of the household cleaners. He said the cans exploded at 120 degrees Fahrenheit—and that was how they were finally going to get rid of Solimine. Castaldo was about to put it all together for them.

Everyone listened as he explained his plan. The group would put the aerosol can in Solimine's gas tank. If the encyclopedia was correct, then the gas inside the tank must reach temperatures of at least 120 degrees. On a hot summer day, the tank had to be 90 degrees anyway. So as the gas tank heated up, the aerosol can heated up, too. The can would explode, then the gas tank would explode and then the car would explode. Solimine would go *poof*. The blast would leave no evidence; they wouldn't even be able to figure out for a while who Solimine was.

Wanger, Carboni, and Strelka nodded eagerly. No one said the plan would really work. But no one objected that it wouldn't, either. On camping trips with relatives in Yugoslavia, Stooge had thrown aerosol cans into the fire and watched them explode. He, for one, thought Castaldo's idea might work. Of course, they would have to find a can small enough to fit inside the car's gas nozzle. Carboni didn't say one way or the other whether he thought it would work, but he was beaming at the thought of causing a fire.

"Let's try it," they said.

Everybody had decided that it would take about five minutes to work after Solimine started his car. But Carboni, of all people, suddenly got second thoughts.

"That wouldn't be a good idea," Carboni said. He said Solimine could be going down the road when the aerosol can exploded and that could set off a chain reaction that might blow up the other cars nearby. They could kill some innocent people, Carboni said.

"Yeah, that's a good point," Castaldo said, and everyone else chimed in with his two cents. After discussing it a while more, however, Castaldo made up his mind, and he didn't care to hear any more objections.

"Forget it," Castaldo said. "We're just going to do it."

"What about the innocent bystanders?" someone asked again.

"I don't care, as long as Solimine's dead," Castaldo said.

That weekend, on January 25, 1992, the group decided to carry out the aerosol can plan. It was about 10:30 P.M. Saturday night when they left Stooge's and drove to the Pathmark grocery store around the corner. They crossed under the iron railroad bridge. A faded green sign proclaimed: "Kids—AIM HIGH! DON'T GET HIGH!" They turned into the parking lot of the grocery store at Paulison and Clifton avenues. On the corner nearby stood a whitewashed cinder-block building with a handpainted sign saying "BRAKES."

"I'm going," Carboni said.

"I'm going with you," Wanger said.

The Pathmark store was dated: The aisles were fairly short and close together, and there was an open-walled office above the registers where the manager could keep an eye on things. Wanger and Carboni walked into the store, past a hot table with roasted chickens in foil pans and plastic, past aisles packed with boxes of Captain Crunch and Cocoa Puffs, and past the aisle with the frozen foods. There were tons of aerosol cans in housewares, but all of them were way too big to go inside a gas line. They walked to the farthest aisle on the right inside the store, past the pharmacy and the video rental counter.

There, over in the personal-hygiene section, on a shelf between the baby bottles, baby powder, and other baby stuff, and the feminine napkins and Tampax boxes, the boys found what they needed. It was a 1½-ounce metal can of FDS feminine deodorant spray. The small can, which was approximately four inches long, was displayed in a cardboard package next to a combination douche, enema, and water bottle system.

Carboni smoothly boosted the can, slipping it inside a pocket under his coat, and they walked to the checkouts. Wanger picked up a pack of chewing gum and paid for it, so as not to attract any suspicion from store security. Then they walked out to Strelka's car and got in.

"I got it," Carboni said.

"Got what!" Castaldo said. "What'd you get?"

Carboni brandished the can. In the glow from the parking lot's lights, they could all see what it was. This was certainly amusing to Castaldo.

You need the extra time-release protection, the can said, in script letters with curlicues. *Confidence, every day.*

And below that, in plain type:

Avoid spraying in eyes. Contents under pressure. Do not puncture or incinerate. Flammable. Do not store at temperatures above 120 degrees Fahrenheit. Keep out of the reach of children.

Strelka started the car and bounced out of the parking lot. Everyone was game, but Carboni was especially hopped up.

"This is my chance," Carboni said, "to make a really big fire."

* * *

Strelka hightailed it up to Solimine's place in North Haledon where Rob was living. It would be a trickier venture there, since the police station was right next door, but they weren't going to let that stop them. They drove past Solimine's house on Overlook Avenue, a tidy little colonial that sat beside the municipal building, the public library, and an elementary school. They couldn't see his car, so Strelka headed back to Clifton to see if Rob's car was at his mother's place on Seventh Street.

Stooge had no idea where Solimine lived. He knew Solimine lived with his father in North Haledon, and he knew that Solimine's mother lived about a block from Strelka's, but that was about it. He assumed that everyone else knew, although Carboni wasn't too sure, either.

"Here's his mom's house," Strelka said, and everyone looked out the window at the small aluminum-sheathed dwelling. Strelka slowed the Buick, and they spotted Solimine's white hatchback in the driveway. A light was burning in a second-floor window over the driveway. Strelka pulled around the corner onto Vernon Avenue and parked in front of the Lakeview Heights Reformed Church, a Tudor-style building painted buff and brown. The church had a boxy outline and a squat bell tower capped with a weather vane.

"It's best you two go," Castaldo said, speaking to Wanger and Carboni. "You got black on. No one will see you."

"You got black on, too," Carboni said.

Castaldo looked down at his shirt. He was wearing a black leather jacket and dark pants, but the shirt was no good.

"I got a white shirt on," he said.

Strelka, who was wearing a green flannel shirt and jeans, didn't say anything. He was the wheelman anyway. He wasn't going.

Castaldo, who was in the front passenger seat, watched Wanger and Carboni crawl out of the car behind Strelka. Stooge stayed put. The three of them watched Carboni and Wanger walk down the street in their black trench coats until their heads disappeared behind some parked cars. Half an hour later, they returned. Their faces said it all.

"There's some kind of lock on the gas tank," Carboni said. He looked hard and angry. "I couldn't get inside."

Wanger, all hangdog and solemn, had nothing to say, but he too was visibly angry. He climbed into the backseat beside Stooge, and Carboni followed. Carboni had known Solimine's car would be locked—the kid didn't leave it anywhere without locking it up—but they hadn't expected the flapper door to be locked, too. Carboni pried at the flapper with the blade of his knife while Wanger stood behind him breathing down his neck, but it was no good. Carboni thought that if he could work the blade inside the door slit and get it behind the locking pin, he might he able to spring the pin and pop the flap. But it was no use.

"He got away!" Castaldo said, and then *BOOM*, he exploded, punching his fist into the roof of Strelka's car. Strelka slammed his hands on the steering wheel but said nothing.

"Someone's looking out for him!" Castaldo said. "There's someone on his side." At first it wasn't clear to Stooge if Castaldo was talking about a traitor in their midst or some supernatural force.

"Every time we try something," Castaldo said, "nothing happens. It's like he has someone on his side helping him. I'm telling you, someone's watching over that kid. Someone's definitely watching over him."

As Castaldo thrashed around the car in anger, Stooge started worrying. Every time Castaldo went off like that, it stirred up his insides with a panic attack, the way his father's tantrums always did. The mere mention that there could be a traitor in the group heightened his insecurity, because it seemed only logical that, since he was the weakest, maybe they would suspect him.

"Let's go up to Annie's Road," Castaldo said.

"What for?" Strelka said.

"Just do it. Drive up there."

Strelka, who wasn't in the mood to drive to Annie's Road for some reason, wanted to know why.

"We gotta see if the spirit's there. The shadow in the window," Castaldo said. "Every time the shadow's in the window and we try something, it don't happen. Solimine gets away every time, and it's because the spirit is looking over him. Drive up to Annie's Road and we'll see if it's there."

Reluctantly, Strelka drove out Route 46. He turned in at the marquee for Cinema 46 and into the Holiday Inn lot and snaked behind the hotel to the road below. They sped along over the rough road, the Buick's lights jogging up and down as they approached Dead Man's Curve. Blue ice shrouded the river and reflected dully the lights on the opposite bank. Strelka slowed down and swung into the bend at Dead Man's Curve. As they drove past, they searched the window in the house that was almost directly below the Route 80 overpass.

There it was. The spirit was in the window. Solimine's guardian angel.

"That's it!" Castaldo said. "The spirit! Look!" Everyone saw it. It was the figure of a lady, a dark shadow that seemed to tremble in the panes of glass.

Strelka sped up and drove to the stores by the Hillery Street bridge, where he turned around, and they drove past again, only this time faster. She was still there. The spirit was still in the window. They all saw her.

Not long after their first unsuccessful attempt with the aerosol can, Strelka was driving like crazy to beat Solimine and Wanger to Annie's Road as part of a new plan. Strelka was driving Stooge, Carboni, and Castaldo. Wanger was in Solimine's car. They drove out Route 46 to the cemetery. With a beer buzzing in their heads and the car pushing the speed limit, it sometimes felt as if the car zoomed along Route 46 like a raft through a canyon of colored lights. There was a certain beauty to the strip in the darkness. During the day, the ride was a depressing trip through suburban sprawl. Strelka was weaving through the line of red taillights ahead of them, past neon signs and floodlights and marquees. There were American flags, so enormous they could be measured in acreage, fluttering like sails above the car dealerships. They drove past a long line of fast-food joints and corporate chains: Burger King, Taco Bell, Caldor, Pathmark, Chili's, Shoe Town, Pizza Hut. The stream of cars bottomed out in the valley right about where the Golden Star Diner stood with its ancient sign and the cement building folded over like pastry dough. Strelka had to get off on the Little Falls side to make the U-turn for the divided highway.

The plan, about a week or so after the first aerosol can attempt, involved going up to Annie's Road and once more trying to plant the aerosol can in Solimine's gas tank. This time, Wanger would be with Solimine in order to gain access to the gas tank. Somewhat like the earlier scheme, where the two parties split up and one sneaked back to Solimine's car with a knife, this plan required Wanger to leave the others on the pretext that he had forgotten his hat inside Solimine's car. While everyone else, including Solimine, remained in the cemetery, Wanger would return to Solimine's car, plant the aerosol can, and rejoin the group. Since Solimine would have to give Wanger his keys, Wanger could pop the gas flap, using the button inside the vehicle. When it was time to leave Annie's Road, everyone except Solimine would take off in Strelka's car. A few minutes after Solimine turned over the engine and started for home, he'd be blown to smithereens.

Everything came together for the new attempt on Monday night, February 10. Wanger and Solimine drove to Annie's Road and parked on the U-shaped street in Midgetville. Strelka, who was driving Castaldo and the others, parked somewhere nearby on Annie's Road. They all climbed the embankment beside the overpass, climbed the broken fence, and went inside. They were milling around Annie's tomb a few minutes when Wanger slapped his forehead.

Wanger told Solimine he needed to get his cap. Solimine handed Wanger his keys. There were four keys on the ring, a Bacardi rum plastic key tag, and a tiny penknife. Wanger strode off toward the road below. He did, in fact, leave his cap in Solimine's car, so as to make sure the cover story worked. But he also had the can of FDS deodorant spray in his pocket.

William Geil had lived happily in a flood zone for thirteen years. He had all the peace and quiet a man could ask for, except when the kids and the drug dealers and a certain element came around.

Geil lived on Norwood Terrace, among the other tiny houses that people referred to as Midgetville or Midget Town, on the bank of the Passaic River. Geil had heard the disparaging nickname for the little street himself. He'd heard for many a year. He had seen them with his own eyes come driving through the narrow streets in the little section of Totowa, mostly teenagers, leaning out the windows and yelling and carrying on.

"Look, there's a midget!" the kids would shout, but there would be only some puzzled child who lived there playing in his yard looking up to see who had yelled at him. The kids who screamed and carried on almost always came from elsewhere. But then, everyone came here because of Annie's Road. It was Annie's ghost that brought them here. Geil knew that as well as anyone. People who lived on Norwood Terrace, which was located just below the cemetery on the river bank, told tales about hearing doors slamming mysteriously and footsteps treading up stairs where no one was to be found.

As a teenager, Geil himself had been a grave digger in the cemetery. Even before that, he had heard of Annie's Ghost.

Geil had heard the stories since he was a kid, growing up in the 1950s, and every bunch that had a story about Annie had a different place inside the cemetery where they said she was buried. Some said she was buried under the elk—the life-size monument, inscribed with the word "CHARITY," erected by the Paterson Elks Club. Still others chose one of the various mausoleums inside the cemetery, such as the one with the stained-glass window that Wanger and the others visited.

A yapping dog brought Geil out on the porch that Monday night, and he saw a bunch of kids walking toward the overpass. They had parked a small white hatchback on Geil's street, in front of a vacant lot next to his house. The lot belonged to a woman who had wanted to build a house but couldn't because the government stopped issuing permits for the flood zone. So she kept a garden there instead.

But it didn't matter, because Geil wouldn't have anybody from outside parking anywhere around there. What Geil didn't like was the way drug deals and all sorts of things happened right there in front of his house and how it got his dog all riled up. There were always kids coming around, spray-painting the bridge abutments and the retaining wall with graffiti and holding black masses or what have you. The kids who had parked the hatchback by his house were out of earshot. Geil was thinking about calling the cops right then and there. But then he went back inside, and he had hardly sat down again when the dog started up a second time. This time, he saw one of the kids fooling around over near the car. It looked like he was getting his hat out of the front seat.

"Hey!" Geil said, and the boy turned around, startled. "Get that car out of here or I'll call the cops!"

"Okay," the kid said. "Let me get my friends."

The kid started walking back toward the overpass.

"You go get your friends and get them back here," Geil called after him, "because I'm going to call the cops and get it taken out of here."

"Okay," the kid said.

The kid hustled off. Geil waited awhile. But the kids never showed. So he called the cops.

Not fifteen minutes later, Castaldo and Strelka heard Wanger coming and rushed over to the fence to see how things had gone. Wanger was huffing from the climb and from excitement.

"What happened?"

"Some guy down in Midgetville saw me and threatened to call the cops."

"Where's the can?"

"It's stuck."

"What do you mean it's stuck?" Castaldo said.

"It's stuck. It's down inside the nozzle. They guy came out and shouted while I was near the gas tank, and I took off. I couldn't get the can out of the tank."

Castaldo couldn't believe it.

"How could you be so stupid to get the can stuck and leave it back there?" Castaldo said. "Did he see you come up the hill?"

Wanger had to admit that the guy had probably seen him huffing up the hill.

"How could you be so stupid to come running back up the hill so he can see where we are?" Castaldo said, and he started cursing. Pretty soon the cops came and everyone scrambled deeper inside the cemetery.

In fact, within only a few minutes of Geil's call, the Totowa Police Department sent out a car to check on the report of a suspicious vehicle. When Borough Patrolman Stephen J. Foster showed up at Geil's house, Geil told him what had happened. Geil said he saw one of the kids doing something to the car. Then Geil said the teenager fled. Geil complained about how the people on Norwood Terrace were sick of it with these kids coming around, and he complained that the Borough never did anything to stop them.

Foster took a look at the little white Plymouth hatchback. The passenger-side window was rolled down entirely, and the door was unlocked. Headquarters ran the plate, which came back to Robert J. Solimine in North Haledon. They called Mr. Solimine, who said his son had the car and was probably inside the cemetery.

Foster wrote a summons for failure to have a current inspection sticker and slipped it under the windshield wiper. There wasn't a whole lot more he could do. It was well known that kids went inside the cemetery to goof off, drink, hang out, and sometimes wreck things, but who was going to try chasing some kids around ninety-three acres of a cemetery in the dark? The Plymouth was left on a borough road, and it wasn't blocking traffic. Foster wrote up the ticket for the old inspection sticker and pulled out. The time was about 8:20 on a Monday night. The court date was put down for February 24. Mr. Solimine and his kid were looking at maybe $42 plus costs for this foolishness. Foster didn't notice that the gas flap was open or that a small can of FDS deodorant spray was lodged in the nozzle.

From up on the hill inside the cemetery, the boys watched what they thought was one of several police cars swarming around down by the overpass. A robotic voice sounded from the car's public address system.

"MR. SOLIMINE," the voice said. "THIS IS THE TOTOWA POLICE. RETURN TO YOUR VEHICLE IMMEDIATELY. YOUR CAR IS PARKED ILLEGALLY. RETURN TO YOUR VEHICLE."

A spotlight raked the trestled under Route 80 and bobbed crazily over the garbage-strewn embankment, and the boys went running like hell through the graveyard. They scampered behind tombstones and crouched behind Annie's tomb, looking for more cops.

All the while, Wanger appeared to be sweating—and he had cause: first, because the cops might catch on to the aerosol can in Solimine's gas tank, and, second, if the cops didn't spot it, maybe Solimine would. There was no way to get down there to get the can out of Solimine's gas tank before Solimine could return to the car.

Eventually, they crept back to the fence and peered out to see if the coast was clear. They caught sight of a police car heading up Annie's Road and scurried back inside and waited some more before venturing out again. Another patrol car sat on the other side of the locked gate near the cemetery's Totowa Road entrance. As time passed, it began to seem as if this was a big sport to the borough cops. At least an hour passed before the boys finally got down to the cars.

Strelka, Stooge, and Castaldo were walking to the Buick,

and Solimine walked to his. Carboni was trying to distract him, and Wanger was hunting for a chance to get to the gas tank and get the aerosol can. Luckily, Rob spotted the summons curled under the windshield wiper. He tore it off the car in anger.

"I can't believe this!" Solimine said, showing the others the ticket. "I'm not going to pay this."

Solimine waved the ticket around in disgust. Still fuming as he got into his car, he didn't pay attention to what Wanger was doing by the open gas flap. Of course, Wanger was trying to get the FDS can out of the nozzle. The can was stuck pretty tightly, and Solimine—what with the ticket and the cops circling around—was getting antsy to leave. Wanger stalled, telling Rob he needed to tie his shoe, and Carboni kept smooth-talking, too, until Wanger finally wriggled the aerosol can free from the gas nozzle and dropped it inside the pocket of his trench coat. Wanger got in the car and Solimine pulled out. Everyone's nerves were jangling, and they felt relieved to take off from Annie's Road. They had come very close to success, and they had come very close to being caught.

Carboni and Stooge got suspended after tangling with a teacher they both hated. Carboni hated her so much that he once filled a notebook page with the sentence "Kill the Bitch." He had written it at least fifty times. The school called Carboni's parents and Stooge's mom.

It was up to the parents whether they wanted the boys to spend the suspension at home or in school. Carboni got to go home for his suspension, so Mary agreed to let Stooge stay home, too.

Stooge went up to his room to watch television on the twelve-inch black-and-white TV he kept on his desk. Mary heard him walking around, although his TV was on very loud. In fact, the TV seemed to have gotten louder the longer Stooge was sitting in there.

But Stooge, in fact, had split. He already had sneaked out

and gone over to Carboni's. When Mary looked in on him and discovered that her son had given her the slip, she was livid. She stomped downstairs to the telephone in the kitchen and dialed the Carbonis'. Frank's mother came to the telephone.

"Do my son is there?" Mary asked in broken English, and Carboni's mother said Stooge had just left with her own son.

"What you mean he just left?" Mary said.

"They just left," Carboni's mother said.

"Where?"

"I don't know. Maybe my cousin's house," Mrs. Carboni said.

Mary called the Castaldo house and asked if her son was there.

"No," the voice said, and hung up.

Mary was furious. She grabbed her car keys and stormed out the door. She didn't know where the Castaldos lived, but she knew the name of the street, and for some reason she knew they lived in a white house beside a vacant lot. But she would go door to door if she had to, and she would settle things not only with her son, but with this Castaldo. Before Stooge met Castaldo, he had been an extremely compliant young man. He was a bighearted kid who helped around the house, watched his little brother, and even helped take care of her in little ways, like the time he followed the cookbook and baked her muffins from scratch and brought them to the factory. As he got older, they still talked, and she felt he had no secrets from her. She had an idea of how hard it was to grow up, particularly without having a father around. She gave him some slack about smoking cigarettes, things like that. She only insisted that he let her buy his cigarettes, because she feared someone would lace his with drugs or put some marijuana in the pack. She worried so much about drugs that from time to time she searched his room.

Now, however, Stooge was full of backtalk. Full of deceitful stunts. If she told him he couldn't go out, he would raise his voice and yell at her and sometimes just push open the door and go. If she called sometimes at Castaldo's and asked for him, and one of the kids answered the phone, they might say no—although she would find out later from Stooge himself that that's where he had been the whole time.

Mary pulled into Prescott Avenue and went up to the house. She didn't know which doorbell to push, the first- or second-floor apartment, so she pushed both. Frank Castaldo came to the door.

"Is Tommy here?" Mary asked.

Castaldo said nothing. He opened the door and stepped inside.

Mary saw two women and she saw Carboni sitting on the couch. For a moment, she considered that perhaps Stooge was not here. But there, just behind the door, with his back pressed against the wall as if trying to become invisible, stood Stooge. Mary saw only the profile of his nose and his aviator glasses. Without a word she stepped through the door and slapped him across the face. The blow knocked his glasses off his face. One of the lenses broke.

"You come home this instant! Get in that car!" Mary said.

"Why did you hit me?" Stooge cried. "What's that for! I didn't do anything!"

"You don't want to stay in school? You stay home!"

"I just went to Carboni's house, and he asked me to come over to Castaldo's house."

Stooge picked up his glasses and stalked into the Castaldo's kitchen and sat down, his mother following close behind. When she was calm her thoughts would sometimes tumble out in loose-fitting phrases and jumbled syntax, but now her frustration poured out in angry torrents on her son.

"Why did you sneak out?" Mary was saying. "What's going on? You know you don't have a father. You have to listen to me! I'm your father *and* your mother! What are you thinking? You don't want to stay in school, then you stay home."

Mrs. Castaldo and her daughter Angie tried to intercede, saying, "Calm down, calm down. Everything will be okay." Castaldo had stepped in, too. He told Mary that it would be best if she went home, and he would bring her son home in a little while.

Mary told her son she wanted him in the car out on the street in ten minutes. She walked outside to the car, sat down and smoked a cigarette, and waited. After a while, Stooge appeared with Castaldo and Carboni, and they walked off down the street. Mary couldn't believe it. He was still defying her. She waited a few minutes and drove off.

Half an hour later Stooge showed up in his kitchen. When he came through the door, Mary saw that Castaldo was still with him.

"No," Mary said angrily, pointing at Castaldo. "I want him out. I want him out of here right now. Right now, Tommy. Out."

"No," Stooge said.

Castaldo gestured to Mary to calm down. Then all three sat down at the kitchen table to talk. Castaldo assumed the role of peacemaker and counselor. They talked for a while. Mary told her son he would be grounded for two weeks. She promised him that he would not get away with treating her like that. By the next day, however, Stooge had been ungrounded. It was hard for his mother to stay mad for very long.

7

BY FEBRUARY, THE GROUP'S GOAL OF ELIMINATING SOLIMINE, as opposed to messing up his car, had become firmly established, although their plans shifted daily and sometimes several times daily. A scheme that seemed the solution to all their previous failures might be hatched and cast aside moments after its inception, and several days could pass where no one plotted anything at all. Then, suddenly, there would be an intense conversation about getting Solimine. Stooge, for one, was never really sure how much was goofing around and having adventures, and how much was for real.

On Saturday, February 15, 1992, the five boys gathered at Castaldo's. Soon they got around to discussing their hatred of Solimine and what to do about it. After pulling the door closed to Stevie Castaldo's room, they talked once more about how to get rid of him. Stooge was clicking the buttons on the Nintendo machine, while Wanger and Carboni suggested a new variation on the plot to kill Solimine. They had the idea of handcuffing Solimine to his steering wheel and blowing up the car. All they had to do was get the handcuffs. Whose idea it was wasn't entirely clear. But it seemed, in the telling of it, as if Carboni and Wanger had booted around the idea between themselves. Maybe Castaldo had toyed with the idea too. It certainly bore Carboni's signature. Being the firebug of the group, Carboni must have come up with the idea of blowing up the car, because he also insisted on handling the details of incinerating it.

To begin with, they agreed that Solimine's gas tank would be full. As the idea took shape, they also decided they needed some kind of fuse or wick, such as a twisted piece of cloth rag, to ignite the gas tank. For good measure they would douse the rag with lighter fluid. It might burn quicker, and leave them less time to get away, but the flaming rag also would be sure to ignite the gasoline down inside the tank—and the explosion would be all the more enormous. Solimine would be cinders, they told themselves, and there would be nothing left to incriminate them. Nothing. Not a fingerprint. Indeed, the beauty of this new plan was its simplicity. Unlike everything they had tried until now, the only problem in this venture would be getting Solimine into the handcuffs. Carboni and Wanger decided that the way to get the handcuffs on would be to sell Solimine on the idea that the handcuffs were trick handcuffs, like something Houdini had used to make his underwater escapes. They would tell Solimine that the handcuffs could be unlocked if you twisted them around the right way and found the secret release mechanism. Of course, the handcuffs were nothing of the kind, and Carboni had a key to prove it. The whole scheme seemed ingeniously simple.

Castaldo liked the idea and said so.

"If you're going to do it, then go ahead and do it," Castaldo said, and he too seemed to mean business.

That Saturday afternoon, Robbie Solimine drove by his mother's house in Clifton. He had started a new job, working at a Friendly's restaurant in Bergen County, and he was in high spirits. He had a heart-shaped Valentine's Day card for his mother, rimmed in lace.

"With love, Mother, from your son," the card said. And inside: "No matter how grown up I may be, or how independent I feel, no matter the distance between us, or the time between visits, there's one thing that you can always be sure of... how very much I love you. Happy Valentine's Day."

Maggie took Robbie shopping for some pants, which he needed for his new job at Friendly's. Before parting, Maggie gave him a can of cookies and a Jets sweatshirt. It was a sweet visit. It was also the last time she would see him alive.

Across town at Castaldo's, the day was swallowed up sitting in front of the TV set and driving all over the place in Strelka's car. There was no clear focus on anything. Everybody loafed at Castaldo's for a while, and then they decided to go to Fun 'N Games. They hung out at the arcade for an hour, and then drove to the Robin Hood Inn to pick up Wanger, and then back to Castaldo's, where everybody loafed some more. Around 3:30 in the afternoon Melanie showed up after doing some baby-sitting for a relative, and that distracted Castaldo for a time. Now and then someone griped about Solimine, but, because Melanie was around, there was no more discussion about doing something to him. The day crossed over into darkness.

That evening around 9 o'clock, Solimine rang the doorbell. Someone let him in, and he stood in the living room of the Castaldo house, wearing a polyester uniform that appeared dopey in the extreme. Solimine told them about his new job. He had liked it so much already that he had asked for additional hours, and he was even going back tomorrow, he said. Solimine suggested that everyone come to his dad's place in North Haledon because his father was in Pennsylvania and he had the house to himself. He also wanted to change clothes. So everyone got back into the cars and sped up to Solimine's house. Wanger and Solimine rode in Solimine's car, while everyone else took Strelka's.

The meandering course of the day at Castaldo's had wiped away the earlier discussion about burning Solimine alive inside his car, at least for Stooge. But as Strelka parked the LeSabre in the municipal lot beside Solimine's house in North Haledon, it became clear that the group actually planned to carry it out. On the way, Strelka made a stop at Carboni's house. Without saying what he was doing, Carboni ran inside to get a pair of handcuffs. There was nothing special about them: They were silver, and they were operable. Carboni had purchased them at one of the Main Avenue fairs. He also fetched an old T-shirt. Carboni ripped a strip of fabric from the shirt to make a wick, and he grabbed a 4½-ounce aluminum can of Zippo lighter fluid, putting everything inside his coat. Carboni kept quiet about what he had, because Melanie was in the car, but he couldn't resist pulling out the handcuffs. They were sitting beside Solimine's house, parked in the lot of the North Haledon Police Department, waiting for Solimine, when Carboni drew the handcuffs out of his coat, dangling them from a fingertip.

"What are those for?" Melanie said.

Carboni smirked.

"You're not going to try more tricks with Rob, are you?" Melanie said.

Big grins from Carboni and the other guys.

"Why do you keep hanging out with Rob if you don't like him?" she said. It wasn't so much that Melanie cared whether Solimine was played the fool, because she too found Solimine annoying, but she just couldn't get it: Why let him come around when there were enough people at Castaldo's house, including her, competing for his attention? Castaldo told Carboni to put the cuffs away.

Solimine showed up and let everyone inside. They turned on the tube and clicked channels until they found a spring break movie with plenty of sand, suds, and sex. But the movie sucked, everyone had seen it anyway, and Melanie wanted to go home, or at least go to Castaldo's house. Melanie said she had to baby-sit the next morning, and she needed to go to sleep. So they left. Wanger and Carboni got in Solimine's car, and Strelka followed them.

Before they left North Haledon, they needed to get gasoline. Both cars pulled into a station near Solimine's house. Strelka's car was tanked, so he pulled to the side of the gas islands. They all made sure Solimine had his car filled up. When it was done, Wanger paid for it. For some reason, Solimine insisted on paying one cent, and the total came to $15.01. Then they took off again, heading to Castaldo's to drop off Melanie.

The cars zoomed down McLean Boulevard to Main Avenue, then over to Prescott. When they arrived at Castaldo's house, Frank went inside with Melanie. Solimine, meanwhile, peeled out in his car and carried on like a lunatic, ripping up and down Prescott Avenue and making such a fuss, with the tires screeching and smoking, that Mrs. Castaldo came out into the cold to scold them for making so much noise. They were going to wake up the neighborhood, she yelled, and she told them to come in or knock it off.

Castaldo came back out without Melanie and both cars took off, heading south on Main Avenue toward Wanger's part of town, under the yellow railroad bridge, past the cemetery and the church Wanger attended, and then under Route 3 heading toward Nutley and Bloomfield. First Solimine would lead, until Strelka caught him, and then Strelka would follow, and the game of car tag continued until they jumped onto Kingsland Street, driving behind a tower of pale blue glass at Hoffman La Roche and then over to the broad, tree-lined avenues of Bloomfield. They passed over the Garden State Parkway, drove past the blazing neon sign for Eye Drive, past an IHOP and well-tended suburban homes. They turned and turned again, past a sign that said Brookdale Park, a place Stooge had never seen before. The park opened at dawn and was supposed to close at 9 P.M. But it was obvious that Castaldo and the others weren't the only people who came after hours.

Entering the park, they passed through an alley of low-hanging trees, then spilled onto a smooth roadway that circled a great rolling plain. There were playing fields and meadows and huge shade trees towering overhead. In the daylight hours, the park's roadways and paths were crowded with joggers, skaters, and people walking dogs. The boys drove to a parking area near a duck pond and a playground. Nearby there was a stone wall, which enclosed a football field's grandstand. Streams of geese crossed the dark sky, their passing marked by a chorus of weird insistent shrieks.

Solimine parked on one side of the small parking lot and Strelka parked on the other. The cars ticked in the cool air as the boys got out to stretch. They smoked cigarettes and listened to the quiet all around them. It seemed like the right place to carry out the plan. Wanger had offered to do the talking. If anyone could get Solimine to go along, Wanger could. Then, after the pest was cuffed, they would pop the gas flap, run a rag down into the gas tank, and light it. As proof that they had covered all the angles, Wanger and Carboni agreed to disconnect the horn on Solimine's car. Solimine could scream and bang on the horn all he wanted, and it wouldn't make a peep.

Solimine slipped into the shadows to take a leak, and the others stood around smoking cigarettes. When Carboni was sure that Solimine wasn't looking, he jumped back into Solimine's car and shut the door. Carboni lifted off the plastic cover to the horn, poked around among the wires inside the steering wheel, and disconnected them. Wanger stood nearby to run interference. Disconnecting the car horn took only a minute or two, and when Carboni got out of the car he spoke a few words in Italian to Wanger. Wanger walked over to Solimine, who was standing by his car. The handcuffs lay in Wanger's hands. Wanger showed them to Solimine.

"Hey, Rob," Wanger said. "I know this trick."

Wanger's sales pitch was smooth—very low-key and patient, as if it wouldn't matter one way or another what Solimine decided to; but Solimine wanted no part of it.

Just then, another car pulled into the lot, and some other kids got out of the car, making noise and goofing off. Castaldo watched the newcomers warily. There were too many people to keep going.

"Let's go," Castaldo said.

Everyone agreed. Wanger and Carboni got back into

Solimine's car, and the others climbed into the Buick. Solimine, who almost invariably peeled rubber or fooled around in the car when he had to go anywhere, jammed on the steering column with the heel of his hand. But the horn didn't work, of course. The lid was loose, and Solimine realized that someone had unplugged the horn.

"Goddammit!" he hollered. "Who's been fucking with my car?"

"Easy, Rob," Wanger said, holding his palms up. He had a big disingenuous smile on his face. "We was just screwing around, playing a trick on you."

Solimine railed for a while until Wanger and Carboni cooled him off and Carboni reconnected the horn. They passed off tampering with Solimine's horn as a gag, nothing more, and eventually Solimine let it go.

They left the park, and Strelka followed Solimine's car as it snaked its way back through the suburban streets to Clifton. They went up Broad Street past the radio towers and under Route 3 again to the Grand Union grocery store, where Solimine wanted to get some No Doz. They drove into Wanger's neighborhood, down South Parkway past Wanger's house, then past a weedy soccer field and playground at the end of Wanger's street, which ended at Route 21. They all turned off at Entin Road, a small industrial complex in the Delawanna section of town. Both sides of the pothole-filled roadway were lined with factories, truck lots, and warehouses. The complex wasn't far from the site of the old railroad station. There were five or six companies there, including the Greater New York Box Co., SK Products Corp., and Gemini Industries, a consumer electronics company. The boys drove past one of the Gemini buildings and came to a dead end at the slope of the old Delaware, Lackawanna and Western railroad embankment. The wooded embankment, which now carried New Jersey Transit commuter trains, rose about thirty feet above the lot, and there was plenty of room in the lot below for tractor trailers to park or turn around. The Gemini plant at the end of the street was lit up as if it were midday.

Solimine pulled in and stopped with the car running. Strelka pulled up too. Enormous wooden spools, emptied of their electric cables, were stacked in a jumble. Nearby was a truck. The more the boys watched the truck, the more they became convinced—or at least Solimine became convinced—that the van belonged to a private security firm. Solimine saw the truck and the surveillance cameras on the buildings and the lights inside the factory, and he got the jitters. He rolled down the window of his car and called to Strelka.

"Let's get out of here," he said. "I don't want to get in trouble." Solimine said he was worried they would be picked up for trespassing.

As they drove out from the factories, Castaldo decided to throw in the towel. He told Strelka he had to go home because his uncle from New York was coming the next morning to visit. Very early, like 6 o'clock or 6:30.

"It's just not going to happen tonight," Castaldo said. He was annoyed that another opportunity seemed to be evaporating. It was the spirit Solimine had hovering over his life.

So Strelka headed across town toward Prescott Avenue. He flagged down Solimine to tell him they had to stop at Castaldo's, and then drove on. Solimine, who had only Wanger in the car, took off after them.

It was about 2:45 A.M. when the radio in Lieutenant Richard Less's patrol car reverberated with a fuzzy voice. Less was driving through the parking lot by two bars around closing time when the dispatch came over: Be on the lookout for a motor vehicle with New Jersey license plate registration number GZY-98G. By coincidence, just as he heard the dispatch, Less saw the plate in question on the back of a white hatchback at the corner of Main and Madison avenues—about a block north of Castaldo's house. There were two occupants in the vehicle. Less decided to go after the car, but his cruiser got jammed up behind traffic. The car turned off on Clifton Avenue, and he lost it.

But not more than ten minutes later the hatchback swung

into view again, turning off Van Winkle Place—now about seven blocks from Castaldo's. Less hit the cherrytops. He came up close behind the Plymouth with the police lights flashing and pulled the car over at the corner of Lexington and Lake.

Solimine was alone in the car now. He took out his wallet with the United States Navy's insignia on it. He handed Less his license, which listed the North Haledon address.

"What are you doing over here?" Less asked.

"I just dropped a buddy off around the corner," Solimine said.

Less returned to his car to check things out. After talking with headquarters, Less realized he had pulled over Solimine by mistake. Another patrolman evidently had called in a license-plate number identical to Solimine's but for one digit, which explained why the number was supposed to come back to a gray van, not a Plymouth Laser. Less looked things over, and everything seemed in order. Walking back to the hatchback, however, Less's eye was drawn to the right rear quarter panel of Solimine's car. Less walked around the back of the car. Then he came back around and stood by the driver's window, handing Solimine his license back.

"You know your gas flap was open?" Less said.

Solimine said he didn't know.

Well, it was, Less said. The officer made some remark about taking care with such things. But Less also said Solimine didn't have to worry about it, because Less already had closed it for him. Solimine was free to go.

Solimine caught up with Strelka again in the Dutch section shortly after Less had pulled him over, and he told them what had happened. They all wanted to go somewhere, especially Wanger, who told Solimine to follow Strelka.

Strelka drove around some more until he turned up Gregory Avenue toward Weasel Brook Park. Just before the park, Strelka's taillights brightened, and the Buick turned in at the elementary school on Gregory Avenue. It was School No. 15, a dull and imposing two-story brick structure built in 1923 on the brow of a little hill overlooking the city and the park.

Strelka's car coasted up the driveway to the left of the schoolhouse. The driveway covered a shallow grade almost 200 feet to the crest of the hill, then bent right toward a concrete playground in the building's rear. Just beyond the bend in the driveway was a small plot of muddy grass. Smack in the center of the lot, which measured about fifty feet long and fifty feet wide, stood a Dumpster. A single streetlamp nearby cast a lemony glow over the yard and the school. Farther behind the school grounds, and almost concealed by trees, were condominiums. To the left, down a slope screened by a thin copse of red oaks, elms, ashes, and mulberries, lay Weasel Brook Park. Down the middle was a filthy stream that had given the county park its name. Geese and ducks paddled around in the water, and in the warmer months, especially in the spring, wedding parties posed for photographs by the stone bridge. Carboni's house was just on the other side of the park.

Strelka parked near the Dumpster, but Solimine wouldn't stop spinning his tires, so Strelka was going to have to move. Solimine was flooring the car until fantails of mud and grass shot up from the wheels. As the wheels spun, the car sailed very slowly through the muck until the wheels bit the macadam and jolted him forward. Disgusted by Solimine's antics, Strelka moved his car up to the steps beside the school. Carboni pointed out that this was a better spot anyway: Parked here by the steps on the side of the building, Strelka's car would block Solimine's car from being seen from the street below. What's more, the distance from Solimine's car would give Strelka a jump on getting away before Solimine's car exploded. Meanwhile, as they all got of Strelka's car, Solimine kept going up and down the driveway, goofing off in the mud. Wanger was becoming impatient that he wouldn't stop. It was not exactly the kind of commotion they needed for their plans to succeed.

Finally, Solimine shut off the engine and opened the car

door and dangled a foot on the ground. The others gathered in a semicircle around him as Solimine searched for good songs on the radio. This time, Carboni was taking a crack. He held the handcuffs up to Solimine and started talking.

"Hey, Rob," Carboni said. "Check it out. These really are trick handcuffs like James was trying to show you. Why don't you see if you can figure out how they work?"

"No," Solimine said.

"Come on, Rob. We tried it. It's easy. We ain't going to do nothing. Just see if you can figure it out without the key. It's no big deal. What are you scared of? Don't be a baby."

"I'm not going to try," Solimine said, and it sounded as if he was long past making up his mind. He kept shaking his head, scrunching up his face and repeating that he wasn't interested.

When Wanger decided to try again, he took the cuffs from Carboni and moved closer to Solimine, imploring him to give the trick a chance. Maybe Solimine could handcuff just one wrist to the steering wheel? But Solimine was no more interested in taking up Wanger's challenge than he had been when Carboni was doing the talking.

"Come on, Rob," Wanger said "It's just a magic trick. They're my grandfather's cuffs. I seen him do it a couple of times. He can get out of them in, like, thirty seconds. It's like something almost anybody can do. You can trust us. You don't got nothing to worry about."

"No. I will not put the handcuffs on," Solimine said. "You'll handcuff me to the steering wheel and leave me here."

"Rob, come on," Wanger said, pleading now, almost begging. Carboni kept joining in, and now and then Strelka tried.

Solimine was getting frazzled. But he wasn't going to be backed into it.

"Look, Rob, if you can't get out in a couple minutes we'll unlock them," Wanger said.

"Ain't nobody handcuffing me to the steering wheel," Solimine said.

"Yo, Rob. Look—we got the key right here," Wanger said.

To demonstrate, Wanger snapped the handcuffs shut and asked Carboni for the key to show that the cuffs would open again with the key.

"You can't try this?" Wanger said. "Just once. We'll just lock you to the wheel, and we'll give you, like, five minutes. That's all. We won't go nowheres. We won't do nothing. We'll turn our backs, give you five minutes, and that's it."

"No, I said!"

"Look, Rob," Wanger said, taking a different tack. "Step out of the car. Watch Stooge, see how he does it."

Solimine got out of the driver's seat and Stooge took his place, smiling nervously. Wanger cuffed Stooge's right wrist with one loop, braided the stubby chain through the wheel, and locked the second loop to the steering wheel. Like a circus bear, Stooge shook the handcuffs around in a curious dumb show.

"See, he's getting it," Wanger said. "He's done it before."

"You're cutting the circulation off," Stooge said.

They unlocked Stooge.

"Okay?" Wanger said. "See, Rob? That's all I wanted to do. No big deal."

"I'm not doing it," Solimine said.

"Rob, put on the cuffs," Wanger said. "You are going to put on the cuffs."

Solimine pulled in his foot and slammed the door. He knocked the button down, locking the car, and rolled up the window. He turned the engine over as the boys called to him through the window. Strelka went around to the passenger side, rapping on the glass and asking Solimine to open up. Solimine inched the car up. The group stepped up beside the car, and Solimine backed up the other way. In an absurd two-step, the car and the boys alternated their movements back and forth. Strelka kept pounding on the window.

"Come on, Rob! Let me in."

Strelka told Wanger and the others to step back, give Solimine some room. Solimine sat with the car idling in the spongy earth, as if he was thinking. Then he reached across the car and unlocked the passenger side so that Strelka could get in.

"Take it easy, Rob," Strelka told him. "Everything's all right."

Solimine's eyes were bright with alarm.

"What's going on? What is Wanger up to?"

"Nothing's going on," Strelka said. "Wanger's just fooling around. You know Wanger, he just wanted to show you something."

"Wanger's acting too weird. I don't know what's going on, but I think I'm going to leave."

"He's just pissed he didn't get to show you the trick."

"Well, I don't like the way he's acting. I don't know what he's up to, but I think I'm going to leave."

"Take it easy," Strelka said.

It took a while, but Solimine calmed down and Strelka got into his own car and they left School 15. They decided to go get something to eat. Wanger offered to pay, as a kind of goodwill gesture.

At Dunkin' Donuts on Main Avenue a few minutes later, they walked past the floodlit racks of doughnuts behind the counter and took seats on the stools—each of them careful, in manly fashion, to sit one or two seats apart from each other. It seemed as if they took up the entire store. Stooge sat between Strelka and Carboni in the far corner. Solimine and Wanger sat close to each other near the door. The huge glass windows afforded a view of the original Clifton City Hall, a gas station, and a Palmer video store. The billiard hall was just down the street. As they drank sodas and ate, Solimine seemed to have put aside the confrontation at the school.

Wanger was quietly seething, however. Although he seemed calm enough, he must have decided that he had had enough of the ruses, the stratagems, and the plots. The time had come to carry out the job that had to be done, and to get it over with. He would kill Solimine himself and he would simplify things immeasurably. Having stayed nearly an hour, the group decided to leave. They were going out the door when Wanger grabbed Stooge.

"Stooge," Wanger said under his breath. "Give me your boot lace."

Stooge looked down at his work boots.

"What for?"

"I'm going to strangle that idiot at the next red light."

Without questions, Stooge knelt down and pretended to be tying his boot as he undid the lace and handed it to Wanger.

Stooge, who had given Wanger the boot lace partially because he wouldn't have known how to refuse, told Carboni what had just happened as they were getting into Strelka's car. Carboni said nothing.

They all got in and followed Solimine.

After a while, they all drove to Carboni's house. Stooge was going to spend the night there, and Wanger was going to call a taxi. Strelka and Solimine dropped off their passengers and took off to Solimine's father's house in North Haledon, where Strelka was going to sleep over. Before he parted from the others for the night, Wanger came up to Stooge and pressed the boot lace into his hand.

"What happened?" Stooge said, relacing his boot.

"I couldn't do it because Carboni got into the wrong car," Wanger said. "Carboni has to be in the car for me to do it."

As was their habit after a night of carousing, Carboni and Stooge slept in on Sunday. Stooge was up first, and he snapped on the TV. Carboni, who finally stirred sometime around 1:30, went downstairs to take a shower and shave. Stooge watched TV while Carboni got ready, and then they headed for Castaldo's on foot. By the time they were at Prescott Avenue, it was almost 3 o'clock in the afternoon.

Castaldo was up and let them in. He was in an owlish mood because of something with Melanie. Carboni and Stooge sat down on the couch in front of the TV while Castaldo fumed and the rest of the Castaldos bustled about talking or carping at each other. Mrs. Castaldo was working in the kitchen. Mr.

Castaldo was in his room or ghosting about, as usual, while Angie and Stevie popped in and out of the living room or talked with the kids dropping by.

People seemed always to be coming and going and doing their own thing at Castaldo's but now there was a heightened sense of anticipation in the air. For most school students, Sunday was generally a lazy day, the mood wavering between relief because it was a day off from school and gathering dread, since Monday and the return to school were almost here. But February 17 marked the beginning of winter break for the Clifton School District, and the kids who came by the Castaldo house were excited. On the calendar in Stooge's bedroom there was a single entry: "NO SCHOOL," written in Magic Marker through the squares Monday through Friday. Although everyone they knew practically had been partying since the last day of school on Friday, now they were on the eve of an entire week without teachers or other grown-ups telling them what to do, and there was much discussion about how the week could be put to good use.

Soon Strelka showed up. He had spent the night at Solimine's house in North Haledon, but he couldn't remember a whole lot about what had happened. He remembered following Solimine in the door, sitting down on the couch in front of the TV, Solimine saying he had to take a leak, Solimine heading for the bathroom, and then . . . boom. Sleep hit him, and Strelka snored until midmorning Sunday. He blinked his eyes, saw Solimine getting dressed to go to work or someplace, and then Strelka went home, where he crawled into his own bed and slept some more. By the time he had awakened and showered and gotten to Frank's, it was 4 o'clock, and the commotion around the Castaldo household was steadily rising. Strelka himself barely was through Castaldo's door when Wanger called from the Robin Hood Inn asking for a ride, and then Melanie showed up for Round 1 with Frank in the kitchen. Carboni let Melanie in the front door, and she went to the kitchen, where it wasn't long before Frank and Melanie were screaming at each other as the boys and Castaldo's brother and sister sat in the living room.

By that time Strelka had gone and returned with Wanger, who had been complaining on the ride to Castaldo's house about how crowded the restaurant was. When they walked into the living room, Castaldo and Melanie were sitting at the dining-room table, giving each other the silent treatment. As they had all been able to determine with their own ears, Castaldo was furious with Melanie because, as usual, she had shown up late. In fact, she hadn't even shown up. Although she had been the one to call him, tracking him down at the pool hall after calling his house, and although she had told him to come meet her on Main Avenue in twenty minutes or a half hour, her hair and makeup and so on had made her half an hour late. Castaldo left the pool hall and went to the corner, but after a while, when Melanie didn't show, he walked on home by himself, and by that time the other guys had shown up.

"Let's go outside," Castaldo said, and Wanger followed him. With a toss of his head, Castaldo directed the others to follow him. They stepped into the front hall, pulling the door to the living room closed.

"So what happened?" Castaldo asked.

"Rob wouldn't go for it," Wanger said. His voice was filled with anger and regret, a kind of regret that made him just a little sheepish as he explained what happened.

"We tried to get the handcuffs on him, but he wouldn't let us. He just—he got away again," Wanger said.

"He got away again," Castaldo said. "He got away again."

Castaldo muttered the words a few times, balling his fists. His whole body seemed to coil and tighten.

"We tried, but Rob just wouldn't do it," Wanger said.

"I can't believe it. Somebody's really looking out for him," Castaldo said, his voice echoing in the small foyer. He grit his teeth and shook his head, then looked away, as if he had discerned at last in the dim hallway that Solimine's fate had been decided by a force larger than himself. The tension seemed to drain from Castaldo's face and arms.

"Look," he said. "I don't care anymore. I don't care what you do. I'm sick of it. I'm sick of this bullshit. I'm sick of Solimine. I'm sick of trying stuff and it never works. The kid has someone looking out for him."

Wanger was shaking his head in solemn agreement.

"Every time you guys go out to do it, nothing happens," Castaldo said. "Forget about it. Just forget about it."

"No, it's going to happen," Wanger said. "It's going to happen tonight. I am definitely going to do it."

Castaldo made a dismissive gesture with his hand, and they went back inside the living room.

Melanie was talking on the telephone with a girlfriend. With an indifferent air—and only because discussion of a party would not violate their vow of silence or other terms of the conflict—Melanie turned to Castaldo, covered the receiver for a moment with her hand, and asked him if he knew about a party in Bloomfield. Castaldo said he did, and they resumed their standoff—although everyone listening realized that they would probably be going to the party after patching up their feud.

Melanie told her girlfriend to come by Castaldo's house and hung up the telephone. Then she and Castaldo walked out to the front porch to settle things.

Strelka picked up Castaldo's phone and started dialing Solimine's number. The other guys were fooling around with him, jabbing at the buttons as he waited for the phone to ring, and goofing off so loud Strelka had to strain to hear and be heard. The dog was barking, too.

On the other end of the line Strelka got Solimine's answering machine, which greeted everyone with an intro of some heavy-metal music, and then he waited for the beep.

"Ha! Solimine!" Strelka said. Expecting that Solimine was sitting there half asleep or just monitoring the call, Strelka was stalling, dragging things out, waiting for Solimine to pick up.

"Solimine, C-O-M-E ONNNN . . ."

Beep.

Strelka turned around.

"Who pressed the button?" he said.

It was Wanger, being obnoxious, reaching around him, poking at the buttons, as Stooge and Carboni horsed around in the background laughing and making noise. The Castaldos' dog was yapping, too.

"C-o-m-e onnnn," Strelka said.

Beep.

"Come on, Rob. Come on."

Beeeeeep.

"Oh, Rob," Strelka said, his voice rising into a falsetto as he mimicked his idea of what a woman having an orgasm sounds like. "Oh . . . oh . . ."

Beep. Beep.

"Come to the phone," Strelka said. "Well, if you come home, I'm by Frank, so call and . . . we'll do something, okay? The time is now 6:35 and 15 seconds, and Angie wants to give you a big hug when ya come."

Beep.

"So do I!" Wanger bellowed in the background. "So do I!"

"Bye," Strelka said, and hung up.

Someone suggested taking a ride up to the mall or Annie's Road. Melanie had to wait for her girlfriend to show up. Everyone else piled into Strelka's car for a drive to the mall and Annie's Road. They soon returned, however, because the mall was dead and no one had felt like even getting out of the car at Annie's Road.

When the group returned, Melanie and Stevie were playing cards at the dining-room table with Melanie's girlfriend, who had walked over to the Castaldos' by herself. There was no sign of Solimine. Castaldo asked Melanie what she wanted to do, and Melanie told him that she wanted to go to this party over in Bloomfield. In fact, she said that their friend Tony already was on the way over to pick them up.

"Where's the party?" Stooge asked.

"It's at Sue Scrudato's," Castaldo said.

"Where's that?"

"Bloomfield."

There was talk about whether Strelka and Carboni and the others wanted to come. Carboni couldn't because his cousins had a birthday party and he felt he should make an appearance later, but Stooge was voting to go along. First, though, Stooge had to go home because he was expecting a long-distance phone call from his father, but after that they could go to the party. Castaldo cut him off, saying he didn't think it was right that he could invite other people to someone else's party. Outside, Tony had shown up to give Castaldo and Melanie a ride.

Wanger was watching Castaldo intently as Castaldo got ready to go. He and Strelka, Stooge, and Carboni followed Castaldo outside onto the brick steps. Wanger touched Castaldo's arm as the others huddled around. Everyone else was getting into Tony's car.

"It's definitely going to happen," Wanger said to Castaldo. Wanger spoke so that no one outside the group could hear.

Castaldo made a sour face, an expression almost impossible to read, as he tugged on his coat. It was hard to tell if he had lost interest in the venture, if he doubted anything would come of Wanger's big talk again, or if he was just angry that the prior attempts, including last night's, had turned out so badly.

"If you're going to do it," Castaldo said, "do it tonight."

"Definitely," Wanger said. "I'm going to do it."

"You better. Or don't bother coming back," Castaldo said.

"I'll see what I can do," Wanger said.

The first thing Strelka did when he came in the door to Stooge's basement was call Solimine at his mother's, leaving a message for Solimine to stop by. But Solimine didn't need a message. Around 7 o'clock, Solimine found everyone at Stooge's. He had found them on his own, without getting the messages on his machine in North Haledon or from his mother's house.

Stooge was waiting to hear from his father. The telephone call was supposed to come at eight, but he watched the hands move around to the hour on the small cuckoo clock with the growing realization that the telephone wouldn't ring for him after all. Everyone hung out, watching TV in Stooge's basement apartment, when they started feeling antsy to cruise around. Solimine said he had to go up to his house. He needed to change out of his work clothes or something—Stooge wasn't quite sure.

So Wanger got into Solimine's car, and everyone else—Stooge, Strelka, and Carboni—got into Strelka's car. They went tearing off toward Solimine's house, screaming up Route 17 and playing cat and mouse until somewhere near the Marcal factory in Elmwood Park, Solimine lost them. He and Wanger just vanished.

Around 8:30, Wanger buzzed the Castaldo house and Stevie Castaldo let him in. Wanger said hello to everyone in the living room—Mrs. Castaldo and a couple of Stevie's friends who were watching TV. Stevie told Wanger that Frank was still at the party with Melanie.

"I know," Wanger said. "Come on outside."

Stevie and a friend followed Wanger outside onto the porch. Solimine, who was snarfing up french fries from a paper bag, blasted the horn through the window of the driver's door and walked up onto the porch. Stevie said hello. They all talked for a minute or two, and Solimine started saying something to Stevie's friend. Wanger took Stevie aside.

"I need an electrical cord," Wanger said. Wanger made his request as matter-of-factly and politely as Wanger always asked for things, but for some reason, he was speaking in hushed tones.

"What for?" Stevie said.

"My grandma got me a new stereo and it doesn't reach the outlet."

Stevie told him they might have one downstairs.

Stevie Castaldo and Wanger went inside and down the

basement stairs into a phantasmagoric heap of junk. Clothes, newspapers, old kitchen stuff, tools, you name it, spilled out of broken cardboard boxes and paper bags. Stevie rummaged around awhile, as Wanger looked over his shoulder.

"Hold on a second," Stevie said. "I gotta take a leak."

Stevie went into the toilet in the basement, and Wanger kept digging around. When Stevie came out, he started looking again and eventually found a cord.

"Here," Stevie said, wadding it up.

Wanger thanked him and stuffed the cord into his trench coat and followed Stevie up the stairs.

Strelka drove all the way up to Solimine's father's house in North Haledon, but with no luck. They all drove back to Stooge's. About an hour later, around 9 o'clock, Solimine and Wanger showed up. Wanger said they had been driving around for a while and then bought some hamburgers at the Roy Rogers on Main Avenue. Wanger told them they had even stopped by Castaldo's house for a while, but Frank wasn't there. Only his parents and brother and sister, Wanger said. Wanger said he and Solimine sat on the couch waiting for the others and when no one showed up, they came back to Stooge's, where they hung out in front of the TV some more.

As they sat in Stooge's living room, Strelka noticed that there was something strange about Wanger. Wanger, who was beside Solimine on the small blue couch in front of the television, would be very quiet for a long period of time—which was unusual for him—and then all of a sudden he'd start chattering at the top of his lungs. One moment, Wanger was lost in thought about something, and the next, his voice would boom with some silly remark. There also was an inexplicable aura about him, as if of some impending, exuberant joy that he could only barely stifle. Strelka felt like asking him what was so funny.

Stooge's mom, who wasn't feeling well, called to him to come upstairs. She wanted to know who was in the basement making a racket.

"My friends," Stooge said, and he went back down.

Wanger stood up from the couch. He asked Strelka to give him a lift to the Quik Pick 'Ns, a convenience store on Clifton Avenue a few blocks from Stooge's house. Wanger said he wanted to buy some smokes.

An unlikely couple walked through the door of the Quik Pick 'Ns Super Deli on Clifton Avenue a little after 9 o'clock.

There was a tall preppy-looking guy in tinted glasses and a long dark coat whom Lauren Doczi had never seen before, and he came in with a younger kid with light hair and an attitude. Doczi, who was eighteen years old, thought she recognized the younger kid as she worked behind the register. The younger kid looked like the leather-jacket type—kind of disgruntled, a bad character. Each of them looked strange, and they looked even stranger together. They both walked halfway into the store and stopped near the bread.

Doczi was alone in the store. Clerks in the convenience store were expected to make sandwiches, keep the coffee fresh, and keep an eye on the kids who came into the store to goof off or shoplift. She was sure now the runtier kid had been in the store before. In fact, he had been one of the kids who tried to buy cigarettes underage, and Doczi refused him. She remembered the kid leaving and coming back with someone who was old enough to purchase cigarettes legally, a kid who spoke with an Italian accent.

"Excuse me," the preppy one said.

He was standing by the bread, calling across the store. He didn't have to shout because the store wasn't big—it was laid out almost like a triangle, with bubble gum–colored counters by the register and a wall of full-length refrigerator cases opposite—but his voice carried loudly. There were no other customers in the store.

"Do you have any twist ties?" the preppy one said.

"Twist ties?"

"Or anything to tie something up with?"

Doczi gave them a doubtful look.

"You mean like . . ."

"Twist ties," the preppy one said. "Like what you'd tie up plastic bags with."

Doczi explained that the store didn't sell any twist ties, which came with the garbage bags and maybe the bread. But not separately.

"We have string," she said in a questioning tone, and she showed them the aisle.

The preppy walked over to the aisle, which wasn't in view of the register, and disappeared. The short kid with the sharp features gazed around the store. Then he walked past the wall filled with refrigerator cases, under the frosty blue neon signs that said "Dairy," "Ice Cream," "Frozen Food," and "Soda Fountain," and disappeared in the same aisle with his friend. They were there awhile.

Then the short one went to the coffee counter and poured himself a cup of hot cocoa and stood sipping his drink near the salad bar. A moment later the preppy came up to the counter. He laid down two packages of beige shoelaces. Odd, Doczi thought.

The tall kid also bought a bottle of Gatorade and some cigarettes. Doczi rang everything up, including the hot cocoa in the short kid's hand. The total came to $5.02. The preppy handed over a twenty-dollar bill and two pennies.

Doczi gave him his change, put the stuff in the bag, and the boys left.

Very odd, Doczi thought.

"Take me somewhere quiet," Wanger said when they got inside the Buick, and Strelka pulled out of the parking lot at Quik Pick 'Ns and drove through the Municipal Center, past the police department and the recycling center, and then down Colfax Avenue to the high school. The ride was short. Strelka turned into the high school's gate, drove past the brick pillar with the school's name, turned left into the seniors' parking lot, and shut the car off under one of the towering oak trees. They could see up Colfax as far as the old blue Shulton plant.

As Strelka watched in the darkened car, Wanger reached into a pocket of his trench coat—where he had a religious medal in a plastic envelope, a scapular, and prescription bottle of Tegritol, an anticonvulsant—and pulled out a wadded-up electrical cord. Wanger said he had got the cord from Stevie Castaldo.

"I told him I needed it for my stereo," Wanger said.

The cord, which was kind of ratty looking, was an outdoor extension cord that must have been at least twenty-five feet long. Wanger started doubling it back and forth until the coil formed an oval loop about four feet long. Explaining as he went along, Wanger smoothed out the coil on his lap so that all the strands lay evenly, and then he pulled it taut, making a single, neat loop.

Then Wanger tore open the plastic bubble on a package of shoelaces. He took the first twenty-seven-inch-long lace and lashed it crosswise around the coiled-up electrical cord, the way a person might wrap a final length of rope around its middle before putting it away. He tied the laces securely, explaining to Strelka which kinds of knots he was using and how he had learned this knot or that knot in the Sea Cadets.

Then Wanger took out another shoelace and wrapped it the same way at another point farther along the coil. He did the same with a third shoelace. Then he was done. The electrical cord was shaped like a figure eight with two big loops and a long middle where the strands of cord were bound tightly together with the shoelaces. A fourth shoelace from the package dropped to the floor of the car, but it wasn't needed anyway.

With three shoelaces Wanger had transformed the electrical cord into a clever weapon. The shoelaces held the device together so that Wanger could slip his hands through the loops on each end—like straps on a ski pole—and grasp the thick bundle of cords in the middle. This middle part of the cord would do the work. The loops at each end ensured that he wouldn't lose his grip on the garrote even if his palms became sweaty, and the multiple strands guaranteed that the device wouldn't snap—an unlikely event—or fall across only part of the neck, or across the chin, perhaps blocking the full potential of force. The weight of the multiple strands gave it enough heft to make it more maneuverable—he would need to whip it quickly over Solimine's head in a cramped space—and the added thickness would cut into his own wrists less sharply than a single cord, thereby minimizing any discomfort or pain he might feel when the cord took hold.

Wanger slipped his hands into the garrote and flexed it as Strelka watched. Strelka had been silent the whole time, amazed and impressed at what he was seeing. He didn't ask Wanger what he planned to do, because he didn't have to ask—it was obvious what Wanger had in mind. Wanger folded up the garrote and stuffed it as best he could inside the pocket of his trench coat.

"Okay. Let's go back to Stooge's," he said, and Strelka did.

Back at Stooge's, Carboni was wondering where Strelka was, because now he needed a ride too. Carboni's cousins, twins who also happened to be Castaldo's cousins, were having a birthday party, and he felt he should put in an appearance. Not going, Carboni felt, would be disrespectful. So as soon as Strelka pulled up, he asked for a ride, and Strelka had no problem giving him one. Wanger went along.

Strelka was driving down Clifton Avenue to drop off Carboni somewhere on Hudson Street when Wanger piped up from the backseat.

"Look, I got it."

Carboni didn't say anything. He didn't feel like turning around.

"Put your head back," Wanger said.

Carboni lifted his chin a little, put his head back. Wanger dropped the garrote over Carboni's head and gave a gentle tug.

"See?"

"Yeah," Carboni said, feeling a bit nervous. He didn't like the feel of the cord around his neck.

"See?"

Strelka was watching the whole time without saying anything. Carboni knew what was coming. He felt it in his gut. Strelka felt it in his gut. It was going to happen this way now, soon perhaps, with this weapon, with Wanger alone, somewhere out there in the night still ahead of them. Wanger took the cord from around Carboni's head, and there was the sound of rustling as he inserted it in the pocket of his trench coat again. The lights streamed over the hood of the Buick. They drove back to Stooge's, although they knew they would have to turn right around and come back because Carboni said he wanted to stay only a half hour.

About a half an hour later, everyone was outside the house where Carboni and Castaldo's cousins were celebrating a birthday. Strelka laid into the horn a few times, and Carboni strolled out. He came over to the window of Strelka's car, saw Wanger wasn't there because he was riding with Solimine, and got into Solimine's car himself. Then they took off. Someone said they were heading for Brookdale Park again, and soon enough they were driving down Clifton Avenue to Broad Street, past the shopping plaza and Ploch's Garden Center, where Stooge and Carboni had been hauling Christmas trees a few weeks earlier.

Stooge had been watching the tube with Solimine when Strelka and Wanger got back from Quik Pick 'Ns. They sat a few minutes, joking around and goofing off before going to get Carboni. Everyone was being nice to Solimine—or at least treating him like he was one of the gang, and doing it in a way that didn't seem like acting. Solimine didn't seem half bad, either, and it was enough to make Stooge forget all about the talk of killing him. Who knew what to make of all that, anyway? Last night, they could have just forced Solimine into the cuffs if they wanted to, and Wanger—he took the boot lace, yes, but nothing happened—was always acting strange. Solimine seemed to be having an all-right time of it now. Wanger was being normal, and Castaldo—despite his last remarks, which could be taken almost any way, if you thought about it—wasn't even here.

As they drove to Brookdale Park, down Broad Street past the BASF plant and the radio station and its blinking red towers, Stooge thought about their discussions that day and couldn't remember anyone—other than Castaldo—bringing up the idea of the handcuffs again or anything else. What the hell, he thought. They were cruising around. They were going places.

8

IT WAS DÉJÀ VU—THE SAME ROUTINE AS THE NIGHT BEFORE when the handcuffing plan seemed to develop of its own will before petering out at dawn. Once again, and moving at almost an identical pace, the night unfolded with two cars full of boys on an aimless course through the suburbs, past gas stations and minimalls, past factories and parks, to the same places, almost to the very same street corners they had visited less than twenty-four hours earlier. They drove to Brookdale Park, surveyed the same parking lot, and, again finding too many people there despite the late hour, didn't bother to stop. They kept driving, cruising through Bloomfield to Nutley to Clifton, before returning to the factories two blocks below Wanger's house in the tiny industrial complex. They drove to the end of factories by the railroad cut, saw the lights on again at the Gemini plant and the security cameras, and turned right around without stopping. It was déjà vu the way Solimine jerked the window down in his car, sticking his head into the cold night to say that he didn't like the place, that he was too nervous to stay.

After leaving the factories near Wanger's house, they crossed into Carboni's neighborhood and soon turned off Gregory Avenue and drove up the asphalt driveway beside School

15. The yellow light flooded the small plot of grass. The muddy tracks from last night, when Solimine kept gunning his car up and down the macadam driveway, were faintly visible. Solimine backed his car onto the grass at the top of the asphalt driveway and parked near the Dumpster. Strelka pulled in almost beside him, facing the same way. That way, the boys could see the street below.

It was as though he couldn't resist: Solimine started doing skids in the soft earth—peeling out, spinning his wheels backward, now forward, now backward, gobs of mud roostertailing this way and that. Some of it spattered Strelka's car. Then he backed onto the grass under the streetlamp. It was as if they were following a script. Just as they had the night before, Strelka parked by the steps so that they could haul ass before Solimine's car blew. But Solimine kept pulling forward, pulling back. Mud everywhere. And then he started hitting doughnuts in the tiny lot.

"What an idiot," Wanger said under his breath, as Solimine gunned the car and it pinwheeled in circles, flicking out grass bits and glop.

"Yo! Rob! Cut it out!" Wanger said.

Solimine stopped spinning mud finally, and got out of his car. The Laser, its white sides dappled with mud and bits of grass, came to rest beside the Dumpster. Strelka and Stooge got out of the Buick and walked back to Solimine's car. They all went off, except Solimine, to take a leak in the bushes. Stooge could hear Wanger mumbling something to Carboni.

There were trees at the rear of the lot and trees that stood along the driveway and dropped over the hill to the park. They screened the condominiums below. When the trees had leaves, the small lot had almost a gladelike feel to it. In a matter of weeks, they would be budding. Tonight, however, the air had a bite to it. The street light beside the Dumpster picked up a sheen of moisture in the mud. The light was almost theatrical. Over behind School 15—Carboni's old school—the city lights hit the sky with a faint orange glow and a vivid moon hung over their heads.

Wanger and Carboni walked back to Solimine's car and stood by the driver's door. The others joined them in a semicircle around Solimine's car. Solimine turned on the radio, which was usually set to a hard-rock station like Z100, dangling one foot outside the car as the boys talked and the radio played. It was cold enough to be uncomfortable standing outside, and Stooge wanted to go back to Strelka's car to get warm. Wanger got into the back of the hatchback behind Solimine, his neck goosed a bit to fit his huge head, and Carboni walked around to the passenger side and sat in the front, flicking his bangs. It was getting on to midnight. Strelka asked Wanger when they were leaving, because he was beginning to worry about his curfew.

"Let's stay another fifteen or twenty minutes," Wanger said. "I want to listen to the birds."

Wanger mentioned something about the crickets, too. Outside they could hear the swoosh of traffic from behind the condominiums or the dawdling drone of a jet overhead. Stooge looked at Strelka with a face you use to show that some idiot had said something unbelievably stupid. Birds? Crickets? It was February. Nobody could hear a thing. It was a strange wish, but what the hell, Stooge thought, Wanger always seemed to like nature and being outdoors. But Stooge also had a feeling something was going to happen. Stooge and Strelka walked back to the Buick by the school stairs.

"We can't leave because Wanger wants to listen to the birds," Strelka muttered. They got into Strelka's car and he lit a cigarette and they waited. A few minutes passed and Strelka worried more.

"I got to get home," Strelka said. "I got to get home, or I'm going to be in trouble." He kept looking back at Solimine's car and piddling around with the dials on the radio, as if he might get lucky and find a new station. Solimine's car showed no signs of life. It just sat there. But Solimine wanted to leave too. He put his seat belt on.

"This is no fun," Solimine said. "What's there to do up here? Come on, let's go."

"Hold on, Rob. Relax," Wanger said.

"This is stupid. Let's just go," Solimine said.

Their heads were dark shapes. Wanger seemed to be shrinking inside the cramped darkness behind Solimine's seat. Cool air leaked through Solimine's window, which was cracked open slightly.

"Adesso," Wanger said. It was almost a whisper.

"No," Carboni said—although he had idea what Wanger meant.

"Adesso," Wanger said again.

Carboni knew Wanger was saying something in Italian but couldn't figure out what it meant. This time, though, Wanger's voice carried a tone of insistence. Whatever it was Wanger was saying, he didn't want "no" as an answer.

"Sí," Carboni said.

"Let's go," Solimine said. "I'm getting out of here."

"No, no," Wanger said. "Wait! Listen to the sounds."

Wanger was stalling. Everyone else, it seemed, was ready to go. Strelka and Stooge sat in Strelka's car up ahead grumbling to themselves; their heads kept turning back toward Solimine's car.

"What the fuck are those guys doing?" Strelka said. "Can you see what's going on back there?"

Stooge looked and saw a car sitting there, still.

"I'm going to see what Wanger's up to," Strelka said, and he got out of his car and stalked back to Solimine's hatchback, stiff-legged.

"I gotta get out of here," Strelka said to the trio in Solimine's car, and he bent his face toward the small opening on the driver's window.

Wanger was hunched over behind Solimine's seat, holding something to his gut—the electric cord that he had tied off into loops with some shoelaces back at the high school, maybe, but Strelka couldn't tell.

"Just wait a few minutes," Wanger said. "We're listening to the sounds."

Strelka snorted. Here we go with the crickets and birds again. He told them he was leaving.

They watched Strelka trudge back to the Buick.

"I'm ready to get out of here," Solimine said.

"Just a couple minutes more," Wanger said.

"This is stupid!" Solimine said. Now he was annoyed, and he raised his voice. "Let's go!" he said. "We're wasting our time."

"Come on—can't you just do it for me?" Wanger said. "You can't do me a favor?"

"No," Solimine said. "We're leaving right now." Solimine reached for the keys in the ignition.

"All right, all right, all right," Wanger said. "I promise. We'll leave. Let's just say a prayer before we leave."

"Huh?"

Wanger wanted to say a Hail Mary. Solimine didn't want to. He didn't want to do anything except start up his car and go somewhere else.

"Please? Come on. Just do it. Just once. Say it after me," Wanger said. "Just once."

Wanger started it.

Hail Mary . . .

Solimine argued some more, and Wanger began again.

Hail Mary . . .

Wanger got Carboni to go along too, and Carboni followed, repeating the first words. Confined inside the car, their voices droned with a weird sound. Wanger wanted the two of them to say the prayer in unison, repeating after him. Solimine kept protesting, but Wanger continued.

Hail Mary, full of grace . . .

This time all three started the prayer, as Wanger wanted. But Solimine took a wise tone and kept interrupting, and Wanger took them back to the beginning of the line and started over.

Hail Mary, full of grace

The Lord is with thee . . .

Now they saw Strelka throw open the door of the Buick

and walk toward them. Another interruption. There was a look of disgust on Strelka's face when he came to the window. His hands were dug into his pockets.

"Look, I gotta get of here," Strelka said.

"All right, all right," Wanger said. "We're saying a Hail Mary."

Strelka turned away before Wanger could say more, walked back to the car, careful not to slip, and got in.

"I think he's going to do it!" Strelka told Stooge.

"What's going on?" Stooge said.

"Wanger has them saying the Hail Mary," Strelka said. He slammed the car door shut and Stooge swiveled his head around, straining to see through the rear window what was going on.

"One more time," Wanger said.

Hail Mary, full of grace,
The Lord is with thee.
Blessed art Thou among women,
And blessed is the fruit of thy womb, Jesus.

Wanger intoned each line. Solimine and Carboni followed. Solimine's still head was bowed. Carboni's eyes were tightly closed and his head rested backward against the car seat. The three voices chanted together. They were almost done, a line or two from the end.

Holy Mary, Mother of God,
Pray for us sinners now
And at the hour of our death.

There was a rustle of clothing, Carboni heard the soft *plap* of the cord as it swiped Solimine's Jets cap, and then he felt the hat on his lap. There was a dull jolt, as if something was thumping somewhere deep inside the car—and then frenzy. Carboni opened his eyes and saw the cord around Solimine's neck.

Wanger had whipped the electric cord over Solimine's head and lunged backward in the seat, pulling with all his might. The cord ran under the headrest to Wanger's hands and around the forearms, cutting into the wrists. Solimine's head was pinned to the headrest, and he was driving his chin down to his chest as if to work it under the cord. He was spitting, tearing with his fingers at the cord, trying to get under it. His eyes were squeezed shut and short moans, almost like grunts, rose from deep in his chest. Wanger dug the heels of his tennis shoes into the bottom of the seat, bracing them for more leverage.

Solimine thrashed now, but the seat belt pinned him. His legs were kicking and the right leg flew up, making spastic jerks, fishlike, against the windshield glass. His arms flailed around inside the car, reaching for the cord, reaching for something, and he got ahold of Carboni and raked his stubby fingernails into the back of Carboni's neck. Wanger's body was still pulling, his upper body veering away from Solimine into the opposite side of the rear seat, as Strelka walked back to Solimine's car to see what was happening. When he peered in the window, he couldn't believe it. He ran back to his car.

"He's being killed!"

Stooge looked at him, a blank face of unrecognition.

"Wanger's killing Rob!" Strelka said. "He's really doing it this time!"

Stooge jumped out. The two Tommys ran up to Solimine's car on the driver's side. At first they couldn't see what was going on because of the glare on the window. Strelka opened the driver's door, and the door alarm inside Solimine's car began beeping. Wanger was pulling with all he could muster. The space inside the car seemed very small and dark, but Stooge could see the light gray electrical cord—it almost appeared white—around Solimine's neck. The cord was round like an outdoor cord, about as thick as a dime, and it was wrapped in Wanger's fists. Crossing his wrists over each other as he pulled, Wanger scrunched up his body into a tiny area, his feet wedged against the seat, yanking on the cord.

"James! Stop it! James! Stop!" they screamed.

But it was almost over. Solimine moved more slowly. He kept picking at the cord, almost dreamily now. His arms had slackened, were dropping away from his throat. Wanger screamed at Strelka to get the baseball bat from his car and bash in Solimine's head, but the other boys just kept yelling at him to stop.

"Get the bat!" Wanger screamed. "Hit him over the head to make sure he's dead!"

"Hell no!" Strelka said.

"I knew you would turn on me! I knew I couldn't trust youse!" Wanger yelled. "I knew I couldn't trust youse!"

But Wanger didn't need a bat. Solimine's body seemed to loosen. The thrashing was gone and all the fight had left him. His eyes were open now. Solimine's tongue stuck out, as if he had vomited it. His skin seemed remarkably pale, and Stooge thought he was already dead.

"Stop! Stop! Stop!" the three boys yelled. They shouted into the car, but none grabbed for the cord or for Wanger's hand. Solimine was motionless. His head was tilted, as if his neck had snapped. His torso leaned toward the passenger side. At the least tug, Solimine's head bobbed. Wanger would pull, release, pull again, and Solimine's head bobbed like a toy's. A tear rolled down his cheek.

Carboni felt Solimine's throat and panicked.

"He's dead!" Carboni said. "He's not breathing! I don't feel a pulse! Stop!"

Then Carboni felt the wrist. Nothing. He jumped out of the passenger side and ran around the car to Solimine's door. He touched the throat for a pulse again, and patted his hand inside Solimine's shirt to see if his heart was beating. He pushed on the chest and air escaped—for a moment making Carboni think that Solimine might still be alive, might be breathing. But Solimine was dead.

Meanwhile, Stooge turned to stone. His face was white, and he couldn't move. Strelka had to grab Stooge and shove him toward the Buick. They got to Strelka's car and slammed the doors. Strelka gunned the engine. The car lurched into gear, bit the macadam, and tore down the driveway. Wanger and Carboni had told Strelka to wait for them, but Strelka and Stooge waited only two seconds at the bottom of the drive, and looked at each other. Wanger and Carboni were still back at Solimine's car.

"I'm not waiting!" Strelka said, and he sped off. He took a left out of the driveway in front of the school and headed down Gregory Avenue.

Up on the hill, Wanger had gotten out by then and come around by the driver's side to pop open the gas flap with the button inside the car. Then he went back to the gas tank nozzle. All the while Solimine's car kept beeping, because the driver's door was flung open. Carboni, now certain that Solimine was dead, plucked the car keys from the ignition and flung them onto the dashboard to stop the alarm's noise. Then Carboni snatched the electric cord from around Solimine's neck and pitched it across the roof of the car to Wanger. Wanger grabbed it and stuffed it inside his trench coat. Leaving Solimine's body, Carboni went around the car again to the passenger side—but before he did, he also grabbed the keys from the dashboard. Carboni was about to bolt through the woods in the direction of Weasel Brook Park and his house beyond, but Wanger was working on the gas cap.

"Frank, where's the lighter?" Wanger said.

Wanger was at the rear of the Laser unscrewing the gas cap, then spearing a tip of white rag down the gas pipe. Carboni doused the rag with lighter fluid from the can in his pocket. His fingers were digging for the Zippo lighter, then fumbling to open the lighter, and then he snapped the flint. The rag started to burn. At the first sight of the flames racing up the rag, the boys ran into the darkness. Carboni first, then Wanger. Behind them the rag flared white for a moment, then settled, smoking, charring the white paint, and dying. Both boys, already down the hill through the trees, expected the car to blow any second.

Carboni and Wanger crashed through the bare branches and down the wooded slope on a footpath. They raced toward a footbridge—lungs huffing, hearts beating, waiting to hear the car blow—and crossed over the stream. They hurried in a semicircle to Third Street. Then they slowed down to walk so as to look inconspicuous and catch their breath.

At the same time that Wanger and Carboni were running through the park, Strelka and Stooge were driving in circles in Strelka's car. They drove past the school at least twice. They went down Clifton Avenue to Main, where they thought they heard an explosion.

"I wonder if that was the car," Strelka said. They cruised up Gregory Avenue past the school one more time and they could see that the car was still intact. There was no sign of Wanger and Carboni.

"Drive by one more time," Stooge said.

"No," Strelka said, "I don't want to keep driving by. Someone might see the car passing and it might look suspicious."

Stooge couldn't think. He felt horrified. He had known something was going to happen, he understood that Solimine was about to be killed, but he had no idea what the truth of it might feel like. Up until then, he hadn't really cared if Solimine got killed. He didn't even know Solimine, really, so nothing registered. Until the killing, he hadn't seen the electrical cord, and he had no idea what Wanger had in store for Solimine. It was as if a failure of the imagination, some frail and almost insignificant ability to foresee the outcome of all the cartoon-strip plans, had concealed a monumental evil. Now Stooge felt frightened about what was coming next, frightened because he was in the group, frightened because they could get caught. Wanger, who would never hurt a fly, had killed another human being with his bare hands, and Stooge was scared out of his wits. He didn't want to wait around for anything. He and Strelka circled in the Buick for twenty minutes. They were panicky. They didn't know what to do next, so they decided to find the others.

"Go past Carboni's house—they might be there," Stooge said. They turned down Third Street and then onto Clinton to see if the lights were on in Carboni's bedroom.

Meanwhile, Carboni and Wanger reached Clinton Street and bolted up Carboni's front stairs as quietly as they could.

Carboni opened the door and they passed the living room, where Carboni's father was on the couch watching television, and headed to the kitchen. Wanger was thirsty. Carboni made a quick telephone call. The time was about 11:30 P.M. when he dialed Stooge's number. Stooge's mother answered, thinking it was probably her son calling to say he was coming home and why he might be late. Carboni's voice, without a greeting of any kind, took her by surprise.

"Is Stooge home?" he said.

"No," Mary answered, and she was thrown off for a moment. Her son was supposed to be with Carboni, so where was he?

"Where is he?" she asked.

"I don't know," Carboni said. "I lost him."

Then Carboni hung up—no "good-bye," just hung up—and Mary started half wondering, half worrying where Stooge was. She thought he was staying at Carboni's house, but he wasn't there, and if he wasn't there, he should have been home by now. Or he had better be on his way.

In Carboni's house, nothing seemed out of place. Carboni's father was watching something on television in the living room.

"Hi. What's up?" Carboni said. He gestured to his father, who looked up but didn't say anything.

Carboni was making himself seem calm, trying not to show how out of breath he was. He and Wanger went to the kitchen in the next room and filled a glass of water for themselves from the tap. Wanger couldn't contain himself, even though Carboni's father was just on the other side of the wall.

"We got rid of him! We finally got rid of him!" Wanger said. He was trying to whisper, stage whisper, but it seemed as if he was screaming with exuberance. "We did it!" Wanger said.

"Shut up!" Carboni hissed. "Shut up!"

Wanger got the message on the third try and quieted down, and they clomped upstairs to Carboni's bedroom on the third floor. Carboni's little brother and little sister were with relatives. Carboni closed the door, and—to his surprise—Wanger uncorked again.

"Yes!" Wanger cried. "Yes!"

Wanger punched the air, almost capered around the room.

"I can't believe that idiot's dead! I got rid of the pest! We got him! We finally did it!"

"Shut up!" Carboni said. He was worried his father would hear.

Carboni sat on his bed, opened a window, and lit a cigarette. He almost couldn't light the cigarette because his hands were trembling. The keys and the gas cap were spread like trophies on the floor against the wall. It was almost midnight. There was noise on the stairs, someone coming, and then the two Tommys appeared. Stooge had seen the light burning in Carboni's room. Carboni's mom answered the door, and said Carboni couldn't come out because it was past midnight, but she let them in.

Stooge stared at the gas cap and the keys. As they stepped into Carboni's room Wanger, who was sitting on the floor with the glass of water, started up again, a big shit-eating grin across his face. He was stomping around, banging on the floor. "Let's celebrate! It's on me!" Wanger said.

"What the fuck are you talking about?" Strelka was saying.

Wanger suggested they throw a party, treat themselves to a diner, do something, and he even had a box of assorted cookies he had left in Strelka's car that he wanted to bring upstairs for the celebration.

Strelka was wide-eyed with terror. Stooge needed both hands to use his cigarette lighter and still couldn't work it. All three boys were telling Wanger to pipe down.

"Why'd you do it?" Strelka said.

Yet a flicker of satisfaction streaked through Stooge because they had accomplished their mission. Then he realized the enormity of what had occurred. The thoughts in his head flowed in wild circles, as if each rush of joy—there was no other way to describe it—carried a huge fear of what was next. They were looking at each other with fear and with questions in their eyes about what to do now. Carboni was trying to think of a story to save themselves. Wanger told them they needed an alibi. Somebody else proposed telling the cops that they hadn't seen Solimine all night, but that got shot down. Everyone agreed to say that they had seen Solimine, they had been hanging out, and then everyone split up at 10 o'clock and left. That settled, it was time to tell someone else.

"Let's go see Frank," Wanger said.

Before they left, however. Wanger called his grandmother to see if he could stay over at Carboni's house. The other guys couldn't hear what she was saying, but it was obvious she was saying "no."

"Please, Grandma?" Wanger pleaded. "Come on, Grandma, let me stay over. I just want to stay over tonight. Let me stay. All right."

Then he hung up the telephone.

As they were getting ready to go, Wanger asked for a bag of some kind to hide the electric cord and the gas cap. Carboni handed him one of the plastic grocery bags that he kept to line the wastebasket in his room. Wanger stuffed the gray electrical cord and the gas cap inside and shoved everything deep inside the pocket of his trench coat. Carboni caught only a glimpse of the electrical cord before it went into the bag. He kept Solimine's keys.

The lights were on at Castaldo's when the four teenagers arrived in Strelka's car. Strelka parked in the driveway. They buzzed the doorbell and Castaldo came to the door. Melanie was on the couch watching TV, looking bored as usual, as the boys trooped into the living room. Mrs. Castaldo, Angie, and Steve were there. Castaldo sized up the group and could tell something was up, but they all sat down on the couch.

Mrs. Castaldo ducked her head out from the kitchen.

"Oh, you back again?" she asked, and returned to the kitchen.

Wanger followed her. He had taken off his cap, but he was walking around in his black trench coat. Mrs. Castaldo was in the kitchen washing some of the dishes that had piled up with all the kids around. Wanger went in, the unzippered trench coat flapping around him, and sat down at the small kitchen table. He asked how Mrs. Castaldo was and if she minded making him a cup of espresso.

"Fine, James, fine," Mrs. Castaldo answered absently, and she stepped away from the sink to brew the coffee for him. As she measured out the coffee and water, Wanger started fooling with the half-breed Chihuahua, until the yapping got on Mrs. Castaldo's nerves.

"Stop, James!" she said. "Stop, you're making him bark."

Wanger apologized, but it was obvious he thought he was being funny with the dog. Castaldo walked in to see what was going on. The other guys were acting weird on the couch, as if the cat had got their tongue.

"James," Mrs. Castaldo said, "I thought I told you I don't like this Solimine kid. I no want you to bring Solimine around here no more. Understand me? I don't like the way that boy carry on around here. You hear what I'm telling you?"

"Don't worry, Mrs. Castaldo," Wanger said brightly. "I had a long talk with Rob. He won't be bothering you anymore."

It was obvious he had something to say and was looking for a chance to take Castaldo aside.

Castaldo jerked his head, and he and Wanger walked out of the kitchen into the dining room. The other guys were watching from the couch.

"We gotta talk to you, Frank," Wanger said.

"All right, let's go outside and talk," Castaldo told the others.

Castaldo put on his sneakers and coat. He told Melanie to stay put. Then Castaldo and the boys stepped outside onto the brick stoop. They stood on the lower set of stairs farthest from the house. Castaldo stood on the top step, and the others peered up at him. The moon was very bright in the deep blue sky. They all started talking at once.

"Quiet down!" Castaldo said. "One at a time."

Castaldo drew himself up, tilted his head, and fixed Wanger with a look.

"He's dead," Wanger said.

Castaldo seemed to be unable to believe it. He looked at Strelka.

"Is he dead?"

"Yeah," Strelka said.

Now Stooge.

"Is he dead?"

"Yeah," Stooge said.

Castaldo smirked.

Afterward, the boys would describe Castaldo's smile as a sign of satisfaction, approval of a job well done. That was how police understood the moment, although there had also been something ambiguous about his expression, as if he couldn't believe that Solimine had been killed, and the news of it was so unbelievable as to be ridiculous.

Castaldo reached into his shirt pocket for a cigarette and fired it up. Everybody went back up on the porch; they were retelling parts, correcting each other, wondering what to do with some of the evidence. They were edgy, scared, proud of what they had done, and talking in businesslike tones to conceal their fear. Stooge had never been a part of anything like their group in his life, and he had never accomplished anything so momentous—but he was terrified, too. They talked a few minutes more, and then Stooge and Carboni said they had to leave. They asked Strelka to drive them home, and Frank asked if Strelka could take Melanie, too.

Wanger told Castaldo that they still had the murder weapon, the gas cap, and Solimine's keys in a bag inside his coat. Carboni said they should toss the plastic bag with the cord and the gas cap over by Royal Silk, over where there was a little stream. Castaldo suggested that they could also just pitch the stuff in the garbage because the collection was tomorrow.

Carboni fished the keys out of his pocket and flipped them over to Castaldo.

"What am I supposed to do with these?" Castaldo said.

Castaldo looked at them intently, as if they contained something of Solimine himself: four keys and a penknife on a ring with a plastic Bacardi rum key tab.

"Keep them as a souvenir," Wanger said.

"They're going in the river," Castaldo said.

Strelka was heading for his car. He was Carboni's ride, and he was going to drive Stooge and Melanie home, as well. Nobody said anything in the car.

"What's everybody so quiet about?" Melanie asked.

"Tired," Strelka said.

Strelka dropped off Carboni and Stooge first. Then he drove Melanie home. Wanger walked back inside Castaldo's house and called Clifton Taxi for a ride.

Carboni and Stooge crept upstairs to Carboni's room on the third floor. Carboni flipped on a light. Stooge turned on the TV. There was a desk at one end of the room, the bed and dressers at the other, and TV and stereo equipment in between. They were restless, smoked cigarettes, fidgeted, but couldn't talk. The events of the night seemed to be knotted up inside.

Stooge was on the couch, where he always slept when he stayed at Carboni's, nodding off in front of some TV show. Stooge kept hearing police sirens and expected to hear an explosion. None came.

Carboni lay down on his bed. He shut his eyes, but everything seemed to be shaking: The room was shaking, the bed was shaking, and he pressed his eyes shut harder. He couldn't make it stop. His head seemed to be rattling. Every time he lay down, the shakes grew worse. Everything in front of his eyes were going back and forth, very fast, left to right. So he sat up. He sat up on his bed, everything shaking, and eventually disappeared inside a deep sleep.

There had been two cabs on duty at Clifton Taxi that night, one responsible for Wayne and one for Clifton, so it took a little while for the radio car to show up. The cab finally came at 1:35 A.M. The driver beeped the horn, and Wanger and Castaldo went out on the stoop. Castaldo didn't bother to put on his coat, but stood in the cold in his jeans and T-shirt, hunched over with the hands thrust deep in his pockets. He and Wanger talked for a moment, and then Wanger shot out his hand. Castaldo put out his hand and they shook before parting.

Wanger went around to the back of the cab while the driver was scribbling in the log. The driver was a young guy, and even sitting down you could see he was short, a chubby guy with a closely clipped black beard that wreathed his round face and gathered at the chin in a neat Van Dyke. Wanger got into the back of the cab and slammed the door, and the driver radioed back to headquarters that he had made his pickup at Prescott Avenue.

"South Parkway," Wanger said, and he told the driver the address.

Although the driver, a guy named Michael Holly, had lived in Clifton all his life, he had been a hack in the city only for about a year, usually working for his father-in-law at Clifton Taxi on the three-to-three shift, and sometimes he needed some directions. He knew South Parkway was cut in two by the old Delawanna rail line, so he asked the kid with the glasses and the derby hat how to get there.

Wanger gave him a general description, and the driver put the car in gear. Wanger scrunched down low in the seat. The driver didn't exactly watch his fares while he was driving, for obvious reasons. What was there to see? But Holly couldn't help noticing how the kid with the glasses appeared to be keeping a low profile on purpose, as if he didn't want anyone to see him. Wanger was leaning against the car door, gazing through the window as they drove across town. He watched the houses and streets going past in a blur and kept an eye ahead on the road, saying nothing except for the monosyllabic directions to his house. He kept his hands in the pockets of the trench coat.

Holly pulled the cab up in front of Wanger's house. There was a small pine tree and an American-made car in the driveway. The car was clean.

"That's five dollars," Holly said.

Wanger handed him the fare and a dollar tip.

"Thanks," Holly said, and he radioed the South Parkway drop-off. The time was 1:44 A.M. as the kid walked to the front door and disappeared inside.

Strelka slipped in the door. The ground seemed to be wobbling. He turned on a light and then the TV. Then he looked around. There was a strange distance to everything in the house, as if the proportions were off. Ordinary objects seemed different now, almost weird: The "Home Sweet Home" sampler with the little wooden bears. The ceramic duck on the kitchen counter with the utensils poking out. Strelka turned on the TV and sat on the sofa in front of it, the light washing over him, and he tried to get a grip. He lit a cigarette. His mother and father had only recently given in on this, and now he was allowed to smoke openly. He just needed to get a grip. He wanted to go back to the school. He wanted to go back and see what had happened in the parking lot, but he knew he couldn't. If he were found there he might be accused of murder. The TV talked, but he couldn't follow what it was saying for very long. His mind seethed over the same spot like ants. His head wouldn't stop. It kept going, but without direction. The thing had gotten ahold of him.

Susie came downstairs. Strelka said hi and drifted back inside to the place in his head that was roiling with images so fresh they couldn't really be called memories yet. His mother asked him where he had been. Strelka said he had been with Mark. He meant in his head Mark Yacono, a friend of his, but he just said Mark. He did not want to betray his nervousness to his mother, but he was so pale that Susie knew something was wrong. He must have banged up the car, she thought. She became a little alarmed but remained outwardly cool.

"Tommy, did everyone get home?"

"Yes."

"What did you do? Smack up the car again?"

"No," Strelka said.

Strelka was all yeses and nos. He was ashen and glassy-eyed, but Susie couldn't tell why. She prodded him, but she couldn't get it out of him. They smoked cigarettes, she on one sofa and he on the other. Strelka kept saying nothing was the matter.

"All right," she said. "I'm going to talk to you in the morning."

Strelka stayed on the sofa for a while. He felt like crying and turned out the light, although he wanted it on because he was afraid. He wanted to go back to the parking lot. The answer might be there. Fear closed in on him in the darkened living room, lit now by the colorful maw of the TV, and he cried. He cried very quietly for a little while until his eyes closed and everything that had happened at the school had vanished without a trace.

Robert Solimine, Sr. and Robert Solimine, Jr. *(Peter Serling)*

James Wanger with his grandfather, Paul Columbo, displays his prize-winning poster in an anti-drug campaign.
(Peter Serling)

Wanger receives the Boy Scouts' religious medal.
(Peter Serling)

Wanger poses in his Sea Cadets uniform.
(Peter Serling)

Paula Wanger and son James.
(Peter Serling)

Robbie Solimine (middle row, far left) and the Clifton High volleyball team pose for their 1991 yearbook photo. (Bergen Record)

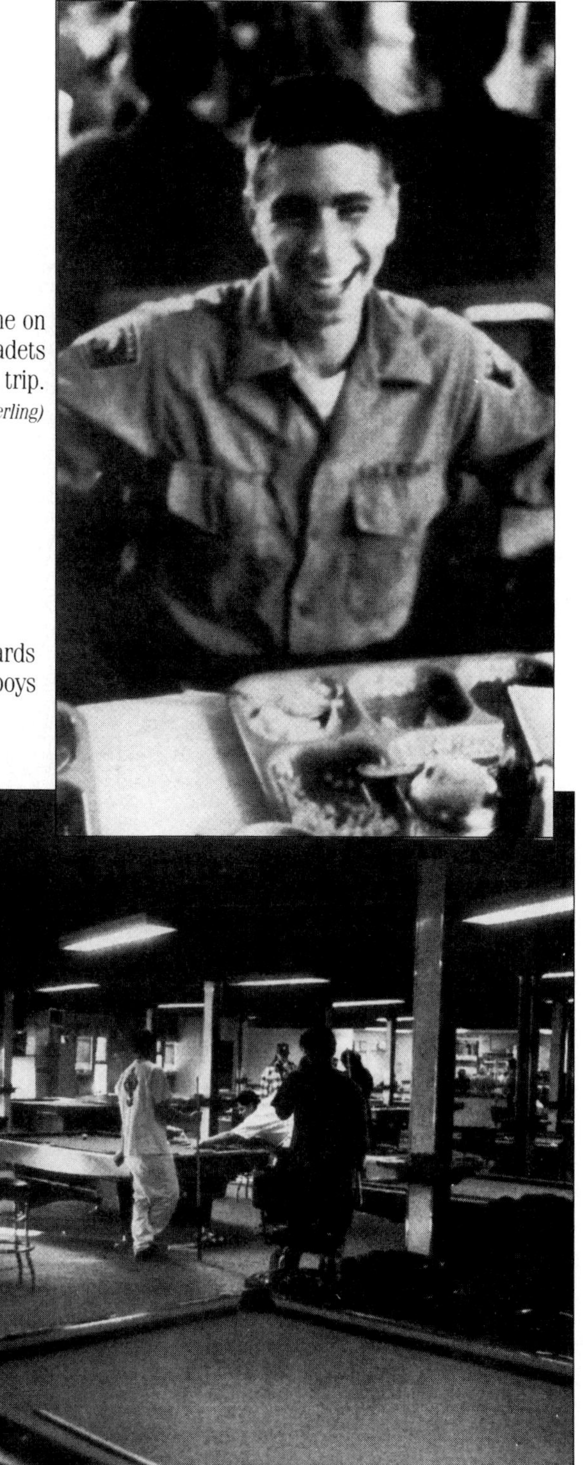

Robbie Solimine on a Sea Cadets field trip.
(Peter Serling)

The Clifton billiards hall where the boys shot pool.

This mausoleum, which the boys knew as "Annie's Tomb," in the Laurel Grove Cemetery in Totowa, NJ, was an almost nightly destination.

The boys believed "Annie" had lived in this house, on Dead Man's Curve, of Riverview Drive—also known as "Annie's Road"—in Totowa, NJ.

The Castaldo home at 18 Prescott Avenue, Clifton, NJ

St. Clare's Roman Catholic Church in Clifton, where Wanger had served as altar boy and lector.

Robbie Solimine's 1991 Clifton High School yearbook photo.
(Peter Serling)

James Wanger's 1991 high school yearbook photo. (Bergen Record)

Robert Solimine's Plymouth Laser. The area around the open gas flap is charred from the boys' attempt to burn the car. *(Passaic County Prosecutor's Office)*

Investigators search for clues at School 15 in Clifton hours after the murder. *(Passaic County Prosecutor's Office)*

Robert Solimine, Jr.'s funeral.
(*John Decker*, Bergen Record)

Margaret Chircop, pictured with the Valentine Robbie had given her the day before his murder.
(Peter Serling)

Frank Castaldo, at a bail hearing, shortly after his arrest. (*Klaus-Peter Steitz,* Bergen Record)

Tommy Strelka's sketch of the murder scene. *(Clifton Police Department)*

Margaret Chircop delivers petitions to the Passaic County Probation Department. (*Danielle P. Richards*, Bergen Record)

John A. Snowdon, Jr., Chief Asst. Passaic County Prosecutor.

James Wanger inspects a facsimile of the garrote during his testimony at his trial. *(Carmine Galasso,* Bergen Record)

Wanger testifies. *(Carmine Galasso,* Bergen Record*)*

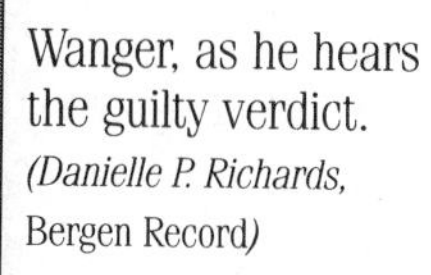

Wanger, as he hears the guilty verdict. *(Danielle P. Richards,* Bergen Record*)*

Martha and Paul Colombo, Wanger's grandparents, as the guilty verdict is read. *(Danielle Richards,* Bergen Record*)*

Robbie Solimine's grandparents, Lee and William Yakal, and his mother, Margaret Chircop, as Wanger's guilty verdict is read. *(Danielle Richards,* Bergen Record*)*

Alfonsina Castaldo, on her son Frank's day of sentencing. *(Ed Hill,* Bergen Record*)*

Margaret Chircop in front of the Passaic County Courthouse after Wanger's verdict. *(Ed Hill,* Bergen Record*)*

Robert Solimine, Sr., holding his son Robbie's 1992 yearbook photo. *(Peter Serling)*

9

It was getting on toward midnight, not long after Patrolman Christian Vassoler had headed out on the eleven-to-seven shift, and the city was quiet. Sunday night, after all, was the slowest night of the week in most towns, and Clifton was no different. Vassoler, who had been a cop six years, was in the patrol division, assigned to car No. 3 on Post 3 in the center of Clifton. The borders of his patrol formed the shape of a lopsided hourglass drawn between four points: Main Avenue, the city of Passaic's border, Van Houten Avenue, and state highway Route 46. In the middle of the assigned area—about where the hourglass narrowed—was Weasel Brook Park. Because it was dark and out of the way, kids liked to hang out there. Vassoler liked to move them along. He also usually checked School 15, because kids liked to hang out there, too, almost as much as they liked to hang out in the park just down the hill.

Vassoler drove on the winding road over the stone bridge that crossed Weasel Brook, then up a small hill where the canopy of tree limbs passed overhead, and onto Gregory Avenue. School 15 was on his left. As he rode past he almost didn't see anything at first. But there, just barely visible at the top of the school's driveway, was the nose of a small car whose lights were blacked out. It was parked at the crest of the hill. Vassoler had been around enough to know you could often catch people, particularly teenagers, parking up there in the shadows behind the school, smoking pot, doing drugs, drinking, making out, whatever. He decided to see what he would find.

Vassoler rolled farther down Gregory Avenue to the next street, Highland Avenue, and made a U-turn. Driving back up Gregory Avenue toward the park, he approached the school on his right. To achieve an element of surprise, Vassoler cut the lights on the patrol car before making the turn into the driveway. The police car glided up the slope until Vassoler was about thirty feet from the other car. Then he snapped on the headlights. The police car drifted another ten feet and came to a stop a short distance from the small white car. It was a two-door hatchback, parked near a green Dumpster and a light on a wooden pole. It was somewhat unusual. Vassoler didn't recognize the car's make. Because the seats looked as if they were reclined, Vassoler suspected that he was about to surprise some lovers necking in the moonlight—but it also occurred to him that someone might be burglarizing the school. Vassoler took his walkie-talkie and got out. The other car's front wheels were on the grassy patch about five feet off the macadam. His legs chopped through the beams of the cruiser's headlights as he crossed toward the driver's door of the other vehicle. There was no sign of anyone inside it.

Then the beam of Vassoler's flashlight picked out the driver, who was sitting behind the steering wheel, slumped toward the passenger's side, his head tilted back. The person looked as if he was sleeping. Maybe drunk, Vassoler thought. As he got closer, Vassoler saw it was a young person. Probably the kid had just started driving.

The driver's-side window was cracked maybe an inch or two. Vassoler threw the flashlight's beam onto the driver's face and neck. Vassoler saw at least five stripes. They were angry red stripes, like welts, that ran from the Adam's apple to the young man's ear, which was pierced with a tiny gold stud. They were very thin red lines that almost appeared to have been cut into the boy's skin.

It can't be, Vassoler thought. Holy shit.

Vassoler knew almost at once what he had, but he didn't want to believe it. He rapped on the window.

"Wake up, you," Vassoler said. He held the flashlight on the young man's face, as if the light would stir him, but there was no response.

"Hey, pal, wake up," Vassoler said. But the stripes on the boy's neck said everything.

Vassoler opened the driver's door—using the tip of his index finger so as not to mar any crime scene with his own fingerprints—and he touched the young man, as if to jostle him, but there was nothing. Then Vassoler checked for vital signs. The body was warm to the touch and the skin was still soft, but Vassoler found no pulse. Seeing the young man's eyes open a crack, Vassoler shone the flashlight into them, but the light produced nothing, no movement whatsoever. The pupils in the kid's eyes were fixed. The kid was dead.

Vassoler kept himself steady, although he was excited. Standing with his walkie-talkie beside the white compact, Vassoler radioed headquarters. He didn't want to broadcast in plain English that he had found a body—it would be sure to attract rubberneckers with police scanners—but he couldn't remember the Clifton P.D.'s 10-code for a homicide. So he told headquarters he had a 10-42, the code for a DOA. The time was twenty-six minutes past midnight. Surveying the entire site around the car, Vassoler took a careful path from the driver's door to the chain-link fence that surrounded the playground and walked on the concrete edge to the patrol car. There were tire tracks in the soft earth and footprints all over the place, especially near the driver's door. Vassoler had realized that they could be important evidence, which might help find the person or persons who had killed the young Caucasian male.

Within only a minute or two, the first backup units appeared and cops began to assemble on the muddy square of grass. Having learned at the police academy the importance of preserving a crime scene, Vassoler warned the other officers of the footprints and tire tracks and told them to stick to the same path he had taken to the car. By 12:30 A.M., three patrol cars and two sergeants had arrived to take a look at the Plymouth Laser. Clifton Ambulance was summoned, too, but it would be clear even before they arrived that there was no need for them.

As Vassoler and the other officers inspected the site, they saw that the entire car was spattered with mud. The wipers had smeared two brown ribbons on the windshield. There was mud caked on the wheels and in the wheel housings, and mud peppered the sides. Along the passenger side was a deep track that seemed to have been left by a second car. It was then Vassoler spotted the open gas flap. Someone had tried to torch the car. The right rear quarter panel around the gas nozzle was charred, the white paint had peeled and blistered, and there was some burnt matter on the ground below. The passenger door hadn't closed completely, but it had been slammed shut enough for the latch to grab. The license plate on the car—New Jersey registration GZY-98G—came back to a 1985 Plymouth Laser owned by a Robert J. Solimine, Sr., 119 Overlook Avenue, North Haledon.

After the body was found, Captain James Territo was one of the first Clifton cops called out of bed. Territo, who ran the Detective Bureau, had been a cop for more than twenty-five years. A short, dark-featured man with heavy eyelids, Territo affected a pencil-thin black mustache and had a habit of mumbling out of the side of his mouth—traits that produced almost a film noir effect. Territo had arrived in the Detective Bureau in 1988 as a captain who had last served in administrative services. When he worked a major crime, such as a homicide, he kept two things in mind: the victim's family and the rapid half-life of evidence. He saw his job of solving a murder as being of paramount importance to the family itself, and he believed that the best way to track down a killer was to throw every available cop into the hunt. He could wake up the entire Detective Bureau if he had to, to press the trail before it turned cold.

Territo's first decision was to pick George O'Brien to act as lead detective. A balding man with sharp Irish features and a high-bridged nose, O'Brien was well known around local law-enforcement circles for his fastidiousness. While most investigators toted around notebooks, O'Brien appeared at homicide scenes with a briefcase, and he had a penchant for speaking in curlicues and officialese. But he had a hawk's eye for details, and he noted them carefully as he went. He had learned over the years that little things that seemed insignificant could later corroborate a substantial element of the case. He was proud of his profession, confident of his skills, and unafraid of bringing logic and order to the most complex and far-flung cases.

Meanwhile, as Territo summoned more help, the detectives and police officers already at the school scoured the area and canvassed the neighborhood for clues. In a garbage can on Gregory Avenue they found a thin hemp rope—perhaps the murder weapon—along with some greasy rags and a broken bag of cement. A detective sketched a diagram of the area. Police officers rang doorbells in the apartments behind the school to see if anyone had seen or heard anything suspicious, but no one had. A gray Lincoln two-door with three young men kept circling suspiciously watching the police until the police stopped them and questioned them and took down their names. The three—a twenty-year-old Paterson man at the wheel and two teenagers—had heard the job on the scanner. Their names were taken and they left.

When O'Brien arrived, he called in a special police truck with high-intensity lights to illuminate the scene, and he began to take notes. No one wanted to get too close to the scene until the body was taken care of. Dr. Robert Briggs made the official pronouncement of death at 1:15 A.M. on February 17, 1992. After that, O'Brien joined a procession of detectives who gingerly approached the car and looked in to survey the scene. He took notes of what he found, recording Solimine's attire in almost minute detail, and he photographed the scene with Polaroid and 35mm cameras. He noticed that the ignition keys and the gas cap to the filler nozzle were missing. He noted the existence of a penknife, its blade closed, lying on the floor of the front passenger seat, and a wooden baseball bat under the seat near it. He wrote in his report that the hatchback contained debris like clothing and a bowling bag. O'Brien described in detail the number and appearance of the red welts left by the ligature on the young man's neck. He wrote that the headrest was in the raised position.

Right away, O'Brien understood a few things. For starters, this evidently was no suicide. It was obvious that the boy had been asphyxiated with a string or cord of some kind, and he had almost certainly been killed by someone else. A suicide could not, of course, have removed the cord he had hanged himself with. A suicide would not have taken the car keys. At this point, it was possible that the boy had died accidentally, and perhaps in front of innocent witnesses who panicked and left him here—but that did not explain the char marks on the gas tank.

The char marks were the most obvious evidence that the young man had been murdered for some reason. The flames had burned inside the mouth of the nozzle. But the fire had not burned down inside the filler neck, probably dying from lack of oxygen. A wadded-up chunk of material, probably a cloth rag, remained inside the nozzle. As O'Brien took in the entire scene—the sneaker prints in the mud, the torn-up grass where somebody had been spinning doughnuts in a car—another thing seemed obvious: A bunch of boys had been having fun at some point, and somewhere in the middle of it, perhaps after a fight, this teenager had been killed by another teenager.

O'Brien had worked his share of homicides over the years. All his life, he had wanted to be a cop. After graduation from Clifton High School, he moved to Virginia and traveled across the Potomac River to work for J. Edgar Hoover's FBI in the clerical section, earning two commendations along the way from the G-man of all G-men because of his administrative efficiency.

As he moved around the murder scene, O'Brien carried out his work clinically, at an emotional distance from the brutality of murder so that he could focus on the facts. He noted the Jets insignia on the boys' clothing and the gold stud in his left ear, all the while composing notes on the posture of the body. Yet it was not lost on him that the person who had been killed was very young, almost exactly the age of one of O'Brien's two sons. His son and the victim might have gone to school together, he thought. With another year of high school and then college in store for him, his son's life was just beginning, and this young man's had ended. Could it have been a fight over a girlfriend? A fight that escalated out of control? Under New Jersey law, it was not necessary to prove the existence of a motive to convict someone of murder. But O'Brien regarded the motive as something that was as important as fact, because a motive could help illuminate the facts. Having a theory about why someone was killed could suggest new avenues of inquiry and reveal patterns among the data already collected. The likelihood that the boy had been strangled also suggested that his killer had been close to him, literally and perhaps figuratively. O'Brien and the other detectives would have to find out who this boy's friends were. Who his enemies were. About forty minutes after O'Brien's arrival, Lieutenant Richard J. Less radioed O'Brien from headquarters with an interesting piece of information.

"I know who that is," Less said. "Robert Solimine was driving that car last night."

Less told O'Brien about his encounter the night before with Solimine. He told O'Brien about the gas flap being open. The license-plate registration and Less's recollection all but confirmed that the teenager was Robert Solimine, Jr., but the identification still wasn't official, and police had not been able to reach the car's owner. Someone was sent to the Solimine household in North Haledon, but no one was home.

One of the other detectives Territo called out that night was Detective Carl Matonak, who was central casting's idea of a cop, right down to his powder-blue double-knit jackets, his shiny polyester ties, and his wide leather belt. He was built like a bear, with thick arms and thinning silver hair swept back toward the crown of his head. He was plainspoken and oddly rustic for a place like Clifton. When he took the stand to testify in criminal cases, he fielded questions from prosecutors and defense attorneys alike with the same unfeigned indifference: The facts were the facts, and there wasn't a whole lot more to say about it. Having been a cop for more than twenty-five years, the last seven in the Youth Services Bureau, he was an old-timer who had spent a lot of time with kids, so he came off a little like a stern but compassionate father. Now and then his temper would show, but he had a lot of patience and a very useful gift for appearing interested in what a suspect had to say, even if the person was lying. His pale-turquoise eyes seemed filled with infinite patience.

Following Captain Territo's orders, the desk sergeant called Matonak just before 2:30 A.M. with news that a kid had been found dead at School 15. A half hour later Matonak arrived at headquarters, a bit groggy after only three hours' sleep. Territo told Matonak that they had a tentative I.D. on the victim from the license registration and asked Matonak to search the juvenile records for any prior contacts with Solimine. Detective Michael Kotora, another old hand in the juvenile bureau, was to help. He, too, had gotten the call from the desk sergeant and headed in, but he was praying that whatever he did would not screw up his plans for a vacation in Mexico. He had tickets to fly out of New Jersey on Saturday.

Matonak searched the file cabinets and soon found index cards listing two previous encounters with Solimine. One was a missing persons report that had been filed after Solimine had run away from home almost to the day a year earlier. The second involved a criminal mischief investigation involving Solimine two days before he had been reported missing. But no juvenile delinquency complaint had been filed. Like all of the index cards, Solimine's cards included his pedigree—date of birth and so forth—his parents' names, his school, and a summary of their encounter with the police. Matonak had been the detective on the runaway job, so he recollected a little about it. Deciding to look up the full reports later, Matonak and Kotora went to the murder scene.

It was about 3 A.M. when Matonak and Kotora showed up. Other detectives—Captain Territo and Lieutenant Frank Chasar, their superior in the Juvenile Bureau—brought them up to date. Matonak asked if they could take a look in the car without disturbing the other detectives who were gathering evidence at the scene. Kotora took a quick look. Matonak, too, glanced in the car windows at the dead kid, and it seemed unreal—the setting, the distorted face, the kid's young age. Matonak reconnoitered the site, sketching a diagram of the school's layout and measuring the width of the tire tracks in the spongy earth, beside Solimine's car. Judging from the tracks, Matonak decided that the second car was big. It had a nearly six-foot wheelbase. The second car also had been less than five feet from Solimine's vehicle, and it was a safe bet that the second car would be covered with mud too.

After Matonak and Kotora had taken a look, Captain Territo and Lieutenant Chasar told them to find out everything they could about Solimine's friends. See if the friends could help them figure out what Solimine had been up to the previous night. Digging out the full report on the missing persons incident last year would be a start. Also, he was to see if any of Solimine's friends owned large muddy cars.

Although the police had peeked inside the car since it had been discovered, no one touched its interior until a local judge signed a search warrant and Dr. Lyla Perez, an assistant state medical examiner, removed the body. Like the others, Perez felt a jolt seeing such a young murder victim. Although one look at the marks on the young man's neck also gave her more than a good idea about what had happened, she set to work documenting medical evidence that could verify to a legal certainty how he had died. With a flashlight she could detect signs of petechial hemorrhages—prickly red dots on the boy's face that brought a peculiar blush to the surface, as if he were wearing makeup—that were caused by pinpoint ruptures of capillaries under the skin and in the whites of his eyes. It was more evidence the cause of death had been asphyxia from the application of a ligature. Perez had logged more than 4,000 autopsies in her career, which began in New York City. If there's an unusual way to die—or a gruesome one—she had probably seen it.

But strangulation was fairly unusual—particularly for males—and she had generally encountered it in situations of rape and homicide, or a fatal episode of domestic violence. It required the killer or killers to move in close, of course. And despite the Mafia movies, she had never once seen it used by mobsters in real life. But police would need to know without a doubt—and probably, down the line, a jury, too—not only whether asphyxia had indeed been the cause of death, but the approximate time of death, the type of ligature, whether the victim had struggled, and whether there were defensive wounds or not. At the autopsy, she might be able to fix an approximate time of death by measuring such quantifiable elements as the victim's body temperature, the stomach contents, and the body's lividity. The furrows on the youth's neck would require close inspection for clues as to what kind of ligature was used: A hemp rope, for example, might create braided impressions, and a sash might leave behind fibers. An electrical cord might make a distinct parallel track created by the groove that ran between the two strands that carried the electrical current.

Following standard procedure, Dr. Perez bagged the fingers of the victim to preserve any blood under the fingernails from fighting with his killer—although as she did this, she also noticed that the victim's fingernails were bitten to the quick, thereby reducing the odds of picking up any scrapings from them. Dr. Perez also took the temperature of the body, which registered at 80 degrees Fahrenheit, and she measured the outside temperature, which was 40 degrees.

Around 4:30 A.M., Perez supervised the removal of Solimine's body from the car. O'Brien and an assistant medical examiner placed the body on a gurney. The body was still pliant—they had found the victim before complete rigor mortis had set in. Before zippering the corpse inside a body bag, Perez and the detectives slipped the wallet from Solimine's back pocket. It was made of blue nylon and bore the insignia of the United States Navy. O'Brien, wearing latex gloves, examined its contents. To no one's surprise, the driver's license confirmed the victim's identity as Robert A. Solimine, of the same North Haledon address as the license-plate registration. According to the D.O.B., the kid had just turned seventeen in August. A few hours ago, the kid on the gurney with the sallow face had been the kid in the photograph with the lazy grin, a good-looking kid with a long face, a prominent nose, short straight brown hair, and an almost wiseass, ironic grin as he looked askance at the camera. There were also six one-dollar bills inside. *There goes all doubt that a robbery was involved,* O'Brien thought.

Back at headquarters, Matonak was hunched over the file cabinets near the interview rooms inside the Youth Services Bureau. Two wooden display cases, the sides showing the wear of countless visits to city schools, sat atop the cabinets. One display case contained an array of handguns and one case contained knives. The handguns were facsimiles, which had been molded from plastic or metal with remarkable precision and accuracy. The knives, including switchblades, butterfly knives, and throwing stars, were real. Both were props designed to grab the attention of schoolchildren when police visited them and talked to them about staying out of the kind of trouble that filled the filing cabinets with thousands of indexed reports on juvenile delinquents.

It took only a few minutes for Matonak to yank Solimine's missing person reports. The papers identified Solimine's mother as a Margaret Chircop, who lived at 216 East Seventh Street in Clifton. In fact, she was the one who had filed the missing person report on February 11, 1991, after she and her son had quarreled. The missing person report had been filed about 8 P.M. and said her son had not gone to school that day and she had no idea where he was. On the line to explain background about the missing person, Mrs. Chircop had written, "Parent & child disagreement do [sic] to his disrespectful attitude with his mouth."

The reports noted that Solimine eventually had been located, the day after his mother had filed the missing person report, at the home of Christine Bachelle, a fifteen-year-old girl who also had a troubled background. In fact, Matonak recognized her name. Matonak called Christine Bachelle's mother to see if he could speak to the young woman. Chrissie's mother said Chrissie was sleeping over with a friend in Passaic. Matonak called the Passaic number next, but Chrissie wasn't there. The girl who came to the phone in Passaic said Chrissie actually was staying with another friend on Rosalie Avenue in Clifton. Chrissie had played the teenage shell game to stay somewhere her parents didn't know about.

Matonak and Kotora decided to head over to Rosalie Avenue. Matonak rang the doorbell. A parent of the girl who lived there answered the door in her bathrobe. Matonak flipped out a shield.

"Why are you waking us up at four A.M.?" the woman said.

"If it wasn't important, we wouldn't be here," Matonak said.

The woman went back inside and summoned a girl with blond hair. Chrissie was in pajamas or sweatpants or something and she was half asleep, but she appeared very surprised to see policemen at that hour.

Matonak was a talker by nature, so he did most of the talking. He wanted to ask questions in a way that would let Chrissie know something had happened but without letting on that Rob had been killed. Chrissie looked at them bleary-eyed, half wondering if this was something about her. Matonak said the detectives had awakened her because of something important. It concerned Rob, they said. She assumed he was missing.

"It's very important we speak with people who might have seen Rob in the last day or so. Do you know where we might find some of his friends?" Matonak said. "We're trying to talk to his friends. See if his friends know anything."

"I can't believe Rob ran away again," Chrissie said, and she somehow got the impression from the detectives that his mother was freaking out about it.

Although the detectives didn't want word about the homicide out yet, Chrissie kept turning their questions back on them, prying to find out what was up. Finally, Chrissie said she hadn't seen Rob in two months. As Matonak later remembered it, he pressed, her, asking not only if she would pass on the names of Rob's friends, but if she also knew anyone who might want to harm Rob.

"Try Frank Castaldo and Tommy Strelka," Chrissie said. "They know Rob. They might be angry with him."

"Why?"

"Because he talked about them."

"Does either of these guys drive?"

"Yes."

Later, Chrissie would recall only that she gave the detectives the names of three people who knew Rob, including Castaldo's, Strelka's, and a girl's.

After getting the addresses of Castaldo and Strelka from Chrissie, Matonak and Kotora piled into the police car. It wasn't much as far as leads go, but at least they had a couple of names. Neither name produced much of a reaction. Castaldo was known around the police department as a troublemaker and a punk, but he had no criminal record. Matonak was perhaps one of the few officers who hadn't heard of him before. There was nothing on this Strelka kid either. But Matonak and Kotora decided to take a ride past the boys' houses to see what they could see. Perhaps, they decided, they might find another muddy car like Solimine's.

The detectives swung past Castaldo's first. They drove up and down Prescott Avenue but saw nothing unusual. They drove across town to the Lakeview Section where Strelka lived. It also happened to be the neighborhood where Detective Sergeant Thomas Surowiec lived. Surowiec, a wisecracking investigator who was working the four-to-twelve shift, would stay on and help with the investigation. Captain Territo considered him an extremely capable detective and a good supervisor. Surowiec could help coordinate the detective's movements.

At the corner of Gordon Street and East Eighth, near where Strelka lived, the detectives spotted a muddy car. It was a silver-gray Buick LeSabre, chipped paint, mud all over the place: in the wheel wells, on the tires, on the fenders, on the sides. The detectives got out and inspected the car more closely. Matonak had no idea to whom it belonged. But the plate came back to a Raymond Strelka.

Bingo. It had to be.

The detectives called headquarters for some cameras. They also told Territo what they had, and the captain came out to have a look. Surowiec came too. When the cameras arrived, Kotora started shooting the car with a 35mm and Matonak took pictures with a Polaroid. Kotora scraped samples of mud from the vehicle's rear fender for comparison with mud at the scene. The doors were locked, but Matonak and Kotora peeped through the windows. They saw a brown paper bag lying on its side on the front passenger seat. Inside the bag was a bottle of Gatorade. Inside the bag was also an unopened pack of tan shoelaces.

The detectives talked over what to do next. Hunting for the mud appeared now to have been one of those inspired hunches that paid off. Odds were that this Strelka kid had been with Solimine around the time of the homicide or shortly before, when they were monkeying around in the mud spinning doughnuts. Much later, however, the police would realize that what had seemed like a stroke of genius had been just dumb luck, because the mud on Strelka's LeSabre hadn't come from the earth at School 15. Laboratory analysis would show that it had come from elsewhere, perhaps Garret Mountain or wherever else Strelka said he had been with Rob that weekend. At the time, however, the spatters of mud closed a circle.

"Get the kid," Territo said. "Let's see what he knows."

In the meantime, someone had to get the word to the victim's family. Territo hated the way the media swarmed around crime victims or their families. In homicide cases especially, Territo felt protective of the families and wanted to shield them from the microphones and the tape recorders and the klieg lights and the stupid questions. Likewise, he wanted to make it easy on the families when they heard the news. It was never easy, of course, but it had to be done. So Territo sent Matonak to speak with Solimine's mother.

Matonak and Detective Richard Onorevole knocked at the door of the Chircop residence around 6:19 A.M. Billy Solimine opened the door. He was a light sleeper. When he saw cops with flashlights standing at his front door, his heart started pounding. The night before, he and some friends had been goofing off at the Wallington bridge over the Passaic River. As a prank one of them had closed a gate on the bridge. Maybe, he thought, their stunt had caused an accident.

"Your parents home?" Matonak asked.

Billy said he would get them. Normally, his mom slept on the couch because of the fighting between her and Manny, but this morning she was upstairs. He went upstairs and told his parents that there were two cops downstairs who wanted to talk to them. Soon Manny and Margaret were up. Margaret came downstairs in a funk, but as her head cleared she grew steadily more alarmed at the way the police were acting.

"Mrs. Chircop? You have a son Robert Solimine?" Matonak said.

"What happened? Has there been an accident or something?"

"Can we sit down?"

The detectives were led to the dining room and everyone took seats at the polished table. There were businesslike introductions.

"Is this about Rob?" the Chircops asked.

"Yes," Matonak said. "When was the last time you saw him?"

Billy said he had last seen his brother on Sunday.

"Is there anything wrong? What happened?" Mrs. Chircop said.

This was never easy, Matonak thought, and he could see that they were reading his face for a sign of what they already knew must be grim news. That was indeed what Matonak had come to divulge, of course—and he was hesitating. Onorevole cleared his throat and stepped in.

"I been doing this twenty-five years," Onorevole said, "and there's no easy way of telling you what I have to tell, so I don't want to prolong your agony—but your son's dead."

The words seemed to paralyze the Chircops for a moment and take their breath away. No one noticed that he referred to Robbie as Bobby as he continued to talk. Margaret Chircop seemed to be drawing deep inside herself, while her husband and son attempted to comfort her. She wept, and then with the tears and gasps of surprise came the questions, the obvious ones: How did he die? When? What had happened? This part was worse even than notifying a family of an accidental death, Matonak thought.

"We believe he's been murdered," Onorevole said.

Then Margaret went to pieces, and more questions flew.

"Where?" she asked. "Where? Was he shot?"

Billy had imagined a traffic accident.

Matonak and Onorevole explained that Robbie had been strangled. They said they needed to ask some questions to try to find his killer or killers. They asked if anyone knew anything about Rob's friends or girlfriends. The Chircops listed his friends and acquaintances, mentioning Strelka more than once. As to Rob's whereabouts, Billy told the detectives that he had last seen his brother at the bowling alley in Fair Lawn on Sunday.

"Tommy would be the one," Margaret said. "Tommy was his best friend. He should have been with Tommy."

By this point, Margaret nearly collapsed. She told them that she and Rob's father had been divorced for some time now, and that Rob had moved in with his father in May 1991. But she broke down. The police officers realized they couldn't talk to her now. Manny was trying to console her, and someone summoned the next-door neighbor, who was a nurse.

Billy shook his head in disbelief. He was horrified that his brother had been killed purposely by someone. It was all the more disconcerting to think that he had been strangled. In this day and age, Billy's first thought was that his brother had been shot. But strangled? By someone who could get that close? Everyone was stunned, and everyone was stumped for clues.

"That's why we'd like to talk to his friends," Onorevole said. "We need to find out if he had any enemies."

"Tommy's his best friend," the family said. "You've got to find Tommy."

Billy told the detectives a little more about what he could remember from talking with Rob on the previous afternoon. They had been at the Brunswick Fair Lawn Lanes on Maple Avenue. They had played three league games against a couple whom they didn't know. Rob had said something about a party he was planning on going to that night. He was wearing a nice shirt, and a nice pair of pants—a shirt he wouldn't normally wear, anyway, because the bowling balls left black streaks on them. Rob had mentioned to Billy that Tommy Strelka had slept over with him at their father's place in North Haledon. Billy said he didn't know a whole lot about Rob's friends, but he knew Strelka. Strelka was Rob's best friend, Billy said, and he might know what Rob had been up to.

"Who do you think did it?" Billy asked.

* * *

The Strelkas lived in a neatly kept frame house that was painted sunny yellow and sat on a street that was nearly, but not quite, a dead end. It was 6:20 A.M., and the streets were just barely stirring, when Detective Kotora and Detective John Barr stood on the rattan welcome mat that said "Go Away!" and rapped loudly on the door. The white storm door held the black metal stencil of a horse and buggy. Finally, a blond kid with stringy hair came to the door. He had broad Slavic cheekbones and a pointy nose. He was wearing street clothes, and it was obvious that he had just been sleeping.

The detectives asked if his parents were around. Although it was early, Strelka's father had already gone to work, but his mother was home, and so were his little brother and sister. The detectives waited for the teenager to go get his mother. Susie wasn't pleased to hear that the police were in her living room. As Strelka thumped down the carpeted stairs with her, out of earshot of the detectives, she poked at his back and whispered under her breath.

"What'd you do this time? What the hell did you do this time, Tommy?" she said, giving him a shove that was only a little playful. It involved the car, probably: She guessed they were going to tell her that Strelka had hit something last night and took off.

By nature, Susie was a nervous person who seemed to be fidgeting and moving all the time: lighting a cigarette, touching her hands to her hair, moving around the hall of her home or her kitchen as she talked. With a birdlike quality she regarded the two police officers, tilting her head to the side and fixing them with a guarded look from her pale-blue eyes. *Now what?* she thought.

The detectives identified themselves and asked to speak with her and her son. They explained that they were working on an important investigation, but they said almost nothing else. She invited them into the kitchen, asking if they wanted a cup of coffee. The detectives declined. They asked Strelka to excuse them for a moment while they talked to his mother in the kitchen. Strelka went upstairs to get changed.

"Why my son?" Mrs. Strelka asked them. She thought Strelka was a good kid all in all. But she also had few illusions. She knew he wasn't an angel. Still, Strelka had never been in trouble with the police.

Kotora told her that the investigation involved a friend of Strelka's.

"I'm not supposed to tell you this," he said, "but Robert Solimine, Jr., was found dead last night. We believe it was a homicide."

They needed to find out who Robert's friends were, Kotora said. Would she be willing to come to headquarters with her son? Mrs. Strelka was thunderstruck. She had known Rob as long as her son had, and she couldn't believe the teenager could be dead. Having known Rob that long, she also thought—she couldn't help thinking—that perhaps it was actually a suicide. After all, the kid must have threatened to kill himself a dozen times, and he tried it at least once as far as she knew. Tommy told her Rob once held a gun to his head at his father's house and threatened to blow his brains out. And if it was a homicide, in a way it was no wonder: She had always thought that Rob would someday provoke the wrong person and he would get shot.

Mrs. Strelka agreed to let her son speak to the police, and the police drove them downtown. Tommy could be a jerky kid, but the thought never entered her head that her son might have anything to do with a homicide.

At the Youth Services Bureau in the Clifton Police Department, Strelka was taken to a cramped room for an interview. He walked past the file cabinets whose records had helped the detectives track him down and took a seat at the head of a small table. The room was paneled like someone's rec room in the 1970s, and the ceiling and the upper part of the walls were covered in white panels that supposedly were soundproof. Because they were not all that soundproof, and the second interview room in the Juvenile Bureau was on the other side of a wall with a two-way mirror, the detectives kept a stereo just outside the door to drown out any particularly loud discussions. Having returned from the Chircops, Matonak agreed to help with the interview.

Matonak had never met Strelka before, and his first impression of the teenager left him puzzled. Strelka looked like a scrawny little kid. Butter wouldn't melt in his mouth. How could this kid know anything about a homicide? Matonak wondered. But Strelka agreed to tell them what he could about Rob. Mrs. Strelka, who smoked cigarettes nearly end to end when she was nervous, sat nearby in the Juvenile Bureau's office.

At first, the detectives played things in a cagy way so as not to tip Strelka about what they were interested in. They told Strelka they were investigating a serious matter involving one of his friends, Robert Solimine, Jr. Did he know what kind of car Rob drove? What kind of cigarettes he smoked? What he had been up to that weekend? Matonak made it clear that they were discussing a criminal investigation, but he told Strelka he wasn't at liberty to go into details. What they were after was information about whom Rob might have seen that weekend. Strelka seemed game to help.

"When did you see Rob last?" the detectives asked.

"I last saw Rob Thursday."

"Thursday?"

"Around ten o'clock," Strelka said. "Rob came over to my house with James Wanger."

Strelka explained who James was, and he told the detectives he worked part-time with Wanger at the Robin Hood Inn.

"I picked up James's paycheck at work, so Rob drove James over to my house to pick it up," Strelka said. "Rob invited me to a party for Sunday night, but I told him I didn't want to go. It was supposed to be a really big party."

Already Matonak knew the kid was hiding something, because he had just left the Chircops and William Solimine had told him Strelka and Rob had slept over together Saturday night. But Matonak let the kid talk. As Strelka unwound his tale, Matonak became more and more convinced that Strelka was feeding him a line of crap, and he wasn't sure why. Kids sometimes protected other kids, and no one liked a rat. But Matonak feigned interest, scribbled notes on his legal pad, and had Strelka spell things that Matonak already knew how to spell.

"Tommy, we need to verify your movements over the weekend," Matonak said. "Can you tell us where you were?"

Strelka explained that he had spent the entire weekend with Mark Yacono, a local kid whose father was a lawyer. Strelka said Yacono had spent Friday night at Strelka's place, and Strelka had spent Saturday night at Yacono's. Matonak asked him if he had driven over any dirt roads or patches of mud lately that might explain why there was mud on his car. Strelka said he hadn't.

"How do you account for the mud on your car?" Matonak asked.

Strelka thought things over.

"Tommy, this is a very serious matter here. Rob's dead. It looks like he was murdered. There's mud all over your car," Matonak said, "and there's mud all over Rob's. You want to go over your story again?"

Strelka said he now recalled that on Friday night he and Rob had driven their cars to a dirt road in the county park on Garret Mountain in West Paterson. Rob's car got stuck in the mud, which had formed from the snowfall the night before. Strelka said his car got smeared with mud too but hadn't gotten stuck. They had been with James Wanger that night, too.

By this time, Strelka had become a little more tense. At first when they had started talking, Strelka blabbed and blabbed, almost as if he had rehearsed his story, but when he started talking again now, he picked his way through the interview more carefully. Matonak kept writing. Barr took notes, too, catching details that Matonak didn't. Although Strelka's story about Garret Mountain sounded convenient, Matonak had no way of knowing if it was a lie. True, there was mud on

Strelka's car and there was mud on Rob's car, but it could have come from someplace besides School 15.

Barr asked Strelka to walk him through the events of Sunday, February 16. Strelka said he had left home about 4 P.M. for a Bradlees, where he purchased some antifreeze. He poured the antifreeze into his car's radiator in the Bradlees parking lot, then drove over to Yacono's house on Allwood Road. Around 4:30, Wanger called him at Yacono's. Wanger needed a lift from the Robin Hood Inn. Strelka said he picked Wanger up, dropped Wanger at Tommy "Stooge" Stujinski's house, and returned to the Yacono residence. He left the Yacono's about 7 o'clock and headed out to Fun 'N Games at the Willowbrook Mall.

"You were alone?" Barr asked.

"Yes," Strelka said.

"Anyone see you there?"

"I saw a kid named Chris. I know him from work, but I don't know his last name," Strelka said. Strelka also said he saw a kid named Jim from the high school, but he couldn't remember that kid's last name, either.

Continuing his story, Strelka said he left the video arcade about 9 o'clock. He drove to Stooge's house, where he met Wanger, Stooge, and Carboni, and then he drove those guys over to Carboni's house. About 11 o'clock, Strelka and Wanger left Carboni's and went out together to get some burgers at the White Castle on Main Avenue. Then, Strelka said, he dropped off Wanger at Carboni's house and headed home himself. Since his 12 o'clock curfew had passed, Strelka stopped at a pay phone to call his parents and let them know that he was on the way. The call, he said, was placed about 12:15 A.M.

Barr wrote it all down, although he didn't believe the kid was telling the truth. Matonak was also doubtful. Matonak homed in on the issue of where Strelka had been staying on Saturday and Sunday. Strelka insisted he had been with Mark Yacono. Matonak decided to squeeze him.

"You sure you want to stick to that story?" Matonak asked.

"Yeah," Strelka said, "that's what happened."

"Well," Matonak said, "we got information that you stayed up at Rob's house."

Strelka paused. There was a look of shock in his face: How did this cop know this? Then he admitted that he had been with Rob on Saturday night. And he admitted lying. He had opened up just a crack, and Matonak knew that now the momentum was going in the detectives' favor. Strelka needed to explain to Matonak that he lied because his mother didn't like him hanging around Rob. Now Matonak and Barr pushed him about Sunday, and they returned to the subject of this party Rob was supposed to have gone to. Strelka kept insisting there was a party, but all he knew was that it was somewhere in Ridgewood.

"Fine," Matonak said. "I'm going to check it out."

Matonak was skeptical about the story, but who knows? He thought he would take a shot in the dark and see if there had been any complaints of a large party. He dialed the Ridgewood Police Department and spoke with a Detective James Rice. Just like a police department: Matonak was put on hold. As Matonak stepped out to call the Ridgewood Police Department, Surowiec and Kotora went into the conference room.

Surowiec was monitoring the investigation with one eye and keeping the other one on the paperwork at his desk. He had heard that they were bringing in Tommy Strelka, whose mother was one of Surowiec's best friends. He wanted to check on the kid, see how the interview was going, but he also wanted to stay clear of any entanglements. He especially wanted to see how Susie was holding up. He asked her how Strelka was doing, and she asked if he would go inside and see.

"Hey, Tommy, how's everything going?" Surowiec said when he came into the room.

"I'm doing okay," Strelka said, and they made small talk. At first, Strelka impressed Surowiec with his calm. He had been chatting with the other detectives as Surowiec walked in.

But as Surowiec and Strelka talked more, Surowiec felt something funny going on. Strelka wouldn't look him in the eye. The sergeant had known the kid thirteen years, and although he wasn't the kid's godfather or anything, he knew him well enough to know that something was eating at the kid.

"What's the matter?" Surowiec said. "Do you know something about this?"

Strelka looked away. His eyes were roving all over the place, around the walls, up to the ceiling, down at the floor.

"Tommy, if you know something about this, help these investigators out," Surowiec said. "If you know the truth, tell them. Don't hide anything."

Surowiec hit a nerve. Strelka sat there a moment, appearing flustered. Fidgety.

"By all means," Surowiec said. "If there's something you know, tell us."

"Well," Strelka said, "I do."

"What?"

Strelka looked at the floor. He looked at the ceiling. His face flushed a deep scarlet. His legs jiggled up and down and he rubbed his hands on his thighs.

"James did it," Strelka said.

"How do you know?" Surowiec said.

"Because I was there."

The interview was stopped. Strelka was advised of his Constitutional rights. Someone told his mother that Strelka had become more than an acquaintance of Solimine's. He had become a witness and, perhaps, a suspect.

Matonak was outside the room on the telephone, still waiting on hold, when Kotora came over.

"Tommy just admitted he was at the scene," Kotora said. "He says James Wanger did it."

Strelka gave the detectives their first glimpse into the events that occurred the night before at School 15. Strelka sketched a crude diagram of where the two cars were parked. Using the style of a police report, Strelka drew a rectangle with a point on it showing which way he had been facing, and a second shape to show where Solimine's car was parked. Then he initialed it. Soon he was giving a sworn written statement. Matonak propounded the questions. Strelka answered. A secretary typed his responses. The prose jolted around, obviously failing to record everything he had said, and it glided over many important details, but it told for the first time the story of how Solimine had been strangled inside his car.

But that was about all it told. The statement fingered Wanger—just Wanger—for the murder, giving only enough detail to corroborate what the police had found independently. And it pinned Carboni down as at least an accomplice after the fact, since Strelka told the police that Carboni had helped trying to blow up the car and ditch the stuff by Royal Silk. Strelka had rendered up a version of events that made it seem as if James Wanger had, without any warning, flipped out and strangled his friend while they were hanging out in their cars, and it was over too fast for anyone to do anything.

There were, however, telltale points in Strelka's story that raised questions. There were times where he had ventured into areas that could have tripped him up. Strelka mentioned the trip into Quick Pick 'N's, for example, but said nothing about Wanger buying any shoelaces or riding with Strelka to the parking lot of the Clifton High School to build a garrote. He helpfully gave the detectives a shoelace he found in his car. He mentioned that it was Wanger's idea to go to School 15 because he had wanted to go there the night before—without letting on why he had gone there the previous night. On closer inspection, parts of Strelka's account were completely absurd, as in his reconstruction of the act of strangulation in Solimine's car:

"I opened the driver's side door, and I saw James with an extension cord tied around Rob's neck," Strelka said to the police in his statement. "I tried to stop James from choking Rob by pulling the cord from Rob's neck. James let go of the extension cord with his left hand and pushed me away from the car. James shut the door and locked it."

Asked why he returned to Carboni's, Strelka said he and Stooge didn't know what to do and they wanted to see where Carboni and Wanger would end up. No one pressed him as to why he and the others failed to summon the police or call for an ambulance. And the trip to Castaldo's house raised still more questions. But the detectives were inclined to explain the omissions by the fact that they were dealing with teenagers, who seemed to operate by their own logic in the best of circumstances and would be all the more scattered and selective in their reporting about something stressful. What's more, the detectives believed that Strelka had lied at first because he was afraid to tell on another kid. That, they assumed, was the universal code of teenager conduct, and it was useful in explaining some of Strelka's behavior after the event. That could also, to some extent, explain Carboni's behavior. Perhaps Strelka and the boy went to Castaldo the way all teenagers these days turned to other teenagers when they got in a jam.

All the same, the detectives held plenty of suspicions. Strelka's account of attempting to stop Wanger made perfect sense—until you considered that it was three boys on one, and they should have been able to overpower the kid. The business with the position of the cars just didn't sit right with Matonak, either. Strelka's explanation about not wanting his car to get covered with mud was okay, as far as it went, but Strelka's car *was* covered with mud. He himself had been talking about driving around Garret Mountain on dirt roads, as if four-wheeling in a beat-up Buick came naturally, and he had driven into the spongy grass lot beside Solimine's car. Why did he get so particular about flying mud all of a sudden at School 15?

10

STRELKA WAS STILL TALKING WITH MATONAK AND COMPANY AT headquarters when Territo sent detectives to pick up the boys who had been at the school with him and Wanger and Solimine. Kotora and Detective Ralph Pennella left headquarters a little before 11 o'clock A.M. to find Carboni. They were looking for a green house—Strelka had given the police Carboni's street and the general vicinity where he lived, but not the street address—and when they found the mailbox, they knocked on the door. Mrs. Carboni answered the door. Her husband had already left for work. They asked about her son, and she told the detectives that Frank Carboni was upstairs with Tommy Stujinski. Kotora explained that the police had reason to believe that her son had witnessed the death of a friend, and they wanted to speak to him.

Mrs. Carboni led the detectives upstairs to Carboni's bedroom on the third floor where the boys were sleeping. Carboni who had fallen asleep sitting up a few hours earlier, had already awakened. He went downstairs to take a shower when he realized there was no towel. He stepped out and got a towel and saw his mother heading up the stairs with two guys. One was carrying a folder and a walkie-talkie. Carboni bolted back into the bathroom, put his robe on. Oh, shit, he thought. The detectives went upstairs and shook Stujinski, who had to be shaken quite a bit because he was a heavy sleeper. The detectives told Stooge they needed to take him down to the police station because he was a witness to a crime.

"You're not in any trouble. Don't worry about it," one of them said. "We just want to ask you some questions."

When Carboni came back from the shower, the detectives explained what they wanted. The boys got dressed and went downstairs to the kitchen. They didn't talk to each other in front of the detectives. One team of detectives was to take Carboni in. Another team of detectives showed up to take Stooge to headquarters. Before they put Stooge in the car, they told him he was being taken in because of the murder of Robert Solimine.

"We know what happened to Bobby," one of the detectives said from the front of the car. "Don't try lying about it. Don't try to hide it. We know he's dead."

The other detectives waited a while longer to see if Mr. Carboni could be reached at work and if he would return home. Mrs. Carboni called her husband at the chemical plant. She was a short woman, somewhat plump, with glasses and brown hair. She told the detectives her husband was going to come home right away. When Mr. Carboni arrived—a short, intense-looking man with a thick black mustache—he took his son into the front room of the house and asked what happened. Carboni made like he didn't know. His father told him to tell the truth. Whatever happened, Mr. Carboni said, it was important that Carboni tell the truth. Carboni, although already appearing a little scared, played dumb.

The police drove Carboni in the backseat of their unmarked car, and his father followed in his truck. It was noon when Carboni and his father arrived at the police station. The detectives walked to the second floor of the department and led Carboni and his father into a small room in the Adult Detective Bureau. There were desks along one of the walls and in the center of the room, and the police radio buzzed and jabbered over an intercom. Inside the conference room there was a table, a steel desk—which was like a study carrel from a library—and a two-way mirror. A sign on the wall said, "USE HANDCUFF BAR." Although he looked a little edgy, Carboni was acting unconcerned; his father's face already was shining with drops of sweat. Everyone came in and took a seat and prepared to talk. When Carboni opened his mouth for the first time around the detectives, his voice seemed too deep and jaded for a kid only fourteen years old.

"Hey, Dad," Carboni said. "Can I have a smoke?"

Mr. Carboni fished a cigarette from his pocket and handed it to his son. Kotora advised them of their Miranda rights, and the interview began. Detective Richard Onorevole sat in and scribbled notes. The detectives told the Carbonis that they were investigating the death of Robert Solimine, Jr., and that it was a suspected homicide. They told Carboni they understood he had been present when Solimine died. They asked Carboni if he could relate to them where he had been.

As he started to talk, the detectives observed the faintest glint of fear in his dark eyes. But Carboni looked like a runt. He seemed too young even for the mustache that was scattered like iron filings over his upper lip. Around 8 o'clock Sunday, Carboni said, he hooked up with Solimine and some other guys. It was the night before a school break and they planned to go out, goof around. Solimine was there, of course, and so were Tommy Strelka, Tommy "Stooge" Stujinski, and James Wanger. They all were in two cars—Strelka's LeSabre and Solimine's car, which Carboni referred to as a Dodge Charger—and they spent much of the night chasing each other, switching back and forth between the cars, stopping at gas stations, and so on. Around 9:30 P.M., Carboni continued, he was dropped off by Strelka at his cousin's house for a birthday party. Around 10:15 P.M., the guys returned to pick up Carboni. Carboni said he got in the backseat of Solimine's car, and Wanger rode in the front. Stujinski rode with Strelka. They drove up to School 15. They all got out, and Solimine was skidding around in the mud by himself. At some point, Wanger and Solimine got into the car together.

"James started talking about the Virgin Mary," Carboni said. Growing nervous the more he talked and the closer he got to the killing, Carboni started stuttering and stammering and using a mixture of grunts and hand gestures to convey what happened. The detectives pressed closer: Here was a boy who had just placed himself in the car with a homicide victim. It was rare to have any eyewitnesses in homicide cases, let alone a few inches away.

"Then James put an extension cord around Rob's neck," Carboni said. "He was only supposed to scare him, but he went crazy and killed him."

As he spoke, Mr. Carboni, bathed in sweat, kept shaking his head in disbelief. Mr. Carboni seemed to be running low on oxygen, and the longer his son talked, the more Mr. Carboni's eyes widened and widened and virtually bulged with horror. Carboni's story more or less corroborated what Strelka had said earlier, Kotora realized. So the kid seemed to be telling the truth—although his story emerged, as with Strelka, in almost telegraphic fashion compared with everything that had been omitted. But the next part seemed to take everyone in the room, except Carboni, by surprise. Carboni flicked his bangs nervously and then explained how he had taken a white rag out of his pocket and given it to Wanger. The rag was doused with lighter fluid, Carboni said.

"James put it in the gas tank," Carboni said, "and I did it."

"What do you mean, 'I did it'?" Kotora asked.

Glum-faced, Carboni raised his arm and flicked his thumb as if striking an imaginary lighter. Mr. Carboni had heard enough.

"Stop," Mr. Carboni said. He waved his hands, "Stop everything."

Mr. Carboni was looking from his son to the police officers and back to his son, as if all of them were complete strangers.

"Okay," Kotora said.

"We understand," said Onorevole.

Kotora and Onorevole said nothing more. They rose from their chairs and left the little green room. They stepped outside into the hall. They invited Mr. Carboni to talk in the hall outside.

"Gentlemen, I've got to stop you," Mr. Carboni said, and he sounded apologetic. "I can't believe what I'm hearing. I can't believe what my son is saying. I don't want to hear any more. I respect you, but I've got to get my son a lawyer."

Kotora agreed that would be a wise move. He explained to Mr. Carboni that his son would probably face arrest, now that he had admitted lighting the rag. At best, Frank Carboni was an accomplice after the fact. At worst, he was a coconspirator in another boy's murder.

Mr. Carboni nodded. Before leaving headquarters to get a lawyer, he wanted to speak with his son again. The detectives agreed. Now that the Carbonis had invoked their constitutional rights against self-incrimination—late though it was—the police were obligated to cease questioning the boy. Mr. Carboni stepped inside. When the door shut behind him, Mr. Carboni looked at his son with disbelief. He was utterly amazed.

"Why?" Carboni's father asked. "Why? Why?"

After a few minutes the detectives came back. As Kotora had said, there was now probable cause to charge Carboni with the homicide. Detective Matonak was drawing up juvenile complaints for murder, arson, and evidence-tampering. To preserve them as evidence, the police took Carboni's black Reebok high-top sneakers (size 10) and his long dark coat, which carried a label saying "The Clother." After explaining that he would get a lawyer, Mr. Carboni opened the door to leave. The boy looked sullen, very frightened, and barely able to keep the tough pose together, but he was trying.

"Make sure you bring me cigarettes," Carboni said. "Bring three or four packs. I'm going to be needing a lot of cigarettes."

Carboni stayed in the conference room for a long time. Then he was led to the holding cell in the bureau a few feet away. It was even smaller.

* * *

Stooge waited an hour before his mother showed up. He was very scared but trying to keep it under control, and he was smoking a lot. A detective kept coming by to see how Stooge was doing, giving little updates about when his mother would probably arrive, although there really wasn't anything new to say about the matter. The fear made him cold.

Mary Stujinski arrived at headquarters with a grim expression on her face. The Friday before she had been in a car accident and hurt her back. So she had gone to the doctor's that Monday morning to see about it. When she came home, her younger son told her that a detective had been looking for her and that Stooge was at headquarters. They lived only a few blocks from the Municipal Center, so Mary got to the station in a matter of minutes. In the short period of time it took to get there, her mind raced with possibilities. She thought Stooge had been in a car accident, given that the kids drove all over the place like maniacs, and then it occurred to her that he was in trouble with the law. Shoplifting or something stupid. Detective Kotora met her in the hallway outside the Youth Services Bureau.

"What is the problem, Officer?" Mary said.

"We have a serious problem," Kotora said. "Rob Solimine's dead."

"What you mean dead?" Mary said. "Car accident?"

"No. Murder."

"Oh my God," she said.

"Don't worry, Mrs. Stujinski," the detective continued. "Rob Solimine was killed in his car, and James Wanger and Frank Carboni were inside the car with him. Your son was in another car with Strelka, and we believe he knew nothing was going on."

By now, the investigation was moving faster. A suspect already had been named. In chasing down some of the other details the boys had related, detectives had driven past Royal Silk to look for the electrical cord in the plastic bag. It was as good a hiding place as any. The business had opened in the late 1970s with a half-page ad in *Cosmopolitan* magazine offering silk shirts for $22 a pop, postage paid, and then climbed to a multimillion-dollar catalog company before going bust in the 1980s. Now the headquarters for the mail-order company, which had once kept 170 people busy, was just a heap of red bricks surrounded by weeds. The detectives drove around the building looking for plastic bags. They saw a lot of them in the weeds or on the driveways or blowing around. None with cords.

Meanwhile, Stooge was in the Youth Services Bureau's second interview room, adjacent to the one where Strelka had been talking to the detectives. This room was larger, had a few posters taped to the walls, and seemed blindingly white because of the fluorescent lighting. Stooge, whose shaggy black eyebrows flexed up and down when he was nervous, perked up when his mother entered the room. They talked very quickly in Serbian—they hardly had time to say anything at all—and the questioning began. Just like that. Mary wanted to get to the bottom of what happened as much as they did.

"Tell them everything you know," Mary told her son. "Don't lie."

Without any fuss, Stooge gave a statement to the police, and his went into considerably more detail than Strelka's. It was the first time in his life Stooge had ever been interviewed by a police officer about anything. His mother had at least talked to the cops the time his dad was arrested. As Kotora and Detective Jeffrey Shom listened, Stooge sketched out what had happened, corroborating Strelka's and Carboni's stories about Wanger strangling Solimine. But for all the detail that Stooge had remembered, he too had shaded events and omitted parts of the story. Stooge opened his account of the murder by beginning a few hours before it occurred. He stepped around questions about why they had gone to Brookdale Park before going to School 15, and what they had been doing there. But he nearly put his foot into it while describing an exchange with Carboni in Carboni's bedroom. In relating that part of the story, Stooge accidentally revealed his foreknowledge. The detectives caught the slip and followed it up but did not pursue it aggressively. Stooge recovered his balance.

"I saw a gas cap and keys on the floor," Stooge explained as a secretary clattered away at a typewriter. "James took a plastic bag out of his coat—it said either 'Pathmark' or 'Foodtown' on it—put the gas cap and keys in the bag, and put the bag inside of his coat, a U.S. Navy pea coat."

Stooge described the objects, and the detectives asked him to continue.

"Frank Carboni asked if the car blew up already. We said, 'No, it didn't, or not yet anyway,'" Stooge said.

"Can you explain to me what you meant by that last statement?" one of the detectives said.

"The gas cap was on the floor with the lighter fluid in Frank's bedroom, so I figured they tried to blow it up when he asked me if the car blew up," Stooge said. "Frank said he had a white rag and that James doused it with lighter fluid, and they put it in the gas valve and lit it, but they wouldn't say which one lit it."

Now and then, his mother stepped outside to smoke a cigarette and Stooge continued giving his statement alone. The cops fed him lunch and treated him nicely. The danger seemed to lift. The detectives asked him to go over his written statement, initial any changes, and sign it. Mary signed too. Then the detectives took it out of the room to confer with Territo and the others. About fifteen minutes after taking his signed statement out of the room, the detectives came back and informed him and his mother that they could both leave.

Of course, Stooge had covered his own tracks no less than Strelka had. Only Carboni had damned himself. In his written and oral statements to the police, Stooge had said nothing about Castaldo—except to mention that the whole crew drove there after meeting up in Carboni's house—and nothing about the prior homicide attempts or conspiracies. He knew that he wasn't being wholly truthful—yet he also failed to comprehend the extent of his liability. And although guilt tugged at him, the idea that he bore legal responsibility for anything that happened was entirely alien. In his mind, he had left out the parts about himself because he felt they were irrelevant. He had been sitting in another car minding his business when Wanger flipped out. For the same reason, he left the parts out about Castaldo because that didn't seem important, either. Castaldo may have wanted the kid dead, but so what—everybody did. Stooge didn't really care. And Castaldo hadn't even been there. The cops wanted to know who killed Robert Solimine, and in his head, that was very simple: It was James Wanger.

By 1:30 P.M. Monday, Detective Matonak was drawing up the complaints to arrest James Wanger for the murder of Robert Solimine, Jr. Based on Carboni's oral admission and Strelka's statements alone, the police had found sufficient probable cause—a legal threshold that means a crime probably has been committed and a suspect has probably committed it—to file murder charges against Wanger. Not to mention that Stujinski—whom virtually everyone now referred to as Stooge because it was hard keeping the two Tommys straight—had given a statement to Detectives Jeffrey Shom and Kotora that also implicated Wanger. It was three against one. The boys' statements, which had been taken separately at headquarters, corroborated each other in their basic elements. That is, all three agreed that Wanger had strangled Solimine, and he had committed the murder with an electric cord in the parking lot of School 15.

A little before 2 P.M., five detectives, including Matonak and Onorevole, drove to Wanger's house at 120 South Parkway. Wanger and his grandparents occupied the second floor of the house, and his aunt lived downstairs. A skiff was stored in the backyard and there was a blue and white statue of the Virgin Mary near a birdbath. The grandmother, Martha Colombo, answered the door, her hair towering upward in a papery gray beehive.

"Is your grandson home?" Matonak asked. "We're the

Clifton police, ma'am, and we're here for Jimmy. We have a warrant for his arrest."

Mrs. Colombo became flustered.

"For what?" she said.

"Homicide."

"Who?"

"Robert Solimine, Jr."

"Impossible!" Mrs. Colombo said. "They're friends!"

Mrs. Colombo showed the detectives the way up the narrow staircase, in her astonishment saying the same thing over and over. "They're friends! Why would he kill his friend?"

Wanger was in his undershirt, lying on the sofa, watching television. The rest of the house looked a little like a cluttered shrine. The dining-room table was unusable for all the religious books, pamphlets, and papers strewn across it. There were some religious statues here and there, and the dining-room floor was covered with shopping bags because Wanger's mother was selling items at the church flea market. Wanger said nothing when the detectives walked in and identified themselves as police officers.

"Stand up," Matonak said, and Wanger stood.

"You are under arrest for the murder of Robert Solimine, Jr.," Matonak said, and he started reciting Wanger's Miranda rights. His grandmother, meanwhile, became more and more hysterical.

"James, what do you know about this? What did you have to do with this?" Mrs. Colombo said. She stood in the kitchen doorway, looking at her grandson and demanding that he look her in the eye, but Wanger kept his eyes glued to the floor. Coming to the end, Matonak asked Wanger if he understood each of his five Constitutional rights, and Wanger said he did.

"Jimmy," his grandmother shrieked, "look me in the eye and tell me you didn't do it! Look me in the eye! Tell me they're lying!"

Wanger kept silent.

Matonak let the grandmother sputter. Who knows, Matonak thought, she might elicit something from Wanger, and he had been read his Miranda rights already. But Wanger didn't say boo, and that made a lasting impression on Matonak. The kid didn't even seem shocked. Then, as if in a gesture of saying "Don't bother," Wanger raised the palm of one hand and spoke to his grandmother

"Take it easy, Grandma," Wanger said. "Before you have a heart attack."

Matonak told Wanger, who was wearing only a pair of dress pants and an undershirt, to get dressed. Then Matonak put the handcuffs on. He told Mrs. Colombo that the detectives wanted the clothes Wanger had been wearing from the night before, and his sneakers. Mrs. Colombo went into another room. When she returned, she handed the detectives a size-38 Navy pea coat, so blue in color that it appeared almost black, and a pair of black high-top sneakers with orange trim. The soles contained the design of a man playing basketball. Matonak was surprised to see there was no mud on the shoes.

Onorevole and Detective William Cooke took Wanger outside and put him in the police car for the ride downtown. Wanger was amiable, extremely so, striking up a conversation about how he admired police officers and how once he had given some thought to becoming a police officer. Onorevole decided the kid was on another planet. Matonak and two detectives stayed behind at the Colombo's in the hope of locating the murder weapon, the gas cap to Solimine's car, and Solimine's car keys. Matonak explained what they wanted, saying they were looking for specific items in a white plastic shopping bag, but Mrs. Colombo seemed confused. She didn't know what to do.

"I gotta call my husband," she said.

"You're under no obligation at this point to let us look around," Matonak said.

"I don't know what to do," she said. She asked the detectives to wait until her husband, Paul Colombo, came home from the hospital. He was visiting their daughter, Wanger's mother, who had undergone back surgery. Matonak and the detectives agreed to wait. They waited about half an hour. But

Mr. Colombo still hadn't returned, so the detectives returned to headquarters. They came back later with a search warrant.

The first thing Detective O'Brien noticed when he walked into the interview room with James Wanger was the hands and the wrists. Investigator James Wood, a detective from the Passaic County prosecutor's office, who had joined the investigation saw it too. Wanger was seated at a large walnut veneer table, and both hands were folded right there on the tabletop, plain as day. Big knobby hands with bony wrists jabbing out of the cuffs of his Izod sweater. Around the wrists were twisted red lines. They were similar to the stripes O'Brien had seen on Solimine's neck, though they were not as vivid. Obviously, they had come from the same source. Stupidity counts, O'Brien thought. And he wondered: Whatever possessed Wanger to display his hands so prominently? Was he stupid? Was he flaunting it? Did he have some kind of unconscious desire to make sure he wouldn't get away with it? O'Brien made a note to himself to photograph the wrists during the interview. He sat down, directly opposite Wanger.

O'Brien introduced himself. He shook hands with the grandfather and with Wanger. Then he went through Wanger's Constitutional rights. Although he didn't doubt that Wanger had been given his rights when the other guys picked him up, it didn't cost anything to read someone's rights more than once. O'Brien was polite, exceedingly so. He studied the grandfather, who didn't say much but nonetheless seemed like a sweet old man, and asked Wanger how he knew Robert Solimine and when he had last seen him.

Wanger began in a matter-of-fact tone, unsmiling, his saga devoid of almost all inflection. As he spoke, he seemed to be talking from miles away, as if he were floating outside himself—and yet he exuded self-confidence, even a sense of superiority in the presence of the officers questioning him. The account Wanger gave suggested that the believed he could convince the police a simple misunderstanding had led him to the police station. He told a story filled with banal details, as if it were calculated to seem nonchalant.

"Well," Wanger began, "we go to school together at Clifton High School. I am in the gifted program. I've known Rob since we were in school together at Christopher Columbus, and we knew each other from Sea Cadets."

"Can you tell us about the events concerning yesterday and today?" O'Brien asked.

"When I woke up yesterday, my grandma made me breakfast. It was toast with cream cheese, and ziti. I had some espresso with a lemon twist. At eleven in the morning," Wanger continued, "I went to work at the Robin Hood Inn, busing tables. That was till about four o'clock. Tommy Strelka picked me up and took me to Tommy Stujinski's house on Fornelius Avenue. It was me and Carboni, Stooge, and Strelka. We hung out at Stooge's, played cards, watched television, stuff like that, till about ten o'clock. About ten o'clock, Rob left. We didn't see him after that."

O'Brien dashed out notes as Wanger spoke. The bit about the espresso and the lemon twist amused him. Then, politely, with the stiff locution of a lifelong police officer, O'Brien confronted Wanger across the table.

"What you are reporting to us, James, is inconsistent with what has been represented to us by other parties," O'Brien said.

Wanger looked O'Brien in the face. No reaction registered. Then Wanger asked for a lawyer.

It was a request that made O'Brien's day. O'Brien didn't need him to answer any more questions. In his mind, it meant he had Wanger in the bag. The case was coming down, all the doors were slamming, Wanger was locked in, and his arrogance had just clinched it. What a cold fish, O'Brien thought. This kid didn't even have enough humanity in his gut to say something that might later cause someone to shed some mercy on him. No remorse, nothing. The kid had fish blood in his veins.

Wanger's grandfather appeared dazed, passive.

"We'll get a lawyer," Mr. Colombo agreed.

O'Brien confiscated Wanger's wallet. Then O'Brien and Wood got a camera. They wrote Wanger's name, the case number, and the date on ribbons of clear plastic tape and stuck these to Wanger's wrists. Then they took photographs. The detectives directed Wanger to remove his shirt, and O'Brien snapped more photos of Wanger standing against the cinder-block wall, arms dangling akimbo in a vaguely James Dean kind of way, eyes peering unemotionally through his tinted shades. There was a gold religious medal dangling from his neck. Then Wanger was taken for fingerprinting.

Detective Onorevole drove over to Castaldo's house about 3:30 P.M. that Monday. Detective Joseph Genchi, an easygoing guy who liked to joke around and kept the mood light around headquarters, went along. Captain Territo told them to see what this kid Castaldo knew, since Solimine was said to have stopped by Castaldo's house hours before the homicide. What's more, two of the kids who had given up Wanger had mentioned going to Castaldo's house before and afterward. Maybe Castaldo knew something, maybe he didn't.

Genchi and Onorevole parked at the curb in front of the Castaldo house, and both of them made it for a dump. Tobacco Road, Onorevole thought. There was a jalopy of some kind parked in front, the brick steps seemed to be peeling away from the mortar, the small window in the front door was busted, and the grass appeared to have survived the entire summer and fall without being cut. Heaps of garbage were stacked up in front of the house waiting for pickup.

The detectives walked past the garbage and up the stairs and buzzed the doorbell. Castaldo came to the door, a suspicious, squinty look on his face, and asked the detectives who they were. They identified themselves, and explained why they had come.

"We're investigating the death of Robert Solimine, Jr.,"

Onorevole said. "We understand you knew this party, and we'd like to ask you some questions."

"Okay."

"Would you be willing to come to headquarters to make a statement?"

"Can I go back in and get some cigarettes?" Castaldo said.

By this time, Mr. and Mrs. Castaldo had come to the door, too, and Mrs. Castaldo started asking what was going on. Frank Castaldo had come back with his coat. He told his parents he was going to headquarters to talk to the police, and that he would be back in a while.

Downtown, Castaldo seemed calm. Although he had no juvenile record, because of some scrapes that had not resulted in arrests, he recognized some of the officers. For once, however, the cops weren't treating him as if he was in trouble. No one enunciated his constitutional rights for him, and unlike the other juveniles in the station for the Solimine homicide that day, Castaldo wasn't asked to sign a written waiver of his Miranda rights.

Genchi and Onorevole led Castaldo into the same interview room where Castaldo's cousin, Carboni, had been earlier that day. Castaldo sat down at the small table under the chalkboard. He folded his hands on the table, sometimes lacing the fingers and sometimes laying them straight across the top as if they were wooden. In the beginning, Castaldo was polite and deferential. He was the good citizen wanting to help out if he could.

But as the interview went on, Castaldo seemed increasingly recalcitrant. He kept saying he couldn't remember this or that. He and Genchi, in particular, started to grate on each other as Castaldo's memory started to dry up. Castaldo propped his elbows on the table, hands over his mouth, and looked away with a trace of a sneer as Genchi pressed him to remember times and places. Onorevole, playing the Good Cop in the well-worn ritual of Bad Cop–Good Cop, had to pose each question at least twice before Castaldo would stir with a reply, and Genchi kept poking at him to be more cooperative. But

Castaldo only became more defensive. At times he was hostile, bobbing his head gently as he spoke, the tough-guy pose, as if he found it distasteful to be in the same room with a police officer. The detectives couldn't even get a reliable answer about how long Solimine had been at Castaldo's house. Castaldo just didn't know.

"Hey, look," Genchi finally snapped. "Don't jerk us around. Just tell us the truth."

"I am telling the truth," Castaldo said. "What do you want me to tell you? You want me to make stuff up?"

The cop and Castaldo traded a few more shots, and Onorevole suggested Genchi leave the two of them alone. Genchi agreed, but he was a little hot. Castaldo gave him a defiant look as Genchi got up to leave the conference room.

"Okay, Frank," Genchi said. "I'm leaving. But I got a feeling we'll be getting to know each other better here."

But other than mentioning that Solimine had been rude to Castaldo's mother when he stopped by, and that Wanger had said some pretty incriminating remarks to Castaldo's mother, Castaldo didn't have much to offer.

"How well did you know Robert Solimine?"

"Pretty good," Castaldo said.

But Castaldo said he and his girlfriend didn't spend much time with this group because they had a party to go to in Bloomfield. He told Onorevole that a bunch of kids—Strelka, Carboni, Stooge, and Wanger—had come by around 7 o'clock to hang out. Solimine was with them also. When he and his girlfriend got back from the party around 9 o'clock, neither the group nor Solimine was there. Castaldo said he played a game of bingo or something with his family and Melanie until about 11:45 P.M. when the group showed up again, minus Solimine.

"Someone told me he left earlier," Castaldo said. "I don't remember who, but they said it was about 10:30 P.M."

"You don't remember who told you that?"

"No," Castaldo said.

No one had said anything about harming Solimine,

Castaldo continued, and the only unusual thing he could recall was that Strelka was acting real quiet. Castaldo said he asked Strelka to drive his girlfriend home, and Strelka did. Wanger stuck around and called a cab from Clifton Taxi about 12:30, and it took about an hour for the taxi to come. Everyone else left with Strelka, Castaldo said. That was about it. Shrug.

"Was there anything wrong?" Onorevole asked.

"What do you mean?"

"You know, was anybody acting unusual? Was anyone angry at Robert?"

"I don't remember. No."

"No," Onorevole said. "There were no problems? Nothing at all that would lead someone to do anything out of the ordinary?"

"No," Castaldo said. "The only thing I can think of Rob did, is he was rude to my mother, and he was annoying Angie, my sister. Messing around with her."

"At any time before he left, did any conversation come up between James Wanger and anyone else about Rob Solimine?"

"Yes," Castaldo said. "Me and my mother were in the kitchen with James when he told her that Rob wouldn't be bothering her anymore."

"Did he say why?"

"No."

After a while, Onorevole asked if Castaldo would agree to give a written statement about some of the things they just discussed Castaldo agreed. They went back over the same ground again, this time in writing, as Onorevole banged at the keyboard and posed questions.

"The Clifton police are investigating the homicidal death of a Robert A. Solimine, age seventeen," Onorevole said. "Do you know him?"

"Yes," Castaldo replied. "I did."

Mary started to make dinner when she and Stooge got home from police headquarters, bustling around the small kitchen as the anger and anxiety and shock worked through her. Mary was still pushing Tommy to tell her everything he might know or could even guess about, that might involve the Solimine homicide.

"Tommy, what's going on?" Mary kept saying. "What you know about this Solimine death?" The moment they had come home from police headquarters she started asking him.

"Ma, it's nothing," Stooge said. "I don't know what happened. Wanger grabbed Solimine, he just grabbed him from behind, and it happened. I don't know why."

Then Stooge clammed up; he didn't want to talk about it. He went about his business. Mary continued preparing dinner. But it kept going through her head that Tommy wasn't telling the truth. He had changed so much since he had started hanging out with this crew, and she could tell he was keeping something from her. But Tommy denied it.

When the telephone on the wall in the kitchen rang, she answered it.

"Hi," a voice said. "Is Stooge there?"

Mary heard a girl's voice she didn't recognize.

"Wait a minute," Mary said, and she handed the phone to her son.

Stooge put the phone to his ear, and he appeared to be jolted. It was Angie Castaldo. Stooge took the telephone receiver and stretched the cord as far as it would go, walking around the wall from the kitchen to the boiler room near the steps.

"Hold on—Frank wants to talk to you," Angie said, and then there was a pause before Castaldo came on.

"Strelka ratted us out. Get over here right away," Castaldo said. "And don't tell anyone where you're going."

Castaldo said they needed to get their stories together. Stooge told him he'd try to be right over.

Around the corner of the dining room and kitchen wall, Mary couldn't hear what Stooge was saying. When he came back to hang up the telephone, he picked up his jacket and started for the door.

"Where are you going?" Mary asked.

"I need to go to Castaldo's house," Stooge said. He was nearly out the door when Mary stopped him.

"Wait, wait, wait, wait," Mary said. "You need to go where?"

"Castaldo's."

"What for?"

"Ma, I just gotta go over there."

"No," Mary said, her voice rising in anger. "No, you do not need to go to Castaldo house. What are you kids doing? You involved in the trouble, you show up at the police, they asking questions. I don't need this, Tommy. You in enough trouble already." Stooge started to hop around the kitchen.

"Ma, I have to go to Castaldo's," he said. "He needs me over there."

Mary put down what she was doing, grabbed him by the jacket, and blocked the door.

"No!" Mary said. "Tommy, one kid is dead! It's done already. You stay here."

Stooge could see his mother was not going to back down, so he took off his coat. He called Castaldo back to tell him that his mother had put her foot down, that he wouldn't be able to make it. Castaldo and Stooge talked for a little while on the telephone, but Castaldo was wary. He told Stooge he hadn't said anything to the cops. They talked a little more, and then hung up.

Andy Blair knew his way around Clifton's City Hall and around the police department. He knew the boys in uniform, and they knew him. Like most of the cops, Blair had grown up in Clifton. He had known some of the old-timers as a kid, and now—several years into establishing his law practice—he had come to know the cops while handling drunk-driving cases and other minor stuff in the Municipal Court downtown. If there was a warrant out for one of his clients, the cops would be decent enough to call him up and let him know so he could surrender the guy instead of having somebody busting down doors in the middle of the night. Blair had also been doing a fair amount of pool work, particularly with juveniles in the state Superior Court at the county courthouse, so he had gotten to know Detective Kotora and the other guys in the Youth Services Bureau. All in all, they had a good working relationship, and the detectives greeted Blair merrily when he walked into their second-floor office asking to see his client.

"How'd you get this one?" Detective Guy Petix said with a chuckle.

How Andrew J. Blair, Esquire, had gotten the case of a lifetime was a fluke. Earlier that afternoon, he had been putzing around the office catching up on some minor affairs when the telephone rang and a man who introduced himself as Stephen Carboni asked to talk with him. Carboni said the lawyer who had done the closing on Carboni's house had referred him to Blair; Carboni wanted to know if he could come by. He said his son was in trouble, and he told Blair what the charge was, but not a whole lot more about the case.

A few minutes later, Mr. Carboni walked through the door, wafting a powerful smell of cigarette smoke. The office was standard American lawyer with a collegiate touch: radiant color photographs of Blair's young family, professional sports paraphernalia—including a team photo of the 1990 Super Bowl champion New York Giants and an autographed picture of New York Yankees slugger Don Mattingly (No. 23—The Hit Man)—golf toys, and huge frames bearing sheepskins. On the wall there was also a grip-and-grin picture of Blair and his grandfather, who was a judge—but not just any judge. This was state Supreme Court Justice Morris Pashman. In the picture, Pashman was shaking his grandson's hand and grinning with obvious pride, the Juris Doctor diploma he was presenting gripped hard in the other fist. After all, he had had something to do with steering Blair down the road toward that career. A legendary jurist in Passaic County, Pashman informed his grandson that he was going to study the law and be admitted to the bar—and not work at one, as Blair had been doing since his graduation from college.

As Carboni sat down and began to talk, Blair was struck by two things: the way the man moved directly to the point without drama or tears, and the fact that he was very scared—deeply terrified about what his son had gotten himself into. Mr. Carboni's eyes widened as he plunged into the story, telling everything he knew from the moment the police came to his house, to the moment that his son flicked his thumb like a cigarette lighter.

Blair agreed on the spot to take the case. He told Carboni what would come next procedurally—what to expect and so on—but the most important thing would be to talk to the boy. Blair said he would call the police and arrange a first meeting at headquarters and find out what had happened. Blair didn't feel comfortable saying everything would be all right.

Down at headquarters, the kid was pacing back and forth in the conference room like a caged beast. Blair sat at the table as the boy passed back and forth, back and forth, smoking cigarettes and looking just as terrified as his father had looked earlier that Monday afternoon in his office. Blair tried reassuring the teenager that he was in good hands.

"This is all I do," Blair said. He explained to Carboni that his entire practice was devoted to handling criminal cases, and he gave him an overview of what was coming.

"I didn't have nothing to do with this," Carboni said.

Blair nodded, kept calming him down.

"My cousin can't go to the county," Carboni said.

The remark seemed to fly out of nowhere. Then the kid said it again, and Blair had no idea what the kid was talking about or even who the cousin was. Blair was curious but decided to let it go. He didn't want to get into the case yet, anyway. He only wanted to calm his kid down. Blair could see this wouldn't be easy. He kept focusing on what would happen next: there would be a hearing tomorrow morning in Family Court. There would be an arraignment, a probable cause hearing, and a detention hearing. The probation department would investigate Carboni's family and background and determine whether it was feasible for Carboni to remain home while the charges were pending.

Carboni kept pacing.

"Frank," Blair said, "calm down. I don't want to get into the facts of the case with you yet. We'll have time to do that later. Just don't worry. You're only fourteen. You're a juvenile."

The kid kept lighting cigarettes and moving. The smoke whirled around his head. The kid would sit down, stand up, sit down again, then start pacing around. It was as if he couldn't stop. He couldn't stop pacing and he couldn't stop smoking, filling the little room with smoke.

Around 6:30 P.M., the police returned to Wanger's house on South Parkway. This time they had a search warrant in hand. Detectives Nick Donato, Matonak, Barr, and investigator Wood from the county prosecutor's office looked through the house and told Mrs. Colombo what they were looking for again. They wanted the extension cord, the gas cap, and the keys from Solimine's car. The detectives showed Wanger's grandmother the search warrant, and she seemed eager to comply. But there was no extension cord, no gas cap, no keys, no white plastic bag that presumably carried the items away from the murder scene.

The police told Wanger's grandmother they also were looking for a black trench coat that Wanger had been wearing the night before. Although they had already received his Navy pea coat—which one of the boys had recalled Wanger wearing—his familiar black trench coat had come up in other interviews. This time, Mrs. Colombo handed the detectives Wanger's black London Fog trench coat. It was hanging on a coat hanger in the shower stall in the bathroom. Barr checked the pockets: The right one was ripped slightly. Inside, the police found a prescription bottle of the drug Tegritol, the anticonvulsant medication Wanger took for brain seizures. There were also St. Jude and St. Joseph medals, shining gold and silver, inside the trench coat pocket. There was a scapular, too, which bore the illegible name of a saint and the phrase "Pray for Us."

"You kids are a bunch of idiots," Susie Strelka said. "I told you something was going to happen. All this fooling around."

Cooking was out—Susie couldn't think straight after the ordeal at the police station—so they ordered in. Everything was racing through her mind. She wanted to talk things over, but she had no idea whom to talk things over with. The cops had said not to discuss it with anyone. At one point, Susie called up Mrs. Chircop to offer her apologies. Meanwhile, Strelka kept saying to his mother that it had all been a big prank. No one had wanted to kill Solimine. Sure, everyone joked around about it, but who would think Wanger would actually do it. Strelka told his mother he had even warned Solimine the night before the murder that Wanger was acting a little nuts. Meanwhile, Chrissie Bachelle stopped by to visit with a girlfriend. She had called her mother, who worked for a lawyer, asking oblique questions about things like murder conspiracy. Now she passed on her mother's advice to Susie.

"My mom says you should get a lawyer," Chrissie said, but Susie shrugged her off. In the end she had to have faith in her son, this gangly kid she had raised for seventeen mostly happy and ordinary years. There was just no way he was any more involved than being a bystander. It all came down to Wanger being a lunatic, she thought, and she recalled a weird exchange she had had with him only a few days before Solimine's death. There was snow on the ground, and Tommy had taken his little sister to their grandmother's house. Susie was beginning to worry about the roads and when they would get back, and once they did, she told him he wouldn't be going out anymore because it was so bad. Then who should come driving up in the middle of the night—it was actually about 10:30 P.M.—but Solimine and Wanger and a car full of boys, including Castaldo. Wanger rang the doorbell and asked for Strelka, who came out on the porch in his stocking feet. In no time, the street in front of the Strelka house was like a frat party. Boys were outside the car pelting each other with snowballs, and Solimine was fishtailing around in the snow and spinning out. Music blared from his car. Susie kept coming out on the porch and yelling at them to pipe down because of the neighbors, and Solimine kept carrying on with the car, no matter how annoyed Mrs. Strelka got.

"Rob, you're going to end up killing yourself!" Susie said. "You're driving like a maniac!"

"He deserves to die," Wanger said. It came out as matter-of-factly as you please. The remark seemed so out of the ordinary—and somehow knowing—that Susie felt an uncanny sensation, a chill that was unrelated to the snowy evening and difficult to explain.

"Nobody deserves to die, James," Mrs. Strelka snapped. "You're just as stupid as him driving around the ice the way youse drive."

Then, standing in the doorway, she shouted into the street again.

"Rob, you better knock the crap off, or I'm going to come out there and kill you!"

"Oh, don't worry about it," Wanger said. "I'm going to do it one of these days." This, too, Wanger said nonchalantly, but the irony now seemed clear.

Now, hours after police had questioned her son, Susie Strelka sat on one couch in her living room, and her son sat on the other, smoking cigarettes together. Strelka told her about things like Annie's Road, which she herself had visited as a teenager, and about the high-speed chases, and the pranks, and she marveled about what her son had been up to and how little she had known of it.

"My God, you kids were doing stupid shit," Susie said.

Eventually, Susie went upstairs to bed. Strelka stayed on the couch. Her mind hopped here and there, consoled by the one undeniable fact that her son had not been in Solimine's car. Her son hadn't murdered anyone.

* * *

Hours later, before he finally called it quits for the day, O'Brien unbolted the flap over the small window on the green metal door of the holding cell where Carboni was being kept and peeked inside. It was a tiny room, painted a sulfurous yellow, with stenciled letters saying "No Smoking" on all four walls. There was a very small wooden bench—maybe three feet long and two and a half feet wide, if that—next to a stainless-steel toilet, whose streamlined configuration resembled a piece of modern art and functioned about as efficiently.

Amazing, O'Brien thought. Carboni had curled up on the bench and gone to sleep. Here's a kid, all of fourteen years old, locked up for taking part in a heinous crime. One kid's dead, and at least another kid is looking at spending the rest of his life behind bars in a room not much bigger than this one, and this kid's sleeping. Sound asleep. That is one cool customer, O'Brien thought.

11

WHEN SOMEONE GETS KILLED IN PASSAIC COUNTY, SENIOR ASSISTANT prosecutor William J. Purdy, Jr., is one of the first people to know about it, and it generally doesn't matter if it's his day off, or the middle of the night, or a national holiday—which it was. On Monday, February 17, 1992, it was Presidents' Day, and most public servants were still sleeping when Purdy got investigator Wood's call at home. There was a homicide working, and Wood had caught it. The job involved a juvenile. There was an autopsy scheduled that morning. Wood would get back to him when there was more to report.

That was it, but it was an important heads-up. The Passaic County Prosecutor's Office required local police departments to notify its investigators of any homicides ASAP, and the investigators alerted Purdy, who was the head of the homicide squad. Throughout that Monday, Purdy kept tabs on the investigation as it proceeded, but he hadn't seen firsthand any of the reports or statements until that evening when he went down to the Clifton police headquarters to have a look. By the time Wanger had been arrested on Monday afternoon, everything seemed well in hand. The detectives on the case felt confident. They had begun the case early Monday morning, shortly after midnight, with just a body in a car and no idea who might have done it, and now they had two juvenile suspects under arrest. They had gotten over the hump. One of the suspects in custody had incriminated himself, and the other two juveniles had given pretty good statements. Since all of the suspects and witnesses were juveniles, Purdy took time out to call Michael O'Shea, the chief assistant Passaic County prosecutor who headed the juvenile delinquency unit, to advise him too. O'Shea, who had been painting a laundry room when Purdy called, offered to come down, but Purdy told him there wasn't any need. Already, Purdy thought, the police had done a very competent job in working the case. They had Wanger to rights, no doubt. Before returning home, Purdy took a peek at the two boys charged with the crime. They were not very criminal-looking or impressive. Carboni, in particular, seemed like just a scrawny kid who was scared to death.

Yet Purdy, a round-faced Irishman with a pinkish-blond complexion, was uneasy. Part of it was his personality. Part of it was the facts. When Purdy reported to work on Tuesday at the county's DeGrasse Street offices behind St. John's Cathedral, he read the statements and reports over and over. Wood came into his office and answered questions. They were a good team, both very low key. As a very cautious man, Purdy felt that enough was never enough in a criminal case. A defendant might give an airtight confession, but Purdy was the kind of prosecutor who worried that the statement would be tossed out by a judge, rare though such rulings are. What's more, juries need to have almost everything wrapped up nicely and presented to them in a neat package. The more serious the crime, the more significant the little details, and Purdy wanted to make sure nothing was missing here. So he looked over the reports and talked things over with Wood and read the statements again. It was difficult imagining how Wanger and his lawyer would be able to get past them.

But Wanger was denying the murder. If Wanger had broken down and confessed, Purdy might have felt more comfortable with things as they stood on Tuesday morning. But Wanger had hung tough—the only one in the entire case to keep his trap shut—and now he had a lawyer. He would say the others blamed it on him to hide their own complicity. So Purdy wanted more. And the reports and statements suggested there was more.

Where was the motive? Was it drugs? Was it a girl? What?

Another thing kept jumping out at him: Why had there been three witnesses to this homicide, or at least to parts of this homicide, who did almost nothing to stop it? Supposing the three juveniles had the benefit of the doubt—Wanger could have ambushed Solimine so quickly with the cord that no one could have saved him—Purdy still couldn't understand something else: Why had none of the boys rendered assistance to Solimine afterward? Or called the police? Called an ambulance? Told a parent?

"Something's missing," Purdy told Wood. "We need to get these kids in here and talk to them again."

On Tuesday morning, February 18, 1992, Wanger and Carboni shuffled into the long blue room where the Honorable Carmen A. Ferrante, Judge of the Superior Court, presiding judge of the Chancery Division, Family Part, held court. The room was long and narrow with high ceilings and wooden pews in close ranks. The boys seemed dazed as they stared upward at the imposing figure on the bench.

Wanger shuffled in wearing shackles over his khaki pants and handcuffs attached to a thick leather waist restraint, which resembled a weight lifter's belt. Wanger appeared pale and soft and very young. The high-top white tennis shoes seemed to accentuate his youth. His grandfather stood nearby. Carboni came in too, shackled and restrained the same way. He appeared solemn and flicked his long black hair nervously from his eyes. His parents, who sat in the front row, were crying.

Ferrante seemed to be studying the boys carefully from his perch as he went through the litany of the charges they faced and the rights that they held under the law. It was a very short proceeding. Then Ferrante entered not guilty pleas on the boys' behalf and ordered them held at the Passaic County Juvenile Detention Center pending a probable cause hearing. Ferrante also ordered psychiatric evaluations.

Purdy returned to Clifton police headquarters following the probable cause hearing in Paterson for Carboni and Wanger because he wanted to participate in the second series of interviews with the juveniles. It was Tuesday afternoon by the time they arrived at headquarters.

Following the hearing in Ferrante's courtroom, Purdy and Wood picked up Carboni, gave him a Diet Coke, and drove to Clifton. Arrangements had been made to bring the other boys to headquarters too. Before leaving the courthouse in Paterson, Purdy and Wood had spoken briefly with Andy Blair about the possibility of a deal. His kid could get leniency if he cooperated. Blair was interested. He was very interested, in fact. To the prosecution, Carboni was key, because he was the only one besides Wanger who had been inside the car with Solimine during the murder. But to Blair, he was looking at a fourteen-year-old kid facing the rest of his life in prison. If his kid went down on the murder rap as an adult—and the state was talking about trying the kid as an adult—he would have to do at least thirty years before parole. So Blair agreed to let his kid go back to police headquarters for more discussions.

As Purdy, O'Shea, and Wood met with the police detectives at headquarters, Purdy discovered that Matonak also felt that the three youngest boys had been more deeply involved than they had admitted. Bleary-eyed from working the case on the previous day, Matonak showed them the sketch that Strelka had drawn of his car in relation to Solimine's. Matonak felt sure that the distance between the cars was not a coincidence; Strelka and Stujinski must have been acting as lookouts in the Buick. His hunch made sense, but the possibility of a wider conspiracy also seemed incredible. O'Shea, for one, almost didn't want to believe that the case was more than a deranged kid going nuts and killing a friend, and another kid helping him to get rid of the evidence. Could a bunch of teenagers, who otherwise seemed ordinary, all participate in a murder conspiracy?

Strelka and Stujinski arrived at headquarters with their mothers, and the police kept them apart. Preparing for the second round of interviews, the detectives and Purdy talked about their approach to each kid. Purdy most wanted to hear what Strelka had to say. As the next eldest to Wanger, Strelka presumably knew more than Stooge. Strelka also posed a mystery. Everyone, including the victim's family, had described Strelka as Solimine's best friend. Why hadn't he called for help? He had stonewalled the cops at first. Why?

Strelka and his mother were introduced to Purdy. Everyone took their places in cafeteria chairs around the table in the Juvenile Bureau, and there was barely enough room to move. Strelka had walked into the room seeming distracted and a little nervous. His hair looked as if it hadn't been washed and he was wearing a white sweatshirt with a Bart Simpson cartoon on it.

"I have an announcement to make," Bart was saying, arms folded smart-ass fashion across his chest. "I'm bored."

Strelka sat down and Susie sat beside him, to her son's right. O'Brien introduced himself and sat directly across from Strelka. Matonak sat across from Susie. Matonak wasn't running the show like yesterday, because O'Brien and Purdy were.

O'Brien explained that they had wanted to talk to Strelka again because there were certain "inconsistencies" in his statement, and he asked Strelka if he would be willing to give the police a second statement pertaining to the events of Sunday night. As O'Brien talked—sounding, as was sometimes his habit, like a lease agreement—Susie detected an ominous note in the air, but reassured herself once more that, although Strelka was wrapped up with the characters who had done this terrible thing, he couldn't have been in on the murder. They were after something here, she thought. But she trusted them too. They knew what they were doing. They were the police.

"Tommy, tell us again about your actions on this date," O'Brien said. "Can you tell us what happened when you get to the school?"

Strelka explained what happened again briefly: where he had parked, what he had seen standing outside the window of Solimine's car, what had happened afterward.

"Why did you park near the steps?" O'Brien asked. If the boys were hanging out, as Tommy said, wouldn't the cars have been closer together?

"I wanted to park there," Strelka said.

"Why park so far away from Rob's car?"

"We just stopped there."

O'Brien pushed him a little now. Why hang out with a buddy in two cars so far apart that you have to keep walking back and forth to chitchat?

Strelka said they were still able to talk. They were talking at the school and hanging out and that was it.

"Fifty feet away from each other?" O'Brien said. "It doesn't conform to human nature."

Strelka grew more and more edgy, and O'Brien was getting more insistent. Voices were rising. Why, O'Brien wanted to know, would anyone keep coming out of his car on a cold February night to see what was happening with Solimine? Why not just leave when he had to leave because of his curfew? He started going over other details and inconsistencies.

"It doesn't add up," O'Brien kept saying. "It's not logical. You were there for one reason. You were the lookout."

But Strelka kept saying that he had moved his car up by the steps because Solimine had been peeling out and spattering his car with mud. O'Brien moved on to another area, prodding Strelka about why he and Stooge had driven all over Clifton following the murder without bothering to alert anyone.

"You were Rob's friend, right?" O'Brien said.

"Yeah."

"You were his best friend, right?"

"Okay."

"You just saw your best friend get strangled, right? By another friend. Well, why didn't you stop him?" O'Brien said.

"We tried to stop him. We couldn't."

"Three guys couldn't stop Wanger?"

Strelka insisted that he had been surprised by Wanger's act and had tried to get him to stop. But even if he was telling the truth, it didn't explain why Strelka went to Carboni's house and then Castaldo's house afterward. What was that for? the detectives asked.

"Well, we didn't know what to do."

"Well," Purdy chimed in, "why didn't you call an ambulance? Why wasn't that your first call? You must have passed about ten phone booths on the way.

"I don't know," Strelka said.

The questions started to fly now from all directions. O'Brien would push, then Matonak would ask something, and then Purdy would pose something else. Strelka hunkered down, but he was nervous. His knee was bobbing up and down, as if his foot were pumping a kick drum. His entire body trembled. And he was smoking a ton of cigarettes, sucking in deep bursts of smoke and jerking the butts away from his mouth. His mother was nervous too. Strelka got up as if he was about to leave. Then he sat down.

"I don't know if I should say anything," Strelka said. He was rubbing his hands on his thighs, as if to wipe away the perspiration. As the pressure from O'Brien increased, Matonak would slow things down and calm down the Strelkas.

"I'm getting really nervous," Susie announced. She said she wanted to go out in the hall and stretch her legs and smoke a cigarette. No one minded that she left, of course—and in fact there was relief around the table that maybe now Strelka might talk more freely without his mother around. The chairs scraped on the floor, and Purdy looked at Strelka across the table.

"Now, Tommy, your mom is out of the room," Purdy said. "Is there anything you want to tell us that you were afraid to say with your mom in the room?" His tone suggested that his puzzlement was genuine. He still had nothing that might explain why the murder happened and why the boys had acted the way they had afterward.

"Is there sex, or drugs, or what here?" Purdy asked.

Strelka looked around the room, hands going on his thighs. "The meetings," he said.

That was it. That was all he said, but it was an enormous revelation. Purdy wanted to leap out of his chair. He looked around the table at Matonak and O'Brien. They were poker-faced.

"Okay," O'Brien said. "What can you tell us about the meetings?"

Now it started to flow. Strelka told the detectives about gathering in Stevie Castaldo's room and discussing, for at least three weeks previous to the murder, how the band of kids wanted to kill Solimine. Strelka told how there had been discussion about the murder hours before it happened.

What's more, for the first time, Castaldo appeared as the prime mover behind Solimine's murder—which also explained the boys' movements in the hours after Solimine's murder. Strelka told them how Wanger and Castaldo had a Mafia infatuation; how Wanger had been learning Italian; how Castaldo had always boasted that his uncle was in the Mafia; how Castaldo had promised Wanger a place in the mob if "James did stuff for him"; how Castaldo had ordered Wanger around and once asked Wanger to beat some other kid up for him. Strelka told about how Wanger had fashioned the garrote in the high-school parking lot and how he had demanded that the other kids hit Solimine with the baseball bat to make sure he was dead. He told the detectives how he had seen Wanger bracing his feet against the bottom of the driver's seat to gain purchase with his whole body as he yanked on the garrote. He gave flesh to suspicions the cops had had all along—that the boys had been in league with each other, if not in conspiring to kill Solimine, then at least in abetting the crime afterward, and that Castaldo played an important role. But then Strelka delivered the bombshell of bombshells. He described how Wanger had asked Solimine to recite the Hail Mary in the car.

The detectives took notes. Everything Strelka said was carried out of the room and bounced off the other two boys to test its veracity. Without revealing exactly what Strelka said, the detectives took tidbits of his account and posed new questions to Carboni and Stooge, using what they had as levers to pry more information out of the teenagers. In the room across the hall, for example, Stooge told detectives about Wanger's dispensation of the medals, a point that Strelka had neglected to mention. Asked about the St. Joseph medals, Strelka explained their significance. He said his was home in the filing cabinet in his bedroom.

Steadily the story unfolded, creating news waves of astonishment among the several detectives, who had thought they had heard everything. The last thing Strelka would admit was that he had been a lookout, but eventually he conceded this too, and the detectives arranged to take his written statement.

As the interrogation intensified, Susie had stepped outside in the hall to have a cigarette. Her ears were buzzing and her eyes were blurry. The cops had her all worked up, and she felt torn between protecting her son and demanding that he tell them everything because she thought that was the only proper thing to do. One minute she was trying to get a cop to back off. The next minute she was yelling at her son. Her head was spinning, and she wondered what she should do.

She drew the cigarette smoke deeply into her lungs, trying to hold it in, to hold on to it. At times it seemed as if Strelka was in control of everything, giving out this bit of information and then that, capriciously, but then of course she realized the police were in control. Someone besides her was in control.

The young detective—she didn't know him—and another guy she didn't know came up close to her face and she lowered her eyes.

"Mrs. Strelka, does Tommy have candles in his room?"

"Yeah," she said. *Where's this going?* she thought.

"Where does he keep them?"

"In his room."

"How about crosses?"

"No."

Uh-oh, Susie thought. *Here it is now. They think Tommy is a Satan worshiper.*

"But he has candles?" the detective said.

"Yeah," Susie said.

"Can you describe them?"

Susie's mind had been getting foggier as the day wore on, but she had the answer in her mind and could even see the candles very clearly after thinking about it for a moment, thinking about where they were and whether Strelka had ever even lit them.

"He has two candles in his room, I think."

"Could you describe them, please?" the detective said. He was holding his pad and pen, ready to get this all down.

"One's Garfield," Susie said. "One's Odie."

The written statement began at 5:15 P.M., and Susie was barely holding herself together. The discussion in the juvenile conference room had lasted nearly three hours, and now they were preparing for yet another session. Once again, Strelka ran over the same ground they had already covered as a typewriter clacked beside him. Listening to her son speaking and the cops reading back his answers, Susie had the sense that the cops were taking liberties. If not exactly putting words in Strelka's mouth, the detectives were altering what he had said, not by much, but enough, so that it conformed more closely with what they wanted. Words like "group" took on an unexpected importance. His exact words were smoothed over and the concepts reduced, so that what was left still resembled the original, but it was different—there was no doubt in her mind it was different, and it made her nervous. But who was she to question the procedure? She believed it was all in the service of getting Wanger, as the cops had put it, so she clenched her teeth and kept on.

"Is there anything that you would like to add to this statement?" O'Brien asked.

"I should have taken this matter seriously from the beginning and told someone about it," Strelka said, as a secretary tapped out the words. "I regret what happened because I never wanted things to turn out this way. If I knew that they were really serious, I would have told."

"Do you believe in God?" O'Brien asked.

"Yes."

A last question made it clear to Strelka that he and his mother would have an opportunity to read over the document for errors and omissions. Strelka's story was committed to writing by 6:31 P.M. Strelka signed the police statement, and so did his mother. Strelka also initialed the statement at the top and bottom of each page.

Susie stepped out into the hall for another cigarette. Strelka waited inside while one of the detectives strode off somewhere with the statement in hand. A few minutes later, O'Brien came back with a camera. Susie watched him as he went inside the room. She had a quizzical look on her face; her heart pounding faster and faster. The camera's flash exploded in cold white light. Again. Then another flash, and it suddenly hit her: They were arresting Strelka. Her son was being charged with a crime. It was too late. She heard this voice in her head saying it was too late, and she suddenly felt foolish. He had signed the paper, she had signed the paper, and it was too late. And then everything went blank.

"She's down," someone said, and O'Brien turned around from the camera to see Mrs. Strelka curled up on the floor of the police department in a fetal position. The officers were trying to help her, but she wasn't talking. Her eyes were open, but she was unresponsive, like a catatonic. She seemed unable to move her limbs.

Uh-oh, O'Brien thought, *she's heading for the flight deck.*

Someone called for an ambulance. The ambulance came and she was put on a stretcher and wheeled outside. She was taken to St. Mary's Hospital for examination. It had been obvious from the start that she was high-strung, but it looked now as if she had cracked up. It was a shame, O'Brien thought. It made it all the more clear that he had been dealing with kids in this crime, not adults. O'Brien hadn't known any of these characters for very long, but he had had the sense the boys had been able to stay out of trouble until now. Sure, they were misfits, but O'Brien figured they probably had been pretty good kids until the day they met each other. They weren't angels, but they were the last kids you'd expect to see in the middle of something like this. Their parents had loved them and tried to provide for them and raise them right, but something went wrong. God knows why they found each other. Probably the parents had been too permissive, too understanding. They didn't put their feet down when the boys were driving all over the county and staying out all hours of the night and hanging around with the likes of this Castaldo kid. And now they were paying for it, too, he thought.

The room where the detectives were trying to talk to Stooge was fogged with smoke: Mrs. Stujinski was smoking, investigator Wood was smoking, Stooge was smoking cigarettes almost end to end, and the grayish-yellow smoke hung in wavy layers near the lights. Purdy had left Strelka's interview for the formal written statement to see what Stujinski had to say, and Matonak came too. O'Shea did not want to become a participant in the interviews; court rules barred attorneys from litigating a matter to which they were also witnesses. Instead, O'Shea watched the boys through the small, porthole like windows with the two-way mirrors.

"We know about the group," Purdy said. "So you might as well just tell us who was in it, and what you guys did."

Stooge stared up at them, his brown eyes floating around the huge buglike frames of his tinted glasses. With mild derision Purdy noted Stooge's black T-shirt with the logo for Megadeth or ACDC or some other such group, and put him down as a headbanger. Mrs. Stujinski was watching with a look of concern on her face. Wood was pounding the coffee down, and coffee was offered to the Stujinskis too.

The detectives were using what Strelka had said as leverage to pry facts out of Stujinski, and the interview seemed to be going more or less smoothly. The kid went back over what he had said during the interviews the day before, adding fresh details here and there about the night before. But even as he discussed his own involvement, he seemed guarded. At first he didn't mention the St. Joseph medals. He also didn't mention Castaldo's telephone call after he had gotten home. As Mary listened, she grew more agitated. She realized her son was holding back and stopped the interview herself. They had only been talking about fifteen minutes before she broke off the session.

"He's lying," Mary said. This came as no great surprise to them, but they appeared astonished for a moment that it was Stujinski's mother who was pointing it out to them. "I know he's lying."

The detectives agreed to leave her alone with Stooge for a few minutes and left.

"I don't know what you kids is doing outside during the day, during the night, hanging out, drinking, driving the cars, racing on the road—now it's time to tell the truth," Mary said. Her voice always became screechy as she became angry or indignant, and she bore down on her son in the small room. "That's not a Nintendo game where you push the button, you kill the guy, and the next minute the guy is still alive. This is real, Tommy. This is real life. You have to face it."

"Ma," Stooge said, "I'm involved."

"You're involved, you need to pay," Mary said.

The detectives and Purdy returned. Once more, their pitch was simply that they knew everything already and only wanted to hear it from Stooge himself. They wanted to understand this group in which he was a member.

Just like that, Stooge started to talk, but now with greater detail than even Strelka had gone into. It took almost nothing to get him going. He began to explain how the group came together, who its leader was, what they were up to, and Purdy and Wood listened and took notes. Purdy especially was struck by how nonchalant the kid was as he described his circle of friends and their activities. The most jarring new piece of information Stooge surrendered concerned the medals. The police had found some religious junk in Wanger's trench-coat pocket, but no one knew what to make of it until Stooge explained its significance.

"James gave us these medals to show that we were a group and you could never leave no matter what," Stooge said.

"Who'd he give them to?" Purdy asked.

"Everyone got one."

Purdy turned to the detectives. "Go back and tell Strelka about the medals."

Stooge's written statement commenced at 6:08 P.M. Perhaps worn down by the long wait at headquarters and the oral interview, Stooge gave monosyllabic answers. He told everything he knew, and he seemed whipped. The compression of his replies and the jumbled organization of his ideas created problems and impressions in the statement that even the prosecution would later downplay. For one thing, Stooge conveyed the impression that the meetings in Castaldo's house were both informal affairs—a bunch of kids drinking soda around a table and talking about things—and discussions apropos of a board meeting, where the boys had organized solely to get rid of Rob. What's more, Stooge made it seem as if the group was somehow a religious cult when he related the time that Wanger quoted the Bible to make Melanie listen to Frank.

But the most startling admission of all, made in utter honesty, would haunt Stooge the rest of his days and almost anyone who came in contact with the case. It would figure in the plea bargain, in the sentencing, and in the arguments by both the defense and the prosecution at the future trials of Wanger and Castaldo.

The police simply asked Stooge what he felt at the moment

that he and Strelka came back to Rob's car and realized he was dead. With bracing candor, Stooge replied:

"At first I was glad that we accomplished our mission, and afterwards when I realized what happened, and that me and Tommy were pressured into doing this, me and Tommy went back to Tommy's car and drove off."

"Did anyone else have that feeling of accomplishment?"

"We all did."

Carboni wasn't going to give it up without a fight. He was the only kid at headquarters with legal counsel—legal counsel that was virtually bashing him over the head to cooperate with the police—and yet he was holding back, refusing to budge either out of stubbornness, honor, or fear of his cousin. Blair stayed in the conference room in the adult Detective Bureau with his client, who would not speak directly to the police. Mr Carboni also was present. To protect the younger Carboni's Fifth Amendment rights, Blair was going to act as a conduit for the detectives' questions and his client's answers. The detectives posed their questions for Carboni to Andy Blair, and Andy Blair got Carboni's story of what had transpired and gave it to the detectives.

What happened next in police headquarters was something akin to a race to get to the bottom of the homicide. In other interrogation rooms, the other two young boys, Stooge and Strelka, were talking away. Neither of them had a lawyer. As the day wore on, Blair would have a chance to see the way the police were working the other boys—and it was either impressive or disturbing, depending on one's point of view. The detectives were dive-bombing the other kids with questions, firing the same question or slight variations of it again and again, accusing the boys, soothing them, getting their mothers worked up, going over the same ground over and over again, demanding that the boys admit what the boys either did not want to admit or could not admit. Then at the typewriter the detectives banged away until they had got it all down. This put all the more pressure on Blair and his kid to catch up. Blair could see the whole case was coming down, and he didn't want his kid to be shut out. But the detectives were growing impatient with Carboni.

When the detectives came over to the conference room, they gave Blair a taste of what the other boys were saying, and Blair would see what Carboni would say. Carboni would give the answer. But not without Blair and Carboni's father cajoling, pleading and arguing with Carboni to tell the whole story. The kid kept sketching broad strokes and the cops wanted details.

"Well, he's saying this," Blair told them, and he would relay Carboni's account.

"Andy," O'Shea told him, "We know a heck of a lot more. If your kid wants the benefit of a deal, he's going to have to tell you everything."

Back inside he'd go, and so on. Then some of the detectives knocked on the conference door, and Blair opened it.

"What about the meetings?"

"Meetings?" Blair said. "What meetings?"

The detectives told him the other two boys had confessed that the group discussed killing Solimine on several occasions before Sunday night. The story was pouring out now, they said, of a premeditated murder. There was a wider conspiracy here, and it also involved Castaldo. After they left, Blair shut the door.

"What the fuck is this?" he said.

Carboni had tears in his eyes. The point had finally come where he could not hold back anymore. He either had to fess up to everything, or watch the deal go out the window. Carboni had been trying to keep Castaldo out of this mess, and his face showed the strain, but now his own father was pushing him to tell the truth, even if it meant that his own nephew and Carboni's cousin would go to prison. Carboni told Blair the story. Blair told the cops. By dinnertime, the story was out about the meetings, the conspiracy, the prior attempts, and Castaldo.

Yet the detectives had nothing, technically, as far as Carboni was concerned. His version of the story had been related through Blair. As far as the law was concerned, he had said nothing since his statement concluded the previous day. So now the detectives and Purdy and O'Shea told Blair that they wanted a written statement from Carboni. Blair told the detectives that he would let his kid talk face-to-face with the detectives, and he would let his kid give a signed, sworn, written statement—but only for something in return.

Purdy and O'Shea said they would have to talk things over with the boss. Passaic County Prosecutor Ronald S. Fava, the county's top law-enforcement official, was supposed to come to police headquarters. In the meantime, Carboni needed something to eat. Somebody ran out to Burger King to get the kid a burger.

It was very late at night when Fava came. He was dressed casually, a look that suited his laid-back demeanor much more than the customary dark suits and conservative ties. The son of Paterson's Finance Commission chairman, Fava had been a rising star in the county's Republican Party, having become one of the youngest legislators in state history to win a state assembly seat. At the time of that victory, he was twenty-six years old. He was handsome, photogenic, and, if this is possible, hip in a square sort of way. Before joining the legislature, he had served as an assistant Passaic County prosecutor in 1973 and 1974. He was married and the father of a daughter and a son. After losing his bid for reelection in 1977, Fava went on to serve as a part-time municipal prosecutor for Paterson, and he was later promoted to Municipal Court, which handles mostly traffic offenses and petty crimes. In 1988, Governor Thomas Kean nominated Fava to become the county prosecutor. Virtually everyone quoted in newspapers lauded Fava's selection: They praised him for his scruples, his decency, his administrative acumen, and above all, his fairness. He was, everyone said, a good guy. He took over the county prosecutor's office with a pledge to be tough on crime, and he was, particularly on drug offenses. As the Hail Mary murder story unfolded, mobs of media crowded into his office. Fava accommodated them all, often one at a time, instead of calling a big press conference.

"What's going on?" Fava said, shaking Blair's hand.

"My guy's ready to talk," Blair said. "He'll tell you exactly what you need to know, but I cannot put the noose around my guy's neck without some kind of guarantee."

Blair wanted Carboni to remain a juvenile. He wanted that guarantee rock solid. He waited as Fava huddled in private with Purdy and O'Shea. Blair knew Fava from Fava's days as a municipal court judge, and Blair liked the man and trusted him.

"What do I get?" Blair asked.

"We're giving you our word that if your guy talks, we'll guarantee that he'll remain in Juvenile Court," Fava said. "We will not seek a waiver."

At this point, Fava offered his word and his hand.

Now Andy Blair was staking his profession, and his fourteen-year-old client's life, on Ron Fava's integrity. As honorable a man as Fava was, this was still staking a tremendous burden on a handshake. Get it in writing: It's the mantra of the legal profession. But that's what it was to be: a handshake agreement. The two shook hands in police headquarters, and the deal was made.

"Your word is good enough for me," Blair said. "I'm trusting you."

Carboni was talking face-to-face with the detectives about the murder for the first time since the previous morning, and the session was, if possible, less friendly. The procedure was supposed to go like this: Carboni first told the detectives everything all over again, and then he would tell it again all over again for the written statement. Blair, having secured Fava's promise to treat his young client as a juvenile, was sitting in, of course. Wood, who was bleary-eyed, and irritable, worked Carboni. Long afterward, he would recall with disbelief how Carboni hung tough. It took six hours to break him down again. Once he broke, he seemed like a lamb. But even then, Wood thought, the kid told only about ninety percent of what he knew, and Wood dogged him for hours. Fava, unbeknownst to Wood, took turns with O'Shea watching through the tiny window with the two-way mirror.

Wood bore in, his sharp blue eyes fixing hawklike on the boy. At times he was shouting.

"I don't remember," Carboni said.

"Bullshit," Wood said. He slammed his hand on the table. "This event is the biggest event in your life. Don't tell me you don't remember. It just happened."

They would extract a little more, and then they would have to work him over again. Blair watched with a mixture of admiration and disquiet. This was the way cops worked. Badgering and using all the psychological tricks they could to get a guy talking. It confirmed what Blair had suspected and what his clients often complained about. Blair felt most leery about the way the words left his client's mouth and appeared on paper. Everything was slightly askew—but more or less on target. He was glad he and Carboni would have a chance to review the document and make changes before Carboni signed it.

The statement was taking forever, as three and sometimes four grown men worked over a fourteen-year-old to get him to tell the whole story. Carboni's father kept encouraging the kid, reassuring him, and Wood kept getting pissed off every time Carboni's memory swooned.

"Fuck it," he said. "You don't want to do this, you can go rot in jail! Your lawyer is busting his ass, but you can go rot with your cousin in jail."

Wood stormed out. It wasn't purely anger that made him leave. Now and then the cops would leave the room to give Blair some more time with his client. But Wood was surprised to see Fava still there, and he realized his boss had been watching through the window.

"Now I know why I hired you," Fava said.

Back inside, Blair knew his client wasn't completely a believer yet, and it was because of Castaldo.

"Look," Blair said, "you've got to forget this cousin shit. Either way, your cousin's going down. Unless you're going to be with him, you want to help yourself. You've got your mom here, you've got your dad here, you've got to trust us and do what we're telling you to do. This is your life." Carboni's mother wasn't in the room, but she, too, had lent him her support. His father just kept repeating to his son that he loved him, that he stood behind him, that it was something he had to do to help himself. Carboni was bawling his eyes out. Then the detectives came back in and they went around again, tapping out more lines on the statement. Carboni was the last to crack, and he had given them almost everything. But not quite. And he never would.

The detectives, along with Purdy and O'Shea, decided that they could not delay Castaldo's arrest until the morning. Carboni, the last of the three boys to give a written statement, had finished up at 1:47 A.M. After he and his counsel reviewed the statement, they made almost no substantive changes. The detectives had sworn statements alleging not only that Castaldo had gotten the ball rolling in the murder of Robbie Solimine, but that he had kept some of the dead boy's belongings or the murder weapons as trophies. Before they could be destroyed, the detectives wanted to search the house. O'Brien called Municipal Court Judge Harry Fengya, who signed the search warrant.

At 3:10 in the morning on Wednesday, February 19, a small posse descended on the rickety white house where Frank Castaldo and his family lived. Detective O'Brien wanted no fuss. Half a dozen police officers and their cars moved in quietly and secured the perimeter. They parked at either end of Prescott Avenue and walked to the house that stood nearly in the middle of its length.

Paperwork in hand, O'Brien rang the doorbell. Rather promptly, Mrs. Castaldo came to the door in a housedress, and O'Brien identified himself.

"We have a search warrant and an arrest warrant for

Frank," O'Brien said, and he showed her copies of the papers that had been signed by Judge Fengya minutes earlier.

Mrs. Castaldo seemed to be in a fog. She said nothing, but allowed the men inside. Through the open door O'Brien could see Castaldo sleeping on the sofa in his clothes. O'Brien stepped into the living room and stood over him. The detective looked around the living room and around the house, which was a mess. The others, including Assistant Passaic County Prosecutors Purdy and Mike O'Shea, trooped into the cramped room. O'Brien tapped Castaldo on the shoulder.

"Wake up, Frank," O'Brien said. "It's the Clifton Police Department. We have a warrant for your arrest."

Castaldo grunted, so O'Brien jostled him some more and called his name again. Castaldo came to, and O'Brien told him to stand. Castaldo was a little groggy, but he seemed to understand well enough what was going down. Despite the grave circumstances of the situation, O'Brien wasn't the only cop who felt an almost merry delight in arresting the kid who had acted like a punk a little more than thirty-six hours ago.

"Are you awake, Frankie?" O'Brien said, and Castaldo regarded him with a genuine, if sleepy look of alarm. "You're under arrest for the murder of Robert Solimine, Jr."

"You can't arrest me," Castaldo said, "I wasn't there."

Wrong, O'Brien thought.

In its own way, Castaldo's remark was a damning statement that summed up his stupidity and arrogance in the same breath. It was true that Castaldo wasn't at the scene when the murder occurred, but his remark only showed his complicity in the plot, O'Brien thought. An innocent man wouldn't be drawing nice legal distinctions. An innocent man would proclaim his innocence, declare his outrage, and be shouting that the police were making a horrible, grievous mistake, O'Brien thought.

Other family members were awake now. Frank's father, Giuseppe, shambled into the living room, along with Angie and Stevie. They were excited, but nothing beyond the ordinary. O'Brien explained that they had come armed with a search warrant. Castaldo acted as if he couldn't believe this was happening, as O'Brien told him what they were looking for.

"Let's take a walk, Frankie," O'Brien said. "We're looking for a few things—the keys to Robert Solimine's car, the gas cap, the aerosol can you guys used to try to blow up the car, the electrical cord James Wanger used to strangle him, and a gold St. Joseph medal. Let's see your brother's bedroom."

"I threw the medal out," Castaldo said.

"We've got a search warrant," O'Brien continued. "We're going to find the stuff, too. If we have to tear the house apart, we're going to find it."

"Wait," Mrs. Castaldo said, and she rushed into the kitchen. She came back to the living room with a gold St. Joseph medal and handed it to O'Brien.

"I put it on the microwave in the kitchen," she said.

"All right," O'Brien said. "Now, where are the keys? And the gas cap to Solimine's car?"

"The stuff is in the closet in my brother's room," Castaldo said. "It's my closet. My brother just sleeps there."

O'Brien, Kotora, and Castaldo marched into the bedroom. The place was pretty barren: a dresser, a desk, a chair, a Nintendo set. Castaldo sat down on the wooden desk chair. So this is the place where Castaldo held court, O'Brien thought. He stooped over and burrowed through a heap of clothes on the floor of the closet. The pile of clothing stood three feet high at least. Two-thirds of the way down, O'Brien found the keys. He didn't wear gloves or use instruments to pick them up. He just grabbed them: four keys and a small folding knife. There was a Bacardi rum key chain, just as the juveniles had said.

"These are the ones?" O'Brien asked.

"Yes," Castaldo said.

"You recognize them?"

"They're Rob's keys. James gave them to me."

"Okay. Where's the aerosol can? The can of FDS spray used in the attempt to blow up Solimine's car?"

"It's on the kitchen counter next to the bread," Castaldo said.

O'Brien went to the kitchen. The sink was full of dirty dishes. But, lo and behold, there on the counter next to the bread and the toaster and a can of bread crumbs—could there be a more absurd place to find it? O'Brien thought—stood the can of FDS feminine hygiene spray. O'Brien took that, too. They paraded back into the living room. Castaldo's tough-guy pose had started to crumble. He looked very scared.

"Okay, Frank, where's the cord?" O'Brien asked.

"James put it in a plastic garbage bag with the gas cap," Castaldo said. "He put it with the garbage on the curb, and it got hauled away with the garbage yesterday morning."

One of the cops didn't believe him and made a crack about how Castaldo had best not lie in front of the prosecutor, because he could put him away for thirty years. Mr. Castaldo said his son was telling the truth: The garbage had been taken away yesterday. That would be Tuesday, a little more than twenty-four hours after the body had been found. But the detectives continued to search anyway. While O'Brien was in the kitchen, Stevie Castaldo was hovering behind him with a question.

"Is the extension cord I gave to James the one he used to kill Solimine?" Stevie asked.

"We have information to that effect," O'Brien said.

The detectives looked around, asking Mr. Castaldo questions as they poked around the basement and the garage. The garage was stuffed with maybe fifty spools of wire in all shapes and sizes, but it wasn't what the cops were looking for because it wasn't what the juveniles had described. Eventually the search wound down without the murder weapon being found. O'Brien handed a receipt of the seized belongings to Mr. Castaldo and returned to Frank.

"You don't need to say anything else, Frank," O'Brien said. "Detective Onorevole is taking you downtown to headquarters. If you have something else to say, you can say it in writing."

Everybody filed out after Castaldo was taken away. Surowiec came from around the rear of the house, where he had been posted in case someone tried anything funny. He was in a very foul mood.

"I stepped in dog shit," Surowiec said. Surowiec was grumbling at the ridiculousness of it. He wasn't alone, either.

"I think everybody stepped in dog shit," Kotora said. "It was like you couldn't miss it."

Long after the search was over, the detectives couldn't help remarking about what a dump the house was. To the detectives, the clutter seemed a fitting symbol for the values that the entire Castaldo clan, with the possible exception of Stevie, represented. In fact, this seemed to be the detectives' attitude before even arriving at the Castaldos'.

Onorevole whistled at the thought of searching the place from top to bottom trying to find items as easily hidden as a set of keys. "I'm really glad he took us inside and showed us the stuff," Onorevole said, "because we'd still be looking."

"Would you like a cup of coffee, Frank?" O'Brien asked.

Castaldo was seated by the reception desk in the Adult Detective Bureau, one of his hands cuffed to the chair. No, he didn't want coffee, but he agreed to give a statement. He seemed more awake than the detectives, but he was beaten, acting as if the fight had gone out of him. The detectives sensed that he had been stung by the betrayal of his pals, especially his cousin. The detectives—Onorevole, O'Brien, and Wood—went over Castaldo's rights again. Castaldo signed them away and initialed the waiver form. Onorevole sat at the typewriter. He was so fatigued that if Castaldo had said O'Brien had committed the homicide Onorevole would have typed it. After Onorevole typed for a while, the detectives switched and O'Brien had a go at it.

"We are going to ask you questions concerning the homicide of Robert Solimine that occurred on Sunday, February 16, 1992, at 700 Gregory Avenue, Clifton, New Jersey, School

No. 15, to be exact," the statement began. "Do you have any information concerning this incident?"

"Yes, I do," Castaldo answered. The questions and answers alternated back and forth for forty-five minutes. O'Brien, who had been up almost two days straight, was so tired that he forgot to type one of Castaldo's answers.

"What if anything were you told of the prior events that evening?"

"They told me they killed Rob Solimine," Castaldo said. "They told me that first we had to talk, so we went outside and talked."

"Once outside, did you ask each member of your group, individually, is Robert Solimine dead?"

"Yes."

"In the last three weeks, did you take part in any discussion concerning the murder of Robert Solimine?"

"Yes."

"Approximately three weeks ago, standing in your kitchen, did you punch a kitchen cabinet and say, 'I want him dead'?"

"I might have said it in anger."

Castaldo seemed now as if he had been willing to take some of the blame for the crime, but the cops believed he still couldn't tell the truth. O'Brien asked about the 1½-ounce can of FDS spray by the toaster, and Castaldo said Wanger had given it to him.

"James tried to put it in Solimine's gas tank, thinking that it would blow up Rob Solimine's car," Castaldo said. He said he thought Wanger had gotten the can simply by walking into a store and buying it.

"Are you the recognized leader of this group?"

"Yes," Castaldo said.

"At one point in time, did you direct James Wanger to go out and beat up someone else?"

"Yes, I told him I wanted to get even with someone. I was going to take care of the guy, but he volunteered to do it for me."

"At some time in the past, did your parents receive a phone

call from a Naval Cadet lieutenant telling them to stop serving alcohol to kids?"

"Yes."

"Who do you believe told the lieutenant that your parents were serving alcohol?"

"Robert Solimine."

"What, if anything, did James Wanger tell you about the homicide of Robert Solimine?"

"He told me he killed him with an extension cord."

"Did he tell you that Frank Carboni was in the car with him at that time?"

"Yes, he did."

"Did you know that on the previous evening they had plans to handcuff Robert Solimine to his steering wheel and blow up the car with him inside it?"

"Yes."

"Did you know that it was your brother Steven who had given to James the extension cord to choke Robert Solimine with?"

"No, I didn't," Castaldo said. "But later I learned that he did."

"Did you take any action in any form with the members of this group to assist or direct the murder of Robert Solimine?"

"No."

At first Castaldo did not wish to add anything to the statement. After reading it over, however, he added three sentences:

"I was telling them to just leave him alone. I mentioned that my life doesn't revolve around him. Just leave him alone."

12

HUNDREDS OF PEOPLE CROWDED INTO THE NAVE OF ST. PAUL'S Roman Catholic Church in Clifton for Robbie Solimine's funeral on Thursday. Relatives, friends, and the curious mixed with tearful high-school students, many of whom had come down because it was an event. The Sea Cadets were there en masse. The older Sea Cadets, with their polished faces and solemn bearing, were members of an honor guard that attended Solimine's coffin at the altar before the Mass, but the pews contained younger recruits as well. Dressed up in miniature white seamen's caps and Navy blues, some of the littler ones seemed to have only the most distant idea of why they were there.

Solimine's family had requested that there be no media, and certainly no photographers or news cameras, inside the church. But some print reporters got inside. They either committed their observations to memory or unobtrusively penned a few sparse notes about the service. Outside, news reporters and photographers swarmed over the street, interviewing as many young people as they could. The church made a fantastic backdrop for the TV news cameras. Everyone was looking for insights into Solimine, asking how the teenagers knew him, but there was more interest still in Wanger. It was one of the curiosities of reporting about juvenile criminals—everyone in the community knew who they were, and the reporters asked about them by name, but the media weren't permitted to reveal the suspects' identities to their readers. But the young people were only too eager to tell what they knew about the boys, preferably on camera. Many of the young people had come not because they knew Solimine, but because his death had sent shock waves through the school. Of course, the impact was further magnified because his killers had been his classmates. Most of the students knew both boys, but it seemed as if Wanger was the better known of the two.

"He was always being picked on in school," kids said of Wanger.

Or: "He didn't seem to be the type that would kill."

Inside, as "Amazing Grace" thundered over the church organ, the honor guard escorted the coffin to the altar. Solimine's family followed behind, all eyes on them as they entered the church. Through the tears Margaret Chircop's face registered anger. A bouquet of white carnations in the shape of an anchor, which was topped by a red, white, and blue ribbon, stood beside the altar. The Reverend Victor J. Mazza delivered a homily invoking the memory of Christ's betrayal by his friends and seeking to allay the family's grief.

"There is no greater pain in human life than the pain of a parent losing a child," Mazza said. "What makes it even worse is that we have no reason and probably never will."

Jennifer Clayton, who had been one of Rob's best friends in the Sea Cadets, delivered an achingly poignant eulogy, and A. E. Housman's poem, "To an Athlete Dying Young," was read aloud:

The time you won your town the race,
We chaired you through the market-place;
Man and boy stood cheering by,
And home we brought you shoulder-high.

Then the relatives carried the coffin to the hearse outside. As news cameras whirred and clicked, an honor guard of six Sea Cadets escorted the pallbearers to the door and down to the street below. Most of the mourners seemed in shock, and Margaret Chircop seemed in need of support as she walked in the procession, sobbing inconsolably.

Outside, Lieutenant Commander Joseph "Teddy" Hamlisch, appearing distraught and confused, told reporters again and again that it just made no sense that Wanger had killed Solimine. Fresh in his mind was the trip two or three weeks earlier the two boys had made with the unit to tour the USS *Butte*, an ammunition and auxiliary ship. That weekend Wanger and Solimine had driven to southern New Jersey in Robbie's car and they had bunked together aboard the ship. No one had seen the faintest trace of animosity between the boys.

"They loved each other," Hamlisch told a reporter from the *Newark Star-Ledger*. "How do you figure anything like this could ever happen? They were fine. They were like the Bobbsey twins. They were always together."

Lights on at the head of the procession, the hearse left Clifton and drove to Totowa for the burial. The cars turned into the iron gates of the Laurel Grove Cemetery, past the voluptuous sculpture of the Spirit of Resurrection, and crawled slowly up the hill. This was the cemetery that Solimine never liked to visit as much as Wanger and Castaldo and the others. But on a gentle slope a few hundred yards from the mausoleum where Wanger never failed to leave a cigarette for Annie's ghost, Robert A. Solimine was laid to rest, wearing the Sea Cadets uniform that had given him the sense of stature and the feeling of belonging that he had so desperately craved. His plot overlooked the cemetery's Memorial Chapel and the town of Totowa. Billy's knees dropped to the ground beside his brother's casket, and other family members sobbed.

Robbie had been a complicated young man. The traits that had served him so well in Sea Cadets—loyalty and devotion to others—had been his undoing. He was not polished. His talents were not unlimited. He was wracked by doubts and demons. But he had started to sort out a few answers for himself. He thought he had an idea of what he could be. He perhaps did not fit exactly the image of the robust young champion in Houseman's poem. Nor had he achieved in his brief life the wide acclaim of the poet's hero, although Robbie Solimine had touched many lives in his seventeen years. Now, however, the astounding manner of his death had drawn him more attention than he might ever have received otherwise.

That same Thursday, not long before the funeral Mass was to be said, all four of the juveniles—Castaldo would appear in the other part of Superior Court for adults—stood before Judge Carmen A. Ferrante in the Family Part of state Superior Court. Few judges in the state of New Jersey had sat as long in Family Court as Ferrante. And few were as tough as he was. Ferrante had a reputation for running his court in a somewhat imperious manner, and many lawyers found him arrogant. It was said that he had often made up his mind about what to do with a boy before he entered the courtroom. He had been appointed in 1977 as Passaic County's presiding judge of the Juvenile and Domestic Court. In the years since, the division had undergone a name change, a major overhaul of its laws, and the review of at least one task force designed to cope with its many problems. For most judges, sitting in Family Court was a duty best to be done with. Virtually everyone who presided there came to hate the high emotional pitch, the staggering caseload, and the perception that Family Court, sometimes referred to derisively as Kiddie Court, was a second-class venue.

But Ferrante stayed. He spent his entire career in the family courts, hearing cases involving children, battered wives, and rotten marriages. At one time, state Senator Frank X. Graves, Jr., who was also mayor of Paterson and one of the county's strongest politicians, complained that he would block Ferrante's reappointment to the bench because the judge was too soft. By 1982, however, Passaic County's two juvenile judges, including Ferrante, sent more kids to reformatories in a six-month period than any other venue—even more than neighboring Essex County, which had twice Passaic County's population, and five times more than Hudson County, whose population was larger, denser, and more urban. Most were minorities, and some complained that race played a role in deciding who went to prison. But Ferrante would have none of it. These were the crimes, these were the kids who did them, and these were his options: send the kids to the New Jersey Training School for Boys, a youth correctional facility in Jamesburg, or sentence them to probation, which amounted to nothing at all.

But Ferrante liked to see himself as being firm and compassionate. The son of Italian immigrants, Carmen Alfred Ferrante was born December 10, 1935, in Paterson. He served as an altar boy at St. Casimir's Roman Catholic Church and attended the Paterson public schools. He went on to Seton Hall University and the Seton Hall Law School, joining the bar in 1961. Twice divorced and three times married, he was the father of three sons, all of whom would go on to serve the public in the law or social work. In the day-to-day workings of the court, Ferrante took great pleasure in helping to turn around a young person's life. It did not happen all the time, but it happened, and he treasured the letters of thanks they sent him later, letters postmarked from fine colleges or the military bases. Indeed, some of the lawyers who practiced law in Ferrante's courtroom had appeared there years earlier as defendants.

Outside the courtroom, Ferrante worked tirelessly to raise the stature of the Family Court. He served on state Supreme Court committees and chaired statewide conferences for judges and lawyers in the family law division. In August 1984, Ferrante was elected for the first time to the board of trustees of the National Council of Juvenile and Family Court Judges, and he would go on to hold the title of president for one year. Throughout his career, Ferrante labored to persuade the public that children's problems were society's problems, that it was wiser to invest resources in juvenile delinquents sooner rather than later, and that it paid to find the money for options to prison before there was no option but prison.

Over the years, moreover, Ferrante's vantage from the Family Court gave him good reason to be alarmed. He saw the kiddie crime wave coming before most other people did, and he thought he saw the reasons behind it. Every day, children stepped into his courtroom who had had almost no upbringing. Most had fathers who had long ago vanished. Most were raised by single mothers. He saw firsthand the diminishing respect youngsters had for authority or for themselves, all the while that their propensity for violence was growing more extreme. When he was starting out, people were shocked by a teenage purse-snatching. A spate of vandalized mailboxes in Wayne was enough to launch an exposé of juvenile delinquency in the local newspaper. By the mid-1980s, however, nothing was shocking. By then, Ferrante had seen it all. Sheriff's officers routinely herded young adolescents before him who had shot, raped, or killed. Indeed, he thought he had seen it all—until Solimine's alleged killers came through his courtroom.

That Thursday, shortly before Solimine's funeral would get under way in Clifton, all four boys shuffled glumly into Ferrante's courtroom. The sheriff's officers directed them to a long table and they all sat down. O'Shea stood off to the side with Wood. O'Brien had come to court too. It was the second time in court for Wanger and Carboni, the first time for Strelka and Stooge. They sat awkwardly, their hands cuffed behind them.

It was also the very first time that Jay W. McCann, a Paterson lawyer, met his client. McCann shook hands with Strelka after a brief and awkward mix-up. When McCann entered the courtroom, the sheriff's officers mistakenly directed him to Stooge. Never having laid eyes on his client before, McCann introduced himself to Stooge, and then it became clear that Stujinski already was represented by Linda Peterson, a striking young woman who worked as an assistant deputy public defender.

Once that was ironed out, and the courtroom seemed to take in a collective breath to compose itself for the hearing,

McCann had a chance to look all the boys over. It was a jarring experience. He struggled to reconcile the enormity of the charges with the boys' appearance: Each one looked goofier than the next. McCann had been expecting some kind of leather-jacketed hood for a client. Then he met Strelka, who looked as if he belonged in a rec room somewhere rolling dice for a game of Risk. It took some imagination putting the kid into any criminal context, let alone a homicide. The same went for Stujinski and Carboni. They looked like nice boys. Like nerds. Then, when McCann figured out who Wanger was, he was astounded to see that the alleged strangler was the goofiest-looking kid of all.

McCann had only been following the story in the local papers when he got a call from the Strelkas to represent their son. When they came to his office to hire him, Mr. and Mrs. Strelka seemed remarkably calm—until McCann realized they were thoroughly dazed. Sitting in McCann's office, the father seemed remote. The mother seemed on the verge of a nervous breakdown. McCann had heard that she conked out at headquarters. It took most of his effort just to keep them focused on the practical and legal tangles ahead. And there were many—the biggest by far being that his client had given not one, but *two* written statements to the police before a lawyer entered the picture.

McCann had some hope, however. As he appraised the police reports, he got more and more of a picture of illegal police conduct in obtaining the statements. Here's a seventeen-year-old kid in police custody answering a barrage of questions from grown men flashing guns and badges around. The detectives even bring in the old family friend/cop to get the kid to give it up. The kid, who McCann understands is extremely immature, has no one to lean on except Mom, and she goes to the floor. If McCann could prove that the police coerced the statements, he could have them tossed out of court, and the state would have nothing. It seemed like it might be possible. Of course, he might fail, and his client could be charged as an adult and face a minimum of thirty years in prison. But McCann, at this stage in the game, tried to stay hopeful. We're going to have a heck of a suppression hearing, McCann thought. One heck of a suppression hearing.

The probable cause hearing before Ferrante, however, took very little time. The ride from the juvenile detention center in Haledon to Paterson took much longer. McCann and the other attorneys for the juveniles waived their right to a probable cause hearing and entered not guilty pleas, and a tentative trial date was set down.

And then Wanger's lawyer surprised nearly everyone. Conveying a request on behalf of his client, Paul W. Bergrin—who was standing in for Anthony J. Pope, Jr., Wanger's lawyer of record, for the preliminary hearings—said Wanger wished to attend Solimine's funeral. Bergrin requested that the judge issue an order permitting Wanger to leave the juvenile shelter for the day. Ferrante declined.

Castaldo's arrest early on Wednesday morning effectively closed the police investigation. But there were still details to be attended to. Matonak took the car keys recovered from Castaldo's closet to the state police impound where Solimine's car was being stored to confirm, by unlocking the car and starting it, that they belonged to the car. They did. Court orders were obtained to seize the suspects' school records and materials from their school lockers. Wood asked Strelka's father to surrender the baseball bat in his son's car. Police also wanted Strelka's St. Joseph medal, which had been found by his parents in Tommy's bedroom. To ascertain if Rob had been given a medal, Matonak asked Manny Chircop about whether Rob wore any jewelry. Matonak asked Bob Solimine about the same thing. Someone got the Totowa police department to fax a copy of the summons left on Solimine's car at Annie's Road the time Wanger sneaked back to the car with the aerosol can.

The investigators also kept up the search for the electrical cord and the gas cap to Solimine's car, although they knew the chances were diminishing that they would find them. Most detectives believed it had probably ended up being hauled away with the Castaldo's garbage. That Monday, Detective Matonak drove over to Andy Blair's offices to get a pair of black handcuffs that belonged to Carboni. The handcuffs—a working model but not the pair used in the murder attempt the night before the actual homicide—were missing part of the key. Blair confessed that he had been fooling around with them in his office and snapped the key off inside them.

In the hopes of learning more about the boys and how they acted together, the investigators also tracked down secondary witnesses. They gathered statements from anyone who could shed any light on the victim or the odd crew of misfits charged with his murder. The detectives spoke to friends and to old girlfriends. They spoke to teachers and neighbors. Some were helpful and some weren't. One witness who had some interesting things to say happened to be an upstairs tenant of the Castaldos. Her name was Ginny.

Ginny was thirty-eight years old, and she had moved in when Frank Castaldo was about sixteen. The woman, who had a dog that she walked frequently, came to know the Castaldos very well. To her, they seemed like a close family who also were wildly irrational. One minute they were looking out for each other, and the next they were at each other's throats—sometimes literally. Frank and Ginny passed many a summer evening sitting on the front porch talking and smoking cigarettes. She found him very likable, but she was also very wary. She believed he had a split personality. One Frank was the soft-spoken young man who was polite, loyal to friends, and something of a ladies' man. The other Frank was a hot-tempered, loudmouthed jerk who was almost ingenious at being able to get his way with people. As Ginny saw it, Frank Castaldo had a way of expecting things—such as the time he claimed he was stranded at the Willowbrook Mall and asked his neighbor to pick him up. Ginny did, and he didn't so much as thank her. Frank also bummed cigarettes all the time and waxed grandiosely about Italians. He told her the Italians were one of the greatest races on the face of the earth and that they had achieved greatness by sticking together.

In their talks, Frank also confided that everyone feared him because they thought he was a drug dealer and because he was connected to the mob. The neighbor didn't even know if it was true. She certainly saw no evidence of it in Castaldo's lifestyle. She put it down to Frank Castaldo's inflated view of himself.

Over time, however, Ginny's relationship with the Castaldo clan became so bad that she contemplated suing her landlords. She retained a lawyer, and she bought a Radio Shack voice-activated tape recorder to capture any intrigues against her. Mostly, it caught the wild goings-on downstairs. But the detectives took a long statement from her and duly listened to the tape.

In addition to pursuing secondary leads and clues, the investigators also reexamined other evidence and reinterviewed some of the witnesses they had first spoken to. On February 25, Robert Solimine, Sr., went to police headquarters to drop off microcassettes that contained the messages Strelka and the others had left for Rob hours before they killed him. There were two other messages besides on tape. One had been from Rob's father calling from Pennsylvania to say when he would be home. The other was from Chrissie Bachelle. She called on Monday afternoon after the killing because she couldn't believe the news and wanted to find out for herself.

Bob Solimine also gave a written statement to Onorevole. During the interview, Solimine told the detective that his son had never expressed any fear of anyone or any worry about being bothered. He knew pranks had been pulled on Rob—he could recall the time some of the kids had pulled the tire off his son's car—but otherwise he came up blank trying to explain the hatred these kids must have felt for his son. Solimine also shed background on his son: how Rob had taken pills while talking to Tommy Strelka on the telephone and his hospitalization at the Carrier clinic; how Paula Wanger and the Colombos had visited Rob at the clinic and how Paula, in talking with the Solimines, fretted that her son had a drinking problem also; how Rob had moved from Clifton to his father's house because of his mother's dissolving marriage. Solimine told Onorevole that he also seemed to recall hearing talk about someone supplying alcohol to some of the Sea Cadets. But he wasn't sure. In passing, he mentioned that "Current Affair," the TV tabloid show, had sent flowers, and so had the Sally Jessy Raphael show.

Arlene Solimine came in the following day. She, too, was at a loss to explain why someone would want to harm Rob. Although she admitted that Rob could be a handful—she told the detective that Rob had moved in with them because he clashed with Manny Chircop—she said he was a good kid who had recently started a new job at the Friendly's in Waldwick. He seemed to like the job a lot. He had made a very good impression on the other employees there in a very short time. He had worked there the weekend of his death, as a matter of fact.

Arlene also related Rob's brush with the pills and his stay at the Carrier Clinic. Indeed, she related the scene that she had had with Rob when she, Maggie, and Bob had helped him prepare the home contract that required Rob to break with his friends. As she recalled it, Rob more or less agreed that he should, as Arlene suggested, stay away from Wanger. ("Paula Wanger said James was becoming hard to handle," Arlene told Onorevole.) But she also told Onorevole about how Rob went wild when she suggested that he give up Strelka. And he became unusually upset with the notion that he might have to break with Chrissie Bachelle.

Arlene left a box of Rob's stuff with Onorevole. The stuff included Sea Cadet rosters, the get-well cards Paula Wanger had mailed to him at the Carrier clinic, and long handwritten lists of telephone numbers. Most belonged to girls listed by their first names.

On the morning when all the juveniles first appeared in court together for a probable cause hearing before Judge Ferrante, McCann, Blair, and the other lawyers compared notes, and it became clear from the start that the best way out for the teenagers would be rolling over on Castaldo and Wanger.

McCann realized that his kid, Strelka, would almost certainly be waived up to Adult Court if he didn't cooperate—and fast. Andy Blair's kid, Carboni, already had made a deal guaranteeing that he would be treated as a juvenile in exchange for his police statement, but it seemed pretty clear that they were willing to go further to help the state too. Since Stooge was the youngest and, by all accounts, the least involved, Linda Peterson would probably be able to cut a deal also. All the lawyers were sweating for their clients, but McCann probably more than the rest. His kid was the oldest of the juveniles. He was a little more than two weeks younger than Wanger, and Wanger was definitely going up to Adult Court. McCann's kid also had two written statements around his neck. And the mother of the victim already was calling for his kid's head.

McCann had to think beyond the waiver issue to defending the kid at trial, and his defense was this: Strelka did not know that Wanger actually meant to kill. That was his only defense, as McCann saw it. Most kids can't distinguish fantasy from reality at that age, and this kid was young for his years. McCann would have to argue that Strelka was around during the meetings or whatever—it would be pretty hard to suggest otherwise—but he would say Strelka did not share a murderous intent. It was probably even the truth, McCann thought, but he wasn't sure how much weight that argument could hold.

The biggest problem, of course, was the body. A jury might be inclined to give the defendant all benefit of the doubt if the case is pitched right to them, but they are not very forgiving when the state brings them a dead body. What's more, this victim was a kid.

As a result, McCann took it as a given that his kid would go next door to the adult courts, and the odds of success there were not good if he didn't strike a deal guaranteeing him treatment as a juvenile. So McCann wanted a deal. Peterson wanted a deal. Blair wanted a deal. The question was whether the prosecutor's office would go for it.

* * *

The Solimine case was only days old when O'Shea, the chief assistant Passaic County prosecutor, whose job it was to prosecute juvenile criminals, invited in Solimine's parents. O'Shea intended to brief them on the status of the investigation and where, in the days and weeks and years ahead, the case would likely be going. It was not going to be a pleasant meeting—not only for the obvious reasons concerning a homicide victim's family, but because of the lesson O'Shea was about to impart about the criminal justice system. What's more, an ugly misunderstanding had already arisen involving local law enforcement and Bill Yakal, and the clash threatened to set the tone for future dealings between the prosecutor's office and the victim's entire family.

Hardly had the news sunk in when Yakal, seething with rage for the little bastards who had killed his grandson, also fumed at what he perceived to be the indifferent treatment of his family by the authorities. Earlier in the week, before the whole story about the plot was known, Bill and Lee had gone to the Clifton Police Department to learn more about what had happened. Having read Captain Territo's name in the newspaper accounts, Bill Yakal went to the bulletproof window in the downstairs lobby at headquarters to ask for him. Territo came downstairs. Wary by nature, Territo allowed Mr. Yakal only a little way in the door.

"What do you want to know?" Territo asked.

"We heard the body was still warm when the body was discovered," Yakal said. He demanded to know if the police had bothered to summon medical attention. In a querulous tone, Yakal was unmistakably suggesting that the police had allowed his grandson to die.

Territo told Yakal that it would be best for the time being not to second-guess the police. Territo excused himself, saying he would have to go upstairs to supervise a murder investigation. But Yakal felt that he was getting the bum's rush. Then Yakal had to read in the *Record* about a preliminary court hearing involving the boys. He was angry that no one had bothered to tell him or, as far as he knew, anyone else in the family about the proceeding. Grabbing Lee and dashing off to the Passaic County Courthouse in Paterson, Yakal tried to find the hearing. A member of the Passaic County Sheriff's Department, which provided security in the courthouse, agreed to show them the way. While assisting the Yakals, however, the sheriff's officer heard Bill Yakal say something that the officer perceived as a threat—something to do with killing the kids who had killed his grandson. There was an unpleasant exchange, Yakal denied he made any threat, and the upshot was that Yakal was barred from the courtroom.

The incident would excite Bill Yakal for a long time afterward and cause more than one angry exchange between him and officials in the prosecutor's office, who came to view Yakal with a mixture of sympathy and caution. O'Shea, who had been privy to one such confrontation with Mr. Yakal himself, did not want a repetition of it, particularly with the news he was bearing. He called a meeting with Robbie's natural parents only, to explain that the state had no choice but to enter plea agreements with the juveniles in order to secure their cooperation in trying Wanger and Castaldo. That would mean, of course, that the three boys would demand something in return. That something would be leniency.

O'Shea had been a criminal prosecutor fourteen years, almost every day of which had been spent in the family division working with juveniles, and leniency was not a thing one might accuse him of. O'Shea spoke slowly and carefully. He was a cautious man who took his job very seriously, sometimes speaking so prudently in and out of court, and with such polite manners, as to seem almost quaint. He was in his early forties, married and with three kids of his own. Rawboned and sharp-featured, O'Shea wore his hair in a modified flattop. The gunmetal gray had softened to white around the sides of his head, and he had very blue eyes and a very long, very pink face. One eyebrow that always seemed to float higher than the other gave his face a slightly off-center look. He had run the prosecutor's juvenile division in Passaic County nearly as long as he had been a prosecutor. In that time, New

Jersey, like the rest of the nation, had seen an explosion in juvenile crime. During the late 1980s, violent crimes committed by children under the age of eighteen in New Jersey jumped nearly 40 percent in a five-year period. Passaic County, with its dying cities and large numbers of poor, accounted for a disproportionate amount of that surge.

O'Shea, taking his cue from Fava and other officials in the Republican-dominated county, believed that firmness was the answer. Focusing on the victims of crime in poor neighborhoods instead of the perpetrators, Passaic County locked up more kids than all but three of the state's twenty-one counties. The Passaic County Juvenile Detention Center, where the boys were being held pending trial, was among the most crowded correctional facilities in the state, packing several children into cells designed for a single prisoner. In perhaps the most telling statistic of all, Passaic County ranked second in the state in the number of juveniles that were transferred from the family courts to the adult courts to face charges.

Like Judge Ferrante, who also had spent almost all his career in the family court, O'Shea had a reputation statewide for expertise in the field. He and other officials argued that their approach worked, reducing crime dramatically compared with other counties. They argued that the cause for the crime explosion lay beyond the courthouse, that the frightful toll of violence had more to do with a breakdown of the family. With one or both parents out of the picture, children raised themselves, or even other children. The holes in their lives were filled with a few values extracted from a money-crazed, media-driven society that glorified sex, violence, and commercial excess: Criminals had taken the place of Mickey Mantle and Hank Aaron as role models. Matters of life and death had become a game. O'Shea could see it as plain as day in this case. He believed that none of the boys had suffered from too much oversight, and without a doubt O'Shea was convinced that Wanger and the others had stolen their ideas for the murder directly from *The Godfather*. Having observed the juveniles giving their statements at the Clifton Police Department, O'Shea also had been amazed at their coldness. Stooge's mother had been tearful and shaking as she heard the story coming out of her son's mouth, but Stooge didn't seem to register the merest trace of remorse or shame or regret. The same was true of Carboni. Wanger seemed almost bon vivant at headquarters, wondering when he could eat something or see his family.

Now a good deal of the responsibility fell to O'Shea to decide what to do with these boys. Waiving Wanger up to face charges as an adult—that was a no-brainer. But what about the three juveniles? O'Shea, who felt as if he was thinking over the case almost every minute of the day, had realized very early that the prosecutor's office would need the cooperation of the three juveniles to win convictions against Wanger and against Castaldo. Purdy concurred. But the boys would need an incentive of some kind to cooperate. Their lawyers were pushing for no more than five years in prison—about what you'd get for serious welfare fraud. O'Shea and Purdy were thinking more along the lines of twelve-year prison terms. But then there was also the problem of conforming to the demands of the New Jersey Code of Juvenile Justice, which had been enacted in 1982.

Unlike the adult code, whose mission was punitive, the juvenile code was supposed to give troubled kids a chance at rehabilitation. Everything in the code—including whether or not a juvenile avoided prosecution as an adult—was based on the idea of trying to reform them. Let a kid learn from his mistakes and move on, the idea went. The law resorted to doublespeak in certain areas to make this point clear. ("The taking of a juvenile into custody shall not be construed as an arrest but shall be deemed a measure to protect the health, morals and well-being of the juvenile . . .") What's more, the process was supposed to move quickly through the courts. If a juvenile had been confined, the law required the prosecutor to bring the case to trial before the Family Part judge (not a jury) within thirty days, unless good cause was shown to extend it. The telescopic timetable of the Family Court forced the system (theoretically) to deal with a juvenile's problems as soon as possible, but it also forced lawyers to make critical decisions in a fairly short amount of time. O'Shea and Purdy had to commit themselves now.

In comparison, Wanger and Castaldo's trials seemed impossibly far away. If Wanger's lawyers chose to fight the state's motion to waive his status as a juvenile, then it would be a month at least before the matter could go to the grand jury. It took an average of about eighteen months or more between the time a grand jury returned an indictment to bring the matter to trial. A case like Wanger and Castaldo's would probably take longer, given that the stakes were high, there were several codefendants, and both young men had private counsel, a sign that presumably they could afford to spend money on pretrial motions and experts that might draw out the matter still further.

Knowing all this, O'Shea faced a simple dilemma: How could the state make sure that the three juveniles still had an incentive to testify when the time came to move against Wanger and Castaldo? If the boys were sentenced next month to, say, twelve years behind bars, then they could go to Jamesburg and start serving their terms. By the time everything was in place to try Wanger or Castaldo, however, the boys could decide that they really didn't feel like helping out against Wanger and Castaldo after all. The state certainly couldn't go back and ask for more prison time—that would no doubt run afoul of the Constitution's ban on double jeopardy. How could they build in an incentive if the sentence was supposed to be fixed by Ferrante this summer? What was the carrot, and what was the stick?

During the lunch hour, O'Shea took long walks downtown with Charlie Greene, who was one of the cheeriest guys in the office and a shrewd litigator besides, hashing out possible compromises.

"Look," Charlie said. "They start out with the max. You start them at twenty, not twelve. Otherwise, they got no incentive to get up there and testify."

Once they testify, Greene said, you could go back to the judge and ask him to cut the sentences.

O'Shea liked it. Not only would they agree to ask the court to reduce the boys' sentences after they had testified, a prosecutor could ask for specific terms. This would inadvertently solve another problem: They could arrange it so that Strelka would serve more time than the younger boys. At first, the prosecutors and defense lawyers kicked around the idea of sentencing all the boys to fourteen years. But almost from the first day, Mrs. Chircop had focused on Strelka's treachery, blaming him most for her son's betrayal. She singled him out and she wanted him to pay more dearly than the others. O'Shea was inclined to agree with her. Taking into account that Strelka also was nearly as old as Wanger and Castaldo, O'Shea felt Strelka should get a harder sentence. In the end, they agreed that the prosecutor would move to cut Strelka's twenty-year sentence to fifteen years, while the other two boys would receive terms of twelve years each.

It was not something that any of the three boys deserved, but it was the right thing to do, if the real culprits were to get what they deserved. However, knowing what he knew already about Yakal and the other members of the victim's family, O'Shea was aware that leniency was exactly what the Solimine family did not want to hear about just then. There was no good way to tell the parents of a murdered child that it would be necessary to give a break to three of their son's killers, but that was what O'Shea had to do.

O'Shea met with Bob Solimine and Margaret Chircop around a large table in the offices behind St. John's Cathedral on DeGrasse Street. Wood was there, and so was Purdy. It was a chilly affair. O'Shea explained the reasons for making the plea agreements. There were no numbers on the table yet, at the time of the meeting, but he wanted to spell out the principles involved. Bob and Margaret both felt that each of the five boys had played an equal part in killing their son—or that the killing would not have been possible if not for their unanimous approval and their concerted efforts. Therefore, they should all spend the rest of their lives in prison. O'Shea explained that the state could try all the boys as adults and let the chips fall where they may—but he told them that such a strategy risked losing against almost all of them, including the very boy who had wielded the garrote.

O'Shea could see the pain of his words registering in Margaret's face as he told the family what he had to do. Bob and Margaret were cordial, but both could do the math. Most inmates in New Jersey's correctional facilities served only about a third of their maximum sentences before becoming eligible for parole. Even if Ferrante rapped out a twenty-year maximum sentence for the three juveniles, they would probably serve no more than 6⅔ years. Maybe the parole board would turn them down once because it was good form in murder cases. But no one believed the boys would do a day more than ten years in a juvenile facility under the maximum term. To give them something less going in seemed horribly wrong.

O'Shea wanted to please the victim's family if he could, but he and the other prosecutors also had a duty to represent the state of New Jersey, and they had to do everything in their power to make sure that Wanger and Castaldo would not go free. Legally, morally, and ethically, there was only one way to do it.

"Look, we have no choice, and we can't wait any longer. We're going to have to enter into agreements," O'Shea told them. "We're sorry if this is not what you wanted, but this is what we have to do."

Mr. Solimine seemed resigned to the plea bargains. Do what ya gotta do, he seemed to be saying.

Margaret wouldn't yield. Unhappy with the course the prosecutor's office had chosen, Margaret told O'Shea and the others that she would take her case before the court of public opinion.

13

MINUTES BEFORE JUDGE FERRANTE WAS EXPECTED TO ENTER guilty pleas for the three juveniles in the Hail Mary murder, as part of a plea bargain between the state and the juveniles, Margaret Yakal Chircop handed Mike O'Shea a letter addressed to him, to Prosecutor Fava, and to almost every politician or political figure in New Jersey. Without looking, O'Shea could have known what was in it.

It was April 15, 1992, two months to the date after the boys had attempted to handcuff Solimine in his car and blow it up, and the three youngest—Carboni, Stooge, and Strelka—were to appear before Judge Ferrante to enter their guilty pleas. Having been put on notice, O'Shea knew that Margaret Chircop's letter probably would be a ringing condemnation of what they were about to do. He also expected Mr. Solimine to speak out against the plea agreement.

The entire pact had been up in the air until only about ten days earlier, and at times the negotiations had become angry. Andy Blair, who had shaken with Fava on the night of Carboni's arrest over the guarantee that his client would stay in the Family Court, had expected to receive an additional benefit for having his client plead guilty. During one telephone conversation, when the assistant prosecutors were saying that his client had already gotten his break, Blair blew up.

"Fuck you, I got my juvenile protection at headquarters," he said.

"It was never a promise, we only told you we would do our best," they said.

"I'm calling Fava," Blair said. "I don't care. Don't think you're screwing me on this."

Suddenly, it occurred to Blair that he wouldn't be able to do much if they reneged, and he realized with a chill that he had staked his client's future on a handshake. Fava had made the deal, Fava was a man of honor, Fava wouldn't go back on this, Blair told himself—but what was he to make of this now?

"I'll go to the press," Blair screamed. "I'll talk to everybody. That's the deal, and you guys already gave it to me."

But he didn't need to, because Fava had kept his word, and Blair and the other lawyers ironed out a deal on March 4.

Before the court hearing, O'Shea and the defense attorneys met in chambers with Ferrante. They spelled out the agreement, and Ferrante agreed to enter the pleas. Ferrante had already presided over their initial appearances and their home detention hearings. In fact, five days before they were to plead guilty, Ferrante entered an order permitting the trio to return to their homes. The judge freed them under conditions similar to those that allowed Castaldo to remain home on bail. Indeed, Ferrante was persuaded by the argument that if Castaldo should be permitted to be at home on bail pending the outcome of the charges, so should the three juveniles. Like Castaldo, all three had to wear electronic anklets and keep in close contact with the county probation officer.

On the day the boys were to plead guilty, the news media poured into Paterson for the event. The hearing for the guilty pleas was to be held in the courthouse annex, a red and white stone building that resembled a layered cake and had been the city's first post office. The judge had agreed to allow media inside the courtroom so long as the juveniles' identities would not be disclosed. Reporters would be allowed to attend the hearing, although TV crews and photographers were barred. But everyone expected Margaret Chircop and perhaps other family members to speak out about the case on the courthouse steps afterward.

Ferrante took the bench and laid down the ground rules for the media. He also noted that the Solimines, or at least Margaret Chircop, had planned to make a public statement. The judge noted that although New Jersey's Victims' Rights Bill did not guarantee access to a juvenile proceeding, the judge had agreed to permit Solimine's family to attend the hearing and to make a public statement at the end.

Then the trio was led into court. All three were wearing handcuffs shackled to heavy leather belts. They greeted their lawyers with curt nods and sat at a long table directly below the bench. Investigator Wood was nearby, wearing a double-vested royal-blue blazer and silk tie, but he was the only investigator on hand.

Mike O'Shea, the prosecutor, stood to address the court. He was about to read the lengthy plea agreement into the record when Ferrante cut him off. First, he wanted Carboni to stand. Carboni's black shaggy locks had disappeared, although his bangs still fell almost to his eyes. He wore a red tie and an ill-fitting gray suit that seemed to exaggerate his diminutive size. Although he was only about five feet, six inches tall, he stood a few inches taller than his parents. Mrs. Carboni, wearing a brown jacket and a purple dress, took her place behind him. His father, wearing a blue pin-striped suit, folded his hands.

"We have some ground rules first, Mr. Carboni," the judge began. "Listen to me carefully. Number one, you have to keep your voice up at all times. Number two, if there's any question I ask you or Mr. Blair asks you that you don't understand, you tell us. If there's any words or phrases that I use that you're not familiar with, any terms that I use or Mr. Blair uses that you don't understand, don't be ashamed to tell us. Do you understand everything I've said so far?"

"Yes, sir," Carboni answered.

The judge read the complaint charging Carboni with murder.

"Your lawyer has indicated that you intend to plead guilty, is that correct?"

"Yes, sir."

"Do you know what it means to plead guilty?"

"Yes, sir."

"What does it mean to you?"

"That I will be found guilty and charged," Carboni said.

"No," the judge said, "it doesn't mean that. Let me explain it to you and then you tell me if you still want to plead guilty. By pleading guilty, you're admitting to me that what it says in the complaint you did. Do you understand that?"

"Yes, sir."

The judge went through the rest of the colloquy.

"Did anyone make any promises to you to make you plead guilty, with the exception of this agreement that I have in my possession, which Mr. O'Shea will read into the record now? Any other promises of any kind?"

"No, sir."

O'Shea read the agreement into the record, an act that he was to perform in succession for each defendant. The agreement wrapped up the entire case for the three juveniles and also dictated the expectations of them in the future. It provided that all three would plead guilty to first-degree murder, admitting that as accomplices they had intentionally contributed to the death of Robert Solimine, Jr. Each juvenile would face the possibility of receiving a maximum twenty-year sentence in a correctional facility for juveniles. The state would withdraw its motion to charge Stooge and Strelka as adults. The state would dismiss the arson and evidence-tampering charges against Carboni. The agreement also required that all three juveniles cooperate fully with the state.

"Each juvenile agrees to tell the entire truth in the course of any future interviews, statements, and testimony in any future criminal proceedings against the codefendants, including James P. Wanger, juvenile, and Frank Castaldo, adult, including the grand jury presentation and any criminal trial, if so requested by the state," O'Shea said.

"Since it is not feasible to postpone the sentencing of Frank Carboni, Thomas M. Strelka, and Thomas Stujinski indefinitely while the prosecution of James P. Wanger and Frank Castaldo is pending, the state will ask the Family Court to sentence Frank Carboni, Thomas M. Strelka, and Thomas Stujinski without delay. The state will urge the Family Court to sentence Frank Carboni, Thomas M. Strelka, and Thomas Stujinski to be incarcerated for twenty years in a suitable institution maintained by the Department of Corrections for the rehabilitation of delinquents."

The agreement required that if the three met their end of the bargain, the state would ask the Family Court to resentence them to reduced prison terms. The state would ask the court to sentence Carboni and Stooge to twelve years. Reflecting the wishes of the Solimine family, the state would request the court to sentence Strelka to a term of fifteen years. The agreement stipulated that the state would request the lower sentences even if Wanger or Castaldo or both pleaded guilty, thereby making the trio's testimony unnecessary. The same would hold true regardless of the outcome at trial for either Wanger or Castaldo, and the same would hold true if—unlikely as it might be—the charges should be dismissed against Castaldo or Wanger. The agreement provided further that if the three juveniles failed to cooperate in any way, the prosecutor would not only oppose their resentencing, but would go before the parole board and oppose their early release. Finally, the agreement warned the three boys that if they should give any falsehood in a sworn statement or under oath, the state would prosecute them for false swearing to the fullest extent possible.

Ferrante asked Blair if that was the agreement between the prosecutor's office and Blair's client as the attorney had understood it. Blair said it was. The judge ordered Carboni to stand. The teenager was placed under oath—a practice that periodically was taken in cases where the stakes were high and there was a risk that the defendant would try to back out of the agreement later.

"Mr. Carboni," the judge said, addressing the young man before him, "I ask you now, is that the entire agreement that's been reached between you, the prosecutor's office, along with your attorney, Mr. Blair?"

"Yes, sir."

"There's no side agreements, any secret agreements, of any kind?"

"No, sir."

"Any other agreements? Everything that's here is the only agreement you have?"

"Yes."

"Do you further understand that the agreement is only subject to the discretion of the court? Any recommendations that are made by the prosecutor's office, the parole board, or anyone else are not binding on me, you understand that?"

Carboni faltered a moment, stirred in his handcuffs.

"No, I . . ."

"These are recommendations that are being made. In the event that you cooperate and it gets to the point where there's a recommendation that certain terms be reduced by way of resentencing, those would be recommendations to me. There's no guarantee that I go along with that, you understand that?"

Carboni paused. It was clear that this came at him like a curveball, perhaps because he had understood that the agreement was signed, sealed, and delivered like a guarantee: Take down Frank and James, and you get twelve years.

"Yes," Carboni said.

"I'm not bound by that," the judge continued.

"Yes," Carboni said.

"Okay. I'm bound by what I think is appropriate and fair, do you understand that?"

"Yes."

Now it was time for Carboni to admit for the first time in

open court his involvement in the murder conspiracy. The reporters, and perhaps some of the spectators, who were prepared to hear new details about the crime were presently disappointed. In six questions posed by his lawyer, Carboni simply confirmed his participation in the conspiracy and in the crime, although he also admitted that he had brought materials to the scene to destroy the car.

Ferrante again made sure that Carboni understood the implications of everything he was doing. Then the judge brought Carboni's parents up, as well, and asked them if they understood what was happening. Mr. and Mrs. Carboni said they did.

Now it was Strelka's turn. Strelka, his blond hair trailing in limp curls over the collar of his gray suit, stood and listened as O'Shea read the agreement aloud. His father stood by solemnly, and Susie, her frizzy blond hair pulled up in a white hair band, looking as if she were about to die. The judge questioned Strelka about his understanding of the proceedings and the plea agreement.

"Do you know what it means to plead guilty, sir?" Ferrante asked.

"Yes."

"What does it mean to you?"

"That I'm admitting to what I did."

"That you did, in fact, do what it says in the complaint, is that correct?"

"Yes."

"You understand by pleading guilty, you're admitting to me that you and possibly others have conspired and did, in fact, participate in purposely causing the death of Robert Solimine on February 17, 1992, is that correct?"

"Yes."

"Did anybody force you to plead guilty?"

"Yes. I have an agreement with the prosecutor's office."

"No, no," Ferrante said impatiently. "Did anybody force you to plead guilty?"

"No."

"Did anybody— Do you know what 'force' means?"

Strelka nodded.

"Did anybody threaten you in any way to make you plead guilty?"

"No."

"Now someone's promised you something by way of an agreement, though, is that correct?"

"Yes."

"Is that what you were trying to tell me a minute ago?"

"Yes."

"All right," Ferrante said. "Mr. O'Shea, I know this is burdensome, but I think it's necessary."

O'Shea again read the entire document laying out the terms of the plea agreement. At the conclusion, Ferrante questioned Strelka, as he had the first boy, about whether he understood it in all its details. Once again, however, the teenager seemed taken aback by the implication that the agreement by which he was admitting to murder was not airtight.

"Do you further understand that if—if I permit the plea to be accepted today, that I'm not bound by the terms of this agreement?" the judge said.

"I don't understand," Strelka answered.

"You don't understand what being bound means? That I don't have to agree with the sentencing that's recommended in this, do you understand that?"

"Yes."

"I have my own discretion to do as a judge whatever I feel is appropriate under the law, do you understand that?"

Tommy nodded his head and murmured a response that died before reaching the bench.

"I can't hear you, son," the judge said.

"Yes."

As he had done with the Carbonis, Ferrante asked Strelka's mother and father to come forward. They, too, gave their sanction to the agreement. The judge moved to enter the plea when McCann gently reminded him that he had forgotten to have Strelka admit his involvement in court on the record. Using leading questions, McCann led Strelka through a few questions to establish his guilt. Strelka, who also was placed under oath, admitted that he had been in the car with Stooge when the murder took place.

"And what were you doing when you were in that car?" McCann asked.

"We were looking out for other people or the police," Strelka said.

"Okay. And while you were in that car, in the car behind you was Solimine, Wanger, and Carboni, is that right?"

"Yes."

"And you knew that Wanger was going to kill Solimine at that time, is that correct?"

"Yes."

"And that's the reason why you were watching, is that correct?"

"Yes."

Next came Stooge. He stepped forward, wearing a pair of black jeans and a gray sports coat, and stopped. His tinted glasses hiding most of his face, he stood stiffly, as if the wrong person had been planted on the floor there inside an enormous pair of orange and black Nike sneakers. His lawyer, Linda E. Peterson, an assistant deputy public defender, asked the judge to eject the media. The judge, noting that he lacked the authority to overcome the defendant's request, complied.

Stooge, standing taller than most fourteen-year-olds, stared straight ahead as the media left. His white skin poked through a very thin black mustache that trickled over his lip.

For the third and final time, the judge presided over the entering of a guilty plea. As with the other two, Stooge had difficulty grasping some of the concepts that the judge was using to lay out the plea agreement.

"By pleading guilty, you're admitting to me that you participated in the murder of Robert Solimine, do you understand that?"

"Yes, I do."

"And what does it mean to you to plead guilty?"

"That I was—I understand that—I was there, and what happened was partly my fault."

"Does it mean to you that you're admitting to me today, if you plead guilty, that you participated and were involved in purposely causing the death of Robert Solimine on February 17, 1992? I can't hear you, son."

"Yes."

O'Shea read the agreement. Then Peterson began to lead Stooge through his admission.

"Were you an accomplice to this killing, in that you acted as a lookout in a car with Tommy Strelka?"

"Yes, we were."

"Do you know what it means to be an accomplice, that you are just as guilty of murder as the principal actor would be?"

"Yes, I do," Stooge mumbled.

"Speak louder, please," Ferrante said.

"Was it your intent that the plan to kill Robert Solimine would be successful?" Peterson asked.

"Could you please repeat that?"

"Was it your intent that the plan would be successful to kill Robert Solimine?"

"What's that mean—intent?"

"I can't hear you, son," Ferrante said.

"What's 'intent' mean?"

"You don't understand that?" Ferrante said.

"Intent."

"Okay," Ferrante said. "That you meant to do what happened. That you intended that it happened. That you meant it. That you wanted it to happen."

"Yes," Stooge said. "We did. Yes."

After entering the guilty plea for Stujinski, the judge prepared to hear from Solimine's family. Margaret came forward. She stood a moment, uneasily, and then sat down. She appeared incredibly nervous. The judge told her that she had a right to be heard at the disposition—the law's term for what amounted to the sentencing of a juvenile—but that he would hear her now as well.

"Thank you," Margaret said. She spoke extemporaneously, stammering at times in her nervousness. "Judge Ferrante, I implore you not to try these four juveniles . . . of any plea bargaining as juveniles because I feel that they plotted three times to murder my son. Uh, and each of the five . . . I feel also that each of the five boys gave each other the strength to murder him. I feel that one could not have done it, or two. I just feel the whole group, as a group, murdered him."

Then she began to read from her prepared text. It was a long and turgid letter that mixed private grief with political commentary. She sent copies of the letter far and wide: to Prosecutor Ronald Fava, of course, but also to United States Senators Bill Bradley and Frank Lautenberg, to Governor Jim Florio, to the state Attorney General, and to various members of the State Senate and Assembly, including one assemblyman who, the judge pointed out, was no longer an assemblyman.

"On February 16, 1992, not only was my son's life brutally and cold-bloodily extinguished, but on that day my life ended too," she said. As she read, she stumbled over phrases and mixed-up words.

"Ma'am, not to interrupt you," the judge said. "If this is difficult for you to read, perhaps Mr. O'Shea can read it to me because you—you just misread a few words, and I know you're nervous, and I can appreciate that you're nervous, and I can appreciate . . ."

"I also forgot to bring my glasses."

From there, Margaret read on, with the judge interjecting now and then to correct her, as she delivered a bitter indictment of the justice system, accusing the prosecutors and the courts of essentially acting as an accessory after her son's death in allowing the boys to escape justice.

"Already as time goes on, the focus is shifting from the wanton destruction of my son's life to the defendants' array of rights," she said.

It took several minutes to deliver.

When it was over, the judge entered the pleas, called the press back in, and summarized her remarks. That was it. The boys had pleaded guilty.

Outside, on the steps of the courthouse, the media thronged around Solimine's family, taking remarks from Bob Solimine and Billy, but mostly focusing on Margaret's give-'em-hell oratory.

McCann watched from a respectful distance. So did Andy Blair. Both of them were pleased that the deal had been entered and sealed, and they were trying not to show it too much. From their clients' perspective, the crime had been a game that escalated into something else because of Wanger and Castaldo. The deals were not only practically necessary, but just, they said.

Away from the glare of the TV lights, O'Shea also was answering a few reporters' questions with almost painful forthrightness.

"We recognize the victim's family's strong feelings in this case," O'Shea said. "I personally met with the parents many times. There came a point where we also had to examine society's need to be protected from violent criminals. It was the position of this office that this is the most appropriate way to proceed with the prosecution of the alleged actual strangler and of the person who allegedly set this act in motion."

A plane crash in suburbia, a political appointment, and lots of brio brought defense attorney Linda George and Frank Castaldo together for the first time in the warren of tiny Plexiglas visiting rooms inside the Passaic County Jail.

The Passaic County Jail's conference rooms were not much bigger than pay-phone booths. There was barely enough room to spread open a briefcase, and each booth was equipped with a red panic button to summon the guards if a defendant acted up. But Castaldo was still in shock. He was tearful and very upset about being penned up. He also wasn't sure about the idea of having a woman represent him. George did all the talking, almost giving orders, a thing that Frank wasn't used to. For their first meeting, George stuck to the basics: She went over procedure, and she told him to make sure he kept his mouth closed in the lockup. George didn't tell her client that she would move to reduce his bail, which had been set at $500,000, but she planned to file the motion as soon as possible. That was about it. But the first meeting was about as straightforward as the story of how they came together was circuitous.

The plane crash had been one of the worst air disasters in North Jersey. On November 10, 1985, a Falcon 50 corporate jet belonging to Nabisco Brands Inc. collided in midair with a Piper Cherokee owned by the Air Pegasus Flying Club, killing two pilots, a copilot, and two passengers. The flaming wreckage ripped through six buildings on a quiet street in Cliffside Park, killing a person on the ground, and the debris rained over a four-by-eight-block area. One of the houses that was wiped out that day belonged to Giovanni Esposito, a retired Hoboken vendor who also happened to be a relative of Alfonsina Castaldo.

Giovanni Esposito's wife broke her hip trying to get out of the house, but no one—including their two children playing in the yard—was injured. They filed a lawsuit for damages like almost everyone else on the block. Their lawyer won them a fairly nice settlement—at least nice enough that Esposito came to mind as someone who might know how to get a lawyer for Frankie. Around four o'clock on the morning after Frankie's arrest, Alfonsina had called Esposito to get a lawyer for her son; Esposito referred her to the lawyer who had handled the plane-crash claims, and this lawyer referred the Castaldos to his partner. That was how the Castaldos came to hire Kevin T. Rigby, a former assistant Bergen County prosecutor and the former mayor of River Edge. His officemate was Linda George, a young, ambitious, and politically connected lawyer, and she was to be an assistant.

The political appointment came from U.S. Senator Bill Bradley, the former New York Knicks basketball player and

Democratic heavyweight. Ten days after Solimine's murder, and after the Castaldos already had forked over thousands of dollars as a retainer to Rigby, Senator Bradley announced that Rigby would be running the senator's Garden State offices. Rigby stayed on for a little while longer, persuading a judge to halve Castaldo's bail, but eventually the career-making case of *State of New Jersey v. Frank Castaldo* became Linda George's.

The brio was all hers. A Paterson native who lived in East Rutherford, George had only recently been a part-time municipal prosecutor with the City of Paterson, handling DWIs, purse-snatchings, and shoplifters while practicing civil law on the side. Before Castaldo came her way, the biggest criminal case she had ever worked on was an appeal for William Engel, a Bergen County millionaire who hired a hit man to kill his wife because she had the gall to divorce him after a hellish marriage.

Now, as George prepared to handle Castaldo's case, a few macabre echoes from the murder of Xiomara Engel murmured down the years: With the divorce only a couple months old, Engel had lured his ex-wife to his office to collect Christmas gifts for their five-year-old daughter. Then he lit a cigarette and calmly puffed away as the hit man strangled his wife with an electrical cord. For all his troubles, the hit man was to receive $25,000. But he, like the Engels, received life in prison instead.

Having turned thirty-seven years old the previous summer, Linda George was smart, brash, mouthy, and also very pretty in a way that was both delicate and loud. She had a round face with severe eyebrows and a slightly spoiled, Cupid's-bow mouth. With her full lips pursed in a perpetual pout, she looked at times like an unhappy porcelain doll. But George had grown up in Paterson, a tough town by all accounts, and she acted the part. When she strode into court on her stick-like legs and Bergdorf Goodman pumps, her hair in full leonine display, lips splashed in blazing carmine lipstick, and her vividly polished fingernails gripping the briefcase, it was plain she was spoiling for a fight. And was she ever, as the prosecutors in Passaic County were going to find out.

Linda George had come out blazing for Frank Castaldo. She filed every motion that the rules permitted, and then some. She battled to get Frank out on bail, and when the motion failed, she brought it again. When she succeeded in getting Frankie out on bail, she went back again and again asking the court to modify the court order to allow visitors. Often she was not successful, but she just kept coming. She asked the courts to move the trial to another venue, she asked to throw out the indictment, she moved to suppress Castaldo's statements. And in a motion that won her no friends in an office filled with people who already despised her, she had filed a motion to disqualify the entire Passaic County Prosecutor's Office from trying the case. None of the lawyers in the prosecutor's office should be allowed to try Castaldo, she argued, because they had crossed the line in his investigation, taking part in events to which they were now witnesses. Lawyers were not supposed to become parties to the controversies they were litigating, the rules said, and Linda George argued that Purdy and O'Shea's conduct had put them in the same spot as the detectives in Castaldo's house on the night of his arrest. Therefore, she said, the entire office must turn the prosecution over to someone else in the interest of giving Castaldo a fair trial.

Some of the lawyers in the prosecutor's office laughed at the motion, and others seemed offended that she would inject an almost personal tone to the case. There were whispers about some problems that she was having with the legal authorities behind the scenes. In fact, the prosecutor's office was investigating a Mafia-linked gambling operation that allegedly involved a café run by her estranged husband; before it was all over, the investigation ultimately snared George, too, in its web of accusations. George would be indicted on a minor gambling rap herself because, the prosecutor's office said, she had helped to run the store.

Related to the same affair, the *New Jersey Herald & News*

accused her of having mob ties. The paper wrote a story saying that she had asked an alleged mob associate to act as the go-between in paying off a loan shark. But she claimed the article did not make it clear that she had paid off the loan on behalf of her husband, who had skipped town. George filed a libel suit against the newspaper and she filed a federal lawsuit against the county prosecutor, accusing his office of violating federal wiretap laws for allegedly leaking the loan-shark story. It was a classic example of Passaic County politics, corruption, and intrigue, and how Linda George was not afraid of a fight.

The Main Avenue street fair was the spring version of the same event seven months earlier where Stooge and Carboni had bumped into each other before heading over to see Castaldo for the first time in Stooge's life. Now Margaret Chircop stood in the middle of it, a spectacle of grief and outrage, fighting for justice for her son's homicide. She stood for hours, her hands gripping the wooden post of a placard bearing her son's 1991 high-school yearbook photo. Across the placard she had written an appeal in thick letters beseeching bystanders to sign her petitions.

"I am asking for your support in sentencing the three juvenile murderers of my son Rob to twenty years," the petitions said. "These three juveniles must be sentenced to twenty years maximum, no less."

Nearby stood Margaret's mother and father, Lee and Bill Yakal. They also carried placards and clipboards with petitions. Shoppers bunched around Margaret, sometimes waiting in line to take up the clipboards holding the petitions. Their faces twisted by anger or disgust, the passersby praised her for her courage taking on the system and pledged their support. Others expressed sympathy for her loss. Many expressed horror that such a thing had happened in Clifton of all places.

"Give me one of those goddamn signs," an eighty-year-old woman told them. "I'll carry it."

No one in Passaic County had ever done such a thing in recent memory. Margaret Chircop, headstrong and unbending, was doing it. She was working the crowd, putting the clipboard and the ballpoint pen in people's hands, enlisting the local citizenry to her cause. The petitions had been her idea and hers alone. In her anger that the prosecutor's office was proceeding against her wishes with the plea agreements for the juveniles, Margaret decided to take her case directly to the public. Bill Yakal, still burning after his encounter with the prosecutor's office, enthusiastically endorsed the idea, seeing it as the only way to secure justice. They had almost three months to work with. The boys were to be sentenced in June, and the plea bargains, like their criminal convictions, would not be formally entered until the boys were sentenced.

Margaret understood that there was nothing she could do now to save her son. He was gone. But the plea bargains—particularly for Strelka, her son's Judas—struck her like spit in the face. In her anger and pain, she located the cause for her son's death in outwardly spiraling forces beyond her control: First the boys, including the killer whom she and her son had mistaken as his best friend. Then there were the boys' parents. Finally, there was society, and the criminal justice system itself. She got in touch with a champion of victims' rights named Richard Pompelio, whose seventeen-year-old son had been murdered in 1989 by another teenager at a beer party. Incensed at the perception that criminal defendants had greater rights than their victims, Pompelio, a Sussex County lawyer, had joined another victims'-rights crusader in promoting an amendment to New Jersey's constitution that expanded victims' rights. He had also pioneered a controversial effort to hold third parties—such as parents or their homeowners' insurance—financially responsible for a crime. Pompelio took on Chircop's case, and Margaret joined a support group called Parents of Murdered Children. She began the petition drive.

"I never thought I would make a difference on this earth," Margaret told a reporter from the *New York Times*. "I thought it was going to be one of those ordinary routine lives. Now I feel maybe it's my destiny to do something for others and make the justice system see it's wrong. I don't think I could be happy any longer sitting around doing promotional payments. I've gotten so hyper. People used to say, 'Maggie, you could put a bomb under you and you wouldn't move.' Now I can't sit still."

In the petitions, in her interviews with news reporters, and in her pitches to passing residents, Margaret seemed to be pleading her case before the judge himself, asking—almost demanding—that Judge Ferrante sentence the three juveniles to the maximum term of twenty years in a juvenile facility with no hope for parole or early release.

A woman who applauded their efforts told Lee she had seen Castaldo's picture in the newspaper just the other day.

"God, he's got evil written in those eyes," the woman said.

People of all ages picked up the clipboards and signed their names. Newspaper photographers snapped pictures. Eventually, 5,725 people affixed their names to her cause. Bill Yakal glowed with pride at the accomplishment. Without any professional help or experience in organizing such a campaign, he would boast, they had surpassed the abilities of some politicians. They had done better than Ross Perot, he thought.

One of Linda George's first coups was obtaining bail for Frank Castaldo under a home-monitoring program, a relatively new and politically sensitive venture that the county had borrowed from the state. What it amounted to was a high-tech ball and chain: Inmates who were selected for the program wore electronic anklets that set off an alarm if they strayed too far from a monitoring device that was rigged up to the telephone lines in their homes. Government officials were excited about the program for a couple of reasons: For one thing, it involved gee-whiz, brand-spanking-new (or almost) technology, and it also promised to empty the overstuffed prisons and jails in New Jersey. The state Department of Corrections had been using the program with convicts who were nearing the end of their sentences. Passaic County had only recently begun to use the program for minor offenders, but the county had never used it for defendants awaiting trial. Then Castaldo's application came in. He was permitted to try the program for several reasons: He was young, he had no previous criminal record, he had a good chance of beating the rap, and it would be a very long time until his trial. It might take at least eighteen months for his case to come to trial, and should he be acquitted, there might be questions about why a young man had to spend two years of his life locked up for nothing.

Castaldo was admitted to the program under the strictest bail conditions. His family posted $250,000 bail on March 18. This included a court-ordered $50,000 surety to a bail bondsman, whose profit incentive would ensure pursuit if Castaldo fled. The bail conditions demanded that he have no contact with the victim's family, or with his codefendants and their families. He was required to make daily check-ins with the county bail unit, bear the costs of home monitoring, abstain from alcohol, turn in his passport, and sign an extradition waiver so that there would be no court fight if he ran away and got caught in another jurisdiction. Finally, there were to be no visitors except family, unless expressly authorized by the court. Superior Court Judge Sidney H. Reiss, who granted the bail, said it was the most stringent he had ever laid down in fifteen years on the bench. He got no argument from Castaldo, who griped that he had less freedom under the home surveillance program than he might have had at the Passaic County Jail. In the jail, at least, he could get visits from almost anyone he pleased.

All the same, Castaldo returned to his mom's cooking and his own living room after the county probation department fitted him with a sleek black anklet. Stuffed with electronic circuitry, the anklet resembled a bicycle lock that was riveted to his leg. A monitoring station was hooked up through the telephone, and this was connected to another monitoring base in the county probation offices. The anklet was designed to emit an alarm if anyone tried to tamper with it or if Castaldo moved more than 150 feet from the monitoring station in his house. What's more, to make sure someone was checking on him, a computer placed random telephone calls to the Castaldo house as many as five times a day, at any time of the day or night. When someone picked up the telephone, a recording would announce that the monitoring program was calling. Within a certain amount of time, Castaldo would have to state his name, tell the time of day, and plug part of the anklet into a socket on the monitoring station to prove his whereabouts. Never a day went by that there wasn't at least one call, and if someone other than Frank answered the telephone, a frantic alarm of shouts would go up through the Castaldo household: "THE MACHINE! THE MACHINE! THE MACHINE!"

Over time, the home detention became second nature to Castaldo. For months, he bugged and bugged Linda George to obtain permission for Melanie to visit, and when the request got shot down, he screamed at her on the phone, swore a few times, and told her she was fired. Incensed, George got in her car and flew over to Castaldo's house.

"You hung up the phone on me?" George shouted. "No one hangs up the phone on me!"

"Get used to it," Castaldo said.

Sometimes the machine erroneously emitted an alarm, and Frank DiGiaimo, the county probation officer in charge of the local program, would call Castaldo to find out what was going on.

"Frank, you there?" DiGiaimo said, sometimes in the middle of the night.

"Where else am I gonna be?" Castaldo said.

Through no fault of his own, Castaldo's semifreedom under the program threatened to go up in smoke in April after a Paterson teenager, who had been released from prison into the state Correction Department's anklet program after serving most of his prison term for a drug charge, tampered with the anklet, sneaked out of his apartment, and accidentally shot a friend while horsing around with a gun. The Paterson shooting upset the entire anklet program, and it put Passaic County's experiment on red alert. Across the state, politicians fulminated and demanded that such anklet programs be curtailed. The Castaldo family waited nervously for the storm to pass.

Then, on the first weekend of May, someone called the Clifton police and reported that Castaldo was having visitors, despite the court orders forbidding them. The police alerted DiGiaimo, who called Castaldo right away. Castaldo admitted that he had been sitting on the front porch talking to friends on the street. The prosecutor's office moved to revoke Castaldo's bail, which Judge Reiss did on May 7. That same week, New Jersey Bell also shut off telephone service to the Castaldos, claiming the family had not paid its bill. Without keeping up telephone service—whose cost the defendant, of course, was required to pay—Castaldo could not participate in the program.

A full hearing was held before Reiss about whether to revoke Castaldo's bail permanently. Bill Purdy argued that Castaldo was too dangerous to allow out, that he had flouted the rules, and he deserved no second chance. But Linda George pointed out that the two visitors happened to be mutual friends of Castaldo's younger siblings. And she said the telephone company had suspended the Castaldos' telephone service only for an hour, and that the disconnection had been the fault of a clerical error. No matter. Reiss would not reinstate bail.

Over the next two weeks, George fought on two fronts to get Castaldo out of jail again. She appeared before Reiss, who reinstated bail but doubled the amount to $500,000, and she went to the state Appellate Division. Finally, less than two weeks after Castaldo went back in the slammer, the appeals court ordered the original bail reinstated. The prosecutor's office kept him under additional surveillance by its investigators for a month, which Castaldo knew. But

Castaldo was back out, and he would stay out for nearly two years while awaiting trial.

Despite the earlier scrape with visitors, which led to his bail revocation, Castaldo would later say he sneaked in Melanie a couple times. And Castaldo joked about his confinement all the time, mostly because it got on his nerves. A trip to the basement could set the blasted thing off.

"This is my wife," he explained to people. "My ball and chain. You gotta call her all the time, it costs a fortune, and I get no sex. And she nags and complains if you get it wrong. That's my wife."

14

For nearly two months, while all three boys—Strelka, Carboni, and Stooge—lived at home under the electronic-surveillance program, they and their families prepared for an event that no one could really prepare for. On June 8, 1992, the day of sentencing had arrived and they knew that Judge Ferrante would send them to the New Jersey Training School for Boys at Jamesburg for twenty years. And perhaps, just perhaps, it would really be twenty years.

The last court proceeding, when they had admitted taking part in the murder, was more or less like a dress rehearsal for the day of sentencing—or, in the parlance of the juvenile code, the disposition. This time, however, Ferrante refused to toss the press out of the room, despite arguments from Stooge's lawyer, Linda Peterson, that it was wrong to open the proceedings. But the judge granted the defense lawyers' second request: McCann asked that the victim's family have their say first, so that he would know how to respond.

Margaret Chircop stood with a leaf of paper and began to read.

"The last time we met, Judge Ferrante, I read a letter filled with pain, grief, and hope for justice," she said. "I hope this time my appeal to you will show you that I am only looking for justice for the murder of my son Rob."

Although it reprised everything she had said in the courtroom two months earlier, this letter seemed only sharper and more angry than her first, and it thrust at the parents of the boys with more than a few angry jabs.

"Looking back, I feel Rob was trapped," she said. "Trapped between his loyalty to his friends, versus the morals and values of his family upbringing. Rob was just discovering himself and what he stood for, observing and evaluating the interests and activities of his friends, seeing that they didn't conform with his morals and values. He was in conflict. Rob just didn't—just couldn't leave them because of his long-standing ties of friendship, loyalty, and the drive to help them with their problems."

In general, the text contained less anguish over the loss of her son and more fury toward the justice system's treatment of the killers. This time, however, members of the press were taking it down, word for word. The only juvenile she singled out for mention by name was Strelka, who sat with a stricken look on his face nearby.

Then Bob Solimine stood and delivered his remarks. He sputtered with anger and pain and struggled to articulate the ideas running through his mind.

"And what I'd like to express is their intense planning in an assassination. I ain't going to say it's a murder," Bob said, "it's a regular assassination of my son. They planned it, they tried it, it worked . . . They had everything planned. The only thing they didn't plan on is getting caught. They made a pact, and I'm sure if they weren't caught again, they would be planning again to [kill] someone else."

Before taking his seat, Bob Solimine suggested that perhaps the death penalty would be the only appropriate punishment for murder.

Now Strelka stood before the court. He wore black pants, a white dress shirt, and a huge floppy black tie. His hands were locked to the leather waist restraint with a padlock. Although McCann did not request a specific sentence, he described his client for the court.

"How did we come here?" McCann said. "The only thing that I can think of, Your Honor, is that Tommy came from a situation where he was not streetwise, or he was not, in quotes, a smart kid. He was not a kid that would go out and try to impress the other kids with his toughness. He's not a tough kid. He's not a braggadocio kid. He's someone who is really under the influence of his parents. When he got to Clifton High School, I believe in order to enhance his own standing at Clifton High School and show that he was somehow a tough guy, and that he wasn't a meek individual, he started hanging around with Frank Castaldo—who had a reputation for being tough, who had a reputation of having a violent temper, who was a bad kid as opposed to being a good kid. And by hanging around with Frank Castaldo, Tommy Strelka tried to make himself a big guy."

By way of closing, McCann added that the family was devastated.

"Mr. Strelka, anything you'd like to say?" Ferrante asked.

"Yes, Your Honor," Strelka said sheepishly. "I'd just like to say that I am very sorry for what happened and—"

"A little louder, please, Thomas."

"—and if I could do everything over again, I would do things differently. And I know now that I'm going to set my life back on track by helping the Passaic County's Prosecutor's Office as much as I can. And I'd just like to apologize to the Court and to my parents and to Rob's parents for what has happened."

Stooge went next. He wore a T-shirt and sneakers. But Stooge, his long black hair almost appearing spiky as he stood in the well of the court, declined to speak to the court, and his lawyer confined her remarks to the matter of the petitions. Then came Carboni, who was dressed entirely in black. Black jeans. Black T-shirt. Black sneakers. Blair did his spiel, speaking of his faith in the system that would rehabilitate his client and attesting to Carboni's remorse.

"Mr. Carboni, it's your time to talk," Ferrante said. "What would you like to say?"

"I'm sorry this ever happened, and I wish it never did."

"I've read that already," Ferrante snapped. "I've read that in the report here that you said that. You wish it never did. Anything else?"

Carboni bowed his head and became choked up, almost theatrically so.

"I'm sorry for Rob's death. I mean, a person's dead, and I can't even handle it myself under the circumstances also."

"Okay," Ferrante said. "Anything else?"

Before imposing sentence, Ferrante explained the law and reviewed the boys' background reports.

"Mrs. Chircop indicated that the juvenile justice—no, strike that—that the justice systems . . . do not serve enough, that the American people are tired, that penalties are not tough enough in our society," Ferrante said. "Perhaps she's right." Then Ferrante passed sentence, imposing a twenty-year indeterminate term on Carboni, Strelka, and Stujinski. He directed that the boys be transported to Jamesburg immediately, and remarked that all three boys had broken their parents' hearts.

"I'm not going to call this stupid," the judge said, addressing Carboni. "There's too much involved here to call it stupid. I can call this only, as I indicated to your codefendant, a senseless, callous act." And for what? the judge wondered. To imitate movie mobsters? Copying John Gotti? It was an incredibly wanton crime, the judge said, that showed no regard whatsoever for human life.

"You're going to have to say a lot of Hail Marys, my friend, to salvage anything you have left in your life."

Jack Snowdon stood outside Robbie Solimine's Plymouth Laser staring in through the closed window on the driver's side. It was eerie to be around the car, and eerier still inside the thing. Snowdon knew because he had sat in it himself. But now Snowdon watched quietly through the glass window as two men performed a macabre exercise. A young man sitting in the backseat flipped an electrical cord over the driver's head and pulled back hard. The cord tightened against the man's neck and cut off the wind. The young man with the garrote leaned back and braced his feet and pulled harder. He pulled on the cord until it became clear that the driver was fatally pinned. And then, after the driver caught his breath, the young man did it again—because Snowdon, an assistant Passaic County prosecutor, wanted to make sure the thing would work.

Jack Snowdon's vocational interests in life lay in two things: the law and carpentry. Both disciplines required logic. One was palpable, a world of math mixed up in the dust and wood grain, where mistakes were never fatal and the work provided a form of contemplation with one's hands. The other discipline in Jack Snowdon's life required immersion in a world of language: In the law, it was of course all words, words, and more words. From the tortured prose of police reports, written statements and grand jury testimony, to the arcane, elusive, and sometimes majestic concepts of the state code and case law, the truth of a criminal case almost always emerged from a careful study of words. Here, of course, the stakes also were usually very high.

It helped him in his trade that Snowdon had always been a talker. Ask him about a case and he would start talking, the words tumbling out without spaces between them, analyzing a fact, a piece of evidence, or a motive first from one direction and then another. He seemed always interested in taking up an issue from a case and viewing it from several sides. As a carpenter, he put his verbal mind to rest and took things step by step, making sure dovejoints were seamless and the kitchen cabinets and windows all hung level.

Snowdon—whose given name was John, like his father's—had a round, florid face. His small eyes were puffy and close-set, like a creature accustomed to burrowing its way out of difficult spots, and his voice contained a tobacco burr from the cigarettes he smoked relentlessly in his office or in the hallway outside the courtroom. He had a shrewd and caustic wit, which gave him the ability to reduce almost anyone—judge, cop, legal adversary, or news reporter—to a one-liner. In the courtroom, he was sharp and cunning and quick. Yet he had a knack for taking a case full of complexity and giving it to jurors in plain common sense, as if between friends the gravest of controversies could be put right with an open mind and a cup of coffee. He could, if things were going his way, get them chuckling at the absurdity of a defense. If drama was called for, he could almost raise the jurors from their seats in outrage—outrage not only over the crime but (and this would be an unspoken agreement between him and them) the defendant's audacity to proclaim his innocence.

Besides his abundant natural abilities, Snowdon's résumé had given him an edge on most other prosecutors: For most of his career, Snowdon had been a defense lawyer. Reversing the normal progression of a lawyer's career, he had taken the side of the accused, working as a public defender for nearly two decades, until he joined the Passaic County Prosecutor's Office in 1990. This experience gave him valuable skills. For one thing, most prosecutors seldom acquire the skill of cross-examining witnesses. It's the prosecutor's job to present the bulk of the evidence in a criminal trial, since the defendant has no obligation whatsoever to call witnesses in his behalf or present a single exhibit. Whoever calls the witness must present the direct examination with questions that are not leading and allow the witness to put into his or her own words what they know or remember. As a result, they conduct methodical questioning almost along prearranged lines, and they do not have as much opportunity to use leading questions—those long dangerous questions that often require a simple yes or no answer—as a defense lawyer does.

In cross-examination, the lawyer goes on attack. After the witness has stated his position in direct examination, the other side guns in, looping, turning, and dive-bombing the witness from any direction and with propositions that the witness sometimes has almost no choice but to agree and disagree at the same time. Sometimes, the only witness prosecutors cross-examine may be an expert witness, or an alibi witness, and perhaps the defendant. In most trials, the defendant does not take the stand, his silence protected by the Constitution. If the defendant does elect to testify, the cross-examination can be a wild experience navigated almost by the seat of the pants, since the prosecutor often is hearing the defendant's version for the first time.

But Snowdon had questioned many a witness presented by the prosecution. After graduating from Dickinson Law School and a stint on active duty with the National Guard, Snowdon went to work as an assistant deputy public defender in 1972 in the appellate section in Newark. Two and a half years later, he was transferred to the trial section in the Paterson office. As a Passaic County assistant deputy public defender, Snowdon learned to wing it. Whatever case the judge wanted to try, they tried it, and at a ferocious rate. There was no time to prepare, and sometimes he tried as many as two cases a week. Along the way Snowdon had attacked cops, victims, and experts, and he knew how to listen and attack at the same time, often by using sarcasm to shred his target's logic. He also picked up little tricks, such as making sure he stood behind the jury box for his witnesses, who would therefore engage the jurors as they testified, and standing on the opposite side of the courtroom for the other guy's witnesses, so that they would appear to be avoiding the jury.

What's more, as a defense lawyer, Snowdon had been faced hundreds of times with the seemingly hopeless task of finding an angle—some angle, any angle—that would give a guilty man a credible defense. As a prosecutor, he would do the same thing when a new assignment fell into his lap. Almost before deciding how to prosecute the case, he would begin thinking about how the other guy would defend it. By taking this view of his cases, he generally learned how to try to head them off.

So it was when Prosecutor Fava turned to Snowdon in the spring of 1992 and asked him to take the Solimine homicide. The assignment would be immense: It would mean handling not just one high-profile case, but two—to say nothing of the potential legal headaches involving the three juveniles who had pleaded guilty. To Snowdon and others who believed the evidence credible enough, the thought of letting a kid like Wanger walk the streets again after a murder like this was unimaginable. Yet given the awesome consequences for the accused—sending a teenager to live in a box for the rest of his life—the case deserved to be tried with the utmost care. Furthermore, Snowdon would have to try the cases with a view not only to convictions, as the prosecutor believed the evidence warranted, but with a view to being sustained on appeal. That was true, of course, of almost any criminal case—but all the more so in this one.

To make matters worse, the case against Wanger and Castaldo would be more difficult to make than one might think at first glance. To begin with, both trials would depend almost solely on the word of three young boys who had pleaded guilty to murder. In the best of circumstances, juries sometimes found untrustworthy the testimony of coconspirators who had received light sentences in exchange for testifying against their fellow codefendants. Yet these three juveniles had received plea bargains that almost everyone agreed were highly lenient. If a jury believed—as the defense was sure to argue—that these three kids would accuse their own mothers of murder if it could spare them a single day in prison, well, then the jury might just let Wanger and Castaldo go.

Problem number two was that there was almost nothing *besides* the word of these three kids to prove that Wanger had committed the murder. Wanger never cracked. While every other defendant had spilled his guts to the police, Wanger never said a word to implicate himself. Furthermore, despite all the cops on the scene—or perhaps because of all the cops teeming around the scene—not a shred of definitive physical evidence was found in Solimine's car, on Solimine's car, in Wanger's house, or anywhere else that would indisputably link Wanger to the crime. There were no fingerprints, no footprints, no fibers, no blood, nothing. What's more, even if Wanger could be placed in the car, his lawyer would simply argue that it meant nothing anyway since he had been inside Solimine's car many times. As if that weren't enough, Wanger came into court with a good reputation. Sure, there were the antics about hanging the stuffed animals in chemistry class and drinking like a sailor, but he had never been in trouble with the police, he was a lector in the church, and so on. At the same time, he also had a history of nonepileptic seizures and prescription use of an anticonvulsant that could, conceivably, be used to build a diminished-capacity defense. He might even try to plead insanity—a tack that Wanger's lawyer initially took before withdrawing it.

The problems with Castaldo would be more difficult to surmount. Here was a kid who wasn't even *there*. Snowdon would have to prove that although Castaldo was miles away at the time, he had shared the same murderous intent Wanger did. If you believed Wanger held the garrote, then it was no great leap to believe that he intended to kill. But even if you believed Castaldo might have said at one point that he wanted this kid dead, would a jury really believe that he meant it to happen? Castaldo was eighteen years old and therefore, under the law, he was an adult—but he was still a teenager, after all, and not vastly older than the two next-oldest boys in the group. He hadn't been an angel, but he also had no criminal record as a juvenile. Castaldo's case would require proving a state of mind based almost entirely on what he had said, when he said it, and how it was interpreted by the three boys. One could imagine that the case might hinge, in some ways, on what Castaldo's tone of voice had been—for example, as he questioned the boys outside his house less than an hour after the murder. Was he attempting to determine if his directions had been carried out—or was he simply incredulous and trying to find out what had happened?

As Snowdon began to prepare for the biggest case in his life, he decided he had to know everything he could about the case and about the boys. If it meant visiting the cemetery where they were hanging out looking for Annie's ghost, then it meant going to Annie's Road to find the mausoleum they visited, the house where Annie had purportedly lived, and the window where the spirit was. If it meant going out in the rain with Investigator Wood to retrace the kids' path from School 15 to Carboni's house or looking for the plank and the hole where Wanger supposedly stashed his booze—because they thought that might also be the place he hid the murder weapon—then so be it.

So one day Snowdon and Wood, accompanied by investigator William Marotta, drove out to the state police impound lot in Totowa to test the garrote inside the Plymouth Laser. The exterior of the hatchback had turned gray with grime. The char mark around the gas nozzle was plainly visible. But the inside of the car seemed the same.

Wood climbed into the driver's seat. He was to play Solimine. William Marotta, a young and cheerful investigator in the prosecutor's office who also happened to be fairly short, climbed into the backseat. He was to be Wanger. They would use a garrote exactly like Wanger's.

Making the facsimile had been Wood's idea. When they had begun working together, Snowdon encouraged Wood to offer any ideas or suggestions that he could think of that might help their case. As the date of the trial approached, Wood suggested that they make a garrote so that jurors could see for themselves what Wanger had used. A bit of showmanship always perked up the jurors, and the object itself would also provide a powerful exhibit of the degree of Wanger's premeditation.

Marotta took an electrical cord to the Passaic County Juvenile Detention Center and gave it to Strelka to demonstrate how Wanger had fashioned the garrote. When Strelka was done, Marotta was impressed. It was incredible to think that anyone, not to mention a teenager, had come up with such a simple and ingenious weapon. Trying it on and pulling it, Marotta found that the shoelaces, which held the folded cord together, rode out nicely to the ends when pressure was applied, thereby tightening the loops around the wrists. There would be no way the thing would slip off the killer's hands.

Snowdon, too, was impressed. But he wanted to leave nothing to chance, and he wanted to prove for himself that Wanger could have strangled Solimine as the boys had said. In Snowdon's mind was the scene from *Fatal Vision,* the TV movie based on the best-seller by Joe McGinniss about tripler murderer Dr. Jeffrey MacDonald. MacDonald, a doctor with the Green Berets, was suspected of killing his wife and two children, but he told investigators that a drug-crazed band of hippies, à la Charlie Manson, broke in, attacked him with a board and a knife, and massacred his family. In the beginning, MacDonald's father-in-law believes him. Then the father-in-law, played by Karl Malden, acts out MacDonald's version of the crime, and he discovers that it was physically impossible. Snowdon recalled that the key had been a two-by-four that never would have cleared the ceiling and crashed on MacDonald's head, as he had claimed. Snowdon wanted to see if there was any way that Solimine could have saved himself. He also wanted to make sure that the garrote, as they now understood it, could be thrown, quickly and quietly, over the driver's head inside such a cramped space.

Now Snowdon stood outside the car, which had been Robbie Solimine's tomb, peering through its window. Even for Wood, who had worked lots of homicides, the experience was a touch ghoulish. Marotta was to spring the garrote on him, just as it had been sprung on Solimine. Wood wanted no warning.

Gripping the garrote like a jump rope, Marotta found that the cord would move with just a flick of the wrists. Wood sat back in the driver's seat and closed his eyes. Marotta whipped the cord around Wood's neck and pulled. The cord flew over in one quick shot, and Marotta pulled hard enough so that Wood's instinct was to put his feet up on the dashboard, propel himself backward into the seat in a bid to lessen the pressure. But there was no way out. Wood was a dead man. He couldn't get his fingers under the cord. He couldn't reach into the backseat. As Marotta leaned backward, he found that he could brace his feet against two spots on the lower part of the seat. With this leverage, he barely had to exert himself to cut off Wood's air. But Marotta didn't even have to lunge backward in the seat or brace his feet midway down the seat, as Wanger had done. All Marotta had to do was sit there and pull. It was an awesome feeling, how the leverage worked and created a kind of sweet spot where it seemed as if he wasn't really pulling at all. Wood was turning red.

"Holy fuck!" Wood said when Marotta released the cord. Wood touched his neck. He was laughing and joking around, but the cord had shut off his windpipe for a moment. It was not a very comfortable feeling.

The experiment ended. It was, in its way, a harrowing experience for Wood and the others, although it had been entirely staged. But it made it all the more clear what Robbie Solimine's last minutes had been like.

In the early-morning hours of Friday, July 16, 1993, the Paterson and Clifton police departments received word of a serious car accident at the intersection of Dey and Hazel streets. It was a single-vehicle accident involving a Chevrolet Camaro. The car had been traveling north on Hazel Street. The car went into a left-hand turn on a curve, banged into the guardrail, and then shot like a slingshot straight ahead and across the other lane of traffic. Then it slammed into a telephone pole and crumpled.

The driver, who was killed in the crash, was identified at the scene as Paula M. Glus—James Wanger's mother. Toxicology reports later indicated that she had been drinking, and that her blood-alcohol level had been above .10 percent, the threshold that New Jersey state law recognized as the level of intoxication.

Wanger's lawyer, Anthony Pope, asked the court if Wanger would be permitted to leave the detention center to see his mother's funeral. The request was granted. Alone, except for the sheriff's officers watching him, Wanger traveled to the funeral home where his mother lay and paid his final respects.

Driving to Jamesburg on a dreary autumn day when rain lanced through the sky, Snowdon was brought up short by the entrance to the correctional facility. There, in the black wrought-iron arch above the entrance, held aloft by two brick pillars, were the words "State Home For Boys." It was quaint, and not particularly striking or even noteworthy—but in Snowdon's inflamed imagination, what with the atmosphere and the setting and the purpose of his visit, the sign seemed to echo the gates of a concentration camp with their motto of "Arbeit Macht Frei." Inside, housing some of New Jersey's most violent children, was a sprawling campus of ill-heated halls, crowded bunks, and crumbling buildings that resembled what was left after a small, private college had squandered its endowment.

This was the last stage of his preparation for trial. Snowdon and Wood were coming to talk to the three boys whose testimony would make or break the prosecution against Wanger and Castaldo. Snowdon wanted to go over their stories for several reasons: to hear it live for himself, make sure the boys' memories had been refreshed, and also track down any new information or loose ends that might come up before trial. He and Wood had planned to stay at a hotel nearby so they wouldn't have to drive back and forth.

They would meet with one boy a day. Strelka, as the eldest and presumably the most knowledgeable, would be first. Then Stujinski. Carboni would follow last.

Strelka came into the interview room with a strong step and a diffident demeanor. He shook hands with Snowdon and Wood, and he indicated that he was willing to help in any way that he could. Snowdon had been expecting the kid to be hard after a year in the stir. To his surprise, Strelka wasn't. Almost from the first, Strelka came off as a kid who was very scared because he had gotten into something way over his head. He was jumpy—it seemed as if he could not look an adult in the eyes with ease—but almost eager to demonstrate to Snowdon and Wood that he would tell them whatever they needed to know. As Snowdon questioned him and walked him through the prior statements, he would ask questions in such a way that he could test whether Strelka was telling him the truth. For example, Snowdon would pose a question with something false contained inside it to see if Strelka would go along with it or not. Strelka would correct him. And as the interview went on, Strelka periodically stopped, telling the assistant prosecutor and the investigator that he had been mistaken about something he said earlier, and he would tell them the new bit of information. Snowdon came to like Strelka as they talked. A few times, Strelka's eyes welled up with tears. Snowdon was impressed by the kid's change of heart, and he started to feel as if Strelka truly had felt guilty for his role in the murder.

The only area that Strelka seemed unwilling to give on was his relationship to Chrissie Bachelle. As Snowdon had looked into the case he came to feel, as the police had in the investigation's early days, as if she had inadvertently played a much larger role in the murder than anyone would acknowledge. It seemed more and more as if one of the reasons everyone hated Solimine—and why Strelka would take part in tormenting Solimine and conspiring against him—was that Solimine had a crush on Chrissie at the same time Strelka did. But Strelka denied being anything more than friends with her.

The second day, Snowdon and Wood met with Stooge. Stooge also seemed eager to help the prosecution, and it became obvious as they talked that Stooge had been the most passive member of the gang. He was smart and he had a reasonably good memory and he wasn't putting on an attitude—but he seemed to lack the solid grasp of events and places that Strelka had had. As the day went on, he came to seem more and more of a pathetic figure, a patsy who had been swept along with kids who were older and more streetwise than he was. Snowdon could imagine easily the exciting world that had opened up for a fourteen-year-old kid in Stooge's shoes. Strelka had a car; Castaldo and Wanger had booze; there were girls, cigarettes, video games, and wild places like Annie's Road. What red-blooded kid wouldn't have a blast carrying on like that? Snowdon thought. If he had not been hooked up in the conspiracy, Snowdon thought, he would genuinely have liked the kid, whose honesty seemed downright pure. Ask the kid a question, and he seemed like an open book.

Carboni came last, and the moment he walked in, he exuded attitude. Of the three boys, Carboni had absorbed the prison mentality the most. In the look in his eyes, his unhelpful answers, his truncated explanations, he was conveying the disgust that inmates profess to feel for anyone who rats. Snitches get stitches, the inmates say, and all three had been harassed when they first entered the facility after word got out that they had turned state's witnesses. Now Carboni—who had started to hang with the toughs inside the facility, the Latino and black kids from hellholes like Camden and Newark—seemed to be having second thoughts about cooperating. He sat down at the table and lit a cigarette, radiating a cool repugnance for the law officers, as if he had deigned to meet with them despite himself. It was as if the kid was acting the part of Jimmy Cagney or some other Hollywood mobster: "Listen, youse screws, you ain't gettin' nothin' out of me." They started going over Carboni's statement, but the kid wouldn't give. In frank but civil tones, Snowdon explained to Carboni that if he wanted the state to keep its end of the bargain and reduce his sentence, he would have to cooperate.

"I don't remember," Carboni kept saying.

Wood's patience ran out first and he motioned to Snowdon to step outside the interview room.

"Fuck this kid," Wood said. "Let him stay here."

He told Snowdon he had seen Carboni's act before.

"We don't need this kid's testimony. Fuck him. He wants to play it this way, we'll play it that way," Wood say. "I'm not going to get jerked around by this kid anymore."

Fine, Snowdon said. He and Wood went back into the room to break the news.

"Guess we don't need your testimony," Wood said. "You can't remember anything. We got the other two guys. So, since you can't remember anything, there goes your deal down the tubes too. We're out of here."

Carboni was dumbstruck. Snowdon and Wood walked out. As far as they were concerned, that was that. In a parting shot, while checking out with the officials before they left the facility, Wood approached an internal affairs officer. He wondered if there had been any suspicious fires at the compound. There had, the official said. Well, said Wood, you might want to talk to this Carboni kid.

Snowdon and Wood were still on the New Jersey Turnpike driving back when Wood's pager started firing like mad. Wood had expected the change of heart, but he didn't expect it that fast. Wood dialed the number on a cellular phone from the car. It was Andy Blair. Wood could almost see him sweating on the other end of the telephone. Blair had already heard from his client about the detectives' departure. Now Blair was pleading to hold the deal together.

"Please," Blair was saying. "Don't do this to him. Don't do this to the kid."

"I didn't do it to him," Wood said. "He did it himself."

Blair was promising up and down that he could turn Carboni around. He told Wood he would go down to Jamesburg himself and lean on his client to cooperate if need be.

"I don't know if Jack wants to go back down there and waste his time," Wood said, half seriously but mostly unable to resist wringing it out for what it was worth.

"Please," Blair was saying. "He'll come around. I swear to you, he'll come around."

"All right," Wood said. "But you're buying lunch, Andy."

It was a month before Wood and Snowdon got back down to Jamesburg to talk with Carboni again. They wanted it that way just to let Carboni sweat a little bit before they returned. Blair went along this time, too. He bought lunch.

For some time before the Superior Court grand jury handed up indictments against Wanger and Castaldo, there had been a shortage of state judges in the Passaic County courthouse. The governor had not yet nominated lawyers to fill the existing vacancies, the backlog of civil and criminal cases rose precipitously, and the divorce calendar ground nearly to a halt. Of the judges available for criminal trials, only a few possessed the necessary experience or temperament to cope with the size and complexity of the Solimine murder trials—to say nothing of the ability to manage the lawyers and the news media. As a result, although he had been a state judge less than two years, the obvious choice to preside over the trials was Judge Ronald G. Marmo.

Judge Marmo had been a top-flight prosecutor before his elevation to the bench. Having spent twenty-three years as a prosecutor in Passaic County, Marmo had distinguished himself while trying hundreds of cases, including at least one that attracted national attention and another that sent a woman to death row for the first time in New Jersey in half a century. He had a woolly cap of brown hair and heavy-lidded, blue eyes. A trim, affable man who laughed easily, as if in perpetual astonishment or good cheer, he could put almost anyone at ease when he was off the bench. On the bench, Marmo might wisecrack with legal counsel if the courtroom was almost empty and it was a routine matter, but at trial he controlled the courtroom with a firm hand. The son of Paterson silk workers who eventually opened an insurance agency, Marmo drove himself physically and mentally. He came to the courthouse early and left late. He never rode the elevator to his courtroom on the sixth floor, walking up twelve flights of stairs at a brisk pace, sometimes two at a time.

Marmo's professional legal career began in 1968 when he accepted a position with the Passaic County Prosecutor's Office, at a time when the post was still just a part-time job in pinched quarters in the old marble courthouse. The job later changed, and Marmo faced the choice of remaining in the office he loved or making more money as a private lawyer. Marmo stayed. Working under seven different county prosecutors—from John Thevos in 1968 to Ronald S. Fava in 1988—Marmo spent virtually his entire career as a prosecutor inside the same building, the Passaic County courthouse complex, as it grew from the neoclassical domed courthouse, to the adjoining cakelike structure, to a white annex, and then to a cube of black marble in the 1990s. Among the most notorious cases he handled was the 1976 retrial of Rubin "Hurricane" Carter and John Artis for a fatal Paterson barroom shooting. A liberal U.S. District Court judge later set aside the convictions, a reversal that stung Marmo long afterward. Then, in 1984, Marmo prosecuted Marie Moore, whose murder trial would haunt him more than any other.

State of New Jersey v. Marie Moore was arguably one of the most gruesome criminal cases in the annals of New Jersey crime. Moore, a former telephone operator who claimed to suffer from a split personality, was accused of fatally torturing a thirteen-year-old girl. Over a period of more than a year, Moore—in the guise of "Billy Joel," a male spirit that she claimed spoke through her—directed her fourteen-year-old lover and her middle-aged roommate to carry out daily punishments of the girl. The abuse began with beatings from a whiffle ball bat and escalated to unspeakable acts of sexual torture. Before the girl's death in January 1983, she had been beaten, starved, hung by thumb cuffs from the wall, raped, sexually assaulted with various objects, forced to eat animal excrement, and scrubbed with bathroom cleanser. To silence her cries, a clothespin was snapped to the child's tongue. The boy, who cooperated with the state in prosecuting Moore, testified that the girl died when she fell and hit her head on a bathtub. One of the keys to prosecuting the case was understanding how Moore could somehow seduce, brainwash, and command others to do her bidding. Marmo made extensive use of psychiatric testimony to prove that Moore was criminally responsible, and not legally insane, when the crime occurred.

As a prosecutor, Marmo was known for conducting almost flawless trials. He had a low-key manner of addressing jurors and spoke to them in a way that the common man could relate to what he was saying. Without notes, Marmo would stand in the well of the courtroom with his hands folded, and analyze and argue his case for the jury as if he were having a friendly chat. He seldom forgot to ask questions that needed asking, and he didn't ask questions that shouldn't have been asked. He didn't forget to move items of evidence for the jury to consider. No one could remember seeing him flustered or backtracking.

Marmo brought his vast skills as a trial attorney with him to his role as a state judge—an excellent thing or a handicap, depending on one's point of view. On the one hand, Marmo possessed an uncanny instinct for predicting not only a trial's general course, but the many ins and outs of each side's tactics. He could anticipate objections and motions before they were entered by the lawyers, and he was uncowed by the most forceful or arrogant of them. What's more, his grasp of the law allowed him to extemporize complicated legal rulings with impressive clarity and precision, no matter how unruly or broad the case law might be on a certain point. Indeed, it was not unusual for Marmo or his clerks, whom he worked almost as hard as himself, to find citations the lawyers on both sides had overlooked.

However, many attorneys—or at least members of the defense bar—griped that Judge Marmo favored the prosecution.

"Who's the prosecutor in your case?" lawyers asked each other in the halls of the courthouse.

"Prosecutor So-and-so and Judge Marmo," wags sometimes replied.

Whatever the case, Marmo was an extremely cautious and careful litigator who took pains to protect the trial record—that is, ensure the integrity of the proceedings so that a higher court would be able to scrutinize his actions and rulings in the clearest light. To that end, Judge Marmo often granted the benefit of the doubt on close calls to the defendant. And while he often suggested that defense lawyers got away with murder by breaking the court rules, because defense lawyers knew that a judge might chastise the offender but would be extremely reluctant to punish the defendant for his or her lawyer's sins, Marmo, in the last analysis, would also grant the defendant considerable leeway.

Snowdon had racked up thousands of man-hours preparing to prosecute Wanger and Castaldo. His attention to detail, he hoped, would pay off. For one thing, he discovered a key piece of evidence that the police themselves had overlooked. It was easy to see why. Snowdon came across the item while examining evidence collected from Wanger, Castaldo, and the three juveniles.

Going through about twelve boxes of physical evidence one day with Wood, Snowdon dumped the contents of Wanger's wallet out and went through the papers and cards and junk inside. In the hurly-burly at the beginning of the homicide investigation, the wallet's contents had never been catalogued by the police. Sometime after the interview with Wanger, O'Brien had confiscated Wanger's wallet, which was made of synthetic cloth in a camouflage pattern. Standard procedure required that all personal property be inventoried, to guard against accusations of tampering or theft. O'Brien had been up all night driving an investigation that seemed to go every which way at once, and the fatigue had gotten to him. He simply forgot to list the wallet's contents.

But Snowdon went through everything in Wanger's wallet carefully. There was a Blockbuster video card in Wanger's grandfather's name, and there were a couple cards from a barbershop—and there, on the back of a Marine recruiter's business card, was the most startling find of all. The significance of the discovery, however, did not come to him all at once. Printed on the card's face were the name, business address, and telephone number for Sergeant Michael A. Hayward, a Marine Corps recruiter in Clifton. On the reverse was a long handwritten list of words and phrases. The lettering had been done by Wanger in a crabbed, boyish hand. At first, Snowdon thought that he had discovered a crib sheet—something Wanger had written down to help him cheat on a Spanish quiz or something. But slowly, as he turned over the card in his hand, one of the words jumped out at him. There, at the top of the list was the word *adesso*.

Adesso had been the word that Carboni said Wanger uttered just before initiating the recitation of the Hail Mary inside Solimine's car. Carboni not only mentioned that Wanger had used the Italian word, he had said this during his very first interview at police headquarters. He had recalled this odd, seemingly inconsequential detail long before he could have been contaminated by any cross-pollination from the police interrogation of the other juveniles. What's more, Carboni was the only one who could have heard Wanger say the word other than the victim. And here it was again, inside Wanger's wallet.

Only one thing didn't make sense. Carboni's parents spoke Italian in the home. Carboni spoke it with them. Why would Carboni also tell the cops that he didn't recognize the word when Wanger said it the first time?

As the trial date loomed closer, Snowdon became occupied completely with the case. The only respite he had would be to go downstairs to his workroom and bang out a piece of furniture. He read and reread the material, putting up Post-it notes all over the place reminding himself to track down this fact or call this person or ask that question. Phrases for opening arguments came to him when he was driving to work. Solutions to questions that had eluded him for months sometimes seemed to materialize from his subconscious as if by magic. One day, some time after his discovery of the Marine recruiter's business card, Snowdon was in the barbershop for a trim and wondering aloud why a kid who knew Italian wouldn't know an ordinary word such as *adesso.*

"Dialects," the barber told him. The barber, who was Italian, told Snowdon that the kid's family probably spoke a dialect that used a different word for now, such as *mo.*

Sure enough, the next time he prepped the case with Carboni, he asked the kid what word his family used at home to say "now." It was *mo.*

15

On September 15, 1993, the hallway outside Judge Ronald G. Marmo's courtroom on the sixth floor of the Passaic County courthouse in Paterson buzzed with activity, and the last-minute touches were being put in place for James Wanger's murder trial. The jury, having taken their oath of duty the previous evening, gathered in the jury room. There were sixteen panelists in all, ten women and six men. (Only twelve would deliberate the case; the others were alternates who would serve in the event of another juror's removal or absence.)

Members of the Solimine family and the Colombos mixed in the hallway outside the judge's courtroom with a crush of news media. The hall was filled with people smoking cigarettes, carrying Styrofoam cups of coffee, and talking nervously and discreetly in little knots. Snowdon stood in the hallway, chain-smoking with Wood. Bob and Arlene Solimine stood in a group of family members waiting for the trial to get under way. Bill and Lee Yakal were a little way off, standing with Maggie and their grandson Billy. Margaret Chircop had saved up her vacation and personal days to take time from work for the trial. By now, she had compiled three albums of newspaper clippings that told the story of everything that had happened since her son's body was found. Now her son's killer would have his say, she guessed, and she anticipated that the trial would be an ordeal in itself.

Martha and Paul Colombo, Wanger's grandparents, sat in the rear of the courtroom. During jury selection, when the courtroom was so filled with potential jurors that only the lawyers and defendant were allowed in, the Colombos sat on a bench down the hall, outside the courtroom. A reporter from the New York *Post* sat beside them, while the camera crews were taping down wires, setting up monitors, and outdoing each other with blasé patter about chasing the big news. Two sketch artists sat in the front row, their easels sticking out of the forest of tripods holding still and video cameras, and scribbled likenesses of the participants. (The judge had ordered them to sketch the juveniles so that their faces would be obscured.)

Snowdon had dressed conservatively for the occasion: a gray suit and workaday tie held in place with a small chain. Wanger's lawyer, Anthony Pope, Jr., appeared in full battle dress: a double-breasted, royal-blue pin-striped suit with wide lapels that tapered to a dart, and a red shirt with a white collar. Underneath the suit jacket was an audacious set of suspenders that, it seemed, he couldn't wait to show off. Every day Pope wore a new pair that seemed flashier (and sometimes tackier) than the pair he had worn before. One pair featured dice tumbling over a fluorescent yellow background.

At 9 o'clock sharp, Wanger entered the courtroom in a leaden shuffle. He wore a nondescript gray suit and a green tie and a blank expression. His dark wavy hair appeared to have thinned slightly. His shoes were conspicuous. They were big, black, and clunky, and seemed almost too big for Wanger's body, military-style Oxfords buffed to a high-frequency store-bought gloss. He nodded to a sheriff's officer. When he got closer to the defense table, he smiled and shook hands with Pope. By 9:27 A.M., the doors shut, everyone was in place, and Snowdon began his opening statement.

"This case concerns a death," Snowdon said. "It concerns

the death of a young man by the name of Robert Solimine, Jr.—age seventeen years, five months, eighteen days, when he died on February 16, 1992, in his automobile parked by a public school in the city of Clifton, New Jersey. This case is about why Robert Solimine died, how he died, and who caused his death.

"It's not a simple situation," Snowdon continued, "and it doesn't revolve around simply the incident that happened on the night of February sixteenth that actually caused his death. It begins much before that. It involves a group of people that you are going to—I almost said, 'understand.' You are not going to ever understand them, but you are going to come to know them in the course of this trial."

His voice gravelly and low and betraying his nerves, Snowdon started in with thanks to the jurors for their patience in sitting through the process of jury selection, and then a windy disquisition about the justice system. Wanger sat solemnly at the defense table, his fingers laced together on the tabletop. Then Snowdon, his face flushed and shiny from perspiration, settled down to do what he does best: he told the story of the crime from beginning to end. He told it like a storyteller and not a lawyer.

He introduced the boys as a group of misfits who came together by chance and formed a group whose common aim, at first, seemed to be nothing at all. Then he described their animosity toward Solimine and their allegiance to Castaldo. Snowdon, who was fond of historical allusions, cast Castaldo as a kind of dictator who had effectively consolidated his power by focusing the group's hatred for Solimine, whom they considered a pest and a snitch. Snowdon described their plans to damage Solimine's car, and then their plans to kill him. He described how each failure to kill Solimine with one of their elaborate and dramatic schemes increased their frustration and their resolve to carry out the crime, how each boy tried to outdo the others thinking up new creative ways of killing Solimine. First the aerosol can. ("Now, you are probably sitting there saying to yourself, 'Well, that sounds like a pretty stupid plan,' and it was," Snowdon said. "We are not dealing with people here who are rocket scientists. We are dealing with people who think they know probably more than they do know.") Then the plan to handcuff Solimine and burn him alive in the car—a scheme that Snowdon personally felt was more abominable than anything else the group had come up with. ("In fact," Snowdon told the jurors, "if anything can be said that could be considered good about the strangulation death of Robert Solimine, it's that he at least did not die in the way they planned for him to die in the second plan.")

Then Snowdon led the jurors right up to the night of Solimine's murder just outside School 15. He had found the groove, and his pacing slowed and speeded to heighten the effect of his words. He explained how Carboni got into the front seat of Solimine's car next to Solimine and—he thrusted his pointed finger at Wanger—how Wanger had taken his seat behind Solimine.

"It's difficult to imagine what he might have been thinking, but we do know what took place inside the car," Snowdon said.

Snowdon described for them the way Wanger had insisted in leading them through the Hail Mary, summons and response, and how he had started over each time there was an interruption. Until the last time.

"When they came to a certain line in the prayer," Snowdon said, his voice building and his hands gripped an imaginary cord, "James Wanger whipped that cord over Robert Solimine's head, located it on his throat, pushed back in his seat, and pulled Robbie Solimine tight against the back of his own seat. He leaned back, he braced his feet against the bottom of the front seat, and pulled for all he was worth. And he kept pulling and he kept pulling and he kept pulling."

Snowdon, who had been leaning backward as if pulling on the invisible cord with his own two hands, now softened his voice.

"It's not a quick death," Snowdon said. "Carboni sat right

alongside of Robert Solimine, the person he thought was his friend, and watched him die."

Snowdon told the rest of the story to its end. He explained how the boys had been arrested, and he explained how the three juveniles would be the heart of the prosecution's case against Wanger. And he explained their plea bargains, offering an apologia in advance for their leniency. In closing, Snowdon also touched on the central mystery of Robert Solimine's murder.

"One last thing I want to leave you with, one last thought," Snowdon said. "And that is something that I am absolutely positive you have already thought of, because every person that I have ever encountered has always asked the same question about this case. And that question is—why? Why did they do it? Why did James Wanger strangle Robert Solimine to death? What was his motive? What could he possibly have been thinking of during the minutes—not seconds—the minutes that it took for that young boy to die? What could have been going through his head? Why didn't he stop? He had plenty of time to stop—why didn't he?"

The motive, Snowdon said, was that there was none. Or that the motives were so small and so absurd as to constitute no motive. There was no reason, Snowdon said, for Solimine's murder, because Solimine's murder was irrational, and the entire group of boys was irrational. Searching for logic in the case, he told them, would be an exercise in futility.

"The sixteen of you—and all sixteen of you may not all deliberate—the sixteen of you now have to judge the fate of another individual," Pope said in his opening statement. "He's a human being there. That human being has a family. That human being has feelings. That human being has said 'I'm not guilty.' "

Anthony J. Pope was a curious mixture of traits. Having grown up in a tough Italian neighborhood in Newark, he carried himself with just a touch of swagger. He was not tall, but he had an athletic, V-shaped build, like a bantamweight prizefighter. Pope liked fast talk, fast cars, and fast motorcycles. When he got out of school, he joined the Newark city police force, working as an undercover narcotics detective. At night he attended Rutgers Law School. Yet for all his rough edges, Pope also came across as a bit of a dandy. He was articulate, sometimes to the point of being glib, and he was clever. He wore owlish eyeglasses that made him seem bookish, and he never failed to ask a judge if he could remove his jacket in the courtroom. When he did, it always seemed as if the entire courtroom needed a moment to adjust to the wild suspenders he wore underneath. Pope arrived at the courthouse every day in a sports car, and every day he was accompanied by a leggy young woman who rolled her eyes in disgust, without obvious reason, during the proceedings. Outside of court, Pope seldom refused the news cameras, holding court in a phalanx of boom mikes. As a crowd of passersby gathered into a large crowd, Pope served up optimistic sound bites about his client's innocence and the meager case the state had built.

But Pope himself had been bewildered from the moment Wanger's grandfather appeared in his office some nineteen months earlier. Paul Colombo sat in Pope's office and wept. He seemed to Pope like a decent man who was now heartbroken and frightened. Colombo, who had raised and adored his grandson, was nearly at a loss to convey the crime that Wanger now stood accused of doing, and he could not comprehend how his grandson—if the charges were true—would be capable of such a monstrous act. As Mr. Colombo explained what he knew, Pope was struck by two other things: his impression that Wanger had been Solimine's protector, in addition to being his friend, and the utter lack of a motive. But Pope, who claimed an eighty-nine percent record of victory in twenty-two murder trials, told Colombo he would handle his grandson's case. It certainly seemed defensible.

Pope's bewilderment mounted when he visited Wanger at the detention center. Here was a young man who used the word "sir," who was polite, who was deferential, who seemed well-spoken. Over the next few months, when Wanger called his offices, he prefaced questions by saying something like "Gee, I know you're busy, but . . ." After learning about Wanger's involvement in the church and his ambition to enter the Marines, Pope was all the more puzzled. On the other hand, as the months flew by between Wanger's arrest and the beginning of his trial, Pope also was struck by Wanger's uncanny ability to acclimate himself to life in the detention center. Pope had never seen anything like it.

As Pope familiarized himself with the case and reviewed the discovery—a lawyer's term for the reports and evidence that the state and defense turn over to each other in preparing for trial—he began to appreciate the mountain of evidence that would come in against his client. Searching for any possibility of mounting an insanity defense, Pope ordered Wanger to be evaluated by a psychiatrist, but Wanger would not admit anything, even to a shrink. What's more, even if Wanger had admitted the deed, it would have been difficult showing that he did not appreciate the wrongfulness of his actions—the state would be able to present ample proof of Wanger's efforts to cover up the crime, beginning with the attempt to blow up the car. Being a realist, Pope understood the odds against his client. But Wanger had little choice but to go to trial.

A week or so before jury selection, Pope once more felt out the prosecution on a possible plea bargain. The deal on the table was stark: Wanger must plead guilty to the murder. In exchange, the state would ask the judge to sentence Wanger only to the murder, which carried a life sentence with a mandatory requirement that Wanger serve thirty years before he became eligible for parole. Such a deal would spare Wanger only one thing, the possibility that he could be found guilty of the attempted murders and receive consecutive sentences that might extend his minimum period of incarceration to as much as forty years. From Pope's perspective, the alternative to trial was so steep his client had nothing to lose by demanding the state put in its proofs.

Now, as Pope opened to the jury, like Snowdon's, his allocution was slow going at first. It is a common approach among defense lawyers to give jurors a civics lesson, emphasizing a defendant's right to the presumption of innocence and invoking the Bill of Rights and the American legal tradition, and Pope was no different. Despite his slick attire, he spoke informally, with a kind of down-home approach to his work, and his sentences were frosted with lots of "gee"s. Sometimes he spoke as if he were thinking aloud and strung together one thought after another with a tentative "okay?" at the end of them. As he talked, Pope sounded four major themes: his client's irreproachable character, the allegedly slapdash investigation by police, the inconsistent statements of the three juveniles, and the huge incentive they had to lie.

His theory of Wanger's innocence was bold, to say the least. Wanger, Pope said, had been no less betrayed by his friends than Solimine had been. The three juveniles—led by Strelka—had killed Solimine and pinned the crime on Wanger. Wanger had not only been framed, he had been the victim's closest ally as the other boys tormented him. What's more, Wanger had never in his life been in serious trouble. He had been a Sea Cadet almost all his life, an altar boy, and a church lector who read the scriptures in his church. He held a job and he had signed up to join the Marines. Wanger was an outsider no less than Solimine had been, and his plans to depart from the group for the military removed him further from their graces, Pope said. What possible motive would Wanger have to kill his friend? Pope wondered. Even the prosecutor had said there was no motive, and Pope couldn't agree more. On this point, like a judo wrestler who uses his opponent's momentum, Pope turned the case's central absurdities against the state. Could anyone dream up a scenario more bizarre than one that had Wanger and Solimine reciting the Hail Mary? That seemed so far out as to be beyond belief, Pope said.

Finally, although at one time he had filed notice that his client might plead innocent by virtue of insanity, by the time of trial Pope was asserting that his client had been nowhere near the murder scene. While the others were strangling

Solimine, Wanger was walking home, Pope said. While Wanger was walking around, the others were concocting an alibi.

"Let's talk about a time line," Pope said, turning to his charts and his easel.

"I submit to you the following, ladies and gentlemen," Pope said. "These boys already had some of the story put together to tell the police, if it came down to that. Because you are going to see the statement of Frank Carboni, who says, very clearly, 'We went back to my house.' You know what to do? To think of 'a story to save our ourselves.' Remember that. Frank Carboni says that to the police in his statement. 'We went back there to think of a story to save ourselves,' okay?"

The police simply took what the three boys had to say as gospel and investigated no further, Pope said. For example, Strelka handed police the only shoelace that they possessed as evidence—yet no one bothered to search Strelka's house for more shoelaces, Pope said. Strelka had reason to dislike Solimine because of rivalry over Chrissie Bachelle—but Strelka got a bye from the police in the early part of the investigation. What grabbed the courtroom's attention most was Pope's assertion—which would be borne out by the evidence—that there was virtually nothing at the scene and no physical evidence of any kind to prove that Wanger had killed Solimine. This, Pope said, despite his client's grandmother handing the police his clothing and the police conducting a search of Wanger's house.

"And you know what they look for on the search warrant?" Pope asked. "Exactly what they are supposed to look for. They look for blood, hair, fiber, clothing, electrical cord, gas cap, keys, and lighter fluid. All to tie in the murder of Solimine. You know what they found? Nothing," Pope said. "Nothing."

The muddy ground around Solimine's car was riddled with footprints that police linked to the three juveniles—but none of the footprints matched the high-top tennis shoes taken from

Wanger's house. The only physical evidence corroborating the crime, Pope said, had been found at Castaldo's house, not Wanger's. Of course, Pope noted, the garrote and the gas cap were never found.

In closing, Pope focused on the plea agreements that would bring the three juveniles to the witness stand. He told the jurors about how the three boys, whose testimony meant so much for the prosecution, were the same three boys who had lied to the police or given contradictory statements. Pope dwelled on the sweetheart plea deal they had wrung from the state, showing quite clearly that the three boys would have an enormous incentive to lie. Who wouldn't lie if it meant shaving a term in prison from twenty years to fifteen years, let alone to twelve years? Pope said. The boys had already pleaded guilty to murder and admitted to killing a close friend, Pope said, so you had better believe they would set up another one. Wanger would be the scapegoat.

"My position, ladies and gentlemen, is this, on behalf of the defense," Pope said. "Frank Carboni, Tommy Stujinski, Tommy Strelka, and Castaldo wanted Rob dead, okay? They may have talked about it—they didn't talk about it in Wanger's presence—but they wanted him dead. They needed a scapegoat, if caught. Wanger betrayed the group. That was, he was joining the Marines. . . . That's bizarre, and that is crazy, but that's the truth. . . . There's only one verdict in this case, and it's about time, after a year and a half, that those three convicted murderers go back to jail exactly where they belong and that young man go home with his family. And the only verdict that's consistent, ladies and gentlemen, with the evidence is 'not guilty.' "

The first prosecution witnesses were Margaret Chircop and Bob Solimine, who testified about Robbie's friendships, his problems with drinking, and his loyalty to the boys accused of killing him. Pope asked them almost no questions, and they were gone, followed by the police officers who worked on the case. The first police officer to testify was Chris Vassoler. He set the scene in detail, describing for the jurors the layout of the school and Weasel Brook Park and the grassy plot where he found Solimine's car. Vassoler then told about finding Robert Solimine's body, and he described the angry red lesions on Solimine's neck. Snowdon also used Vassoler to introduce as evidence police photographers of the boy's body in the car. When Snowdon passed the pictures to the jury, Margaret Chircop began to cry and stepped out of the courtroom, the first of many times that she left when the testimony became too graphic and unbearable.

Then came Detectives Matonak and Kotora, who told how Tommy Strelka had been located by searching for a muddy car. Detective John Barr related how Strelka had given a phony story about his whereabouts, and finally broke down. With the detectives, Pope now took a more aggressive posture in cross-examination, attempting to emphasize how Strelka had lied to police on several occasions before accusing Wanger and also how the police were willing, to an extent, to overlook the lies. For example, he asked Matonak if he found it unusual that Strelka, like other criminal suspects, had lied to him.

"I expect it," Matonak said.

Tommy "Stooge" Stujinski was the first of the three juveniles to testify in open court about the murder of Robert Solimine, Jr. Snowdon had decided that he wanted to build his case more strongly as he went. He considered Stooge the weakest of the three young witnesses, because he was impressionable, because he was the youngest, and because Stooge had been most on the periphery of the conspiracy. Snowdon wanted to conclude the boys' testimony with Strelka, whom he considered the most mature, the most knowledgeable, and the most contrite of all three.

Knowing that one of the juveniles was to appear, the press had arrived early for court on Tuesday, September 21, 1993. A few minutes after 9 o'clock, the Passaic County sheriff's officers unhooked Stooge's handcuffs in the holding area near the jury box, and Stooge strode into the courtroom. Now sixteen years old, he wore jeans, a white dress shirt, black high-top sneakers, and a black-and-white windbreaker. His face was nearly obscured by the huge, buglike lenses of his tinted aviator glasses. His black hair, longish and shaggy, was parted down the middle—one reporter thought it "Beatle-like"—and he seemed young and sullen. He took the oath with his hand on the Bible. The spectators in the courtroom gawked at him, as if straining to find the recognizable trait of a killer in his face or his posture or his gait as he walked to the witness stand. But Stooge looked entirely ordinary, like any kid in any video arcade at any mall. As he settled into his place on the witness stand, it was clear that he was trying not to look at Wanger.

Snowdon started in with the fundamentals of Stooge's plea bargain, then led Stooge back in time to his first meeting with the other boys. The courtroom was spellbound. When it came time to describe meeting Wanger, Snowdon asked Stooge to point out Wanger in the courtroom. Stooge, licking his lips nervously, barely turned his head and pointed to Wanger.

Snowdon questioned Stooge with delicate patience, drawing out the boy's story as if he were unfolding a brittle map. Stooge was more than compliant. He spoke with a nasal tone and strong New Jersey inflection; the word "with" came out "wit," and words like "they" and "there" came out "dey" and "deh." At one point, he was tripped up by the meaning of the word "contemplate," which he didn't understand. More than once, he mispronounced Wanger's name, calling him "Wagner."

"We just drove around whichever way the car was pointing," Stooge said. He described the group's days hanging out, driving around, playing video games at the mall or Nintendo in Stevie Castaldo's room, and sneaking into the cemetery in Totowa to visit with Annie. After telling how the group had become more cohesive until it became like a ragtag Mafia crew, Stooge also explained how Solimine kept coming around all the time, despite Castaldo's and the group's coldness toward him.

"Was there ever any talk of getting Robbie Solimine into this group?" Snowdon asked.

"No."

"Why was that?"

"He wasn't one of us," Stooge answered. "He could never be one of us. It was just something that everybody knew from the beginning."

"Well," Snowdon said, "was he different from the rest of you?"

"He was—in a way he was," Stooge said, "because he would come around whenever we didn't want it. He was a tagalong, sort of—just show up when you didn't want him around. We'd try to get rid of him, tell him to leave. We'd jump—everybody would jump in Tommy's car and drive off and he would be following us in his car, and he always knew where we would be, where we would go. He was always around when we didn't want him to be."

Stooge described how Solimine's coming around drove Castaldo nuts, and how the group started thinking of things to do to Solimine's car to keep him away. He told about Wanger's phony truce, saying he couldn't be sure if it was part of a plot at the time or if it was because Wanger "was that type of person."

"He didn't like anger," Stooge said.

"But did he take part in these other things that were done to Robbie Solimine?" Snowdon asked.

"He did. That, I didn't understand that, but at the time, I was fourteen. I didn't really care what was going on. I was out having my fun."

Then Stooge recounted the murder plots, beginning with the first time that Wanger had proposed the idea at Romeo's Pizza in Passaic. Then the aerosol can. Then the handcuffing. Then the murder itself. Snowdon sat on the edge of the counsel table, his foot wagging off the end of it, holding the can of

FDS spray, and propounded questions to Stooge in a fatherly manner.

As Stooge told about the moment of Solimine's murder, Margaret Chircop and her mother, Lee Yakal, began to weep. He described coming up to Solimine's window and finding Solimine already half dead. Wanger was shouting to get the baseball bat, and then Stooge found himself bolting with Strelka in the Buick. He told of driving around and around wondering what to do.

"Were you afraid?" Snowdon asked.

"A little bit," Stooge said. "I was afraid because I didn't know what was going to happen next. I didn't know. I saw Wanger as the type that wouldn't hurt a fly. Now I just saw him killing somebody, and the way he was acting, just the way, the look in his eyes, that he could kill anybody at any time now."

"Tommy, as you look back on this, on this whole incident, can you tell us why Robbie Solimine was murdered?" Snowdon asked.

"No," he said, "I can't."

Then it was Pope's turn. Picking up on Stooge's testimony that he believed it had taken ten minutes for Wanger to strangle Solimine, Pope demonstrated his flair for the dramatic by requesting that the courtroom sit silently for ten minutes. There were a few whispers. There was the sound of paper shuffling. Stooge seemed not to know where to look.

It would soon become clear, under Pope's cross-examination, that Stooge was a welter of contradictions. By his own testimony, he did and did not know beforehand that the murder would happen. He still could not grasp, it seemed, the concept of intent. He insisted that he had nothing to do with the murder—although Pope singled out Stooge's damning admission to the police, to the effect that all of them had felt as if they had accomplished their mission. As Pope attacked him, Stooge's attitude became more bitter. He pressed his forefingers together into a little steeple, digging the point into his chin, and stared through dark glasses across the room at his questioner with unmistakable hostility. And one thing seemed clear. He did not care. He seemed utterly indifferent to this other boy's fate. Pope asked how Stooge had felt after the killing, and Stooge, with startling candor, told him.

"I didn't feel anything," Stooge said.

"Well, I mean, you feel bad?"

"In a way I felt bad that he was dead. In a way I felt good because he was dead. It was both," Stooge said.

Even in the courtroom now, after all that time in jail, he spoke with a flat voice that seemed entirely free of any remorse, and perhaps even cloaked an obscure hatred, which came out in a testy exchange about what happened when he and Strelka got out of the Buick and went to Solimine's car.

"He said, 'James is killing Rob,'" Stooge recalled. "I looked at him. He said, 'He's actually killing Rob.' I got out of the car, and we went back there. I walked."

"You walked?" Pope asked.

"I walked."

"Somebody had just told you your friend was being killed and you walked back to the car?"

"He wasn't my friend," Stooge snapped. "He was an acquaintance of mine."

The churlishness of his remark caught everyone by surprise. Only Pope seemed to take any pleasure in it.

"Is it fair to say, then, you didn't care what happened to him?" Pope asked.

"Yes. It is."

"It's fair to say that you have no emotion or remorse whatsoever about what occurred to Rob Solimine?"

"At the time, I didn't."

"Okay. Now you do, though?"

"To a part, yes."

"To a part. But you still really don't care one way or the other, do you?"

"I do care, yeah, but I just said, to a part."

Some of the jurors' faces registered looks of horrified amazement.

* * *

Mary Stujinski was a very affecting witness. Her physical appearance—she was so thin she seemed almost rickety as she placed one hand on the Bible and raised the other—contrasted sharply with her disposition. Thin, intense, and direct, Mary sat on the witness stand and told how her son had changed from being a dutiful young man to a sneak who talked back to her. Her lips trembled slightly, and her Slavic accent more than once tripped up listeners in the courtroom, as she misused verb tenses and spoke in gnarled syntax. The tone of her voice kept rising in a strange singsong. She also told how she instructed Stooge to tell the truth while giving his second police statement. She knew he was holding back, and she confronted him.

"I tell him, one kids is dead, and he need to tell the truth. Even though he's guilty, he need to pay," she said.

Carboni came next, and if anything only deepened the malevolent pallor in the courtroom. His hair was cropped into a crew cut that revealed a low flat brow. His eyes appeared very deep-set, and he had a prominent nose, shaped somewhat like the actor Tom Cruise's. He wore a white polo shirt. Like Stooge, he was now sixteen years old.

Snowdon led Carboni through the same prelude as he had Stooge, beginning with the plea agreement and some background on how he had met the other boys. Scowling through long pauses to collect his thoughts, Carboni answered in half-digested monosyllables, as if he couldn't be bothered with long explanations when burping out a one-word answer would do. The slit of his mouth barely moved when he talked. At times his lips seemed not to move at all, as if someone were talking through him, and a cold smirk played across his lips. He registered pride of authorship, for example, when he explained the first tries at slashing Solimine's tires or when they came up with the idea of blowing up Solimine's car. And he seemed to convey an unmistakable bitterness toward the victim, as if it were Solimine's fault that Carboni was in prison.

"The first night we saw him, I thought Rob was all right. And then they told me to watch him because he acts like he's all that," Carboni said. "I did watch him, and he did act like he was all that. He thought he was the man, you know. Then I just started disliking him. He thought he was great and he wasn't."

Why, Snowdon asked, had they never just told him to go away?

"I guess it would be more fun," Carboni sneered. "Make him look like an idiot."

The most remarkable testimony came when Carboni recreated the events inside the car during the murder, from the moment Wanger had said *adesso*, to the end. Describing how Wanger had led the two of them in the Hail Mary, Carboni leaned far back on the witness stand, closed his eyes, and told the awestruck courtroom about what happened next—how the cord went around Solimine's neck at the words "pray for us sinners," and how Solimine thrashed for his life.

"Were his eyes open?" Snowdon asked softly.

"Yes."

"Was he looking at you?"

"I didn't look into his eyes," Carboni said.

One of the jurors wept. Carboni told how it seemed as if it took a long time for Solimine to die, and he told of lighting the rag at the gas tank and then racing through the woods after seeing it catch fire. With annoyance still in his voice, he also told of Wanger's noisy celebration in the bedroom. Then he, too, as Stooge had on the previous day, related the events leading up to his arrest.

By the time Pope began the cross-examination, Carboni seemed impatient and defensive. Flashes of sarcasm lit up his replies. Sometimes his responses were tagged with phrases such as "Like I told you before . . ." or "I've said that already," or "Do you remember I said that earlier?", and he tended to fix the lawyer with a baleful look. Unlike Stooge, who found it excruciating to lock eyes with Wanger, Carboni turned toward Wanger almost every time he said his name, spitting out the word "James." Talking out the side of his mouth, Carboni became particularly irritable as Pope probed the exact sequence of events at the school. At one point, the subject of prayer came up.

"Do you pray a lot?" Pope asked, almost a throwaway line.

"Not anymore," Carboni said.

"Okay. Did you pray back then?"

"I haven't gone to church in a long time, sir."

At another point, Carboni insisted that he wanted to stop the killing but he was too dumbfounded to react.

"You did?" Pope asked.

"But I didn't. That's just it. Like I told you, I just said, I did not think of it. The only thing running through my head was fear. Scared."

Strelka was the third and final juvenile to testify against Wanger, and although he was the eldest of the three witnesses, he appeared and acted as if he were the youngest of the group. He wore a corded fisherman's sweater over a white shirt and dark pants. The dress shirt, whose collar poked high above the putty-colored sweater, looked as if it had been borrowed from an adult. His long blond hair was gone, and his jug ears stuck out. He seemed very shy, very frail, and very nervous.

By now, the jury had heard more than enough about the group's activities and the grisly details of Solimine's murder. But people studied Strelka the most carefully, it seemed. Perhaps it was because he was easily the most articulate of the three boys and the most forthright. He seemed likable, smart, and respectful. And, by his own account, he had liked Robbie Solimine and had been his friend for six years. As the prosecutor led him through the questioning, Strelka often seemed to gather his thoughts in a reflective way, rubbing his chin or biting the tip of his thumb, before answering. All the same, Strelka's irritation at Solimine lay just beneath the surface. It was most obvious when Strelka talked about Solimine getting him in trouble with his parents over drinking, but it was there when he talked about Solimine's overdose, and it was there when he talked about Solimine hanging around after Solimine came back from the Carrier clinic.

"I just—I just didn't want to be bothered with him anymore," Strelka said. "He stopped drinking, and when he stopped drinking he didn't know what to do with himself, and he just kept coming around, and I kept telling him to go away and he'd just come and keep coming and he wouldn't leave."

The jury listened with evident dismay as Strelka described calming Solimine after the failed handcuffing attempt and luring him to Castaldo's house with the telephone message left on Solimine's answering machine. Strelka, who confessed to spending the night at Solimine's the night before he was killed, also held everyone spellbound with his account of Wanger building the garrote in the parking lot of the Clifton High School. It took Wanger ten minutes of work before stuffing the thing inside his trench coat, Strelka said. He demonstrated for the jury how Wanger had worked the device, too. Then Strelka gave his account of the killing, describing going up to the car and finding Wanger pulling back on the cord with all his might.

"Did you look at Robbie Solimine?" Snowdon asked.

"Yes."

"What did you see?"

"He was—he wasn't moving."

"Did you look at his face?"

"Yes."

"What did you see?"

"His eyes were closed, his tongue was sticking out a little bit, and there was a tear coming out of his eye."

"Did Robbie Solimine say anything?"

"No."

"When you got there, was he moving?"

"No."

Pope had made little headway with the other boys, except to show that they were exceptionally indifferent to the crime they had admitted taking part in. He also had difficulty shaking Strelka from Strelka's basic story, and it seemed more and more a stretch to assert that the boys were blaming Wanger because Wanger had joined the Marines and turned his back on him. The trio's denials of this were more than forceful. They reacted with genuine surprise, as if they had never heard of anything more preposterous.

But Pope did manage to show that Strelka had plenty to do with Solimine's murder, and that he had more than sufficient motive. Indeed, by the time Strelka left the witness stand, it seemed as if he had the strongest motives—or at least the most logical motives—of all. To begin with, he liked Chrissie Bachelle and Solimine liked Chrissie Bachelle. Although Strelka denied that she was his girlfriend, it came through that he was very much attached to her and jealous of Solimine, and during one exchange, when discussing what he had done after his first interview at police headquarters, he referred to her as his girlfriend. Second, Strelka acknowledged that Solimine had got on his nerves. This came through particularly as Pope asked him about the night Solimine overdosed while talking with Strelka on the telephone.

"Did you care whether or not he was taking pills, though, what would happen to him?"

"No," Strelka said, "because I figured there was no need to worry, that he wouldn't take enough pills to try and kill him."

"It's your testimony you would be worried if you thought he was taking more?"

"Yes."

"When did that worrying stop? When you decided to blow up his car, or when you decided to strangle him?"

Strelka's face darkened.

"You want an answer?" he snapped.

"Yes, I ask the questions. You answer them."

"I don't have an answer," Strelka said.

Minutes later, Pope made Strelka lose his temper again, while questioning him about the meetings. Pope wanted to know a date or time for the meeting at which the boys raised the idea of blowing up Solimine's car with the aerosol can.

"I don't remember," Strelka said.

"Okay," Pope said. "It's not something that sticks in your mind?"

"No. It's hard to remember every little tiny meeting."

"Hard to remember what?"

"Every meeting."

"You say, 'tiny little meeting'?"

"Yes."

"Would you refer to blowing someone's car up or killing them as a 'tiny little meeting'?"

"Objection," Snowdon said.

"I'll allow it," said the judge.

As Strelka started to become more rattled, perhaps with good reason, Pope also tried to pin down when he and the other boys had watched *The Godfather* together. Pope wanted specifics, and Strelka kept saying he couldn't remember. ("Are you getting angry, Tommy?" Pope asked. "No, I'm saying, you expect me to remember the date that somebody watched a movie?") Pope also got to Strelka when he asked about why he didn't help Solimine after Wanger had strangled him, or call for an ambulance, or call the police.

"I was scared," Strelka said.

"Did you do anything that night to help Rob Solimine?"

"No," Strelka said. "No."

"But you were concerned about him?" Pope said sarcastically.

Strelka became flustered and angry.

"I was worried to do— If I would have done something to help Rob, I was afraid they would turn on me, too—all right?" Strelka said.

Detective George F. O'Brien was the state's concluding witness. O'Brien, chewing gum, grinning like a rattlesnake, and testifying with almost exaggerated precision, helped pull all the pieces of the case together. It also fell to him to relate Wanger's interview—the one that began with Wanger informing O'Brien that he was in the gifted program at school and explaining what he had eaten the day before (ziti and espresso, with a lemon twist). And perhaps most damning of all, O'Brien testified about the red marks on Wanger's wrists.

Others had come after the boys and before O'Brien: Lauren Doczi, the clerk from Quik Pick 'Ns, testified about the boys buying shoelaces; Stevie Castaldo testified about Wanger asking for an electrical cord—although he insisted that the cord was a small, flat electrical cord like one would use in the home, not the outdoor cord described by the three juveniles; Alfonsina Castaldo testified about Wanger's boastful remark to her that Solimine wouldn't be coming around anymore; Mr. Carboni testified that he saw all the boys in his house around 11:30 P.M.—testimony which was especially crucial, since Vassoler had testified that Solimine's body was found around 12:26 A.M. The three boys testified that the murder happened shortly before 11:30 P.M. Mr. Carboni placed Wanger with the three juveniles in the Carboni household at 11:30 P.M. or so. Leaving aside the boys' testimony, witnesses who seemed unimpeachable placed Wanger with them within the same hour that Solimine died. It would be a difficult time frame to get out of.

When the defense's turn came to call witnesses, Pope called staff sergeant Richard Scilabro, a Marine recruiter. Pope had simply called Scilabro, appearing in a smart-looking uniform and buzz cut, to testify about Wanger's interest in joining the Marines. Perhaps Pope also hoped that some of Scilabro's martial luster would rub off on Wanger. In any case, Scilabro testified that Wanger had signed a Statement of Understanding on January 7, 1992, with a Food Service Option. That is, he wanted to be a cook in the Marine Corps. But before Scilabro left the witness stand, Snowdon asked him about a business card. It wasn't even Scilabro's own business card. The small, white card—which bore the name of Sgt. Michael A. Hayward, a Marine Corps recruiter in the Clifton office—had been found inside the folds of Wanger's wallet. On its face and reverse side were nearly two dozen words and phrases handwritten in Italian—including *adesso,* the word

Wanger had said just before slipping the garrote shoelaces over Solimine's neck.

Snowdon hadn't even mentioned the card. Not in his opening. Not with O'Brien, who had confiscated Wanger's wallet. Not with any of the other officers. Indeed, he had kept the card a closely held secret between him and Wood. Snowdon wanted it that way, hoping that the mini-dictionary would be the booby trap to catch Wanger should Wanger take the witness stand and deny that he even knew the word *adesso.* Snowdon would whip out the card, which held phrases in Italian and their English translations that Wanger had scribbled across the back and front. There were twenty-three entries in all. There was no obvious rhyme or reason to the selection, which included *va bene* ("fine, okay"); *il comune [sic] della cittá* ("City Hall"); *mi puoi dar un passagio* ("Can you give me a ride?"); *non era mia intenzione* ("I didn't mean to"); *sei proprio fortunato* ("You're really lucky"); *fa' in fretta* ("Hurry up"), *non c' é niente* ("There is nothing that can be done), and *ti diverti* ("Are you having a good time?"). At the top of the list was the word *adesso*. At the least, this was a coincidence that would be very difficult to explain.

But Pope was incensed that Snowdon was trying to move it into evidence. Pope argued that he hadn't been aware of the business card until Snowdon sprang it on him, since O'Brien and the other police officers had neglected to inventory the contents of Wanger's wallet.

The arguments became heated. Pope admitted that while preparing for trial he had examined Wanger's camouflage-patterned billfold in the evidence vault of the Clifton Police Department as Wood looked on. But, Pope said, he evidently overlooked the business card. (Afterward, Wood would say that Pope indeed had seen the card while he was in the evidence vault, but in the gamesmanship of trial strategy, pretended not to; evidently, Pope did not want to tip the prosecution to a piece of evidence that perhaps *they* had overlooked.)

Marmo listened to both sides. But he ruled the wallet admissible. In public, at least, Pope shrugged it off, while Snowdon gloated.

"It's an appeal issue," Pope said outside after the day's session had ended.

16

TRIALS ARE OFTEN COMPARED TO PLAYS, AND WITH GOOD REAson. The well of the court functions like a proscenium, and two characters with diametrical aims—the prosecutor and the defendant—use its stage as a platform to air their conflict. The courtroom itself is arranged for a solemn public spectacle with commonplace props: the raised bench for the judge, perhaps the seal of the jurisdiction often displayed over his head, the furled American flag and the heavy wooden gavels that sit atop almost every bench, although judges today seldom if ever use them. Everyone, except the jury, is in costume, beginning with the judge. Members of the public or their representatives fill the spectator section. The victims' families and the defendants' families often take their places—almost always, as if by unwritten rule, seating themselves on opposite sides of the courtroom. Addressing their remarks to a very critical audience of twelve, witnesses take the stage, tell their tales, and depart. Sometimes there are tears and sometimes there are wisecracks. There are moments of great excitement and anger, or of sorrow and regret. There are also long stretches of boredom. Much happens off-stage—hearings, arguments by lawyers, and decisions about what to present to the jury—and everything is closely scripted. There may be a few surprises in the testimony, but not many. Both the prosecutor and the defense lawyer know, almost to the word, what a witness will say because they have read their prior statements or interviewed them in preparation for the trial. In the end, two narratives, and sometimes more, are submitted for a jury's scrutiny. One narrative describes the defendant's guilt; one affirms his innocence. It falls to the jury to judge the reliability of the two narratives and, ultimately, choose between them. At bottom, of course, in most plays and in every trial, lies a conflict and the will to resolve it.

Wanger's decision to testify brought his trial to a dramatic finale. Pope even wore a lavender suit for the occasion. Before the jury came out for the morning session, Wanger shook Pope's hand and blew a kiss at his grandparents in the back row. He buttoned his suit jacket and banged his fists together like a prizefighter. Everyone knew a momentous point in the trial had come. When the jurors took their seats, Marmo invited Pope to call his next witness, and Pope called Wanger.

Wanger virtually snapped to attention, boomed out the oath with his hand on the Bible, and strode to the witness stand with a brisk and purposeful stride. Snowdon had been saying all along that he would love to get Wanger on the stand, but neither he nor anyone else in the courtroom, except Pope, had any idea what Wanger would say. Snowdon half expected Wanger to throw himself on the mercy of the jury, save himself the murder rap, and shoot for a manslaughter verdict by claiming that he was playing a prank that miscarried when Solimine died. Who wouldn't believe that a teenager, particularly one with a clean record and a history of goofing off, had been trying to scare the bejesus out of another kid everyone loved to pick on? That he simply had gone too far?

As Wanger settled in, Snowdon took out a legal pad to scribble notes. Then Wanger started talking. As everyone expected, his speech was sprinkled with "yes sir"s and "no sir"s and other pleasant formalities. But the timbre of his voice came as a complete surprise to many in the courtroom. Snowdon, for example, had been expecting a nerdy-looking geek like Wanger to sound like Mickey Mouse. Instead, Wanger sounded like Sylvester Stallone. His voice was basso profundo, with an almost jolly note to it at times. What's more, his use of the English language was horrible. He swallowed vowels, mangled his sentences, used words like "Yo!" and "youse" and "dose," and laid on the sincerity very, very thickly. He looked like some blue-blood prep school lad and spoke like a loanshark.

Some of the spectators exchanged smiles and members of the press made wisecracks. ("The Vienna Boys Choir meets Stanley Kowalski," one said.) It was hard to believe that a person who had once been in the gifted program could use such tortured grammar and diction, and harder still to imagine him reading from the Gospel of St. Mark in a crowded church with any degree of grace or sensitivity. Then, after a while, he grew casual about testifying, so much so he seemed to forget where he was. Questions that required only a brief explanation could turn into windy essays touching on several irrelevant topics. He became so assertive he seemed cocky, and more than once seemed eager to bait the prosecutor. During seven hours of testimony, he started slumping down in the seat and crossing his legs, as if he were in study hall. More than once, Pope asked him to sit up.

The story Wanger embraced bordered on the fantastic. Although Wanger adopted the framework of the three boys' testimony, he made key alterations. It wasn't Castaldo who led the group, but Carboni. There was a Mafia thing going on, but Wanger had no part of it. Yes, he used to drink with the gang and buy them liquor, but he stopped because he wanted to get physically fit and he didn't want to jeopardize enlisting with the Marines in the food service. (He explained that he wanted to be a cook someday and open a restaurant.) Yes, he knew something about the plans to mess up Solimine's car and so forth—but these, he said, were merely pranks as part of an elaborate initiation rite into the group of teenage boys. As he understood it, they were going to let the air out of Solimine's tires, not slash them. They weren't going to blow up Solimine's car, they were just going to dump something into it to seize it up. And so on. Instead of being one of Solimine's tormentors, Wanger asserted that he actually had been Solimine's guardian angel.

By his own account, Wanger had tried to introduce Solimine into the group and had even advised him about the pranks in advance. Solimine agreed to go along with them, Wanger said. Wanger also explained to the jury that he had betrayed the group because of his plans to enlist in the Marines and because he had stopped drinking—a decision that supposedly infuriated the others, especially Carboni.

"Tell the jury exactly what he said," Pope said.

"He said, 'How could you go into the Marine Corps?' He said, you know, I shouldn't be leaving them. He said why am I going out there and fighting and dying for strangers, and he was upset and he was angry with me. . . . He said, 'If this was *The Godfather* movie, you wouldn't be doing this. You wouldn't be leaving the group.' "

"What was their reaction when you decided to stop drinking?" Pope asked.

"They says, 'Why you stopping? What's wrong with you?' They laughed."

Then Wanger explained the reasoning behind the initiation rites, which included wrecking Solimine's car engine.

"What was the initiation supposed to be if his engine was seized up—how does that initiate someone in a group?" Pope asked.

"Just to see how he would act afterwards towards the group—that was the whole thing."

"What was the point—how he would act?"

"Trying to establish loyalty."

"Loyalty to the group?"

"Make sure he'd be loyal. Yes."

"At any time—I want you to tell this jury—did anybody ever suggest to you to blow up his car?" Pope asked.

"No, nobody ever suggested nothing like that," Wanger said. "They talked about letting air out of his tires, they talked about, you know, mixing the stuff, messing up his gas line, but nobody said nothing about blowing up the car. That was never mentioned to me."

Wanger admitted trying to convince Solimine to put on the handcuffs at School 15, for example, but once more he insisted this was to be merely a prank—that they were going to handcuff Solimine to the car and leave him there for an hour or so. All the stuff about blowing up the car came as a complete surprise to him—as did Stooge's testimony about Wanger's request for his boot lace at the Dunkin' Donuts, so that he could strangle Solimine at the red light.

"I told him that, you know, 'Look, they're going to try to convince you to cuff yourself. You go along with it like it's all right. I'm going to tell you they're trick handcuffs. You do that, we're going to leave—don't worry, we'll be back, though. We come back, they let you go, and then [you'll] be part of the group.'"

"What did Rob say?"

"Rob didn't say nothing. He said he'd get back to me on it."

"Was there ever a discussion, did you ever take a shoelace from Tommy and tell him you wanted to strangle Rob in the car?"

"No, I never said nothing like that," Wanger said.

"Is there any truth to that whatsoever?"

"No truth at all, man, nothing."

Then Pope walked Wanger through the events of Sunday, February 16, 1992, the day of the murder, beginning with the fact that Wanger had gone to church. Pope asked him about his duties there as a lector.

"I taught religion, too," Wanger added. "I taught religion to third-graders."

Pope asked for more details.

"Well, after I got confirmed I had gone to the priest, one of the priests in the parish. I asked, you know, is there anything I could do for the church. Anything. I was the type of person," Wanger said, and here he began to go freestyle, "I like to give things back if I got something, because the church—I didn't consider myself like I was a holy person, that just because I was doing all this I was great or made me great or something—but whenever I had a problem, the church was already there for me, and the priests were there, and they were good—they'd be there for you. And I felt it was a way to kind of give something back by, you know, lectoring. And he talked to me—and I was an altar boy when I was younger—and he told me that they could always use some teachers for religion. And my knowledge wasn't the best, and that's why he gave me a lower grade . . . the year I got locked up, it was a third grade. Cute kids."

"James," Pope interrupted at one point, "if I tell you what time it is, don't tell me how to build a clock. Just answer the question."

Then Pope asked Wanger to explain the medals.

"See, I found a lot of peace with religion," Wanger said, "a lot of peace of mind and it was, it was always a good thing for me and I thought that I just kind of, since I was getting close to them, real close as friends, I wanted them to have some of that too. . . . I don't consider myself a fanatic, but you know, I was religious. I believe in God and all that type of thing."

Now, for all of Wanger's interjections ("I love restaurants!" he said, and beamed a huge smile, after Pope asked where he worked), Pope had arrived at the night of the murder. Wanger began accounting for his time, although if he said it once he said it half a dozen times that he never wore a watch. And he kept trying to account for why he knew nothing about any murder plot although he had spent most of his day with the other boys. He kept saying the other guys were "in their own world." But Wanger had to explain certain facts, and his gloss was transparent. For example, he had to explain why he asked Stevie Castaldo for an electrical cord less than three hours before Solimine had been strangled with one. Wanger testified that Strelka had asked him, Wanger, to ask Castaldo for a cord for Strelka's stereo.

"He just asked me to do it for him and I did it for him. It was no big deal," Wanger said. He couldn't resist adding: "He was kind of cheap, I guess you could say. He wasn't the type who would like to buy stuff if he didn't have to."

Wanger seemed almost to be enjoying the theater of it, as if he were goofing off in science class again. After questioning Wanger about his errand at Quik Pick 'Ns, Pope asked about making the garrote in the school parking lot.

"Did you ever go to Clifton High School?"

"I went there four years, sir," Wanger cracked.

Finally, Wanger had to explain his whereabouts around the time of the murder itself. He admitted driving around with the other boys and arriving in the vicinity of Weasel Brook Park around ten o'clock ("Little after ten, I'd say. A little after ten, probably"). But they soon split up because the gang wanted to drink and he didn't, Wanger said.

"They says, 'Good, we're going to drink now,' " Wanger explained. "Carboni had said that, and I said, 'I don't want to drink. I already quit,' I says. 'You all know I quit. You all know I don't drink.' They said, 'Why did you quit drinking?' They started laughing at me a little bit, stuff like that. Then I said, 'Could you take me home?' and Tommy says, 'No, I can't take you home.' He says, 'We're running too late. I got a curfew.' He didn't want to be bothered with any extra trips he had to make; he wanted to do what he wanted to do. So I got out of the car and started walking."

As he listened to Wanger's account of teenagers drinking on a closely scheduled timetable—and only an hour or so before curfew—Snowdon's face said it all, although he kept it for the most part buried in his legal pad. Now and then Snowdon looked up to see how this was going over with the jury.

Wanger acknowledged that it would take at least an hour to walk to his house from the park. He also mentioned that Carboni let drop that the group would return to his place nearby after drinking. So, Wanger said, he just wandered around in the cold night air with his trench coat for about twenty or twenty-five minutes before he decided that he didn't want to go home after all. Then he walked to Carboni's a few blocks away. When he got there, he waited on the porch for a while because, he said, he didn't want to ring the bell.

"I didn't want to disturb the family," Wanger said, "and plus Carboni don't really like when you go in the house when he ain't around, either, so . . ."

About ten minutes later, lo and behold, his friends showed up again at Carboni's. Carboni got out of Strelka's car, and Strelka and Stooge jetted off to parts unknown. Wanger said he asked Carboni where they had been, and Carboni told him, "Don't worry about it." They went to Carboni's bedroom. Wanger denied the celebration, of course, but he mentioned seeing scratches on Carboni's neck. Carboni wouldn't talk about anything, however.

"He was kind of in his own world," Wanger said.

Wonder of wonders, when Stooge and Strelka returned, none of the other boys would talk, either. Wanger testified that he just assumed they had been caught drinking, they were all so quiet. Because they were in the mood to see Castaldo, however, they all headed over there, and he made no mention of the meeting on Castaldo's front porch. Then, he said, he called a taxi and went home.

"Okay," Pope said. "When you got home, what did you do?"

"When I got home, I got changed, you know, to go to sleep, and I had my grandmother, she cooked for me."

"What did she cook?"

"Some linguine. I had like three plates of that!" Wanger said, busting out in a huge grin. He looked toward his grandparents in the rear of the courtroom.

"Three plates at 1:30?" Pope asked for some reason.

"Oh, yeah!'" Wanger exclaimed. "It's good stuff! She knows. Right? She knows it's good! It's some good stuff."

Wanger said he then got undressed and went to sleep on the couch.

"Was it a pullout?" Pope asked.

"It was just a couch couch."

"That was your bed?"

"Yeah. It was comfortable, though! It was comfortable."

He said he hung his coat in the bathroom because they were all short on closet space, and turned in, sleeping late until he was awakened by the police, who told him he was under arrest for Robert Solimine's homicide.

"What did you think at that point?"

"I was shocked," Wanger said. "I didn't know what to say. I didn't know what to think. I was confused, too. I really . . . I wasn't feeling a lot of things at the same time and I really don't know how to describe how I felt altogether, but I couldn't believe what was going on. It just didn't make no kind of sense to me."

"Were you able to go about the house?"

"Couldn't go about the house. She had to bring everything to me. I couldn't wash my face, brush my teeth. My hair was messy. I had bad breath."

"How did they handcuff you?"

"It was all messed up," Wanger said. "They handcuffed me from behind."

This would explain the marks on his wrists as being caused by the handcuffs. Then he told his side of the brief interview and how O'Brien had taken his wallet.

"Let me ask you a question," Pope said. "Did you speak Italian?"

"I knew some, a little bit."

"How did you know some words?"

"Carboni thought that I should learn Italian."

"Why did he think that?"

"He said that it's important that I knew it."

"Why, though?" Pope said. "Did he say why?"

"He said that it's going to be part of the group—that everybody is going to learn eventually."

"Okay. How did you feel about that? Did you agree with that?"

"Well, I had no problems with it." Wanger said. "It's always good to take on another language, get a little bit more knowledge. Plus there's some restaurants I go to and stuff . . . and maybe a little understanding of things would be good, so, yeah, it was all right to me."

"When he would teach you these words, would you ever write any of them down?" Pope asked.

"Yeah. He told me to."

"Did he teach you the word *adesso*?"

"Yeah, that was among the words."

"What does *adesso* mean?"

"It means 'now.' "

As they went over the card, Pope had Wanger empty out all the papers in his wallet and tell what they were. There was a Blockbuster video rental card, a pack of matches, a card from a local barbershop that his mother had given him. ("Yeah, I used to like to get—every once in a while—I used to go to the barbershop. I used to get straight razor shaves and as a gift—I think it was Christmas—yeah, it was Christmas—as a gift she had gotten me a few cards . . ."). When he got to the card with the Italian phrases, Wanger happily offered an explanation of this too:

"Well, he said, because I was interested in the Marines and whenever I thought about the Marines and I drew the card from the wallet, I would be thinking about this also," he said.

At last, Pope headed for the finale.

"James, I'm going to ask you one more time. When was the first time you knew about Rob Solimine's death?"

"When?"

"Yes."

"When they came to my house and they said, you know, you have the right to remain silent and all that other stuff."

"Did you ever kill Rob Solimine?"

"No, I didn't."

"Did you ever plan to blow up his car?"

"No, I never blew up his car, I never planned to blow up his car."

"Did you ever intend to do any harm to Rob?"

"No. No, sir."

"Did you ever plan it with anybody?"

"To do harm?"

"Yes."

"No, sir."

"Did you ever talk to anybody about it?"

"No, sir, I didn't want to do any harm."

"Look at each one of these jurors. Are you positive as to what you're talking about?"

"Yes, sir."

"Do you swear to what you're saying?"

"I swear to God!" Wanger exclaimed. He looked up one row of jurors and down the others. It was an awkward moment, captured clearly with close-ups for the evening news.

"All right, James. Thank you," Pope said. "I have nothing further."

"Mr. Wanger . . ." Snowdon began.

"Yes, how are you, Mr. Snowdon?" Wanger said.

"I'm just fine," Snowdon said, a note of irritation in his voice. "How are you?"

Thus began Wanger's cross-examination. Wanger had spent approximately two and a half hours in direct examination, answering the friendly questions of his own lawyer. For the next seven hours, however, he would undergo a biting cross-examination from Snowdon that would have been amusing had the subject not been so grave. Using sarcasm and wisecracks, Snowdon slashed at Wanger's story until almost nothing was left of it. For much of his cross-examination, Snowdon went after almost every one of Wanger's assertions and, almost with ease, demonstrated their absurdity.

At first Wanger stood his ground. He came off even more as a smart aleck, and from time to time turned directly to the judge in an appeal to finish an answer that had been cut short by Snowdon's rapid-fire questions. By the end of the day, however, Wanger became hoarse, and he answered Snowdon's questions with questions.

For starters, Snowdon needled Wanger about why he had been hanging out with boys three years his junior and about why everyone looked up to Frank Castaldo, the high-school dropout. Then he caught his rhythm, setting Wanger up with a question so that he would trip a moment later. One moment, for example, Wanger was nodding in agreement that Carboni had been running the group without Castaldo around, and the next minute he was admitting that he wouldn't do everything a fourteen-year-old kid wanted him to do. Snowdon found contradictions everywhere and asked Wanger about them, beginning with Wanger's drinking habits.

"You didn't want to be around doing anything wrong. Is that right?" Snowdon asked.

"Yeah, I wasn't for that," Wanger said.

"So you didn't see anything wrong about obtaining alcohol and giving it to fourteen-year-old kids to drink in the cemetery. Is that right?"

"Well, that—that used to be a place where we used to hang out," Wanger said, and it sounded as if he was gearing up for a filibuster.

"Mr. Wanger, I think the answer is—did you see anything wrong with getting alcohol and giving it to fourteen-year-old boys to drink in the cemetery?"

"Would you allow me to answer?"

"Respond to the question," the judge said.

"Did I see anything wrong with it . . . ?"

"Yes."

"No, I didn't see . . ."

"You didn't see anything wrong with it?"

"I didn't see anything wrong," Wanger continued. "It wasn't like we was drinking a lot, where we was just drunk and off the edge. It wasn't where anybody was being harmed by it, and up until I quit I didn't see anything wrong with it . . ."

"Well, you knew you were doing something illegal when you did this, isn't that true?"

"Illegal?"

"Yes."

"Well, I knew we're really not supposed to buy, no."

Having revealed Wanger's moral relativity on a small

point, Snowdon wouldn't let up. Didn't what he learned in church have an impact on him when he was drinking underage or doing other illegal things?

"Well, the way I seen it, sir, I went to church and I had my job and once in a while after work, I would be carrying a lot of trays and, kind of sore, sit back, relax, have a couple of drinks," Wanger said. "I was working, giving money to my mother, going to church. I was going to school. I had plans for the future. I didn't see any harm in it, personally. I could be wrong. I didn't see any harm in it, sir."

"What—are you telling me because you were working and tired it was okay to go out and lie to somebody in a store, and obtain the alcohol and then give it to fourteen-year-old kids because you were tired and had a tough day?"

"I justified it inside my mind, yes, sir."

"You justified it?"

"Yes, sir."

"Did you justify anything else in your mind?"

"As?"

"Other things that you did that you weren't supposed to do. Were they justified in your mind, too?"

Snowdon also asked Wanger about the way he used a false impression to purchase alcohol, by appearing older than he was.

"You created a similar impression when you had a conversation with Detective O'Brien about this murder, too, didn't you?"

"What type of impression?"

"You created an impression that at ten o'clock you were at Stooge's house, Robbie Solimine left, and that's all you know?"

"That's right."

"That the impression you created, isn't it?"

"That's what happened."

"That's not what happened, Mr. Wanger."

Snowdon went over the medals, and then over the nature of the group itself, as a way of suggesting that the group functioned like any gang, in that its purpose was both to protect each other from violence and carry out violent acts. Wanger denied it, saying they only took care of each other.

"What would you have to take care of each other about?" Snowdon asked.

"About?"

"What was there to take care of, I mean?"

"Well, everything was all right, you know, everything was okay. It was like if anybody was ever in trouble, if anybody was sad or something or needed somebody to talk to, we'd be there for them."

"Give me an example of trouble that the group had to help them out somehow."

"Well, like—let's say, like, there was a time when Tommy missed his curfew and he was in trouble, and he was talking to us about it, and we started talking to him about being able to get done earlier so he'd be able to get home earlier so he'd be able to make it," Wanger said. "Like that."

"So what you're saying is this wasn't like, we're going to protect ourselves, this was more of, like, a group-counseling thing, if someone had some kind of problem?" Snowdon asked sarcastically.

"That was a nice way to say it," Wanger said.

Now Snowdon started on a premise that was central to Wanger's position: the notion that belonging to the group was of such importance that his enlistment with the Marine Corps was viewed as betrayal. Once more, Wanger insisted that the others, particularly Carboni, became furious about Wanger's looming departure because no one could ever leave the group.

"Ever?" Snowdon asked.

"Ever."

"You couldn't get married?"

"Well, you wouldn't be leaving," Wanger said. "You'd still be in it."

"So long as your wife didn't give you too much trouble to go to Annie's Road and Fun 'N Games—" Snowdon cracked.

"I've got to object," Pope shot in. "It's a ridiculous question."

"I'll strike it," Snowdon said. But it was clear he was having fun now. He prodded Wanger about this idea of excessive loyalty and questioned whether it had something to do with the junior Mafia they were running. Wanger said he felt it did have something to do with the Mafia, since Carboni had talked all the time about joining it.

"I didn't take it serious," Wanger said.

"No?"

"I thought it was something that would pass from his head," Wanger continued. "Just something he happened to be interested in. People, like, may be interested in cowboy-and-Indian movies, but they don't buy a horse and move to the prairie. I didn't take it serious."

The longer this went on, the funnier Snowdon's questions became, and the more the logic failed to hold for almost everything Wanger said. The idea that everything had been one big prank that Solimine was going along with, as a kind of initiation, sounded just plain stupid, Snowdon said.

"What was the idea here—that he would be thrilled at having his car destroyed, the engine destroyed, and then want to join your group?"

"No," Wanger said. "It was supposed to see how he'd react after that, if he'd still have a good feeling toward the people . . ."

"How did you think he would react? Did you think he would be happy to have his car engine destroyed?"

"Certainly not."

"Was your so-called group so desirable to be in that someone would write off their car being destroyed in order to be in the group?"

"I doubt it."

"Did you think he was going to say, 'I embrace you all as my close-knit group because you destroyed my vehicle'?"

Snowdon tripped him up at will now. With one question, Wanger admitted he was familiar with the switch that opened the gas flap, although he had never driven Solimine's car. With another, Wanger was at a loss to explain why the other boys would tell the police that they had tried to blow up Solimine's car when Wanger was saying all they wanted to do was spray an aerosol can inside the tank and mess up the engine. By the time Snowdon reviewed Wanger's performance in school—at least as Wanger had related it to Detective O'Brien—the questioning became almost farcical.

"Well," Snowdon asked. "Were you in the gifted program in Clifton High School?"

"Well, I was doing all right in school. I was on the honor roll."

"You were?"

"Yeah."

"And so, did you consider that to be the gifted program? You know what a gifted program is, don't you?"

"Well, everybody has their gifts and talents, sir."

"Mr. Wanger, in school, a gifted program is a certain thing. You know that, don't you?"

"Well, yeah."

"And did you consider yourself to be in the gifted program?"

"I considered myself to be smart, you know? Not really smart, but I considered myself to be smart enough."

Snowdon whipped out the grade reports from Wanger's junior year, which registered Fs and Ds, except for a C in marketing.

"Eleventh grade was a bad year," Wanger said.

Why, Snowdon wondered, had Wanger even gone into his academic performance when O'Brien started questioning him?

"You've been arrested, you just discovered that one of your best friends has been brutally murdered . . ."

"Yes."

"Okay? It must have struck you like a thunderbolt?"

"Yes, sir."

"When you got the news, the only thing worse is that you were being accused of doing it, isn't that true?"

"It was a bad day, sir," Wanger said with a smirk.

"I guess it was."

As the afternoon wore on, Snowdon walked Wanger through the events of the evening. Despite Wanger's protestations that he had no watch, he came up with a framework that seemed to adopt times from other witnesses and leave him in the clear. But he had made a huge mistake. In his recounting of the evening, Wanger had himself leaving the others and arriving at the Carboni household an hour earlier than he did, at least if Mr. Carboni and the boys were to be believed. Wanger's account—which included going to Quik Pick 'Ns (to get twist ties for Strelka, who was supposedly moving and cleaning up at his house) and walking around in the cold for at least half an hour—put him at the Carboni household around 10:30 P.M. But Mr. Carboni testified that his son and the other boys came through the door, and got a glass of water, around about twenty minutes before midnight.

"Well, James," Snowdon asked. "Where were you for that missing hour?"

"Missing hour?"

"Yeah," Snowdon said. "You told us that you left Stooge's a little after ten, you walked around for a half hour, you spend ten minutes waiting for Carboni to return—that brings you to about twenty to eleven. Mr. Carboni says you come into the house at twenty to twelve. Where were you?"

"I must have got the times mixed up, then," Wanger said.

"You were at School 15, that's where you were, James, weren't you?"

"No, I wasn't."

Snowdon re-added the times as Wanger had given them, to show that he couldn't account for a key hour.

"Yeah, I must have messed up on the times, sir."

"I guess so."

"I probably did, sir."

* * *

Outside the courthouse, the cameras and the news reporters crowded around Pope. To judge from the questions, the press seemed to have formed a rough consensus that Wanger had bombed, but Pope put his best face forward.

"I think he did great," Pope said. "Those other juveniles wouldn't even look at the jury."

Pope again pinned the homicide on the three juveniles, particularly Strelka, and scoffed at the prosecution's claim of a missing hour. But several reporters weren't buying it and pressed further, wanting to know why Pope had decided to risk a meltdown, which appeared to have been what just happened.

"I put him on the stand because he wanted to be on the stand," Pope said. "He said, 'Mr. Pope, how can it hurt me? I'm going to tell the truth.' I said go up there and tell the truth."

The next day, Wanger sat through another excruciating session on the witness stand as Snowdon whittled away at the deceptions, great and small, that composed so much of his testimony. Did he really expect people to believe that he used the bathroom in his family's home as a closet all the time? Was that the only reason why he hung the black trench coat there? Why had he possessed instant recall for O'Brien about his breakfast on the day of the killing—right down to the ziti and the espresso with a lemon twist that everyone heard about ad infinitum—when he failed to mention going to Carboni's house, going by Castaldo's house, and borrowing an electrical cord hours before Solimine was strangled with one? Did he really expect the jury to believe it was just dumb luck that his wrists were covered with red marks only hours after someone strangled Solimine with a cord? Did he really expect the jury to believe the handcuffs had created the marks?

From afar, Pope appeared already a beaten man. Wanger was still plucky, although it seemed as if some of the fight from the previous day had been taken out of him, but he still clowned around, particularly when the subject of his school performance came up. ("I have to tell you," Wanger said as Snowdon interrogated him about the *adesso* card and his knowledge of foreign languages, "I wasn't good in Latin at all. I barely survived Latin.") Although there were a few new areas for cross-examination—the business card with *adesso* on it and so on—Snowdon focused one last time on Wanger's alibi at the time of the murder. Characterizing it again as the missing hour, Snowdon returned to the gap of time when Wanger could not account for his whereabouts. Snowdon used maps to show that Wanger had been heading away from his house at the time Wanger said he had decided to walk home.

"And you spent a little time last night I guess thinking about the testimony of the times?"

"Thinking about the testimony of the times?"

"That missing hour?"

"The . . ."

"I'm asking, did you spend some time thinking about that last night?"

"No, sir."

"You didn't?"

"I didn't need to. There was no missing hour on that day, sir."

"Wouldn't it be fair to say that of all the thousands of hours in your entire life that that one hour is the most important of all right now?"

"That hour exists because of my inaccurate time estimates, sir."

One last time, he reminded Snowdon that he didn't have a watch. And then it was over.

At 2:27 P.M. on October 6, 1993, the jury knocked with its verdict. They had deliberated seven hours over two days in a sweltering courtroom after listening to both lawyers' summations. Pope delivered a four-hour summation, trotting out the easel once more to chart all of the inconsistencies in the juveniles' testimony. In his closing statement, Snowdon took two and a half hours to review the testimony and argue for conviction, essentially saying that as preposterous as the allegations might be, the only thing more preposterous was the defense's account of what happened. In a bit of courtroom theater, Snowdon had even slipped on Wanger's black trench coat to demonstrate how he had kept the garrote stuffed inside.

On the first full day of deliberations, the jurors listened to a readback of Wanger's testimony, focusing on the part where he detailed his whereabouts ninety minutes before the homicide. They also listened to the message Strelka left on Solimine's answering machine and heard a readback of Matonak's testimony about seizing Wanger's pea coat and sneakers at the time of his arrest.

Inside the jury room, some of the jurors leaned at first toward acquittal, feeling that it was indeed possible that the three boys had lied and framed Wanger to save their own skins. But the force of the argument for conviction eventually carried them. The *adesso* card, which both sides thought could be of huge importance, figured less in their deliberations than the photographs of the red lines around Wanger's wrists. Using the facsimile of the garrote, one of the jurors wrapped the device around his wrists tightly to demonstrate how the marks could be made—and this had a particularly powerful effect on some of the skeptics. They also sent out two questions, which nearly made Snowdon lose his mind.

Snowdon, virtually overdosing on nicotine while chain-smoking and fretting for a verdict, paced the halls outside or sat in the cafeteria, drinking coffee. He had had a rough night after the jury went an entire day without a decision and ended their deliberations by asking to rehear Wanger's testimony. But after hearing Wanger's testimony again, he calmed down.

One of the questions the jury sent out had spooked him more—until everyone realized that it contained a simple mistake. As the note was initially sent out, it appeared to be asking about count number two in the indictment, whether Wanger could be found guilty of being an accomplice to the conspiracy charge. *Uh-oh,* Snowdon thought, *they must have believed he was not at the scene and are now considering whether he should be responsible for taking part in any discussions of harming Solimine.* But then it turned out that they were considering count eleven, not count two. Marmo had misread the two slashes for the numerals. This suggested that the jury already had decided about the murder charges and were wondering whether Wanger shared the guilt as an accomplice to the arson. In the state's view, he did, since Carboni had lit the fire. In his gut, Snowdon knew that the conviction was coming down. After the law was clarified, the jury deliberated twenty minutes longer, and then they knocked for the final time.

Snowdon poured himself a glass of water. There was a trace of a smile on Wanger's lips as the jury took their seats. Bill Yakal sat in a bench in the spectator section with his hands on his head, and Lee Yakal sat just ahead of him. Martha and Paul Colombo sat in the last pew on the right side of the courtroom. Wanger expressed confidence.

"It's in God's hands," Wanger told Pope as the jury retired to decide his fate. But now Pope looked grave as the jury filed into the courtroom and took their places. The court clerk called the roll.

"Mr. Foreman, please rise," the court clerk said.

The jury foreman, David Ryder, a Clifton resident, stood to deliver the verdict.

"Mr. Foreman, how do you the jury find the defendant, James Wanger, as charged in indictment 92-06-0722, on count one, murder?"

"Guilty," Ryder said.

"Was the verdict unanimous?"

"Yes."

Ryder repeated the word "guilty" ten more times as the clerk read out the indictment. Except for perhaps an instant, Wanger's face remained blank and utterly devoid of expression, as if frozen in the impenetrable dream of the martyr. Wanger clutched a mass card from his mother's funeral.

Asked by the court clerk whether the jury had unanimously agreed that Wanger was guilty of murder as an accomplice or as the strangler, Ryder replied, "James Wanger strangled Robert Solimine to death." He looked at Pope, who did not return the glance, and the corners of Wanger's mouth appeared to sink ever so slightly. Now and then, he slowly craned his neck toward the rear of the courtroom, as if searching for his grandparents.

Almost bent over behind the wooden pew in front of her, Martha Colombo sobbed, filling the courtroom with shuddering gasps, as if each pronouncement of guilt were a fresh blow of physical pain. She dabbed under her huge black sunglasses with a tissue. Paul Colombo held her in his arms and looked across the courtroom with a look of disbelief. Bob Solimine wept, and Arlene put her arm around him, as the clerk went through the remaining counts of the indictment. Margaret Chircop studied Wanger's face for a sign of something, anything, that might reveal his humanity. She saw nothing. For one instant it seemed as if something sank in, turning down the boy's mouth, and she thought to herself, *Cold, cold, cold.*

Pope asked that the jurors be polled. One by one, the counts were read again, and each juror said aloud that he or she agreed with the verdict. Marmo excused the jurors and revoked Wanger's bail, and the young man was led away in handcuffs. The jurors, in tears as they rode the elevator downstairs, were whisked past reporters by sheriff's officers. None wanted to talk.

17

A FEW MONTHS AFTER WANGER'S TRIAL, FRANK CASTALDO went on trial in the same courtroom before the same judge. This time, although Court TV unsuccessfully attempted to broadcast the proceedings on live television, there were fewer news media attending the trial. And those that did attend played the story much less prominently. There was just not as much interest. The story had been told, for one thing. And the allegations against Castaldo—that he had instigated and directed the murder plot from on high—were more abstract, and certainly not as dramatic, or as juicy, as the allegations that Wanger, a seventeen-year-old former Sea Cadet and altar boy, had used his own two hands and an electrical cord to snuff out another teenager's life.

Yet Castaldo's trial was widely expected to be more of a horse race, with more uncertainty of a conviction. Snowdon, who had sweated through a day and a half of deliberations at Wanger's trial, despite knowing that he had put in an enormously strong case, was well aware that Castaldo's odds of acquittal were higher. Everyone agreed that Castaldo was miles away when Solimine died. Snowdon would have to prove that this boy was no less guilty of murder than a mob boss in New York who had ordered his agents to kill someone in Los Angeles—an analogy he made use of in his opening statement. And Castaldo was, in some senses, still a boy. The law recognized that he had become an adult at the age of eighteen—but would a jury hold him to an adult's level of responsibility for what amounted to talk? Would a jury send a young man away to prison for the rest of his life under these circumstances? Because Castaldo told some kids to do a crazy, evil thing, and they did it? Because that's what it also came down to. Talk. Should Castaldo spend the rest of his life in prison because he was talking trash, talking like a tough guy and a crackpot so that Wanger took him seriously?

As expected, the trial unfolded almost as Wanger's had. This time, however, Snowdon seemed more polished and sure of himself. His opening statement seemed more practiced, but also a bit less impassioned. In presenting the three juveniles, he switched the order, going from the strongest to the weakest. Their testimony closely resembled their testimony at Wanger's trial. Only Carboni seemed remarkably different. It was apparent that he was testifying against his cousin only under duress, as it were, although his story changed little from the account he had given at Wanger's trial.

Unlike Pope, however, Linda George seemed to have more success in planting an alternative story in the minds of the jurors. Obviously working with inside information that Castaldo had given her, she used her questions in cross-examination to offer a counterstory. Snowdon frequently objected, demanding to know if a witness would be called who would back up the assertions she had hidden in the guise of questions for the various witnesses. Marmo usually overruled him, but cautioned the jury more than once that the remarks and questions posed by counsel on both sides were not to be considered as evidence, and that they were to decide the case based only on sworn testimony from the witnesses.

George seemed at once both novice and battle-seasoned veteran of the courtroom. Either through temperament or inexperience, she displayed a knack for arguing everything, great and small, in equal measure, but usually with a force of such intensity that she weakened her position overall: She had not learned, it seemed, to pick her battles. As she questioned the witnesses, she also had a habit of asking a clutch of questions all at once, which would prompt Snowdon to object and the judge to sort them out into one question at a time. Sometimes she flirted with a disastrous exchange by violating one of the cardinal rules of lawyering—don't ask questions to which you don't already know the answer—but she managed to get away without being hit in the face with the equivalent of a cream pie.

Yet George attacked with tireless ferocity the idea that the murder conspiracy had progressively developed until it became a cohesive thing. She shook the notion of what a "meeting" was, and even the notion that there was a "group," in the sense of a gang. To that end, she introduced testimony from several other teenagers who also hung out at Castaldo's house. These teenagers, who were closer to Castaldo in age, said they never saw the cohesive unit that had been depicted by the prosecution in Wanger's trial or in Snowdon's opening statements. As the trial progressed, the concept of how the five teenagers acted together became less fixed and more fluid. Again and again, she was also able to show that the three juveniles were often uncertain about what would happen or whether anything would happen at all—particularly Stooge. By the end of his testimony, it seemed he could answer the same question one way for Snowdon and offer exactly the opposite response for George. By casting doubt on the account of a junior Mafia acting in concert, George also undermined the idea that Castaldo was in control of the others, showing that each of the boys was likely to do what he pleased no matter what his parents or Castaldo told them. She also banged at the police and the police investigation more vigorously than had Pope, expressing outrage at the fact that all the detectives confessed to destroying the notes of their initial interviews with the suspects, including Castaldo, after filling out their police reports.

Most intriguing of all, George introduced statements from

the three juveniles—statements they made either to other teenagers or to counselors or to psychiatrists after their arrest—that demonstrated *they* were uncertain about what role, if any, Castaldo had played in Solimine's murder.

The most dramatic moment of the trial occurred when George called Melanie Gardzielik to the witness stand. Her name had barely come up at Wanger's trial. Now she became a critical witness for Castaldo. George attempted to show that Melanie was almost everywhere that Castaldo and the boys were—thereby casting doubt on the idea of a tightly controlled band plotting Solimine's death at all hours of the day and night. It was a good plan, although it nearly backfired and almost implicated Melanie.

Melanie, who was seventeen years old, looked terrified as she sat in the witness box. She wore a black-and-gray stippled jacket with red lapels over a white shirt. A red pocket handkerchief darted out of the breast pocket. The pitiless lighting in the courtroom made her seem especially pale, but she was pretty in an unconventional, almost masculine way, with high cheekbones and a long face. Her hair was long and wavy.

From the start, she shifted the focus of the group's animus for Solimine away from her boyfriend and onto Strelka. Speaking in such a faint voice that the judge kept telling her to speak up, Melanie said Strelka was always complaining about Solimine. Strelka hated Solimine for messing with Chrissie Bachelle, for getting him in trouble with his parents, for being the saint of temperance. She also testified that Castaldo told the others to leave Solimine alone on several occasions and quit with the pranks. What's more, she said Strelka and the other two juveniles tagged along with Castaldo and her to the point that Castaldo would sometimes hide from them so that he and she could be alone. As Linda George asked the questions, Melanie denied up and down hearing anything about group meetings or plans to hurt Solimine, let alone kill him. She also declared that Castaldo wasn't with the group the night the boys tried to handcuff Solimine to the steering wheel or the night of the murder.

When it came Snowdon's turn to ask Melanie questions, he attempted to sow doubt about her story of the boys' innocent pastimes and pranks. Indeed, after Melanie admitted that she knew about the tire-slashing plans, Snowdon all but accused her of knowing a lot more than she was saying—suggesting that she had been aware of the murder plot herself. Snowdon led her to her testimony about being with the group on the night before Solimine's murder, when she saw Carboni pull out the handcuffs.

"At first we were just talking and joking around." Melanie said. "And then Carboni pulled out a pair of handcuffs. Me and Frank Castaldo at the same time said, 'What are those for?' After that I said, 'You know, you are not going to play any tricks with them, are you? Or any jokes?' So Frank Castaldo, as soon as I said that, said, um, 'Why do you, you know, why do you keep hanging out with Rob if you don't like him, if you want to keep playing tricks?' "

But Snowdon got Melanie to admit that she had no idea where Castaldo and the others were the rest of that night. And he pointed out that by her own admission, she had been with the group after they filled Solimine's car with gas and waved the handcuffs around. Melanie became uncomfortable as Snowdon moved in close.

"Is there anything you would like to tell me about what you know about what was going to happen that night?" Snowdon asked quietly.

"I didn't know anything was going to happen that night," she said.

"All of these activities seem completely normal to you? Handcuffs, Wanger paying for gas, kids hanging around outside Mrs. Castaldo's house at two-thirty?"

"Well," she said, "the handcuffs seemed unusual. James would pay for a lot of things. When we would go out to eat, he would pay."

"Is it your testimony that you heard no conversation at all—at all—about what was going to happen later that night?"

"I don't remember hearing anything about doing anything."

"Are you saying you don't remember? Are you sure or not?"

"Yes, I'm positive that I don't remember hearing anything."

"Well, you are positive that there was no conversation? That's what I want to know."

"On that night, no. I don't believe there was."

"You are telling me the truth?"

"Yes."

"Are you concerned about your own part in this?"

"What part do I have in this?"

"Well, you were with them, weren't you?"

"Earlier that night. I wasn't there when this—that happened."

"When what happened?"

"When—that was the night—the morning that they tried to handcuff Rob to the car or whatever."

"No, you weren't there then, but you were there earlier, weren't you?"

"Yes."

"And you knew about the handcuffs?"

"I knew Frank Carboni had handcuffs."

"And you knew Robbie was in the car?"

"Yes. Rob was with us."

"And you knew nobody liked him, right?"

"I guess not."

"And you know that they had already done things to his car?"

"Yes."

"And you knew that Frank was mad about those things not working out?"

"No, he wasn't mad."

"He was annoyed, right?"

"He was annoyed that they kept thinking up things to do."

"And the car was filled with gas?"

"Yes, he got gas."

"Are you concerned about the fact that you were there while all those things were taking place?"

"No. I didn't do anything."

"Is that changing your testimony at all here today, that concern?"

"No."

Eventually, Melanie stepped down, and she cried as she left the courthouse. But her testimony also highlighted a chief difference from Wanger's trial: the almost palpable animosity between the lawyers. Snowdon and George couldn't stand each other, and it appeared as if Marmo shared Snowdon's antipathy toward her. At one point, it descended to Snowdon's calling George an unflattering name in the courtroom while the jury was out.

The exchanges became so acrimonious that they threatened to sidetrack the trial. Indeed, Snowdon tried to bar Melanie from testifying. Claiming George was springing a surprise alibi witness on him at the last minute, Snowdon accused her of not filing the necessary legal papers required by the court rules. He implied that her failure to file a notice of alibi had been intentional. This set off a rancorous argument that verged on a trial-within-a-trial. George, uncertain about whether she had filed the notice of an alibi witness, confessed that perhaps she had forgotten to. But she pointed out that Melanie had been known as a possible witness all along. In fact, George said, Melanie had spoken with police on not just one occasion, but two. Then Snowdon presented an investigator from the office who testified that Melanie and her mother had arranged a date before the trial to speak with the authorities, then canceled it.

But Marmo was hot. He rebuked George for flouting and bending other court rules, all but accusing her of cheating. In a particularly harsh exchange, Marmo also called Melanie back into the courtroom and directed the young woman to stand in the center of the court.

"Do you have any problem speaking to them and answering their questions?" Marmo asked.

"I would rather not, right now."

"Well, I'm directing you to do it," Marmo snapped. "Do you have any problem following my order?"

"No," she whispered.

Melanie submitted to the interview with the prosecutor's office, like it or not. Speaking to them without the assistance of legal counsel—and without the presence even of her mother—Melanie in effect gave a court-ordered statement to prosecutors. Then her testimony resumed. Days later, as it would turn out, the document that Linda George had been accused of not filing would surface. She asked Marmo for a mistrial, a request that was summarily refused.

In the end, however, the jury took approximately the same amount of time to convict Castaldo that it had taken to convict Wanger. They knocked with the verdict at 3:41 P.M. on February 14, 1994, nearly two years to the date of Robert Solimine's murder. Castaldo sat at the defense table, his face drawn, until the foreman stood. At the pronouncement of guilty on all counts, gasps went up from the courtroom, and Castaldo's face turned ashen. His lips quivered, and he appeared to be mumbling to himself and staring in disbelief at the floor just ahead of the counsel's table, when his face contorted as if to cry. But no tears came. Linda George put her arm around his shoulders and patted his back in gentle comfort.

A few rows back in the courtroom, Alfonsina Castaldo started to bawl, then whimper through her hands as she covered her face and sagged down into the seat. As sheriff's officers stood by, mindful of the judge's orders to quell any disturbances, Castaldo's mother buried her head in Joe Castaldo's chest. Marmo revoked Castaldo's bail. Joe shook his head. The entire Castaldo family was there, and they had been holding hands with some of his friends. Melanie

Gardzielik's mother wrapped her daughter in a shielding hug as her daughter heaved and sobbed.

As Castaldo stood to be handcuffed and led away, he reclaimed his composure, and he called over his shoulder to Frank DiGiaimo, the Passaic County probation official who had supervised him all those months while he was on the county's electronic-surveillance program.

"Frank, tell my mother not to forget to buy cigarettes," Castaldo said, and he was gone.

Outside, Alfonsina Castaldo rushed past reporters, but not before shrieking about her nephew Carboni's betrayal of her son.

"He's innocent!" she kept saying. "He's innocent! He tried to protect his cousin!"

Melanie was still crying, too, as she hurried out the door with her mother.

"They just convicted an innocent man!" her mother snapped.

"Can't you leave anyone alone?" bawled Melanie as reporters tailed her with questions.

In preparation for sentencing two and a half months later, probation department officials compiled a report, as they do in all cases, for the court to review. The report said Castaldo had been taking medication for a bleeding ulcer; he also reported being depressed, although he was not suicidal. Interviewed at the Passaic County Jail, Castaldo expressed condolences for Solimine's death, but he continued to deny any involvement with the crime.

"I didn't do anything," Castaldo said. "I really feel bad for the victim's family, but I didn't have anything to do with it."

But Castaldo did not speak the day of sentencing, and Marmo sentenced him to life in prison. By law, Castaldo would have to serve at least thirty years before he could become eligible for a parole review.

18

ON THE MORNING OF NOVEMBER 19, THE DAY OF JAMES Wanger's sentencing, Judge Marmo's courtroom filled until it was virtually standing room only. As it had been during the trial, the heat in the sixth-floor courtroom was stifling. The doors to chambers were opened, so that cool air would circulate through the judge's open windows. By 9:30 A.M., Mr. and Mrs. Yakal were in their seats. Bob, Arlene, Billy, and other relatives took their places in the courtroom, and Margaret Yakal Chircop clutched the piece of paper that contained the remarks she would read to the court. Mr. and Mrs. Colombo, appearing tense and emotionally drained, sat in the rear of the courtroom where they had been during the trial. Today there was a priest with them, sitting in the middle in his black and white clerical shirt. Prosecutors, court clerks, stenographers, defense lawyers, and other familiar faces around the courthouse filled the remaining seats. Besides the same media pack that had attended the trial, Wanger's sentencing brought detectives and others who worked on the case. Purdy was there. Detectives O'Brien and Suroweic and even Captain Territo were there.

Marmo swept onto the bench, and Wanger was led into the courtroom from the holding cells. As was customary, he stood behind the rear rail of the jury box facing the court. The suit and tie were gone. He wore a standard-issue orange jumpsuit from the Passaic County Jail over, a white T-shirt, and he looked thinner and paler than he had during his trial. He wore the same gloomy, indecipherable expression that he had worn for two weeks of testimony, but otherwise showed no emotion. His Adam's apple bobbed up and down as he took big quiet gulps and the hearing got under way.

Pope stood at Wanger's right side. He would speak first. His plea would be simple. Pope could not argue against the weight of evidence that had persuaded a jury to convict Wanger of the charges, but he would remind the court that the entire case was so inexplicable that perhaps the result had been mistaken. And finally, he would ask Marmo to sentence Wanger to the minimum sentence required by law on the murder count and run all the other sentences concurrently. That would mean Wanger would have to serve at least thirty years before he could ever step in front of a parole board. He would be forty-seven years old before he could even hope, realistically, for a shot at freedom.

"I guess since the moment the jury came back with a guilty verdict on this case, there have been many nights and days which I've tried to consider exactly what really occurred here," Pope began. "I see an individual that stands before me to the left of me, which, for the life of me, I cannot understand or figure out or have any clue whatsoever as to what occurred on February 16, 1992.

"I have an individual who lectored Sunday morning at a Catholic church," Pope continued, and his voice rang with a note of unfeigned astonishment. "When I go to church on Sunday myself and I watch people lector and give the Gospel in the sermons, I stare at them now, and I wonder to myself: Is it possible that somebody could actually stand on the altar, read from the Bible, teach catechism, and then that same night go out there and strangle somebody? How do you reconcile those two acts? How do you reconcile the fact that from the time he was born, he's never been in trouble with the law?

There's been no drinking incident that he was arrested for, no stolen cars, no running away from home, no acts of violence."

Pope recapitulated Wanger's record of participating in Sea Cadets and other civic organizations, and he told of Wanger's unfortunate childhood, touching on aspects of Wanger's life that had been reported here and there in the media but had never before been stated openly in court: Wanger's abandonment by his father, his mother working two jobs, his grandparents virtually raising him, and his medical problems. He mentioned that Wanger had been taking Tegritol for about two years because of nonepileptic seizures, but he took the point no further. Then, almost as if speaking off the cuff, Pope offered his own theory of Wanger's soul. This theory came to him, Pope explained, one night while he was watching a TV program about children who had been abandoned by their parents. These children developed "attachment disorders," Pope said.

"When I was watching the program—it was just two nights ago—I was wondering to myself if there was an attachment disorder, if there was an inability to have an emotional connection," Pope said. He took up this theme later, suggesting that perhaps Wanger had been a loser in the genetic lottery—that he suffered from "a mutant gene."

"I can't reconcile the fact that you can get on the stand, deny involvement—if in fact it did happen; we have to accept the jury verdict for this purpose—that you could teach catechism, read from the Bible, join the Marines and do everything that's good," Pope said, "and have no emotion, no remorse or any explanation for the execution-style killing of another young person. None of that makes any sense."

Then, as if to use as leverage his concession that Wanger had shown no remorse, Pope plunged ahead into the most controversial element of the entire case: the plea bargains. If the other juveniles could admit to conspiring to murder someone at the behest of an older, influential young man and then receive sentences of no more than twelve years, didn't

Wanger deserve leniency as well? Wouldn't it be basic fairness? Pope argued.

Marmo cut him off. First commending Pope for his skill in defending Wanger, Marmo launched a defense of the prosecution that seemed almost calculated to make the case—perhaps for the benefit of the media, and thereby the public, or perhaps for Mrs. Chircop, who sat in the audience—that the plea bargains had been unavoidable and that it was time to stop second-guessing the prosecution's strategy.

"If the prosecutor just wanted to get convictions," Marmo said, "he could have just prosecuted the juveniles, waived them up as adults. But they didn't do that. They went after the person they felt was really culpable, the person that put the garrote around the victim's neck, fashioned the garrote, pulled with all his strength and stamina. . . . They didn't have much of a case without the juveniles. You know that as an attorney and an advocate."

On the other hand, Marmo pointed out, the three juveniles were in the bag.

"They were dead. They weren't going to be acquitted," Marmo said.

"But my point—"

"So didn't they do the right thing?" Marmo continued. "Maybe the police should have been tougher. But shouldn't they have dealt—struck deals, as we say, with those people to go after the others, the two older persons?"

Raising once more the idea that Wanger's genes or tortured childhood had brought him to this pass, Pope said he was arguing only that there should be balance for the juveniles and for Wanger, who admittedly should carry more weight than the other three. Pope assured the judge that Wanger did feel sorrow for Solimine's death. Then, in remarks that seemed to suggest that Wanger might privately be admitting what he had denied so publicly, Pope said Wanger had visited with priests in the county jail.

What Wanger most needed was intensive counseling, said Pope, who also surmised that someday there would be a legal defense constructed on the inheritance of the "mutant gene" that made some people incapable of conforming to the rules of society. In his conclusion, he pleaded for the minimum thirty years and anticipated that the prosecution and the Solimine family would make a powerful pitch for much more.

"Mr. Solimine or Mrs. Solimine's family, if they walk out feeling happier that it's forty years or fifty years as opposed to thirty years, you know, the only thing I can say to that is I pray for all of you," Pope said. "Because if tomorrow a loved one of mine was killed and somebody told me that I could put him in jail for fifty years or I could burn him at the cross, it's not going to change my heartbreak. Because once you've killed a loved one, it's over with," he continued. "The loss is the loss, and a pound of flesh, Judge, is nothing more than revenge. And I think revenge is for the Lord—justice is for the Court."

Pope ceased. Marmo thanked him and invited members of Wanger's family to address him if they pleased. Mr. Colombo came forward, pushing through the swinging doors to the well of the court, walking with his head back like a man accustomed to wearing bifocals. James regarded him impassively as Mr. Colombo unfolded a piece of paper and began to read.

"My entire family and I want to thank you and the Court for allowing me to speak to you on behalf of my grandson, James Wanger, who stands before you today awaiting your sentence on the charge of murder," Mr. Colombo said. His voice was a sonorous bass, with just the slightest tremble, and he craned his neck almost painfully upward to the Court. Reporters whose pens had begun to slow halfway through Pope's address now bent over their pads trying to capture Mr. Colombo's every word.

"First off, Your Honor, none of us believe that James is capable of such an act," Mr. Colombo said. "He was raised mainly by my wife, Martha, and myself. His father abandoned him shortly after birth. And his mother, who was killed in an auto accident this past July, had worked to earn a living."

Here Mr. Colombo's voice knotted up and his red eyes appeared to fill with tears. Wanger stared at him. He was sagging at the shoulders, the corners of his mouth, his eyes, but otherwise giving no sign of recognition, no gesture of shared grief with his grandfather. Some spectators in the pewlike seats of the courtroom began to weep as Mr. Colombo faltered a moment, then moved on.

"I would like to add at this point, Your Honor, that my family and I have grieved with the entire family over the loss of their son, Robbie. Robbie Solimine was a fairly frequent visitor at our home and was treated like one of the family. He will be sorely missed by us as well as his family."

Mr. Colombo closed with a plea to limit the prison term his grandson faced. Sobbing, Mr. Colombo told the judge that perhaps someday James might be able to return to society and help young people. Marmo appeared solemnly moved. One of the reporters saw Wanger blink hard and gulp.

"All right," the judge said quietly. "Thank you, sir. Thank you for coming."

Then Judge Marmo turned to Wanger.

"Mr. Wanger, anything you want to say? I'd welcome hearing from you if there is."

"Nothing."

Wanger spoke in a low voice. He couldn't say enough when he testified just a few weeks earlier. He had been so full of himself before, that some of the spectators had been convinced he would speak up. But his response fell dully to the floor, and after a pause, Marmo turned to Snowdon.

"All right. State?" the judge asked.

Now it was time for the victims to be heard. Maggie came first, giving her name to the court reporter as Margaret Yakal Chircop. She held a piece of paper in her hands and began to read. She lifted her head from time to time to look Wanger in the face, but Wanger gazed off in the distance, perhaps toward the judge, perhaps at the ceiling, as Margaret began to speak.

"Since that devastating day, February 16, 1992, when James Wanger made the choice to murder my son Robert Solimine rather than walk away as any normal person would do, he not only destroyed my son's life, but has destroyed all of Rob's family's lives, and destroyed each and every one of his family members' lives. I have been scarred for life by James Wanger's brutal and senseless attack in the taking of my son Rob from me and his family. I am a mother who has been raped of her most sacred of loves, that for her child."

Wanger stared straight ahead.

"James Wanger," she said, calling him out. "You met Rob at the age of fourteen in the Sea Cadets. Rob befriended you by inviting you to his home often enough to know that all Rob wanted was to be a friend to you."

Wanger turned to her. They were looking at each other.

"How dare you play God!" she said. "How dare you extinguish my son's life! Decide that my son has no right to live!"

Margaret felt her anger rising through her voice, and as she looked at Wanger, she sensed him radiating a dull hostility, that his eyes distantly beheld her in anger and returned it. Her voice was quavering, and the papers in her hands shook.

"Instead of saying the Hail Mary, you should have said the Lord's Prayer," Maggie said, and she recited its concluding lines:

Forgive us our trespasses, as we forgive those who trespass against us

Lead us not into temptation, but deliver us from evil.

After chiding him for dragging her family and his own family into this hell of his own making—think of your grandparents, she told him, and how they would be scorned, humiliated, shamed, and aggrieved—she turned to the court, departing from the script.

"James Wanger never showed an ounce of remorse or anxiety for the murder of my son in the three gruesome weeks of this trial," she said. "He came in shaking hands and smiling like this was some kind of ordinary routine day. His attitude towards being arrested for murder is having a bad day.

"For myself, Judge Marmo, I still feel lost, never to be found again," Maggie said, and as her remarks touched on the personal, more people in the courtroom began to weep. "Not to have seen Rob graduate from high school was very painful. I had shut my house windows for weeks so I would not have to hear the car horns of happy graduates of 1992. This was supposed to be one of our happiest moments, to see Rob grow into such a fine young man and go on to marriage and have children. All these things I can never have with my son Rob. And since I can't have them with Rob, all the future Christmases, Easters, Thanksgivings, New Years, etc., are not important any longer."

In closing, she asked the judge to make certain that Wanger would not profit from any book, movie, or magazine piece that might come of the case. If Wanger stood to make money from such a thing, she said, she asked the judge to direct its profits to her son, Billy.

Next came Mr. Solimine. He did not have any written remarks. He stood at first with his hands in his pockets, slouching. Then, speaking in a nasal voice that began quietly in matter-of-fact style, Bob Solimine addressed Wanger with contempt.

"I didn't know whether I wanted to say anything, because to me this is almost open and closed," Bob Solimine began. "We know he's guilty. He knows he's guilty. He deserves to be behind bars. If he wants to be a cook, I'm sure the prison needs cooks. He could make somebody a nice meal once in a while."

Mr. Solimine turned to the detectives and Snowdon, thanking them for their work.

"It's different when complete strangers touch part of your life," he said. "A year and a half ago, I was a regular person doing my thing. Next thing I know, the whole world knows who I am—my family, my divorce over fifteen years ago, my son's personal life. And it's hard to walk past the newsstands, see your picture or your son's picture on the front of the paper, on a magazine, or on TV, eyewitness news, CNN, all over the world. So many people touched my life. Most of them were for our benefit to help us convict the people that murdered my son, as the detectives here."

Mr. Solimine dismissed the high talk about James's religious habit and the musings about an attachment disorder.

"Sure, there's something wrong with him," Mr. Solimine said. "Anybody has to be crazy to kill someone else. I punished James Wanger every night since he killed my son. He's punishing me. Every night I executed him with my hands around his neck. Thirty years—if he gets thirty years without parole, I will still be around when he gets out of jail. My son will definitely be around."

Members of the press corps looked at each other with raised eyebrows at Mr. Solimine's open threat, but he was moving faster now, rolling toward the end.

"He should be put away for the rest of his life," Mr. Solimine said. "He will do it again. These kids planned and carried out an execution Mafia-style. They planned it to the extent, except they didn't plan on getting caught. What would happen if they didn't get caught? Whose turn was it next to kill? You would have had somebody kill somebody. It was your turn. Whose turn was it next? You would have done it and done it until you got caught. And you know I'm right," Mr. Solimine said, almost shouting at Wanger and pointing his finger across the courtroom at him. Then Solimine thanked the court and sat down.

Now it was Snowdon's turn. He asked Marmo to impose a sentence of life imprisonment with at least fifty years before parole. Wanger had robbed Robbie Solimine of those many years and perhaps more of his expected life, and he deserved to pay in kind. He began by explaining how unusual it was to encounter a premeditated murder like this one. Most homicides occur in the flash of gunfire, in the heat of a dispute, over some definable cause, he said.

"It's even more unusual to have a situation where not one, but a group of people participate in extensive planning over an extensive period of time to cause the death of another human being," Snowdon said. "The question that's been raised since this case began is one of motive. And there is no definable motive for this murder. And my position is that that makes this murder even worse. It was a murder basically for fun, Judge, is what it boils down to."

Snowdon told the court that he understood that if Wanger maintained that he had nothing to do with the murder, he couldn't very well express remorse. But, Snowdon said, driving the point in, Wanger expressed nothing at all.

"Mr. Pope calls it an attachment disorder," Snowdon said. "I call it sociopathic behavior. It's a person who has no conscience, a person who knows what to say, how to appear, and present himself in a certain manner. He knows how to stand in church and read from the Bible, but he doesn't appreciate what he's really reading. He doesn't feel it inside him. He is missing a conscience, if you want to call it that. He simply doesn't have it. And he's never going to have it. Counseling for Mr. Wanger? Counseling is not going to change what's missing in Mr. Wanger, Judge."

At last, Marmo spoke. Before going through the complexities of weighing the aggravating and mitigating factors that bear on a sentence, Marmo picked up a sheaf of letters that had been sent to him by relatives and friends of Robbie Solimine. He explained to the crowded courtroom that the letters were too voluminous to read entirely, but he would read excerpts, and as he read, the courtroom seemed to fill with the voices of dozens of different relatives and friends who weren't actually there. In incantatory tones, Judge Marmo began:

" 'This execution-style murder has had a profound effect on Rob's family and me. I will never see our Robbie go on to college or the military. I will never see him marry and raise a family. There will never be hugs and kisses or letting Rob know how much we love him. I will never hear him enter the house, calling out, "Hi Grandma" again, but see that around the table there will always be an empty chair,' " Marmo said.

"That's from Lena Yakal, the grandmother of Robert Solimine," the judge said, and then he went on in like fashion.

" 'There are many day-to-day things that most people don't think about that tear us apart, such as seeing handsome young men standing out on their front yards all dressed up in their prom tuxedos getting their pictures taken, hearing car horns honking on graduation day—things that Robbie never got to do . . .'

"That was from Arlene Solimine, Robbie's stepmother," the judge said.

" 'This murder has put a tremendous strain on the whole Solimine family. We were planning to celebrate my daughter's wedding only two weeks after the murder. The day after Robbie's death, with tears in his eyes, my brother asked if I knew someone who could use the suit they bought for the wedding. Robbie was looking forward to attending. These very sad memories will weigh heavy in my heart for the rest of my life. Our family will never be the same because of the loss of my nephew.'

"That letter was by Anthony Solimine, Jr., Robert Solimine's uncle," the judge said.

" 'We miss Robbie every day, over holidays. Easter, Thanksgiving, Christmas, his birthday are now sad events, not happy events that most people enjoy. The betrayal by his friends' conspiracy . . . makes it even harder for our family to bear our loss. I am left demoralized, angered and have lost faith in human behavior. . . . It was a gross mistake by the prosecutor's office to charge the three as juveniles.'

"That was by William Yakal, one of Robbie Solimine's grandfathers," the judge said.

" 'Robbie was a helpful grandchild. He came over to my house many times to help me cut the lawn, clean up the yard, and we would work on our cars together. He would always ask me to get out a deck of cards so that we could spend some time together—cards was one of his favorite things to do. I ask myself over and over again, why this had to happen to such a goodhearted boy, a boy who never got a chance to be a man. . . . I will be seventy-five years old this summer and my opinion of punishment for crimes might seem outdated by some. However, I feel very strongly that when someone is murdered the punishment should be death. Since that is not possible in this case, I ask you to pass down the most harsh punishment that is within your power. Make these boys feel the pain of confinement for as long as possible . . .'

"That letter was from Anthony Solimine, Sr., Robbie's paternal grandfather," the judge said.

" 'There is not a day that goes by that I do not think of the horror of what happened. I have two children of my own, and I have always been overprotective and cautioned them about the harmful things in this world, but this is unimaginable.'

"Linda Solimine, Robert Solimine's aunt," the judge said.

Then Marmo read how Sharon Johnson, a cousin, wrote to say that her fourteen-year-old daughter, who practically grew up with Robbie, locked herself in her room.

" 'Here is a young girl that spends days in her room writing letters to her murdered cousin,' " the letter says. " 'Written on practically everything in her room is "I miss my cousin"; "Why, why, why,"; "Please, not my cousin"; "I love you, Robbie." ' "

Marmo put the letters aside.

"What sticks out to everyone who looks at this case is the senselessness of this murder," he said. "There is nothing that anyone can point to and identify as any kind of comprehensible reason for what was done except the excitement of it." It was clear, the judge said, that the horrendous nature of the crime outweighed every factor that Wanger could put forth in his favor, namely his youth, his clean record, and his past.

"Furthermore," Marmo continued, "this killing was done with incredible persistence and determination."

The sad-sack expression remained on Wanger's face, and as the judge pointed out that Wanger had worked hard at carrying off the crime, Wanger's morose face seemed to sag further, like wax. Marmo spoke as if in astonishment that nothing could provoke a comprehensible response from the young man before him.

"I have seen, in the course of my involvement in this, not the tiniest indication of remorse and, as incredible as it may seem, not even regret," Marmo said. Then, in an oblique reference perhaps to the influence of Hollywood on Wanger's behavior, he denounced the media culture that bathes society in violence.

At last Marmo pronounced sentence. Tallying up all the aggravating and mitigating factors, Marmo sentenced Wanger to life in prison with no chance of parole for forty years. For the murder, the judge imposed the mandatory sentence of life in prison with at least thirty years before parole. For the attempted murder with the aerosol can on January 25, Marmo sentenced Wanger to 18½ years in prison, to be served after the murder sentence. This sentence carried a minimum period of parole ineligibility of four years. For the attempted murder using the handcuffs, Marmo imposed another 18½-year sentence, this one with a six-year period of parole ineligibility. Wanger swallowed hard when the judge imposed the second attempted murder sentence. As of his day of sentencing, November 19, 1993, Wanger had already served 641 days behind bars. He still had at least 13,949 days to go.

Three years after they had left Solimine's body slumped behind the wheel of his car in a muddy schoolyard, and more than a year after the last of the two adult trials, the three juveniles appeared once more before Judge Ferrante in a tiny courtroom on the top floor of the county's extravagant new administration building. The date was January 20, 1995. The boys had aged appreciably, and except for Carboni, who was still represented by Andy Blair, they had hired new lawyers. Ernest M. Caposela represented Strelka. Michael J. Koribanics represented Stooge. After a long wait, when it seemed as if no one wanted to deal with the issue of their expected sentence reductions, both lawyers, whose offices were in Clifton, had joined with Blair in filing motions seeking to enforce the plea bargain.

The boys' families took seats on the right side of the courtroom. Susie Strelka stared straight ahead at the empty bench, spinning her shiny wedding band on her finger, and glancing nervously at the door behind her. She and the other parents smiled happily at their sons when the young men shuffled into the courtroom, their legs shackled and their wrists handcuffed to the leather waist restraints. Strelka's and Carboni's heads were shaved almost to the skin. Stooge's hair had grown long and shaggy, and he wore a tinted pair of eyeglasses that he had made himself in the prison shop. All three wore parkas over the orange jumpsuits issued by the correctional facility. They greeted their parents warmly and sat down at the defense table, followed by three beefy corrections officers who sat in the front row. Mary Stujinski, now that her son wasn't looking at her, bowed her head a moment at the sight of her son in irons and bit her lip.

A few feet away Margaret Chircop—accompanied by her lawyer, Richard Pompelio, the victims' rights champion—sat in the front row on the left side of the courtroom. Bob and Billy Solimine sat on that side as well, and three reporters from the local newspapers squeezed in beside them, with barely enough room to hold their notepads and take notes. O'Shea stood in the well of the court, and Jack Snowdon waited outside. The three defense lawyers greeted their clients and spoke to them quietly at the defense table.

Blair and Koribanics appeared confident. Before coming into the courtroom, they had been saying that Ferrante had been slow to schedule the hearing and had shown every sign of dragging his feet on the resentencing motion. But both lawyers forecast that he would do it. Although they were wary of Ferrante, who had a reputation for doing almost as he pleased, they expected him to thunder about the leniency of the prosecutor's proposed plea agreement, direct a few disparaging remarks their way, and then reduce the sentences. Blair, for one, believed the judge had no choice.

Only Caposela seemed pessimistic. Before entering the courtroom, he kept shaking his head, dreading the idea that Ferrante was going to send them packing. Although his client's family was pushing him to get their son out of Jamesburg, Caposela had been leery of pressuring the judge by filing motions. Having known the judge for many years—he clerked for him after law school—Caposela sensed that Ferrante would not reduce the boys' sentences, and he was right.

Judge Ferrante strode to the bench, and the hearing began. O'Shea called Snowdon to the witness stand. It was a curious sight: the prosecutor who had worked with the three juveniles to convict Wanger and Castaldo was now testifying in their behalf. He was not on the stand very long, and the thrust of his remarks was simple: it would have been extremely difficult, if not impossible, to convict Wanger and Castaldo without the three boys' assistance. What's more, Snowdon told the court that Wanger and Castaldo had filed appeals in their cases, and should either conviction be reversed, the state would need the boys' testimony again. He said the boys had testified in expectation of reduced prison sentences and, having upheld their end of the bargain, should receive them. In closing, and in making his recommendation for the sentence reduction, Snowdon also noted that the failure to uphold the plea agreement would cast the prosecutor's office in a bad light, which might suggest to other defendants that it would not be able to enforce its future plea agreements. In the interest of justice, Snowdon said, the court should reduce the boys' prison terms in accordance with the plea agreement signed almost three years previously.

"You've indicated that it would not send a good signal, in that the prosecutor's office could not be trusted—if the agreement were not fulfilled, it would be harmful to the prosecutor's office," Ferrante said.

"That's correct," Snowdon said.

"If the prosecutor's office lives up to its part of the agreement by what it's doing today, and the court did something to the contrary of that, then the prosecutor's office would not be subject to criticism, would it?"

"It wouldn't be subject to criticism legally," Snowdon said. "How it would be perceived by the public in general—I don't know that that would be true."

Ferrante's opening remarks revealed plenty—everyone in the courtroom knew where Ferrante was going even before he took up the transcript and started reading from the day in April 1992 when the boys had pleaded guilty. Carboni hung his head as Ferrante read out the passages of the plea hearing in which he had warned everyone that the ultimate discretion for reducing their sentences lay with him.

Although he took pains to practice the verbal bowing and scraping lawyers train to use before a judge, it was apparent that Blair was furious when his turn came to speak. He argued, in effect, that the judge's discretion rested solely on whether he could find that the boys had failed to live up to their part of the agreement, which they had not. The judge could not just toss the agreement out now without cause. By accepting the guilty pleas nearly three years ago, Blair said, the judge had given them his imprimatur. If he hadn't liked the agreement or thought it too lenient, Blair argued, then he should have rejected the boys' pleas back then. The boys could then have withdrawn their guilty pleas, gone to trial, and taken their chances. But now they had no such recourse. They had given the state what was asked of them, and they had already served a good portion of their sentences. A deal is a deal, Blair argued, and it was too late for the judge to back out now. What Blair was telling the judge, to his face, was that Ferrante had no discretion—and all the "most respectfully, Your Honor"s he could utter didn't change this one bit.

"Are you saying to me that your position is that I don't have any discretion as a result of some agreement that your client reached with the prosecutor's office?" the judge said. Ferrante bristled at the idea.

"No, Your Honor," Blair stammered. "I say, most respectfully, that my position is that . . . the way it was worded in writing and signed by the parties, is that it did not leave, most respectfully—and I understand Your Honor has, obviously, the right to make any decision Your Honor sees fit—but under the written plea agreement, as I interpret it, that it did not leave any room for the discretion as to whether or not to accept this application—that the discretion lay in Your Honor's right to accept or reject the plea bargain as a whole . . ."

Then, after more sparring, Ferrante announced that he had received a letter from Mr. Solimine—who essentially said that he was not thrilled with the sentence reductions but now understood the necessity for having made the plea bargains—and that Margaret Yakal wished to read her letter in court. In it, she asked Ferrante to consider keeping Stooge and Carboni locked up to the maximum or at least as long at it took to rehabilitate them, and to consider sending them to boot camp. And then as Margaret attacked Strelka, singling him out once more for harsher punishment because of his age and his betrayal, Susie Strelka became so agitated that she couldn't take it anymore, and left the courtroom. She screamed wildly and cursed Yakal with profanities from the ninth floor to the first in the elevator. Meanwhile, as if to drive home further the point that the boys had received excessively lenient treatment, Ferrante placed on the record his steps to block the trio's release on weekend furloughs home; a practice for which they had become eligible the previous October. Ferrante noted with some asperity that such furloughs had been forbidden to other juveniles convicted of manslaughter, sexual assault, robbery, kidnapping, and aggravated assault. Why, he asked, had they been condoned for convicted murderers?

"It looks like the judge is on our side," whispered Billy Solimine.

"We're paying him," Bob Solimine replied, feeling for once proud as a taxpayer.

Indeed, because of the judge's actions, furloughs were thereafter denied to all violent offenders at Jamesburg. In a final slap at the corrections system, Ferrante read from the boys' progress reports. Each evaluation sounded as if it was written by the same officer about the same boy, as if they had been done by rote.

Smelling certain defeat, Caposela huddled with the other lawyers. They agreed to put off the hearing another month, to allow the authorities to compile more detailed information about the boys' progress. Carboni's head sank nearly to the floor.

Epilogue

THE THREE JUVENILES CONTINUED TO SERVE THEIR TWENTY-year indeterminate sentences at Jamesburg, despite another tumultuous hearing before Judge Ferrante in February 1995. Indeed, the boys' families appealed Ferrante's decision to the Appellate Division of the Superior Court but lost. With the appeals court's decision, their hopes for receiving sentence reductions all but faded. Yet the families—who already had spent substantial sums of money on legal fees to defend their sons against the criminal charges and against a civil suit filed by Margaret Chircop—took their appeal higher, petitioning the New Jersey Supreme Court to hear their case. That request too was denied.

Meanwhile, many of the families moved away. Bob and Arlene left Clifton. The Chircops, since divorced, left Clifton. The Carbonis left Clifton. Susie Strelka talked about moving but had no idea where they might go. Mary Stujinski said she could not leave.

Margaret, her divorce from Manny complete, resumed using the last name of her parents, Yakal, and she pressed forward with lawsuits seeking damages not only against the boys but against their parents—accusing Mary, Susie, and the others of neglect in the care of their children. This inflamed

Susie and Mary to no end, not because of the money—homeowners' insurance bought off the suit for $15,000 per couple—but because of the way they believed Margaret had made herself out to be the Mother of the Year. But Mary and Susie Strelka grew closer during their weekly visits to see their sons in Jamesburg, and their animosity toward Margaret Chircop intensified.

Billy Solimine finished college and talked of becoming a police officer, while Bob and Arlene Solimine settled in a small rural town in another state; Arlene ran an antiques shop and Bob continued to repair airline equipment. All of them treasured the memories they had of Robbie and still felt his spirit now and then when they saw the same sights or took part in the same activities that once amused him.

Maggie remained in the public eye, half by choice and half because now the news media turned to her as a kind of spokeswoman for reforming the justice system. Taking a role in persuading the courts and the legislature to deal more harshly with crime and juvenile offenders, Maggie appeared before the state legislature appealing for laws creating a punitive prison for adult offenders. She was still quoted often in the newspapers. Bill Yakal, too, would be quoted, and he mailed off letters to the editor on the subject.

Bill and Lee Yakal also tried to put the loss behind them, but without forgetting, and in the process an otherworldly experience, an epiphany of sorts, was revealed to them. Lee had attended both trials for the murder of her grandson, and she read the newspapers about new developments in the case, and she got on with her life as best she could. She thought about him all the time. But her grandson's death haunted her in unexpected ways. Robbie had come by their house all the time before his death, just pushing open the back door and calling, "Gram, I'm here." Now, when Billy came by and called through the house, "Gram, I'm here," the sound of his voice confused her. For an instant, it sounded like Robbie, as if he had come by one more time, and Lee felt a stitch in her heart.

Every Sunday, too, Lee went with Maggie, and sometimes

with Bill, to the Laurel Grove Cemetery in Totowa to tend to Robbie's grave. Robbie was buried on a gentle slope, just off one of the looping driveways that crisscrossed the cemetery, overlooking the towns of Totowa and Paterson. The susurration of the highway was faintly audible from over the crest of the hill, and the handsome chapel building stood just below. There were many new graves here and few trees. To the east, along the ridge in the direction of Paterson, was the oldest part of the cemetery, and about two hundred yards or so in that direction stood the grove of trees and the mausoleums where Robbie had visited so many times in the past with the friends who killed him.

Sometimes Maggie and her parents planted flowers or pulled weeds or stood over the bronze plaque that marked his grave, reminiscing. The plaque was decorated with a relief of a mountain vista. The inscription read:

Robert Solimine Jr.
"Robbie"
1974–1992
Died for his morals and values

Before leaving, Lee Yakal always said a prayer for her grandson. All her life she found peace in moments of prayer. As a devout Roman Catholic, Lee had been in the habit of reciting three of the church's common prayers: The Lord's Prayer, which she called the "Our Father"; the Act of Contrition, which begins, "My God, I am sorry for my sins, with all my heart . . ."; and the Hail Mary.

But in her anger and revulsion over her grandson's murder, she had ceased to say the Hail Mary. It was a fearful desecration of holy prayer and seemed to show how demonic Wanger's purpose had been in killing Robbie, and for some time afterward, Lee could not bring herself to repeat the Hail Mary. Time passed, and she would start the prayer, but then she would be unable to complete it. She would hear herself saying it—"Hail Mary, full of grace, the Lord is with thee"—and she would stop. She could not go further.

Then one Sunday Lee and Bill Yakal went to see the cemetery before heading out on vacation. They were going to North Carolina, and Lee wanted to visit Robbie's grave before leaving town. It was a balmy day in September. The leaves were still on the trees, and the sky was radiant. Lee stood over the grave to pray, and for the first time, she said the Hail Mary from beginning to end. Then she got in the car to leave.

"Bye, Robbie," Lee said quietly, and she pressed two of her fingers to her lips in a parting kiss. "I'll see you when I get back."

"I'm here in the car with you, Grandma," a voice said.

Lee heard the voice, felt it through her bones, and knew that her grandson's spirit was with her. She was startled, but not afraid, and looked in the backseat, although she knew she wouldn't see anything there. But a sense of Robbie's spiritual presence filled the car and filled her heart with happiness. A feeling of tranquility descended on her for the first time since his murder, and it stayed with her as they departed. That was the first time that she had finished the Hail Mary. That was the first time she felt his spirit. In the days to come, she would hear his voice again. Robbie's spiritual presence was with her, it was very much alive, and it would be ever afterward in her heart.

Acknowledgments

MY FONDEST GRATITUDE GOES TO MY WIFE, JULIE PHILIPS, AND our daughters, Hannah and Madeleine, for the generous support, patience and love they gave me during my work on this book. They made it possible for me to finish the manuscript in a year's time and retain at least a trace of sanity.

Several members of Robbie Solimine's family—Robert Solimine, Sr., and his wife, Arlene; Billy Solimine; Emanuel Chircop; and Bill and Lee Yakal—courageously revealed much of their private lives despite the pain of revisiting their loss. In the same regard, I cannot thank enough the mothers of D.S. and D.M.S., who brought me closer to the world that their sons inhabited.

I am indebted to Malcolm A. Borg and the entire newspaper family of the *Bergen Record*. Editor Glenn Ritt and Managing Editor Vivian Waixel supported the venture with kind words of encouragement, and Director of Photography Rich Gigli offered immense assistance in acquiring photographs. An enormous debt of gratitude goes to Assistant Managing Editor Mike Semel, whose creative handling of the Passaic County news bureau allowed me to serve two masters at once. Staff writer David Gibson of the *Record*, who as a police reporter covered the story as no one else could, generously opened his notebooks and offered recollections about the case from its earliest days. I am also grateful for the encouraging words offered everyone on the newspaper staff, particularly when so many friends seemed more certain than I that the book would get done. In the world of journalists, I am also grateful to Maria Speidel, of *People Weekly* magazine, who shared her notes and insights, and photographer Peter Serling, who graciously made his work available for reproduction.

Thanks also to the entire Clifton Police Department—especially Detective Captain James Territo, Captain Robert Kelly, and Detectives Carl Matonak and George O'Brien. These officers are true professionals who offered their cooperation wholeheartedly, and I could virtually go down the entire roster naming many others who were eager to help.

Likewise, Passaic County Prosecutor Ronald S. Fava and his staff were unfailingly cooperative throughout the entire project. The office door of Senior Assistant Prosecutor William J. Purdy, Jr., was always open, his wit and insight I valued very much. I am grateful as well to Chief Assistant Prosecutor Michael O'Shea. Chief Assistant Prosecutor John A. Snowdon, Jr., never seemed to tire of hashing over points great and small about the case, and investigator James Wood also deserves special mention for his patience answering countless questions and for hunting down dusty boxes in the evidence vault.

On the other side of the courtroom, I owe an immeasurable debt of gratitude to the defense attorneys. In particular, attorney Linda George offered tremendous help researching the book and made it possible to interview Frank Castaldo in prison. Attorney Michael Koribanics went out of his way to set up visits at Jamesburg, and attorney Ernest M. Caposela encouraged the cooperation of his client. Likewise, my thanks go to attorneys Andrew Blair, Anthony J. Pope, Jr., and Jay W. McCann.

Father Thomas B. Iwanowski, director of the Worship Office of the Archdiocese of Newark, offered his considerable knowledge and wisdom so that I might understand better some of the religious background. Likewise in the spiritual realm, Andrew Weiss provided invaluable insight and guidance in understanding the characters and writing the book.

In writing about Clifton, I must acknowledge my gratitude to *A Clifton Sampler* by Elvira Hessler, David L. Van Dillen, and William J. Wurst. In addition, I also drew on accounts by "Clifton Golden Jubilee 1917–1967," compiled and edited by *Morning Call* reporter Thomas Sullivan.

At Warner Books, I owe much thanks to editor Diane Stockwell, who liked the idea while talking about it at the Mare Chiaro in Little Italy and encouraged me to pursue a book. Without her—and Teddy Jefferson—the book might never have been done.

It would be impossible to name everyone who has offered their time or encouragement to me in carrying out this project, but my gratitude to them is no less heartfelt. A final word of thanks goes to my parents and my family, who offered their long-distance support and care.

About the Author

FREDRICK KUNKLE has been a reporter at the *Bergen Record* in New Jersey for seven years, and a newspaper reporter for eleven years. At the *Record*, he has covered the police beat and general assignment, in addition to the courthouse. He is also a fiction writer. He graduated from Yale College, and lives in New Jersey with his wife and two daughters.